ISAAC ASIMOV'S

THREE LAWS OF ROBOTICS

1.

A robot may not injure a human being, or through inaction, allow a human being to come to harm.

2.

A robot must obey the orders given it by human beings except where such orders would conflict with the First Law.

3.

A robot must protect its own existence, as long as such protection does not conflict with the First or Second Laws.

PRAISE FOR AUTHOR MARK W. TIEDEMANN
AND THE
ISAAC ASIMOV'S ROBOT MYSTERY TRILOGY

"Mark Tiedemann is science fiction's secret weapon: a shrewd and intelligent storyteller, flying in just under the radar. Isaac Asimov would not have been disappointed with his continuation of the Robot series, nor will the Good Doctor's many readers."

—Allen Steele
Hugo and Nebula Award-winning author
of *A King of Infinite Space* and *Oceanspace*

"Tiedemann takes what Asimov imagined and makes it so real you can see the dirt under the fingernails. The mystery is absorbing, the action is fast-paced, the intrigue is enigmatic. What more could you want from a book?"

—Carolyn Ives Gilman
Author of *Halfway Human*

ISAAC ASIMOV'S
ROBOT MYSTERY

AURORA

MARK W. TIEDEMANN

Mark W. Tiedemann's love for science fiction and writing started at an early age, although it was momentarily side-tracked—for over twenty years—by his career as a professional photographer. With the publication of "Targets" in the December 1990 issue of *Asimov's Science Fiction Magazine*, he began selling short stories to various markets; his work has since appeared in *Magazine of Fantasy & Science Fiction*, *Science Fiction Age*, *Tomorrow SF*, and a number of anthologies. His bestselling novel *Mirage*, the first entry in the *Isaac Asimov's Robot Mysteries* series, was released in April 2000; its follow-up, *Chimera*, was published in April 2001. His most recent novel, *Compass Reach*, was nominated for the 2001 Philip K. Dick Memorial Award. Tiedemann lives in St. Louis, Missouri, with his companion, Donna, and their resident alien life form—a dog named Kory.

ISAAC ASIMOV

Isaac Asimov was the author of over 400 books—including three Hugo Award-winners—and numerous bestsellers, as well as countless stories and scientific essays. He was awarded the Grand Master of Science Fiction by the Science Fiction Writers of America in 1985, and he was the man who coined the words robotics, positronic, and psychohistory. He died in 1992.

AVAILABLE NOW

Realtime
by Mark W. Tiedemann

ISAAC ASIMOV ROBOT MYSTERIES
by Mark W. Tiedemann
Mirage
Chimera

ISAAC ASIMOV'S ROBOT CITY
Volume 1
by Michael P. Kube-McDowell and Mike McQuay

Volume 2
by William F. Wu and Arthur Byron Cover

Volume 3
by Rob Chilson and William F. Wu

ISAAC ASIMOV'S ROBOTS AND ALIENS CITY
Volume 1
by Stephen Leigh and Cordell Scotten

Volume 2
by Robert Thurston and Jerry Oltion

ISAAC ASIMOV'S
ROBOT MYSTERY

AURORA

MARK W. TIEDEMANN

ibooks
new york
www.ibooksinc.com

DISTRIBUTED BY SIMON & SCHUSTER, INC

An Original Publication of ibooks, inc.

Copyright © 2002 by Byron Preiss Visual Publications, Inc.

"Chronology of the Robot Empire/Foundation Universe"
copyright © 2001 by Attila Torkos

An ibooks, inc. Book

ibooks, inc.
24 West 25th Street
New York, NY 10010

The ibooks World Wide Web Site Address is:
http://www.ibooksinc.com

ISBN 0-7434-4460-4
First ibooks, inc. printing April 2002
10 9 8 7 6 5 4 3 2 1

Edited by Steven A. Roman

Cover art by Bruce Jensen
Cover design by j. vita

Printed in the U.S.A.

This one is for
Greg, Judy, and Isaac—the Millers,
steadfast friends and good people

AUTHOR'S NOTE

Every book is inspired or assembled or informed by many other books. In writing this series, I used many. To be sure, the wealth of imaginative possibilities latent in Isaac Asimov's original stories about the caves of steel, Spacers and robots, ethics and programming cannot be underestimated. But a lifetime of reading Asimov's science essays must also be stressed, for they established a foundation upon which sound speculation and the breadth of interest necessary for three books such as these could be built.

More currently, I would like to mention a few works that proved essential to the construction of these speculations: Roger Penrose's "The Emperor's New Mind" is a little dated, but still valuable in discussions of AI and other matters Turing; "A History of the Mind" by Nicholas Humphrey; Richard Feyman's prescient essay "Computing Minds in the Future"; "Artificial Life" by Steven Levy; "Climbing Mount Improbable" by Richard Dawkins; and most relevant to the last volume, Laurie Garrett's two works on disease and public health, "The Coming Plague" and "Betrayal of Trust," both works of extreme relevance. Scientific American published an issue devoted to nanotech in September 2001.

Also, I would like to thank Carolyn Ives Gilman, Timons Esaias, Bernadette Harris, and Donna Schultz for their direct input and innumerable conversations during the writing of these books.

Special thanks to my editor, Steven Roman, for an excellent job and remarkable patience and understanding.

Finally, my thanks, appreciation, and love to Donna, without whom none of this would have come to pass.

ISAAC ASIMOV'S
ROBOT MYSTERY

AURORA

Prologue

Record module new file catalogue designation "Operations Adjustment, Relocation, and Program Revision" access code protected pending security verifications running current upload virtual conference reference unlabeled fill visual fill audio status On

T HE THICK man with amber-tinged white hair watched the other chairs around the table become occupied. Eighteen chairs, but after everyone arrived only seven of them were in use. He smiled to himself at the cosmetic masks most of them used. Two of them were shifting blurs, people seen through patterned glass.

The program whispered in his ear that everyone who was going to show up was present. He tapped his fingers lightly on the tabletop. The sound traveled effectively through the environment, as good as a gavel strike, and the attendees stopped their quiet chatter and turned their full attention to their host.

"Our ranks have thinned," he said. "Still, there are more of you than I expected." He looked around at each of them, fixing one after another with a narrow gaze.

"The arrests have been unexpected and embarrassing," he continued. "Alda Mikels is back in prison, pending trial for conspiracy to commit murder. Personally, I believe he will beat the charge, but it no longer matters. This unfortunate turn has rendered him useless to us. That has damaged the organization, but we're not crippled. We can function without Mikels.

"However, our shipping lines have been severely compromised. That is not something as easily survived. We've lost several key operatives in the wave of arrests following the discovery of our Nova Levis operation. Most expensively, we're now short two cyborgs. Our chief operative on Kopernik Station is dead, as are her principal contacts on the ground on Earth. The arrests following these incidents have severely curtailed our ability to funnel material in and out of Earth ports, and our distribution network on Earth has been shut down for the duration."

He smiled grimly. "Would that Heisenberg save us from honest police."

A smattering of dry laughter circled the table.

"The chief problem, however," he resumed after a long pause, "is a matter of information. We don't know how much they know about our operations. We have no idea how much they may understand about our program. As bad as things have been to date, the real catastrophe may yet come.

"I've decided, therefore, to move the timetable up slightly. I look around at our gathering here and see that a useable number of us are still willing to go forward. Your presence here declares your commitment. But that so many others are no longer either able or willing to meet with us urges a sharp departure from our former long-term goals. In the wake of everything that has happened in the previous fourteen months, I believe we should abandon Earth."

Quick looks and muttering followed. He waited till their attention returned to him.

"I know," he said. "Many of you live on Earth. However, it seems clear that Earth has become inhospitable toward us. In time, I'm certain, we can reestablish a base. Till then, though, we should move the center of operations. Reducing Earth to simply one more market rather than pretending that it can be a haven for our activities will hardly damage profits. The freedom of movement we now enjoy among the more recently established Settler colonies will, I believe, more than compensate for the loss of comfort and prestige Earth has offered in the past. The fact remains, however, that our agenda failed when we were unable to displace Aurora from her position as chief legation to Earth. The subsequent restructuring of the law enforcement programs has in some respects strengthened their position on Earth and allowed the Terrans to emerge as a policing force among the older Settler colonies. This is becoming inconvenient.

"We're fortunate, however, that all their attention has been diverted to a demand for ground inspections on Nova Levis. This is leaving most of our operations free to conduct business unfettered over the majority of our range.

"At least, for now. Aurora is agitating for a stronger Spacer presence to assist in the Terran effort to curtail our operations. They're gaining support for this position in the Council of Fifty Worlds. The Theians, as we have seen, are already putting ships at Terran disposal. Who knows how long we have before a majority of Spacer worlds come around to Aurora's point of view?"

"So what do you suggest we do about it?" one of the blurred attendees demanded.

The others looked at the speaker nervously. No one before had ever interrupted the Chairman.

"I suggest," the Chairman said after a time, "that we replace Aurora as chief Spacer world."

"That's been one of your intentions all along," the blur said. "Eighteen months ago you expected exactly that to happen after slaughtering all those diplomats on Earth. What do you propose to do differently?"

The Chairman reached forward and touched a contact on the table.

Abruptly, everyone's appearance changed. The cosmetic "tweaking" most of them employed when attending these meetings vanished, leaving them as they really appeared in life. The two blurred members suddenly snapped into focus. From the sharp intake of breath all around, no one had guessed their identities before.

All of them turned angry glares on the Chairman. His own appearance had altered, though not as completely as the others, giving the impression that the masking program he employed had switched off.

"That's better," he said. "I like to know who is challenging me."

One of the unveiled leaned forward. "You *always* knew who I was!"

"Yes, but now everyone does. So if I'm stabbed in the back, everyone will have a face to remember and a name to accuse."

It amazed him sometimes how well unspoken communications functioned in this noncorporeal place. The tension around the table seemed to tingle over his skin.

"We're moving all operations to Nova Levis," the Chairman said. "From there, we can manage the coming campaign."

"Are we going to war?" one of the others asked.

"We've *been* at war," the Chairman said dryly. "We're simply acknowledging it openly, at least among ourselves. I can't see how this will have a negative effect. We may all become more focussed. I do not require all of you to join me there, though. You each have tasks which will be best carried out from other locations."

"Why Nova Levis?" another asked. "It's blockaded, the place is falling apart—it's hellish."

"Precisely. No one would expect anyone to move a power base *to* such a place. The blockade will give us the ideal blind from cover in which we can carry out our business. It has created tensions between all the factions and even though relations between Terran and Spacer are in some ways better, they are more fragile than ever before. If we damage that, we can compromise Aurora. And when Aurora finally falls, it will become the perfect world from which to orchestrate the final shift in power."

He looked at them. He could see their interest, their avarice, even under their natural reticence and suspicion. *They're all worried what this is going to cost them...*

"You've each been sent data packets since arriving at this meeting. In them you'll find specific instructions. I've taken steps to ensure your safety as far as possible, but nothing worth doing is without risk. You've heard this before, of course, that the rewards are great. You've heard it before, heard it from me, and it has always been true. You've all gained enormous wealth through our association. Power. The only thing worth risking that for is more wealth and power. And status. Right now none of you can actually admit to anyone who you really are and what you really do. When this is finished, you may all step out of the shadows, into the full light of unchallenged status. Dawn is coming."

A few smiles, nods all around, even from the two completely unmasked members.

"Good," the Chairman said, slapping the table. "Let me show you the prize."

Around the table, abruptly, a landscape shimmered into existence. Lush grass stretched away in all directions, toward low hills, fields filled with orchards, golden-barked serpentine oaks, and a cloudless turquoise sky. The Terrans at the table flinched. It had been a long time since their last visit here, and they were no longer used to the open-aired vistas in which the Chairman liked to hold his meetings. This, though, was even more striking. They were Outside, not even the pretense of a structure to shield them from the vastness of unenclosed nature.

"This is the prize," the Chairman announced, standing. He waved around at the limitless sky and the pristine sward. "When we are done, this will be our capital, our home. We will live here." He laughed and looked at them. Even those evidently pleased with the prospect seemed bemused. He laughed louder. "Don't you recognize it? I said dawn was coming. This is what it will look like.

"This is Aurora."

ARIEL BURGESS opened her eyes in the dim room and stared up at the featureless ceiling. Dream images fled, dissipated against the flatness above. Lately her dreams seemed to be taking place from the perspective of a childhood she could not remember. It seemed appropriate that she could, on waking, retain nothing specific about the dreams.

But they had woken her early every morning for the past six weeks.

A heavy sigh, followed by oddly muted smacking sounds, drew her attention. Beside her, Coren rolled tentatively onto his right side, poised unconsciously for a few seconds, then twisted back onto his left side, his face half buried in pillow. He had kicked off his sheet again, though it persistently tangled his calves. Ariel never understood why he bothered with covers—he kept his apartment overly warm. She glanced down at herself, only covered up to her thighs.

Something primal about sleeping with a blanket, she thought. *That must be it...*

Ariel tried to fall back to sleep. It never worked, but Coren sometimes took it as a personal rebuke to wake up alone.

The hell with it, she thought, and eased out of bed.

She went to the kitchen and punched the autochef for coffee. A few seconds later, she took the steaming cup and went to the comm. She tapped in the code for her own apartment in the Spacer embassy enclave.

"Ambassador Burgess's residence," answered the faintly feminine voice of her robot.

"Jennie, it's Ariel. Any messages?"

"Derec Avery wishes to speak with you at your convenience. Hofton called, but left no specific message. Ambassador Setaris wishes to see you as soon as possible."

Ariel shivered briefly. *Setaris...*

"Thank you, Jennie. If Ambassador Setaris calls again, tell her I have not checked in. I'm taking personal time."

"That would be a lie."

"Exactly, Jennie. I am not now officially checking in. Understood?"

"And personal time?"

"Starting yesterday."

"Very well, Ariel."

"Are both Hofton and Derec still on Kopernik Station?"

"Hofton returned from Kopernik last night. Mr. Avery is still on Kopernik."

"Fine. I'll contact Hofton on my own. Patch me through to Derec."

Ariel sipped her coffee while the complex transaction of making a secure connection between Coren Lanra's apartment, through her own apartment in the Spacer embassy, to Derec on Kopernik Station proceeded. It took several seconds before Derec's face appeared on the small screen.

His eyes widened briefly. Ariel leaned forward and adjusted the angle of view, limiting what Derec saw to just her face. Derec smiled.

"Good morning," he said.

"Maybe, maybe not," Ariel answered wryly. "Setaris wants to see me. As soon as possible."

"Ah. Have you spoken to her yet?"

"No. I thought it would be best to talk to you and Hofton first."

Derec nodded. "Where are you?"

"I'm with Coren."

Ariel saw the first hint of a frown, an instant of disapproval in his face, and felt a brief chill. Derec had never looked at her quite that way before. "Is that wise?" he asked.

"Why wouldn't it be?" She laughed self-effacingly. "I always seem to have better luck with Terrans."

Derec looked surprised. "That's not what I mean. Setaris wants to see you. Under current circumstances—*political* circumstances—"

"Oh." Now she felt foolish. "Little late now to worry about that."

"I suppose. Anyway, Hofton is on the ground, finishing up Thales' transferral up here. Approval went through very quickly, so—"

"So it looks like we're getting sent home after all."

"*I* am, at least."

"No, they've been treating us as a package. Every conversation I have with Setaris anymore, it's 'Mr. Avery and you' or 'Derec, you, others.' I don't think Setaris sees us as separate entities. If you're going home, then I am, too. She just hasn't told me yet."

"She wants to see you as soon as possible."

"Of course. Whenever Setaris wants something, it's now. Has she spoken to you?"

"No, not directly, but I haven't been able to talk to the liaison here as freely as I used to."

"Is that why you called? To see if I knew anything?"

"Partly. I wanted you to see if, before you were completely shut out, you could at least sign off on Rana's request for citizenship application." For close to a year, his assistant, Rana Duvan, had been trying to get Auroran citizenship, partly because she hoped to study at the legendary Calvin Institute there. Mostly, however, it was because the troubles she, Derec, and Ariel had found themselves in had made Earth far too politically hot for her to remain.

Ariel tried to ignore the spike of irritation. "I thought that was already done. Hofton could take care of it."

"Evidently not anymore. I received word that he's been transferred out of your service, effective last night."

"Oh." The irritation turned to anger, then faded into a kind of hopeless resignation. "I see. So the shaft finishes its long journey into the heart."

"I'm sorry."

"Not your fault," Ariel said.

"No, but—hell, *somebody* should apologize and the people who did it to us certainly won't."

Ariel laughed. "Well. Look, thanks for caring. I'll see what I can do for Rana. I have a few things I want to do before Setaris gives me my travel orders."

"Talk to Hofton beforehand, all right? And be careful."

"Always."

She touched the disconnect and leaned back in the chair. After a moment, she turned. Coren stood in the doorway, watching her, a cup in his left hand.

"It's almost over," he said. "Isn't it?"

"I—maybe. Probably."

"Setaris is looking for you. Derec's getting final approval to take his Resident Intelligence up to Kopernik—which means Terran authorities have stopped trying to get him out of Auroran embassy space and just want him gone. And Hofton's down here, probably looking for you, but reassigned." He shrugged. "How long do you figure we have?"

The one thing about Coren Lanra she had yet to really understand was his complete lack of self-deception. He could be sentimental, but he always managed to isolate it from reality. Worse, his refusal to lie to himself forced her to a level of honesty that was immediate and unforgiving.

How long did they have? Ariel did not know how to judge. She had originally thought her transfer would come within days of being told she was going back. But that had been nearly two months ago. She knew things moved slowly through Spacer bureaucracy, but...

"Couple days," she said. "At most."

He took a drink from his cup, and came toward her. He stopped and brushed his fingers along the line of her jaw. "So what do you want to do?"

"Do I have options?"

"I could still make some calls, pull in a few favors, get you a Terran citizenship."

"That's a bit unlikely, don't you think?"

"No. Not if you present it to the right people the right way."

"No." She shook her head. "I'm—it wouldn't be comfortable."

"All right. Then what do you want to do?"

Make love, she thought. They had done that nearly every day since Coren's release from the hospital. She glanced at his right arm. The hair was beginning to grow back where the skin grafts had coated his wrist and forearm. Within, she knew, bone had been rebuilt. He had sustained other injuries from the cyborg Gamelin, but the arm had been the hardest to repair, taken the longest to recover.

Thinking about Gamelin, she asked, "Have you heard from Rega Looms lately?"

"No. I'm not on his keep-in-touch list."

Coren's former employer, whom Coren had walked out on, had sent only one communication that Ariel knew about—a large payment Coren assumed was severance pay.

Gamelin had been Rega Looms' son at one time, abandoned in infancy, the victim of a chronic disorder for which there was no cure, only certain death after an undetermined length of time. Looms had kept the infant's existence a secret from everyone, even the sister born a few years later—a sister the reconstructed, transformed, and returned scion had murdered, a sister with whom Coren had been in love once...

Quitting had been the only reasonable option Coren had left. He could not continue being Looms' head of security when he no longer respected or trusted the man. Ariel thought she understood that.

But she had stubbornly refused to resign her own position with the Auroran legation after realizing that her own superiors had lied to her and used her and similarly destroyed her respect for them. She could not bring herself to quit. *Is that a flaw or a virtue?*

The past year and two months had been hellish. Friends killed, her mission on Earth for Aurora altered beyond recognition, old anxieties about her worth to Aurora resurrected. Cyborgs, of all things, appearing out the miasma of impossibility. The best she could do, the best she *had* done, was to simply hold on, ride it out, and do her job the best way she knew. Not that it mattered for her own career—any choice she made had put her more and more on the fast track to dismissal.

What do I want to do...?

Not go home in disgrace.

Coren waited patiently. He possessed that ability in more abundance than any man she had ever known. He knew how to wait. He did it well.

What have I left unfinished? she wondered. *Other than my life...*

She looked up at him. "I want to see Nova Levis."

Coren frowned. "The lab or the planet? There's nothing *in* the lab. It's been closed down for years."

"So we were told."

He pursed his lips thoughtfully. Finally, he nodded. "Get dressed."

They stepped down the ramp from the semiballistic, into the press of the Indones Sector station. Ariel's nose wrinkled at the sharp aromas. Just outside the transition lounge, vendors in kiosks hawked steaming foods, bright scarves that tied around the waist or across the shoulder, souvenir trinkets, and maps to the sector.

The concourse arched over them like the ribs of an ancient promenade. They made their way through the throngs, bags slung over shoulders, to the brightness at the far end.

Ariel and Coren emerged into a vast terminal. The domed ceiling above glowed with pearlescent light. Queues formed at all the desks, for travel either by tube, semiballistic, surface transport, or local service. Coren led the way to the local transport access and quickly secured a cab.

"DyNan Manual Industries local offices," he told the autopilot.

"I thought you resigned from them," Ariel said.

"I did. But I still have friends. I made a couple calls before we left."

He opened his pack and pulled out a palm-sized device. He opened it out till it was nearly a meter square. A grid map appeared on its surface. He tapped a glowing green circle.

"The lab is somewhere in this block of old conversion," he said. "Not sure precisely where, which is why I needed to make those calls." He folded up his screen and slipped it back into the bag. "This whole region is constantly under construction. Most of it is underwater."

"I know," Ariel said. "The Pacific Ocean is above us even now."

"Not yet. Another few kilometers."

Ariel found his hand and squeezed. He turned his hand over and laced his fingers through hers. She had a mental list of things she wanted to say to him. They rode all the way to the DyNan compound in silence.

The cab descended several levels, through narrower avenues lined with people and businesses and apartment blocks that seemed to crowd in even more than typically for Earth. The warrens pulsed with activity. Ariel felt a sudden craving. She *wanted*... but could not define *what* she wanted.

To stay...?

Finally, the cab turned down an empty, private lane sandwiched between two high walls. It stopped at the gate at the end.

"Wait here," Coren said, and got out.

Ariel watched him walk up to the gate and insert a card in the reader slot. A moment later, he used a different card. A door off to his right opened. He turned, grinning, and gestured for her to join him.

Ariel grabbed both packs and slid out of the cab.

Beyond the narrow entrance, they followed a corridor to another doorway, which opened on a garden area. Glass-walled offices lined the opposite side of the arboretum. A man wound his way along the snaking pathway to meet them.

"Coren," the man said, nodding as he stopped before them.

"Green," Coren said.

"Coming back to work, boss?"

Coren looked surprised. "How's that?"

Green looked uncertain then. "We heard you were injured."

"You didn't hear that I resigned?"

"Rumors... nothing anyone took seriously." He frowned deeply. "Did you?"

Coren sighed. "I need a favor, Green. Depending on that we'll see how true which rumors are."

"Okay."

"I need access to an old section in Teluk Tolo."

"I take it you can't get there through public services."

"Let's say I don't want to bother anybody about it."

Green nodded. "Let's see what you need." He glanced at Ariel. "You must be Ambassador Burgess."

"Yes."

"I'm Green Honli, branch security chief," he said, extending a hand. Ariel shook it. "Pleased to meet you."

"There's a snake out for you."

Ariel blinked. "I beg your pardon?"

"How old?" Coren asked.

"Twelve hours," Green said.

"What is a snake?" Ariel asked.

"One step down from a warrant," Coren said. "On the quiet, a request for local authorities to locate and return you to your embassy. Nothing public, but a damn nuisance." He hissed between his teeth. "All we need is a day, Green."

"That shouldn't be a problem. Come on, I've had housekeeping prep the visitor apartment."

Less than a half-hour later, Green took them in a DyNan transport out another exit.

"We used to have a workforce of nearly three thousand," Green explained. He gestured out the window at passing apartment blocks. "We housed them here. That's been a few years. All this is empty. We've been negotiating with the local district housing authority for converting it to public domiciles, but we're having a problem over squatting."

"Can't get them to police it?" Coren asked.

"Basically. Without guarantees and reversion rights, DyNan's not about to let the sector have it. Not surprising. Indones reportedly has the worst warren-squatting on the globe." He shrugged. "Old problem."

"So this is all uninhabited?" Ariel asked, gesturing out the window at the passing blocks.

"A couple businesses rent office and warehouse space," Green said, "but by and large no one lives here."

The transport traveled uncharacteristically empty streets for nearly ten minutes. Green signaled the driver to stop within sight of a boundary wall that shot up to join a tangle of strutwork and supporting columns just below the eaves of a cupola. He gestured for Ariel and Coren to get out.

Green took a disk from his pocket and handed it to Coren. "This is the guide to the site you want. It's about ten kilometers from here, but two down," he emphasized, jabbing a finger toward the pavement. "You might have some trouble actually getting into it. According to sector housing updates, after it was closed it was scheduled to be converted into vat space for waste treatment and gas exchangers. There's nothing to indicate that the conversion actually took place, which isn't uncommon here, either, so it may be just sitting there empty."

"That was quick," Coren said.

"You trained us," Green said with mock indignity. "Actually, stuff like this is fairly easy. Anytime something is scheduled for a conversion, there's a civil court file opened on it in anticipation of legal challenges— competing claims, special interest suits, oversight committee interest... I'll tell you, boss, sometimes I wish I could work in the Horn District or Brasil or even in the Persak. The local bureaucracy here is mind-numbing. But anyway, you just screen for open court files. If they're still open pending a hearing, all the relevant data is there."

"This should have been resolved eighteen years ago," Ariel said.

Green shrugged. "Recently, Imbitek had to rip out an entire distribution center because the file was still open on their license to convert an old hospice center. The center had been abandoned, closed down for twelve years. They petitioned for the space, got preliminary approval, and moved in after waiting a recommended four years to see if anyone would challenge. They neglected to file a claim to seal the approval to amendation. Someone challenged. Now here's the amazing thing: The court told them to restore the space to its original condition pending the hearing. Imbitek could still win the petition, but it won't even be heard while they continue to operate."

Coren shook his head. "Trust me, Indones doesn't have a lock on that kind of thing. I could tell you some stories..." He glanced at Ariel. "But later." He slipped the disk into his reader. "So, we have to do this on foot?"

"Sorry, yes." Green pointed to the nearest building. "This is the access to the maintenance warrens under here. You'll find the path through the link stations connecting the housing plant to the civic infrastructure on the disk. This way you can avoid running into anyone. Do the whole thing through the service tunnels. It'll take longer, but..."

"Perfect," Coren said. "Thanks. We'll be back by morning."

"I'll be here."

Coren walked away. Ariel followed a moment later, glancing back from the door to the maintenance building to see Green Honli climb back into the transport. The vehicle, nearly silent, circled around and headed back the way it had come.

The small anteroom was dark, lit poorly by red guide lights on the floor and around the ceiling.

"Do you trust him?" she asked.

Coren opened his reader and studied the new grid that scrolled across its surface. "As much as anyone else. There's nothing to be gained by him lying to us or turning us in. We haven't done anything illegal and as for Rega—I checked while we were waiting for Green to get us this material and guess what? I *am* still technically an employee of DyNan Manual Industries. I've even been collecting a salary."

"So it wouldn't be practical for him to betray us."

"No, it wouldn't." He looked at her. She could not see his eyes in the dimness. "Look at it this way: Even if he turned you over to the authorities, *I* still haven't done anything. He'd have to deal with me, then, and he knows me." He shook his head. "We have a little time. There's not much I can do to keep you from having to go back to your people. Let's do what you want and stop wasting time on fruitless paranoia."

"Paranoia is a habit."

"Then get over it." He studied the grid. "This way."

He refolded the reader and headed off. For a moment, Ariel considered letting him go and running. It was a peculiar feeling, one she had not experienced in many years. It was fear, she knew, but the kind of fear she had thought long banished from her palette of emotions—fear of finishing.

Things were coming to an end. Following Coren now guaranteed their completion.

And then what?

She hefted her small backpack and lurched after him.

They climbed down a series of ladders, through narrower and narrower passages, until they reached an ancient walkway. Through the gaps in the lattices Ariel made out vague amalgams of machine-shapes, artifacts slowly congealing into organic imitations of landscape, coated with the drippings and growths of centuries of inattention. Her nose wrinkled at a pervasively fetid atmosphere which seemed to alternate between sickly-sweet and musty decay.

The light that surrounded them was a combination of dimming service lights and phosphorescent growths along the walls. They progressed through long stretches of corridor which possessed no light at all. Coren's lamp flicked on then and Ariel followed his silhouette.

He stopped and opened up his reader.

Around them, distant sounds, wet and metallic and combinations of both, echoed, intimating vast spaces beyond the range of their light and vision.

In the glow of the flatscreen, Coren's face looked grim. After studying the map for several seconds, he handed Ariel the reader, unshouldered his pack, and knelt. He took out a handful of tiny devices. He touched each one and, in turn, they glowed faintly. When he dropped them to the ground, they abruptly scattered, scampering off into the darkness.

Coren retrieved the reader from Ariel and tapped the control pad a couple of times.

"Now maybe we can see if this leads where it's supposed to," he muttered.

Ariel suppressed a shudder and watched the screen.

One by one, then in clusters, blue markers appeared on the grid, locating each of the little machines.

The ones scurrying down the path designated by the map stopped. They shifted around for a few moments, then shot off down alternate routes. Finally, one of them blinked red and the others converged on it, running along the new path.

"Okay," Coren said. He sounded relieved. "Let's go."

When they reached the spot where Coren's scouts had stopped, they found that the passage had been sealed off with new construction. Under their lights, the surface of the wall appeared visibly newer than its surroundings.

They followed the scouts.

"Listen," Ariel said.

Coren halted. A faint whispering sound penetrated. "Water," he said.

The path led down again. Ancient steps, a short ladder—Coren checked the map regularly now, as they were well off the route provided by Green Honli—and finally along a narrow corridor that ended at a circular chamber with a hatch in the floor. Several of Coren's machines clustered around it.

He deactivated the tiny vonoomans and scooped them up, returning them to his pack. He checked the flatscreen.

"Under here," he said. "Either we're about to climb into a sewage treatment facility—maybe even a sewage line—or..." He shrugged elaborately.

"Open it," Ariel said.

It was warm in the small room. Sweat trickled along Ariel's spine.

"We're under ocean," Coren said as he began working at the security lock on the hatch. "A kilometer up. Maybe three kilometers from the mainland."

He tapped code into the lock and waited. When nothing happened, he grunted and opened his pack again. He took out a small device and placed it against the hatch, close to the security keypad.

"Ah," he said after a few seconds. He tapped in a new sequence. The seals snapped open with a brittle *snik*. Coren looked up. "Ready?"

Ariel waved him to proceed. Coren removed his scanner and stood up. He touched a plate alongside the hatch with his toe and the entire door swung up with a faint pneumatic hiss.

"Doesn't smell like sewage," Coren said, smiling. He dropped a few of his scouts down the opening. He watched his flatscreen. "Clear."

He folded up the screen and dropped it into his pack. He climbed down the hatch. Ariel drew a deep breath and followed.

She reached bottom in nearly total darkness. An instant later, Coren switched on his light and dragged its beam over the walls of the room. Ariel could make no sense out of the fragments illuminated, but Coren grunted suddenly and walked away.

An instant later, a ceiling light came on.

They stood in an empty, irregularly-shaped space. Faint outlines on the walls showed where shelves or cabinets had been bolted. Two doors led out in opposite directions.

Ariel went to the nearest and pressed the handle. The door opened outward easily.

As she stepped through, lights flickered to life ahead of her, down a short corridor that let onto a balcony.

Below lay a cavernous space. The floor, under the sharp bluish-white light, was littered with debris. Desks stood here and there, drawers pulled out and empty.

Coren knelt beside her and ran a finger over the balcony floor.

"Not much dust," he said. "This hasn't been empty that long."

"Doesn't look much like a sewage plant, either," Ariel said.

"Can't believe everything you read."

Coren let loose the rest of his scouts. A few minutes later he said, "We're the only people here."

Ariel went to the stairs at the far end of the balcony and hurried down to the main level. Close up she could make out footprints still visible under recent layers of dust. Paper scraps gathered in corners, along with bits of metal and plastic, pieces and parts of objects hastily removed.

Recently removed...

Beyond this chamber she found a constellation of other rooms, some smaller, one at least much larger. She went through the smaller ones. She could almost tell what each one had been—this one an office, that one a lab of some sort, over there a storage room.

"Ariel!"

She followed his voice back through the largest chamber and into a long corridor lined on one wall with doors. Most stood open, but a few were closed. She found Coren in the last room.

Two walls were filled with storage drawers. Most were pulled out and empty. Label plaques had been ripped from the wall beside each drawer.

Coren was squatting before a pile of debris. He looked up when she entered and pointed at scattered shafts of pale-yellow vegetation.

"Grass?" Ariel mused.

"That's what it looks like to me."

"Odd place for it." She began pulling out drawers and searching for more traces of what they might have contained. "Did you check the other rooms?"

"Yes. Same arrangement. A lot of storage capacity here."

Ariel yanked a drawer out as far as it would come and peered into the dim recesses. She ran her hand around it and touched a plate set in the top. "Ah-hah. These are stasis boxes. Were, anyway." She surveyed the banks of drawers. "Sample storage."

Coren frowned. "Grass?"

"Did you touch it?"

"No..."

"Don't. Use gloves. It might be worth having it tested."

Ariel opened her pack. She had brought a stack of sample bags, in case any biological samples might still be present. She had actually expected to find nothing. She pulled on a pair of bioprophylaxis gloves and carefully scooped most of the grass blades into the bag.

The facility had been only recently occupied, that much was obvious. The data labeling it as a treatment complex showed a registration and permit date nearly thirteen years old.

"So what were they still doing here?" Coren wondered aloud.

They found a few more traces of material that they thought might be worth analyzing, but by and large the previous occupants had done an impressive job of removing evidence of their activities.

"Disappointed?" Coren asked.

"A little. I thought perhaps..." Ariel shrugged.

"You thought you might find something that would change Aurora's decision."

She nodded, then looked at him.

"I still think I could get you Terran citizenship," he said.

"For that matter, I could still get you a job with us."

He cocked an eyebrow. "Move to Aurora?"

Ariel nodded. "Doesn't appeal to you, does it?"

"No, I–"

"It's all right. Just so you understand."

His frown changed to reluctant acceptance. "Let's get out of here."

Ariel gave the place a last look, then followed Coren back to their entry point.

There was a delay when they returned to the DyNan compound while the limo came to fetch them. Ariel sat with her back to the wall of the small building while Coren did his best not to pace.

"So what happens next?" he asked finally.

"I go back to the embassy," Ariel said. "Setaris tells me how much I've messed things up and that in the best interests of Aurora I must be removed from my post. A trip back to Aurora and a hearing before one or more committees trying to understand things I'm not at all sure I can explain fully."

"You didn't do anything wrong."

"I'm a fulcrum. Events shifted around me, using me as a pivot point, and turned...inconvenient." She shrugged. "Mainly, I'm the one who will have to explain how a cyborg could be made and that I did indeed see one."

"Derec has the corpse, why can't *he* go back?"

"He will." She suppressed a smile. "They can't have two loose cannons out here shouting about monsters. We're being recalled to find out if we can be trusted as much as anything else."

He looked at her for a long moment. "So you might be back?"

"Could very well be back. As long as Earth doesn't do anything too reactionary." She shrugged again. "Even so, the odds are favorable. Why? Would you like that?"

Coren pursed his lips and slowly nodded.

The limo appeared. Coren blinked and shook his head.

The vehicle stopped and Green Honli stepped out. He went quickly up to Coren and drew him aside. Ariel could not hear the words, but she recognized the tone of voice and body language. Coren paled.

"Come on," he said.

Ariel fell into the back of the limo with him. Doors closed and the transport sped back.

"What is it?" she asked.

Coren's jaw flexed as he stared out the window. "Rega Looms is dead."

2

DEREC AVERY glanced up at the two security officers who entered the lab. The new director, a young woman named Per Alis, met them and they stood together now, talking. Per looked toward Derec briefly and he felt the hairs down the back of his neck shift.

He returned his attention to the console and the large robot sitting next to it.

The robot's torso was open, the breast plate removed. Cables connected various components within to the console, on which an array of screens displayed data.

Most of the robot was a dull brassy color, its surface scarred from years of use. The DW-12 had started existence as a laborer and presumably spent most of its early years being used according to its specifications. Eventually it came into the possession of someone who began making upgrades and modifications until it became effectively a more advanced unit, though physically it remained largely unchanged.

A darker, grayish material comprised its arms and shoulders, part of its waist, and the hips: a recent addition. Derec hoped to be able to complete these modifications before—

The two security officers looked his way. He recognized one of them: Fran Olsin, who had taken over the department after Security Chief Sipha Palen's death.

"Thales," Derec said quietly, "do you know what's going on that would bring station security here?"

"There is a restraining order in effect," the Resident Intelligence replied. "The schedule has been moved up, apparently. You are to be sequestered until travel arrangements are complete, then placed on the first available transport to Aurora."

"Did you just learn about this?"

"In the last ten minutes."

"Were you going to tell me?"

"You instructed me not to bother you unless it was a matter of life and death."

Derec felt a stab of annoyance. "You're not always so literal."

"You are not always engaged in a delicate operation."

Derec's irritation turned inward. He *had* been explicit. Installation of the third tier of positronic buffers required close monitoring. He glanced at the set of oblate components now resting in their new rack within the robot's guts. Thales was running the final checks to see if they would link properly to the main positronic matrix.

"Where's Hofton?" he asked.

"Earthside," Thales said. "In the Spacer Embassy, D.C. Sector."

"Let him know what's happening and ask if there is anything he can do."

"Ariel has been formally recalled," Thales said after a few seconds.

The security officers were approaching him now.

"How are we with this, Thales? Can I close it up?"

"Diagnostics indicate no path impedance, optimum through-flow, and matched-specification gate response. You may safely reseal the unit."

"Disengage diagnostics."

As Derec stood, the cables released themselves from within the torso and retracted into the console. Derec lifted the cover plate from the work-table nearby—heavy, nearly twenty kilograms—and, grunting, hefted it into place on the robot. Instantly, tiny sealing mechanisms grasped the edges of the plate, taking over the labor from Derec, and binding the metal to the body.

Derec straightened and picked up a towel from the table.

"Derec," Fran Olsin said. She looked apologetic.

"Hi, Fran."

She looked at the robot. "How's it coming?"

"Not badly. Better than I expected." He wiped his hands with the towel—a habit, more ritual than necessity—and dropped it on the console. "What's going on?"

"Bad news," Fran said. "We've been ordered to confine you till transport is arranged to Aurora."

Even expecting it, Derec felt a moment of outrage and despair. It had been coming for a long time. He knew it, Ariel knew it, they had talked about it. But until official word came they had been able to pretend that it might not—would not—really happen.

"Confine me where?" he asked. "I never leave the embassy area anyway."

Fran scratched her chin absently, frowning. "That's not very clear, so I'm having to make it up on my own." She looked at the robot. "I suppose technically that robot is yours?"

"It is now. I have the ownership documents if you'd like to review them."

"No, no, I had to verify them, remember?" She stared at the robot for a time. "Look, I get the feeling that my superiors and yours would prefer you didn't do any new work on it till you're away from Earth. So I'm going to read these instructions as house arrest orders. Confine yourself to your cabin till we can get you a berth."

"That sounds reasonable." He glanced at the robot. "I think I've done about as much as I can here, anyway. Maybe a trip to Aurora is just what I need to finish it."

"Good."

"I'll leave the robot in Rana's possession till departure time. How's that?"

"That ought to satisfy just about everybody. Sorry, Derec."

He waved a hand. "You're just doing your job." He leaned over the console. "Thales, copy all this to Hofton's attention. Let Rana know Bogard's status. I'll be in my quarters."

"Yes, Derec."

"So," Derec said to Fran. "Do you escort me, or trust me to go to my room?"

Fran lingered in his cabin. She sent her assistant away and shut the door.

"Some nasty fam has broken loose," she said.

Derec thought for a moment before he recognized the slang. Fam: Freefall Anomalous Matter. A spaceworker term for debris, waste, or other garbage that occasionally got loose, sometimes causing problems in construction sites or with small satellites.

"Such as?" he asked.

"We got word a couple hours ago that Rega Looms is dead. Terran Bureau of Investigation is already making enquiries. They paid your Ambassador Setaris a visit."

"This triggered the recall?"

"Sounds like your people want you away from here before more questions get asked about that mess we had over Looms' daughter. Anyway, there's bound to be suggestions of Spacer retribution for—well, for everything Looms stood for, really."

"You don't believe any of that, do you?"

"No. But I have the advantage of a close relationship with human venality," she said sarcastically. "I just wanted to let you know that maybe this is for your own good. There's no telling what TBI and Special Service might stir up. Knowing them, it wouldn't surprise me if you got blamed for Sipha's death."

Derec had witnessed Sipha Palen's death—and the deaths of several of her officers and who knew how many people aboard the shuttle that had exploded in the docking bay, ripping a hole in the body of Kopernik Station—and had felt absolutely helpless and desolate. Perhaps he deserved some blame. Not that he had caused any of it, but he had been involved in the circumstances that led to it.

"Maybe," he agreed. "Maybe it's time we all get out of here. I don't think we're doing any good anymore."

"Meaning Spacers?" Fran shrugged. "Won't happen. Anyway, I just wanted to let you know how deep this could get."

"Thanks."

Ever since Palen's death, her people—Kopernik Station security—had taken care of him. They had collectively decided he was a victim, too, and needed watching out for. In a way, he was like a mascot.

In return, he had helped them upgrade their own AI systems and improved the efficiency of their surveillance net. They had looked out for him. This was likely the last gesture they could make.

"Rega Looms is dead," he said. "How? Murdered, I gather?"

"Why would you assume that?"

"If the TBI is involved..."

"Ah. Yes, you have a point. However, we don't have all the details. Word is he was found crushed to death in his private quarters."

An escort from the Auroran Embassy waited at Coren's apartment when they returned. Coren suppressed an impulse to challenge them. Ariel had talked it over with him on their flight back.

"No scenes," she said. "It won't do any good anyway, and it might get you more attention than you need."

So as their cab pulled up to his building and he saw the embassy limo and the plainclothes security lounging around the area, he squeezed her hand and let her kiss him.

Last one, he thought, tasting her.

She grabbed her pack and stepped out of the cab. He stayed within and watched her surrender herself to embassy security. No one came up to him to ask him anything. Ariel climbed into the embassy transport and within seconds the security vanished and the vehicles rolled quickly away.

He was alone in the back of the cab.

"Do you wish to proceed to another destination?" the autopilot asked.

"Yes," he said after a pause. "DyNan Manual Industries, main head-quarters."

Coren was surprised that his ID still worked. When he had quit he had expected Rega to deactivate his credentials that very day. They had had a very loud and principled parting—Rega had given in to blackmail and ended his campaign for the senate, and he had done so because the blackmail contained truths, facts he had kept from Coren even while expecting Coren to take care of such matters. The relationship, in Coren's mind, became untenable.

Shola Bran met him in the lobby of the main building. She had been one of his personal choices for Rega's security during his abortive run for the senate. He wondered what position she had moved into since.

"Mr. Lanra," she said. "This is unexpected. We thought your hiatus would last longer."

"Rega's death is unexpected as well, I trust."

She frowned. "Is that why you're back?"

"Is that a problem?"

"I've assumed your duties since..."

Coren glanced around the lobby. A few people worked behind information desks. He gave Shola a slight shake of the head. "My office."

She led the way. When they entered, he was surprised to find it much as he had left it. He closed the doors and went to his desk. He was pleased that it still responded to him. He initiated the security walls Rega would have objected to had he known about them.

"All right," he said, sitting down. "You've become head of security, is that what you're saying?" He waved her toward a chair. "You may speak freely, no one can listen in, and I've always expected candor."

"I remember." She clasped her hands behind her back, continuing to stand. "Yes, I have. You walked out. It was necessary."

"Good. At least someone knows what happened."

"I don't know everything that happened. I just know that you quit."

"You kept that out of general circulation."

"I didn't see it as my place to disseminate gossip."

"I'm not going to undercut you. I *did* quit. As far as I'm concerned, when I finish what I have to do, I'm going back to being quit. If you've been head of security, as far as I'm concerned you still are." He leaned forward. "As long as you don't interfere with me till I'm done."

"What are you going to do?"

"I want to find Rega's killer. Plus finish the thing that put us at odds in the first place. Will you help me or fight me?"

"I'll help. Fighting you...I'd lose."

"Maybe. You're very good at what you do."

Her expression softened. "None of us expected...no one knew..."

"When is the funeral?"

"Tomorrow. Closed casket. He didn't want any cosmetics done, you know how he was. But..."

"Who found him?"

"Me and Lio Top."

"Lio. His campaign manager."

"She's been his liaison at board meetings for the last several weeks."

"He stopped attending?"

"Only voice comm. Then even that stopped. We thought, with the senate race over and his daughter's death—"

"I gather you saw him from time to time?"

"No, not really. Once or twice. Mostly it was Lio."

"I want to talk to her. Did anyone else have access to Rega?"

"No..."

"You sound uncertain."

"Well...I could never prove it, but it seemed sometimes that someone was living with Rega."

"Someone...a woman?"

Shola shrugged. "I'm sorry, boss. I could never get close enough and I didn't feel right about using any invasives."

And now he's dead...

Coren kept that thought to himself. "I need to see the recordings of his comm messages over the last couple of months." He drummed his fingers idly on the edge of the desk. "What's the mood?"

"Awful. No one knows what's going to happen next. Rumor has it that Rega never groomed a successor."

"He wasn't that old. I suppose he didn't think he needed to yet."

"The board doesn't know what to do."

Coren found that doubtful: *Someone* would have a plan, an idea what they *wanted* to do if nothing else. But no one would be willing to step forward just yet. "All right. Copy me the arrangements, then let it be known that I'm back. While I'm here I'll walk you through the parts of the job I never told anyone about." He smiled, he hoped reassuringly. "Meanwhile, I've got your support?"

"I'd love to find out who did this."

The edge in Shola's voice made the hairs on Coren's neck bristle. "Then you're it. I've got to catch up now."

"Sure." She went to the door. "Welcome back, boss."

"Thanks."

He requested a department list from his desk. He selected the bio-research division and studied the names appended. After a few minutes' consideration, he tapped one and waited for the link to open.

"Organics. Willis Jay here."

"Mr. Jay, this is Coren Lanra..." He hesitated briefly, then added, "Head of security."

"Yes, Mr. Lanra?"

"Are you available for the next hour? I have something I want to bring over to you for analysis."

"Well...sure, I've got some time."

"You're in your office?"

"My lab. Right next door."

"Be there shortly."

Coren broke the link and opened his pack. He took out the sample bag of grass. Ariel had divided it up before catching the semiballistic back to D.C., giving him a third. He slipped the package into his jacket pocket and headed for the research wing.

The offices of DyNan were usually quiet and a bit overly-serious, but what Coren walked through now felt sepulchral. *To be expected,* he thought. Still, it got to him. By the time he reached the research area and found the department of Organic Research, he felt guilty, almost ashamed.

Willis Jay looked up at Coren's entrance, eyes large and pale green, and slowly rose to his full height, head-and-shoulders above Coren.

"Mr. Jay," Coren said, extending a hand, "I'm—"

"Coren Lanra, yes. What can I do for you?"

Jay's grasp was quick and light and he sat immediately back down. Coren placed the sample bag on his desk.

"I found this. I'd like it analyzed."

Jay picked it up and held it to the overhead light. "Grass."

"I deduced that much."

"Where did you find it?"

"In an abandoned lab. Beyond that, I'd rather not say."

"So there could be contaminants of an unknown type?"

"That's what I'd like you to find out."

Jay set the bag back down. "And I suppose you don't want this to go any further than us."

Coren felt a smile tug at his mouth. "You suppose correctly."

"I don't suppose you could give me any idea what specifically I might be looking for? No? Give me a couple of days, then." He looked up at Coren. "We'd all heard a rumor that you'd quit."

Coren was surprised at the change of topic. "Really. Where did you hear that?"

"Rumor. Talk in the kitchen, that sort of thing."

"I suppose it wasn't true, then."

"It appears not."

"Any other rumors attached to that one?"

Jay sniffed. "You've been seeing an Auroran ambassador."

"Ah. Now that one is true."

"I suppose it's not a rumor, then."

"How long have you been with DyNan, Mr. Jay?"

"Fifteen years, I think." Jay looked thoughtful for a moment. "Are you going to the funeral?"

"I suppose."

"Rumor is that Mr. Looms was crushed to death."

"Can't confirm or deny that. I don't know. Where's he being kept?"

"The morgue, I imagine. The police took the body away."

"When's the funeral?"

"Two days from now. I wonder who will run the company after this." Jay stood again and picked up the bag. "I'll get back to you about your grass by the funeral, Mr. Lanra."

"I appreciate it, Mr. Jay."

"Just Jay."

"Thanks, Jay. Let me know what you find."

Coren returned to his office by a circuitous path. Along the way he looked into open doors, greeted people, paused in earshot of conversations for a few moments—all to get a better feel for the mood in the building. Somber, he decided, but with an edge of anger, as if Looms' death were a personal betrayal. People did not work for Rega Looms just to have a job—if they came to DyNan with that in mind they rarely lasted long—but because they personally believed in what the company did and came to feel the same way about Rega. By the time he sat down at his own desk again, Coren believed that the company by and large would welcome answers to Looms' murder.

It still puzzled him that Rega had not, apparently, accepted his resignation.

For the last couple of months, Coren had begun testing the waters for new employment. He had found more options than he had expected. After Ariel, he had told himself, he would look for a new job. They had both known it would end—she knew her recall by Aurora was inevitable. There was little enough time as it was.

As for Rega...after years of working for the man, they had finally come into ideological conflict.

Coren had been looking for the murderer of Looms' daughter. And Rega had wanted him to stop. Setting aside Coren's personal feelings toward the late Nyom Looms, there was no way he could see this as other than a direct threat to Rega and DyNan. Rega had placed him in an impossible ethical quandary.

It seems Rega had thought it over and decided that I was right...

It would have been wise for Rega to have at least told him.

Maybe he'd still be alive if I'd known I was still working for him...

Coren shoved that thought aside. That way lies madness, he knew. This was in no way his failure.

What now? He *had* resigned. Pretend it had never happened?

No...that would be unethical.

What do I owe you now, Rega?

After a few minutes' thought, Coren decided that his last obligation to Rega Looms was to find out how he had died and if there were anything he could do about it.

He started accessing records to catch up on the last few months.

direct access subroutine category six Thales-to-Bogard evaluation standard in process, copy log, copy sequence, interrogatory systems profile, match template, revise epistatic drift at point zero-one, revised deviation reference initial protocols subheader Bogard

    Query: self-diagnostic

    Engaged

    Assessment

    Deviation on sublevels two, nine, twenty-three, forty-one, and forty-two

Analysis of deviation

Category error in standard definition of subject profile, internal/experiential conformity deviance in basic parameters

Specify category

Three Law base assumptions, BIOS reevaluation in process, inconclusive, repeat function

Define evaluative failure, specify location, specify assumption

Evaluative failure in action prompts, location topologically nonspecific, system-wide, assumption holistic evaluation reducible to question of type

Specify question

Question: What is human?

3

ARIEL CLIMBED out of the embassy limo and started across the garage to the elevators. As she reached the doors, one set opened and Hofton stepped out.

"Ambassador," Hofton greeted her, giving a slight bow from the waist. He took the pack from her and draped it over his left shoulder.

"Hofton. When did you get back?"

"Last night, actually." He looked past her at the embassy security. "I'm to escort Ambassador Burgess directly to Ambassador Setaris. We won't require your presence."

The pair of officers hesitated. Ariel could see that their orders did not allow this much discretion.

"My responsibility," Hofton added. "If she escapes, you may shoot me in public."

Both of the security officers reddened visibly, then nodded.

"Ambassador...?" Hofton waved her into the elevator.

When they doors closed, Ariel slumped back against the wall and closed her eyes. "Bad news first, Hofton."

"As there's no *good* news, your request is easy. Your recall came through two days ago. Ambassador Setaris has been trying to arrange transport for both you and Mr. Avery."

"Derec, too?"

"He's currently under house arrest. Confinement to quarters, really, just a formality. But it was at the request of the Senate Subcommittee on NonTerran Affairs."

Ariel opened her eyes. "Jonis Taprin?"

31

"The very same. He's been all but demanding that the both of you leave Earth in chains."

"I don't understand. We were friends once...I thought..."

"Never underestimate the power of embarrassment."

"Hofton...Rega Looms is dead."

"I just heard a few hours ago," Hofton said. "That hasn't helped the situation. In fact, it only added to Senator Taprin's expostulations. He's blaming us."

That surprised Ariel. "We don't even know how he died."

"Gruesomely, according to the subetherics. Crushed." He glanced sidelong at her. "Sound familiar?"

"Is there anything we can do?"

"At present, staying out of the line of fire might be the best we can hope for. I haven't heard the word 'cyborg' in any of the 'casts, but it's only a matter of time. In any case, Ambassador Setaris will want to tell you the rest." He paused thoughtfully. "Oh. Pon Byris, head of Auroran security, has attached his name to your recall."

"That's a bit heavyhanded, isn't it?"

"Possibly the result of Senator Taprin's extremely loud complaints. Regardless, I doubt anything positive will result if Byris is involved."

The elevator came to a stop and they stepped into the corridor leading to Setaris's offices. Hofton nodded encouragingly to her, and proceeded down the hall.

A pair of aides looked up from their desks when Hofton and Ariel entered. One of them started to stand, but Hofton waved her back.

"We're expected," he announced, and pushed through the double doors to Setaris's private office.

Setaris seemed to be waiting for them, leaning back in her chair, watching their entrance. Ariel realized then that Setaris's ability to always appear to expect whatever happened had annoyed her since she had come to work for the senior ambassador.

"Ariel, how are you?" Setaris asked, smiling thinly.

Ariel sat down before Setaris offered a chair. "Annoyed."

"Really? And why would that be? Have we interrupted something?"

"Not that it matters to you, but yes."

"We apologize for any inconvenience," Setaris said with a clear tone of sarcasm. "Your recall is official. I'm placing you on an Aurora-bound ship day after tomorrow. The...*Wysteria*?" She glanced at Hofton, who had taken a position standing just behind and to Ariel's left.

"That's correct, Ambassador," Hofton said.

"You'll remain here in the embassy till your shuttle departs. Try to clean up any unfinished business you have before then."

Ariel's hands clenched into fists. *You transferred me to the Intelligence branch two months ago. Since then I haven't had a single assignment. There's nothing to clean up.* "May I ask why I'm being recalled now?"

"You may. Three reasons. The first is the Council is convening a hearing on this matter of the cyborgs. That is why your friend Derec Avery is also going back with you. You're both expert witnesses, your testimony is essential. It's a closed door session, so hyperwave link will not be allowed. You have to be there."

You knew that two months ago, Ariel thought impatiently.

Setaris steepled her long fingers under her chin. "The second reason is general unfitness for duty. You've made yourself ineffective here. Keeping you on is pointless."

"Thank you for your confidence in me."

"Don't act the martyr, Ariel, you've brought this on yourself. Your choice in liaisons has been...unfortunate."

Ariel felt heat in her face. "Who I spend my personal time with is my business."

"How it affects your ability to perform your duties is mine. You have an enemy in Senator Taprin. That alone might have been manageable, but your association with Rega Looms' chief of security has made you suspect to the Spacer population. The combination has been too much. Your usefulness...well..."

"My usefulness at what? I haven't had any duties since—" Ariel cut herself off. "How much of this has to do with what happened to Ambassador Chassik?"

"That much," Setaris said, "I'll grant you, was none of your doing. At least, not in any way to be criticized. Chassik hated you, there's no point trying to explain it away. You embarrassed him in this last fiasco. I'm certain that pressure was brought to bear on the Calvin Institute and the Auroran Council by allies Chassik stirred up to have you recalled. I'm sure if they have their way, you'll be disgraced as well. As far as that goes, sending you home now may be the best thing for you personally. We can minimize the damage here and pull the teeth of most of their complaints."

"You're telling me this is in my best interest?"

"Partly. It's certainly in *our* best interest."

Ariel seethed. "You said three reasons."

"I did. Ambassador Chassik was recalled."

"I remember. I was there."

"Three weeks after that hearing, he formally transferred Solarian legation duties to the Keresians as a temporary condition until another Solarian could be found to take his place. He found one reason or another to
stay here till about a week ago. He was finally shipped out."

"Yes," Ariel said tightly. "I remember." Though she had not known he
had remained on Earth for so long. She wondered how he had managed.

"He never arrived," Setaris said. "The ship was attacked and destroyed.
Chassik is presumed dead. Solaria is claiming that we leaked his itinerary
and, because of our relations with Earth, arranged to have this done."

"That's absurd."

"Of course it is and they know it. However, they want to subpoena
you for an inquest. Shipping you to Aurora now may be the only way to
keep you out of their hands."

Ariel thought for a moment. "Are you telling me that *I'm* being
blamed for Gale Chassik's death?"

Setaris scowled and looked out the broad window at the bright blue
sky. "They no more believe that than they believe Aurora colluded with
Terrans to kill him. But they certainly want you for something."

"The cyborgs."

"That would be my guess. We have no way of knowing how deeply
involved Solaria is in that."

"I assumed Solaria had nothing to do with it as a polity, that it was
just Chassik overstepping authority."

"That's our assumption, too. Unfortunately, we have this debacle with
Nova Levis hanging over our heads and easy solutions are not to be
found."

"Are you suggesting Solaria *does* have something to do with this?"

"A faction of them, almost certainly." Setaris sighed. "It's not your
problem anymore, Ariel. You are out of this."

Despite herself, Ariel was forced to agree with Setaris. There was no
other option. She had to go back to Aurora.

She had known it was coming, that some pretext would be found to
recall her, but still she thought she could avoid it. Now that it was real,
she could find no flaw in the reasons.

"Is Hofton still assigned to me?" she asked.

"No. Hofton is staying here. He has duties."

That shook her even more, but she said nothing. After a minute or so,
she stood.

Then: "Why would anyone want to kill Chassik?"

"That's a very good question, Ariel. We're hoping to answer it before all hell breaks loose."

"They did a wonderful job of keeping me in the dark," Ariel commented sourly.

Hofton and she sat at a small table in the embassy lounge, by the broad windows that gave them a view across the roof of the embassy, out to forest in the distance beneath open sky.

"Everyone here is being kept ignorant of Ambassador Chassik's death," he said. "I didn't know till two days ago. And to be fair, you did not exactly inspire our security people. Now that I think of it, maybe that's the reason Byris has involved himself. You're nominally attached to Intelligence, after all, and your actions *have* been questionable. At least to an outsider."

"I'm part of Auroran Intelligence now, Hofton, and I can't find out anything. Don't you find that funny?"

"Riotously."

Ariel was startled at the glumness in his voice. "I'm sorry," she said.

Hofton raised a hand. "Lately, I haven't been my usual frivolous self. As for Ambassador Chassik, I believe only Ambassador Setaris and one or two of her personal staff knew any details of his death. There have been suggestions in certain circles that it was a Terran ship that attacked his liner. The Terrans are blaming pirates—an easy enough target—and since Aurora has been stepping up its presence on the Nova Levis blockade, accusations of collusion are inevitable."

"Hm. What's your opinion?"

"That returning to Aurora might be the safest option for you."

"Thanks. Why did it take so damn long? I expected to be on a ship a week after Chassik's recall."

"Besides the usual glacial pace of Auroran bureaucratic process, the Terrans have been trying to keep you here."

"Why?"

"It went through phases. First, there was the ongoing TBI investigation about the cyborgs. They wanted you as an expert consultant. Then they wanted you as a material witness at the hearings. Failing to get that, they wanted to hire you. It graduated eventually to a demand for your arrest on charges of conspiracy."

"Conspiracy to do what?"

Hofton shrugged eloquently. "They simply don't want you to leave. At least, some of them don't. Senator Taprin is practically manic to get rid of you. The others I can understand—they want a source of information about a threat they don't know anything about. Taprin is just..."

"Taprin," Ariel finished for him. "The problem is, I don't know anything about cyborgs. None of us do."

"Mr. Avery has been learning quite a lot. Before our people seized the cyborg corpse we had on Kopernik, he recorded a great deal."

"Then why aren't the Terran authorities trying to keep *him?*"

"Oh, they have been *trying*. Setaris has successfully fended off every attempt."

Ariel thought about that. "Has it occurred to her that while she's keeping us out of Terran hands they might be thinking her reasons are a bit more sinister than stated?"

"You mean mightn't they think *we* have something to do with the cyborgs?" He nodded. "I'm certain that has occurred to her, but she's acting under orders from Aurora as well. I don't think Ambassador Setaris has been happy with a single decision she's been allowed to make in months."

"It's falling apart, isn't it?"

"In my opinion," Hofton said, "yes. Ever since Humadros was killed and Eliton's conference self-destructed, things have gotten worse. And this Nova Levis thing is just aggravating it. You would have thought when an Auroran ship was attacked the Terrans would find common cause with us, that relations might ease up. But they keep worsening in too many other areas."

They sat in silence for a time, brooding.

"Well," Hofton said finally. "I have duties—"

"Sure," Ariel said. "Um...Hofton, I have a favor to ask."

"If I can help, of course."

"I need some grass analyzed."

Hofton gave her a quizzical look. "Grass?"

4

HE REFITTED cargo hold smelled of ancient oil, sweat, and hot plastic, odors so long embedded in the fabric of the ship that no cleansing could expunge them. That nearly eighty bodies were crammed in the narrow confines created by the false bulkheads—which hid the stacks of travel couches secured against the actual bulkheads—did nothing to make the aroma any more pleasant.

"They told us we'd get used to it," a woman observed sullenly from somewhere above.

Masid Vorian looked up in her direction. He saw her feet dangling over the edge of her rack. "That," he said with mock cheer, "and five credits will buy you any truth you want."

Laughter lightly cascaded around the collection of bunks. It was an old joke, but not so worn that desperately bored people would not find some humor still in it.

Masid stretched on his couch. He estimated that they had been in transit now twelve days. Twice in that time the P.A. had barked at them to be as silent as possible due to imminent boarding. As far as he knew, the freighter had never been boarded. In between such moments of intense fear the time passed like sludge. It was too dark even to see each other clearly. He had heard the sounds of lovemaking a few times, but it was difficult in these cramped quarters to overcome the normal inhibitions against sex in public. Maybe others were simply good at being quiet at it. Conversation dwindled after several days, speculation on their chances of getting through and what it would be like once they arrived exhausting itself in the mix of ignorance and worry. One or two small groups chattered, their conversation ending the moment someone new tried to join in.

Typical Terran cliquishness, Masid thought, *born of equal parts arrogance, stupidity, and paranoia.*

Masid suspected a few of the baleys might be other than Earth-borns, but no one willingly admitted it here. Maybe once they arrived on Nova Levis he might find one or two Settler-born.

If they reached Nova Levis. Masid could not be certain, but he was convinced that the ship had had to change course at least twice, maybe three times. The ten-day transit had increased to twelve so far, and still no word from the crew about when they might arrive.

The rations had been cut as well. Not bad, not yet, but it was not encouraging.

It had already taken him longer to even get started on this trip than any previous one.

Before slipping into this group of baleys, Masid had heard that Aurora was sending ships to reinforce the blockade around Nova Levis. He wondered how much that might have reduced his chances of getting through...

A low, barely audible vibration ran through the hull.

What conversation there was ceased. Masid leaned his head out to peer up into the nearly-lightless spaces above.

A hatch opened, spilling light into the cramped hold, and a man's head and shoulders appeared.

"Another inspection," he called. "Keep it still, everything'll be all right."

The hatch sealed again and immediately the chatter increased.

"The man said *quiet!*" Masid shouted.

Silence fell at once.

Masid adjusted the pack on which he rested his head, settled himself with hands folded over his chest, and closed his eyes. The best way to wait an inspection out was sleep, he believed. Anything more active was a sure way to get found.

He kept track of the various sounds transmitted throughout the ship, the creaks and scrapes and shiftings, and guessed the point at which boarding occurred. There was still a chance they might get past all this, but—

A whisper passed his ear. Masid's eyes snapped open. Air moved. He heard it again, like something small and fast whizzing through the air. He swallowed, knowing—

The hatch opened again and a new voice boomed through the confines.

"Everyone out."

Damn...

Masid took his time. The others climbed up the scaffolding to the hatch, their small bundles clutched in one arm or slung over tired shoulders. Masid felt for them. Most had spent whatever credit they had left to get this far. They had nothing to go back to, nothing to see them through. Depending on who their captors were, they could look forward to internment camps, transition camps, or a quick trip back to their point of origin. And then nothing.

He heard a few sobs.

"Come on, come on," the voice urged from above.

At least they didn't cut the gravity, he thought. *Likely they're Spacers, then, not Terrans...*

"No stragglers, we've got a head count, come on out."

Masid waited until he was nearly the last. Then he rolled out of the couch, finding the footholds on the bracing. He snagged his pack deftly and slung it over his shoulder, then began the climb up to the hatch.

Webbing stretched across the gap between hull and false bulkhead. Some of the older baleys had a little difficulty negotiating it, but when he reached the webbing himself, Masid saw several uniformed officers giving ample help.

Dull reddish-brown uniforms with gold flashings at high collars and waists: Theians.

A strong hand caught his arm and drew him into the corridor. Theians formed a line, handing the baleys along toward the ship's main lock. Masid followed, smiling grimly, looking from face to face. The Theians looked mildly embarrassed about the whole business.

At the hatch to the lock area a pair of robots seemed to monitor the entire procedure.

Masid stepped between them—

—and locked eyes with a Theian officer. He hesitated and let himself smile just a little more.

The officer turned to his aide and whispered. The aide looked at Masid, frowning, and stepped forward.

"Sir," she said. "Would you come with me, please."

"What for?" Masid asked loudly.

"Sir."

"I don't recognize your authority," Masid said.

The aide placed a hand on her stunner and gripped Masid's elbow. "Please, sir."

Masid looked around frantically. The other baleys nearby cast frightened glances at him.

"This isn't fair!"

He stepped out of line and let the Theian lead him away.

She took him past drums strapped against bulkheads, around a narrow makeshift gangway, and into the cargo bay. Overfilled cages of crates, nacelles, and cubes rose from the deck like topiary gone wild, the path of the maze barely discernible.

The aide kept hold of him until they had made their way through the dangerously disorganized stowage and onto the loading deck.

More robots, a few more Theians. The aide led him to an arbitrary spot against a bulkhead.

"Stay here," she said, then signaled for a robot to stand watch over him. Masid suppressed a smile, tempted to point out to her that he was himself not Terran and knew better than to be afraid of a robot. But he nodded mutely, gave the robot what he hoped was a convincingly fearful look, and slid to the deck to wait.

The aide spoke to a couple of the other Theians, then returned the way she had brought him.

Half an hour later, the Theian officer who had recognized him emerged from the maze. He stopped immediately in front of Masid.

"Vorian, what in the hells of space are you doing here?"

Masid glanced at the other Spacers; none of them showed any sign of having heard.

"Trying to be inconspicuous," Masid said. "What are you doing here, Anda?"

"Arresting the crew of this—" he turned and waved disgustedly at the mass of precariously balanced cargo "—this excuse for a freighter. You could have died inconspicuously, you know."

"It's good to see you, too," Masid said, standing. "I'm trying to get to Nova Levis."

"Really. Well, forget it. The blockade became real a few weeks ago, when Aurora finally joined it officially."

"Is *that* what happened? I wondered why my passport wouldn't work with the major carriers." He glanced around again. "Nothing personal against your people, but could we carry this conversation on somewhere more private?"

Anda's eyes narrowed. "You're working, then."

"Amazing powers of deduction you have there. They should promote you."

Anda scowled. "Come with me."

Masid followed the man to the big cargo bay door. The personnel hatch stood open. An umbilical ran a short distance to the Theian cruiser that held the freighter tightly in a tractor grip.

As soon as he stepped out of the umbilical, into the Theian ship, Masid felt physically better. The air was cleaner for one, as were the decks and bulkheads. He suddenly felt a bit self-conscious in his grungy travel-ing clothes. He had been in the baley-hole for twelve days without undressing.

Abruptly, a small sphere appeared over Anda's left shoulder, hovering and slowly revolving. Anda spoke into the air.

"This is Masid Vorian, officially a guest of the ship. Confirm." A few seconds later, he nodded. "Come on," he said to Masid.

Two turns and up one deck, and they entered a spacious, pleasantly-appointed private cabin. A slender, ivory-colored robot met them just inside the door. The sphere hovering at Anda's shoulder shot across the cabin and set itself in a slot in the wall.

"Captain Wilam, welcome back," the robot said, voice slightly femi-nine. "This is ship's guest Vorian?"

"Yes, Laris, this is Masid."

"Welcome, Masid. May I serve you a confection?"

Anda unbuckled his weapons belt and dropped it on a couch. He glanced at Masid. "Drink?"

"Clean water would be wonderful."

"Nothing for me, Laris."

The robot drifted off to a bar on the other side of the room and returned quickly with a tall glass of water.

"If there is anything else you require, Masid, I am at your service."

"Thanks," Masid said, accepting the glass.

"So just what are you doing?" Anda asked.

Masid took several long swallows. "You first. I've been out of the loop for over a month."

"Doing what?"

"Trying to get to Nova Levis. I haven't had this much trouble getting somewhere in—hell, I don't know if I've *ever* had this much trouble."

"What do you want on Nova Levis? It's a sewer."

Masid fingered his collar. "I should fit right in, then."

"We'll fix that later."

"I'm sure." Masid finished his water and handed the glass to the robot. "Please, sir, I want some more. I've been drinking recycled fluid—I won't call it water—with electrolytes added like seasoning for the past two weeks."

"Goes with the job, doesn't it?" Anda asked caustically.

Masid ignored that. "Nova Levis is a sewer, huh? That wouldn't have anything to do with your new and improved blockade, would it?"

"A blockade runner fired on us. You knew about that, didn't you?"

"I heard something about it."

"That was incident the first. Incident the second happened three weeks ago. An Auroran police liner was attacked en route to Solaria. The ship was destroyed, all aboard killed. Including Solarian Ambassador Gale Chassik."

"Oh, shit."

"That was pretty much everyone's reaction. The ships were recorded coming in, and the recordings were transmitted by hyperwave just before the liner was destroyed. They were identified as the same type that have been doing the bulk of the blockade-running off Nova Levis. Solaria was duly outraged and demanded immediate action, Aurora responded by demanding full disclosure from Solaria about their dealings with Nova Levis, and one result was Aurora presence on the blockade itself. No more Solarian ships are getting in anymore, which has one faction of the Solarian Legation mad enough to chew rocks. Once Solaria admitted to still actually owning Nova Levis, even though the Settler government is the one barring on-ground inspections, Earth began making ominous noises about Spacer collusion and we have our present situation. So we're now intercepting ships bound for Nova Levis well in advance of their arrival—to avoid entanglements with overlapping jurisdiction, you understand—and this, too, has Earth in a spasm."

"How intemperate of them."

Laris brought Masid a refilled glass.

"Your turn," Anda said.

"I need to get to Nova Levis." Masid sipped water.

"So you say. Who are you working for this time? Last I heard, you were actually working for Terran security."

"Station security, Kopernik. True enough. Right now I'm exercising my authority as an independent agent and working on behalf of every-body."

"Hah! There's no such authority."

"You didn't get the memo? Damn." He leaned forward. "They're building cyborgs, Anda."

Anda hesitated and stared at Masid. "Who?"

"That's what I have to find out. But they're building them on Nova Levis."

"You know this for a fact?"

"No. But I have reason to believe it. Strong reason."

"There are no such things as cyborgs."

"You wish. I fought one. Be afraid."

"Why Nova Levis? It's under blockade, there's nothing there."

"There's more there than you might think. Besides, you're providing the best cover there could be."

Anda sighed heavily. "Laris, give me a brandy, please." He looked at Masid, eyes narrow and intent. "Tell me about it."

Masid showered in the hygienic cubicle of the stateroom Anda gave him. The spray of water and massage of 'sonics felt like the caresses of sirens to him. He leaned against the wall and closed his eyes.

He had not told Anda very much—mainly the murder on Kopernik and the subsequent entrapment of the cyborg, leaving out all of Derec Avery's and Ariel Burgess's involvement. He tied it in with the baleys through Sipha Palen's death in the explosion of the shuttle delivering the head organizer of the baley traffic. He had had to mention the dead baleys that had prompted the investigation, but that did not give much away. He left Anda with the impression that he was carrying on this investigation independently of most Spacer, Settler, or Terran authority, something Anda knew Masid tended to do from time to time.

Working his way into the baley network had taken far too long and left him far too out of touch with events. Evidently a mess had been made of the whole traffic in the wake of the Kopernik affair. No one seemed to be in charge anymore, and the independents were both too paranoid and too incompetent to fill the void left by the traditional smugglers.

Why would anyone want to kill Ambassador Chassik?

It made no sense. Chassik represented Solaria, which had taken a "no comment" position on the entire Nova Levis situation. There was no motive. All they could hope to achieve would be to irritate the very world that was their only hope of independence.

Chassik had been recalled...what had that all been about?

He had gotten no answers from the Aurorans, who were in charge of the Spacer mission on Earth. He had not pressed for them, either. No time, he had wanted to get moving...

Masid sighed and closed his eyes again. There was nothing he could do about it this minute, anyway. He still needed to get to Nova Levis. He had to be careful what he dug into right now.

If I turn over the wrong rock, I'll be answering questions put by boards of inquiry from now till the Omega point.

The water felt too good to give up just now. If he could only stop thinking for a time.

Mia Daventri looked up from the workstation as the short, thickset man entered the cabin. He stopped just inside the hatch, blinking at her, doubtlessly wondering what an Internal Security inspector was doing in his quarters.

He began to step back through the open door. The pair of security officers flanking the hatchway closed ranks to block him.

"Corf."

The man glared toward the voice, which came from a meter behind and to Mia's right.

"Sir," the thickset man said grudgingly.

Mia heard two steps and then felt the presence of the officer beside her. A slender hand came out and tapped the screen before which Mia sat.

"You've been industrious, Corf," the officer said.

Mia glanced up at him. Tall, almost Spacer slender with smooth skin. Cosmetically enhanced, she knew, to look...not young, so much as healthy and well-aged. It made a more profound impression. As Mia had come to know Lt. Commander Reen, if it would have served him to appear as a hideous, boil-encrusted ogre, he would have had the surgery. His only vanity seemed to lay in his sense of duty.

"Sir," Corf said noncommittally.

"I'm impressed," Reen said, nodding. He caught Mia's eye. "How about you, Lieutenant? When was the last time you saw these kinds of numbers attached to an illicit trade?"

"Not since I was on Earth, sir," Mia admitted, playing along with Reen's game. If he had a fault, it was that he enjoyed teasing people too much.

"And what did you do when you saw those numbers?"

"Shut them down, sir."

Corf scowled at her.

"Completely," she added.

"That's the only way to do it," Reen said. "Let me see..." He leaned closer, making a show of reading the screen. "One hundred seventy-eight thousand credits in the last sixty days. I see cases of antivirals, antibiotics, wine, variable lobe wheat seed..." He looked bemused. "Soap."

Corf frowned uncertainly.

Reen continued reading. "Two isotope analyzers...that's interesting, I wonder where you got them? Perhaps those two missing from Stennis's lab on the *Thessaly*? Two hundred meters of silk, nine thousand meters of polythor thread, and two hundred and thirty-one books."

Reen stepped around the console and stopped before Corf. "I can see a lot of that, but the first two items, the antivirals and 'biotics—what is that about? Those items come under the aegis of humanitarian exception. We let medical supplies through." He waited, but Corf said nothing. "You've probably convinced some profiteer down there that we'll be cutting them off soon. Who knows, maybe the same profiteer is intercepting what legally gets sent down and is selling both your supplies and ours at obscene prices to people who have no choice."

He wheeled on one heel and came back around the console. He slapped the screen sharply with his knuckles, making Mia jump.

"We'll find out," he said. "You could save us time and make your punishment a bit less by providing us names of contacts." He held up his hand. "Not now. Think about it for a day or so. I don't trust quick confessions."

Reen nodded his head, and the security officers clasped Corf's arms and hauled him out of the room.

Mia waited while Reen paced.

"I hate this," he said. "Not bad enough we have to deal with actual pirates, we have to have some of our own decide to try it out. Good work, Daventri. You've copied all this to the main log?"

"Yes, sir."

Reen leaned on the console again, staring at the screen. "Fabric. Medicine and fabric. No food yet."

Mia gestured. "Wine."

"Hardly a necessity." He slapped the console. "We could probably shut all the traffic from our own people down in no time at all. I don't want to. Shut enough of them down to narrow the goods going through military hands. I want to monitor it. When they start importing food—"

"The wheat seed?"

"Seed, Daventri. It means they have time to grow it. They're still eating. When they start buying prepackaged foods through the black market, then we know it's only a matter of time."

"Yes, sir. May I ask a question, though?"

Reen nodded.

"You told Corf that we send medical supplies through as humanitarian goods. Doesn't food qualify?"

"No. We want them pressed, Daventri, but healthy. We don't need epidemics taking root when we intend to occupy and resume relations with a planet. We'll help them stay disease-free, but we won't feed them. Starvation isn't communicable."

He straightened. "See if you can dig any contacts out of these manifests. We'll let Corf worry over his situation for a day or two before we question him. Meantime, if you can come up with some associates…"

"Yes, sir. I'll do what I can."

"Good. Carry on."

Reen strode out of the chamber. The hatch snapped shut.

"Shit," Mia breathed.

The blockade was approaching a year old now, and the Settlers on the ground had given no indication of yielding. It seemed immoral to her to continue this way. Reen's attitude held sway, though, throughout the military, and Earth was backing them.

"Can't have pirates roaming the trade lanes," she said with mock gravity.

Still, as much as she hated what they were doing to the citizens of Nova Levis, she loathed people like Ensign Corf who were more than willing to take advantage of them to make a few extra credits. Finding them and flushing them out felt…fulfilling.

The best use of her talents.

Under these circumstances.

She had trouble deciding about people like Reen who seemed willing to use both the situation and the avarice of Corf to enhance the efficiency of his own job. The end result was not a bad thing, but in the meantime people who should not suffer suffered.

"Maybe I'll understand when I grow up," she mused aloud.

She adjusted herself in the chair and began asking the already compromised system more questions. Corf had stuffed the illicit records in with the routine departmental memos everyone received and no one read, memos concerning recreational activities, uniform inspections, promotions, demotions, policy statements, recommendations for protocol, receptions, and a great many bits of propaganda about the important job the blockade and the Terran Expeditionary Taskforce were doing here. Corf slipped the logs of his black market business into the "Personal

Notes" files attached to these memos. By code, people at Corf's level were not allowed personal datums. Corf's unique use of otherwise public databases impressed Mia. She wondered who had come up with the idea.

Mia tapped instructions into her own personal datum, connected now to the console. The troll program she initiated would scour the entire databank for communications related to the manifest. As thoroughly as the illicit goods were recorded, she felt certain that a trail existed, from source to delivery.

WORKING appeared on her datum screen.

Mia turned in the chair to survey the rest of the small cabin. Ensigns did not receive a great deal of private space on a ship like this. The *Helico* was a mid-range attack cruiser, three hundred crew plus a contingent of officers. It spent most of the time in dock, its primary purpose in life being pursuit and assault.

Consequently, she knew, most of the crew spent as little time as possible on board. The blockade stations, immense and spacious by comparison, offered a wider variety of release from the drudgery of duty. Cabins like this, therefore, tended to be either very neat or very neglected.

Corf kept his neat.

Mia went to his locker. After playing with the code for a few minutes, she took out her passkey and inserted the bit into the receptacle below the touchpad. The lock clicked off and the door slid open.

At first glance it appeared to be a standard kit. Uniforms stacked there—two sets of dress grays still in the shrink wrap—other, personal, clothing in that container; two packs; an extra sidearm locked in a secure storage container; a case of book disks.

Mia pulled out the last item with some effort—twelve or more kilos, at least—and carried it to the console. She unsealed it and removed the transparent lid.

Among the blocks of book disks, Mia found a few printed volumes. Surprised, she gingerly pulled them out and opened the covers. The pages bore faint finger smudges, evidently from frequent reading. Old. Mia brought one close to her face and sniffed. The faintly sweet odor of a preservative could still be detected. She shuffled through the container, pulling out the paper volumes, four in all. She glanced at the titles: *War and Peace, Of Human Bondage, Oliver Twist,* and *Les Miserables.*

Mia went through the disks, but quickly noticed that they were either technical works or contemporary fiction. The paper volumes were the only ancient works. "Classics," her Culture and Diversity Instructor had called them.

Mr. Jayn, she recalled. She had enjoyed his classes and his somewhat trendy disdain for what he called "the contemporary excuse for culture, which is little more than aggressively spinning in place, hoping the scenery changes on the next turn." He had not pushed that line too hard— a little contempt served to keep students interested, while too much could be seen as fomenting disrespect, something apparently only educational oversight committees really worried about—but Mia took enough to heart to find herself continually dissatisfied with most of her choices thereafter.

Becoming a Special Service agent had then seemed the best answer to that dissatisfaction. For a time, she had felt amply fulfilled. Then everything had gone wrong during the Eliton Conference fiasco and she had been in the middle of every possible controversial aspect: personal security for Senator Eliton, Service manager of the only autonomous positronic robot the Service possessed, implicated in the conspiracy to murder Eliton and the chief delegates of the Spacer legations, and then, after, a traitor to the Service for exposing the agents who *had* been involved in the plot...

A mess indeed...

Now, in the logic of the Service, having proven herself capable of policing her own people, she was Internal Security on the Nova Levis blockade, responsible for finding and neutralizing corrupt officers.

She gazed at the four bound volumes. *How corrupt can a man who reads these kinds of books, this way, be...?*

It was tempting to believe refined taste placed one in a special category. Not a common black market operative, surely. A misunderstanding?

Her datum still worked through the comm logs. No, the manifest she had found was clearly Corf's.

Up to this point everything about him fit what she expected. An ensign, passed over for promotion twice due to substandard fitness reports, disciplined once for brawling, twice for "intemperate language to a superior," and with a credit account several hundred credits richer than it should have been. A mediocre cadet, an average crewman, now a problematic officer: he would serve out his time and be discharged with no option for re-enlistment, vested in a small retirement pension. An unexceptional, somewhat dull, short-tempered, progressively bitter man, the perfect profile to be recruited by smugglers. His current duty was in Stores, also ideal, specifically requisitions for shipboard amenities...

Les Miserables...?

Mia grunted and sat down. She tapped her datum for a second task and entered the specifications for the four books. She wanted to know what they would cost.

WORKING

She leafed through *Oliver Twist* while she waited. She stopped at a section to which someone had added a checkmark in the margin:

> *For the next eight or ten months, Oliver was the victim of a systematic course of treachery and deception. He was raised by hand. The hungry and destitute situation of the infant orphan was duly reported by the workhouse authorities to the parish authorities. The parish authorities inquired with dignity of the workhouse authorities, whether there was no female then domiciled in "the house" who was in a situation to impart to Oliver Twist, the consolation and nourishment of which he stood in need. The workhouse authorities replied with humility, that there was not. Upon this, the parish authorities magnanimously and humanely resolved, that Oliver should be "farmed," or, in other words, that he should be despatched to a branch-workhouse some three miles off, where twenty or thirty other juvenile offenders against the poor-laws rolled about the floor all day, without the inconvenience of too much food or too much clothing...*

Mia felt an inexplicable twist of conscience reading this. She looked at her datum.

EXTERNAL SOURCES REQUIRED FOR INQUIRY

She leaned over and pressed the CONTINUE key.

Mia continued leafing through the book. It seemed incredible to her that she should know a few orphans. Here was a story more than a thousand years old about a situation that humanity, in all its progress and through all its various periods of wealth, had never solved.

Curious, she pulled up Corf's record again. No, he had never been an orphan.

She opened the other books to see if any other passages had been checked. She found several, in all of them. The books had clearly not simply adorned a shelf somewhere unread. These volumes had been well used.

No owner's name appeared in any of the books. One, however, had a bookseller's imprint on the inside back cover: OMNE MUNDI COMPLURIUM, ANTIQUITIES, LYZIG.

She added that to the search protocol and set the books aside.

The datum chimed, the first search concluded. She pulled up the results and sat back, dismayed. The trails of communications spread out like a complex algorithm, a web of interconnected associations covering several ships and traversing many levels of command hierarchy.

Mia's mood darkened. *This is going to take days to collate into useful tables...*

"That's why I earn the big money," she said aloud, and began copying everything to a disk.

She resealed the container of book disks and returned it to Corf's locker. The paper volumes she tucked into her pack. She then made another search of the cabin, but she found nothing else out of the expected.

Her datum still read WORKING, so she closed it up for now. It would continue to pursue the search. She slipped it into her pack, closed down Corf's workstation, and left the cabin. She slapped an IS seal on the door and activated it. Only her code now would open Corf's cabin.

Satisfied that she had overlooked nothing—for now—she hoisted her pack over her left shoulder and headed for the ship's personnel lock.

5

DEREC SEALED the last bag and set it by the cabin door with three others. Most of his worldly possessions filled those packs, the bulk having arrived only within the last week, shipped up from Earth. Hofton had managed to get it all through customs without question.

I'm going to miss Hofton, he thought as he sat down to stare at the collection of luggage. Then: *Hell, I'm going to miss* everything...

The door chimed and slid open. Ambassador Yart Leri, branch head of the Kopernik Auroran embassy, stood at the threshold with two security officers. Behind them, in the corridor, was a large porter robot.

"Mr. Avery," Leri said, looking and sounding slightly embarrassed, "the *Wysteria* is boarding. It may be best to go early, before it fills up and becomes a party."

"Of course," Derec said. "Thales and...?"

"Already loaded and secured. My assistant saw to it earlier today."

Derec heaved to his feet. He felt intensely weary. "Fine, then. Shall we get started?"

"Um...of course."

Leri stood aside and gestured. The robot floated on noiseless pivots, entered the cabin, and extruded limbs that deftly hooked all the bags. Thin straps appeared, wrapping instantly around the luggage, securing them firmly to the robot's body. It rolled back into the corridor and waited.

Derec pulled on his jacket, shouldered the case containing his personal datum and a few other items, including passport—newly-issued—and ticket. The ticket was merely a nod to dignity—there was no question of his leaving Kopernik; all that had been taken care of without his consent. He had rarely felt so powerless.

"I'm ready," he said.

Leri walked beside him. The security officers stationed outside his cabin followed, three paces behind, and the robot brought up the rear.

Derec could not stop looking pointedly at everything they passed, as if this were the first time he had seen any of it. It *was* likely the last time he would see it, though there was nothing remarkable about the place. It was a station, like any other found throughout settled space, though flavored by Terran taste. It was possible he would never see *this* particular station again. Ever.

They entered a larger concourse. The few people they encountered gave them a wide berth, staring at the guards and the robot with open curiosity and dismay. Derec avoided direct eye contact, self-consciously keeping his expression neutral.

Leri and one guard boarded a shunt with Derec, the rest of the entourage following in a second car.

"I'd like to express our gratitude again for the work you did here," Leri said. "Unfortunate consequences aside, you saved the branch mission itself from any undeserved blame."

"It was a pleasure to work," Derec said. "Glad I could help."

"Yes, uhm..."

Derec let Leri fumble and lapse into silence. He did not care to indulge in polite conversation. Not during his eviction from Earth territory.

The shunt came to a halt and they emerged onto the broad plaza outside the customs station. Derec could see the boarding gate on the far side. Small collections of people loitered around the shunt platform. A short line passed slowly through the customs archway.

The second shunt arrived and the remaining guard and the robot joined them.

"I'll walk you through, Mr. Avery," Leri said, gesturing toward the arch.

Derec glanced at the shunt monitor to see if another car were about to arrive. It showed none, so, disappointed, Derec walked alongside Leri toward the line.

"I wish..." Leri began.

"So do I, Ambassador," Derec said. "But you've been an excellent host. I have no complaints."

Leri smiled quickly at one of the traditional compliments of Aurora. "Thank you, Mr. Avery. And you've been a perfect guest."

They reached the gate. Leri stepped behind the desk and spoke quickly to the attendant.

"Pass through, sir," she said.

Leri stepped through to the other side. He clasped Derec's hand. "Safe journey, Mr. Avery. I hope we have the opportunity to meet again."

"Given time, I'm sure."

The robot stopped beside him.

Leri handed Derec a disk. "Give this to the bosun as you board. He'll see you to your cabin personally."

Derec nodded. He cast a final look back toward the shunt platform, expectantly. A shunt arrived, opened, and four people he did not recognize got out.

No Rana.

"Take care, Ambassador," he said then, and strode toward the loading gate.

A short umbilical took him into the liner's boarding lounge. A brightly-uniformed crewman greeted him just inside the enormous hatch. Derec handed over the disk from Leri, which the crewman slid into his hand reader.

"Yes, sir," he said. He looked across the chamber and signaled another uniform.

The flashings at the collar of her equally bright blue uniform differed from the crewman's. She looked over the reader and nodded.

"Mr. Avery, I'm Chief Petty Officer Craym. I'll take you directly to your cabin. Is this your robot?"

"No, the station's. That *is* my luggage."

"Let me get another porter."

CPO Craym made the arrangements quickly and efficiently and within minutes she was leading Derec through the narrow corridors of the liner, past other crew and passengers, to a small but comfortable cabin amidships.

"Are you familiar with interstellar travel, Mr. Avery?" she asked as the robot porter deposited his luggage on the deck. It began stowing the bags in the row of cabinets set in the bulkhead, beneath a wall-size subetheric screen.

"I've done some traveling," he said.

"So I need not go over every little detail? Emergency stasis couch is here, menu to shipboard activities and personnel available here, food processor here. We encourage dining in one of the three public commons, but you may easily take your meals in private."

"Sanitizer?"

She crossed the cabin and pressed a contact. A vertical tube swiveled out from the wall. "We recommend decontamination prior to first jump, but as long as you use it before entering Spacer territory it's up to you. How long has it been since you've flown?"

"A few years."

"There have been improvements. It takes slightly less time now, and isn't nearly so invasive."

"But still necessary."

She smiled helpfully.

"That's fine," he said. "Can I find a list of fellow passengers on this?"

"Except for those who have purchased privacy, yes."

The robot finished and whisked silently from the cabin.

"Anything you cannot find listed in the menus, feel free to ask."

The particular pitch of her voice made Derec look at her more critically. She met his gaze with Spacer ease and a faint smile that seemed slightly warmer than standard politeness. When she did not look away or move toward the door, Derec felt an awkward uncertainty.

"You?" he asked.

"Barring other duties, that would be fine."

"Thank you."

She smiled more brightly, and left the cabin. The door sealed. After a few moments, he decided that his imagination was working too hard.

Colluding with my loneliness?

He stood then, still, listening to the distant and ubiquitous thrumming of the ship as to the blood flow of a somnolent beast, absorbing the finality of his position.

It's done... I'm going home... whatever that means...

He shrugged out of his jacket and draped it over the high-backed chair nestled against the small comm station opposite the bed. He sat down and waited.

Three hours. A light winked on above the subetheric screen and a polite, androgynous voice announced:

"The Star Liner *Wysteria* is now leaving Kopernik Station. Please remained seated or reclining until we have reached initial cruising velocity. We will inform you when we will be approaching jump. Thank you for traveling with us. We hope you have a pleasant voyage."

Derec lay back on the narrow bed, arms at his sides, and tried to feel the surge of the engines and the change in *g* from acceleration. He could not tell—it seemed the background sound changed pitch—so he picked a point at which he could tell himself *I've left. I'm gone. I'll arrive...soon enough....*

Coren entered the pavilion atop Looms' Kenya District home, where, per Looms' last wishes, the services were conducted under a transparent geodesic dome that was the only concession to the endemic agoraphobia the visitors exhibited in varying degrees. Coren swallowed hard as he walked out of the shelter of the arcade that rimmed a third of the dome. Ariel's influence showed in his growing ability to cope with rooflessness, but he still felt a profound vulnerability when Outside.

Above, faceted by the thread-like braces of the dome superstructure, gleamed an intense blue and cloudless sky. Its light set the air aglow within the pavilion. Coren estimated perhaps sixty people gathered. Others filled the drawing rooms and halls below, in the labyrinthine main house, unwilling to venture out from the protection of ceilings. Perhaps because of his newly-acquired tolerance, Coren felt the beginnings of contempt toward them.

Subetheric recorders floated around, each sphere colored and marked according to the service to which it belonged. Coren did not see any reporters, though. He could not tell which, then, were personal cameras belonging to any of the guests and which were news feeds.

As he neared the bier and the closed onyx and ebony casket upon it, Coren saw two people he would never have expected here. Myler Towne, the CEO of the newly reformed Imbitek Industries Incorporated, stood off to one side with three of his aides. He nodded slightly at Coren.

The other stood alone by the casket. Coren walked over to greet him.

"Inspector Capel," Coren said as he stopped alongside the police detective. "A little far from your district."

Capel kept his chin tucked down, like most of the Terrans unaccustomed to the Open. "Lanra. Maybe. Looms kept a residence in my jurisdiction, I figure that gives me a small reason to be interested. That and the fact that he died there."

A holograph of a recumbent and cosmetically perfect Rega Looms hovered above the casket.

"I thought you weren't working for him anymore?" Capel asked.

"So did I," Coren admitted. "Somewhere along the line, he forgot to tell anyone else that I quit. I'm still on salary."

"Is that like him to forget?"

"No."

"Did you see the crime scene and autopsy images?"

"No. I've been occupied. I only came back when I heard he was dead."

"I'll show them to you later. I'd like your opinion about something."

That surprised Coren. "Certainly. I'd appreciate that."

"It won't be for free," Capel said. He patted Coren's shoulder and wandered off.

Coren stared at the holograph of his former employer. He resisted the urge to pry open the coffin and look inside.

"My condolences, Mr. Lanra."

Coren turned toward the voice. Myler Towne stood near, hands clasped behind his back. He was a large man, easily twenty-five centimeters taller than Lanra and at least thirty kilos heavier, most of it in his shoulders and chest. He made an unlikely-looking CEO, but there was no question that he made an immediate impression.

"Thank you," Coren said. "And before you ask, I'm still thinking about it. Events have conspired to delay my final decision regarding your offer of employment."

"Oh, unquestionably. I would have it no other way. I trust you intend to find Rega's murderer? Do so. Any assistance I can render, call."

"That's generous."

Towne's mouth turned down slightly. "Generous. Mr. Lanra, there was nothing to be gained by anyone I know of in killing Rega. This threatens us all. This isn't generosity—it's absolute self-interest."

"If I need anything, I promise I'll ask for it."

Towne nodded, apparently satisfied. "What will happen to DyNan now? I understand there are no heirs."

"The will is to be read in two days. We'll all know then."

"You have no guesses?"

"After Nyom—after his daughter died, I was unaware of any contingencies. If he had a back-up plan, he never confided it to me."

"It will be interesting."

"Indeed."

Towne bowed slightly. "If you'll excuse me..."

Coren watched Towne retreat to the company of his aides. They exchanged a few words, then one left, wending a path toward the arcade.

Coren continued to let his gaze drift over the gathered mourners. He saw furtive looks, worry, a few expressions of genuine regret and pain. More than a few overly-pointed looks directed at him.

He worked his way back through the crowd, stopping to speak to people, share a few stories about Rega with old acquaintances, and generally blend in with them. He hated being the center of attention—it was anathema to his job, an impossible position from which to carry on any kind of delicate inquiry.

An hour and a half later, he found himself back beneath the arcade. He took a drink from a passing tray and went down the stairs into the main house.

A wide central corridor led down the center of the butterfly-like superstructure. Doorways opened on large rooms, staircases up and down, alcoves, and other passageways. There were even hidden rooms behind false walls. Nyom had shown him many of them, but he was sure there were several even she had not known about. The house was a vast architectural playground, the ideal hide-and-seek environment for a playful personality few would have guessed Rega to possess.

This was Rega's proudest possession, this manor. Contrary to tradition—and, in some parts of the globe, the law—he had built it "above ground." Rebuilt, in fact, the new layered atop an already-existing structure that predated the expulsion of robots from Earth. It rested in the middle of several thousand acres of natural preserve, accessible by aircraft or a single tube that connected it to Bassa District. There was also an aircar pad, complete with a collection of obsolete and mostly nonworking aircars from previous centuries. Coren had intended bringing Nyom here during Rega's scuttled senate campaign, after getting her away from the baley runners with whom she had been working. Except that she had gone with the last group and given him no chance to extract her from the situation. Her death afterward and the threat of blackmail had ruined Rega's chances for a senate seat. His unwillingness to let Coren proceed with the investigation to find Nyom's killers had driven a wedge between them that had kept Coren away.

Till now, when it was too late to help.

Rega Looms was dead. Coren could not help but feel responsible.

He found Capel in one of the galleries just off the main hall. The detective stared at an ancient abstract painting that Coren had long ago decided was a perversely distorted winged woman trying to fly out of a volcano.

"Enlightenment must be earned," Coren quipped.

"Hm. I'm working at it."

"You want to show me something?"

Capel nodded. "Somewhere we can go?"

Coren pointed, then led the way to one of several offices scattered throughout the multilevel structure.

"I keep wondering," Capel said as Coren locked the door behind them, "what it must be like to have money. Real money. Like this. Considering the cost, I'm glad I don't know."

Coren went to the desk and started up the reader. A flatscreen extruded from the desktop.

"This material is better viewed holographically," Capel said, holding up a disk.

"Not available here," Coren said. "One of Rega's prejudices."

Capel grunted, but handed over the disk.

Coren slipped it into the hopper and tapped the keypad.

A wide image of a spacious apartment bedroom appeared on the screen. The pale walls and expensive furniture bespoke considerable wealth. Coren recognized it as Rega's Baltimor District residence, where, apparently, Rega had sequestered himself for the last several weeks, communicating exclusively by comm.

Someone lay stretched out on the bed.

The next image was a full-length shot of the body.

It was naked, bruised from neck to ankle, horribly purpled with splotches of yellow and green. The face stared blankly at nothing, the tongue swollen, forcing open the mouth.

"This was thirty-six hours after death," Capel said. "Your ex-boss wasn't a complete luddite. He had a pretty up-to-date biomonitor system in place. It had been subverted—we figure the reprogramming took place six, seven weeks ago—but one thing it still did was record Rega Looms' actual living presence. Once that ended without any other indications that he had simply left the apartment, an alarm was triggered."

"Subverted...why?"

"We found evidence that a second person was living in the apartment. All the biomonitor recorded was one. Our people are looking into how the system was hacked. But the catastrophic trauma alarm had been completely switched off. Autopsy showed that Looms had been beaten and tortured continually for most of the last four or five weeks." Capel waved a hand at the screen. "Look familiar?"

"Yes..."

Coren had seen three other corpses with that same kind of bruising, as if someone had systematically crushed their bodies, bursting capillaries, pulverizing bone, bursting organs. Slowly, one area at a time, but not so slowly that the bruising could heal anywhere. He had felt the grip that could inflict this sort of damage. Absently, he rubbed his right forearm where the cyborg had held him, crushing the bone and muscle.

"Gamelin?" Capel prompted.

"Probably. We never recovered the body. It was a mistake to declare him dead, but the TBI were afraid of panicking people."

"So we have to assume he's at large again. Where would he go?"

"I don't know. The baley network he used before is gone, most of the people he worked for are in jail or dead. He could hide in the warrens, I suppose. But sooner or later someone would report him."

"If he was living with Rega, how come none of your people found out?"

"That's a good question," Coren said.

"Are you looking into this?"

"Absolutely."

"You'll share data with me?"

"When I get it. Can you leave this disk?"

"Sure."

Coren switched the view off. "It's possible he could link up with a part of the network we didn't shut down. But for now I'd say he's on his own. Tell your people not to take chances. Use only lethal force if they encounter him."

"I'm going to have another talk with Alda Mikels."

"Do you think he'll tell you anything?"

"Not really," Capel admitted. "But I don't have anyone else to interrogate. Who knows, he might slip."

"Hm."

"What do your Special Service people think about all this?"

"How would I know?" Coren asked, surprised.

"I heard you were reinstated."

"An honorary thing, just for the duration of that last investigation. I suppose I could ask."

"I'd be interested."

"I'm sure you would."

Capel almost smiled. "Call me." He left the office.

Coren sat down at the desk then. After a few minutes, he opened the disk again and studied the images.

6

HE CABIN lights flared brightly and Masid squinted, coming sluggishly awake. He lurched to a sitting position and blinked furiously at the chronometer across the room; he had only been asleep a few hours.

"What—"

"Get your kit together, Vorian," Anda said. "You're leaving."

Masid's eyes adjusted. Two robots stood on either side of the cabin hatch. Anda, hands on hips, loomed over Masid.

"Tired of my company so soon?"

"Come on, we don't have much time. A day at the most. I'm getting you to Nova Levis." He held up a capsule about two centimeters long and four wide. "Take this."

"What is it?"

"Implant. Immune system augment."

Masid came fully awake then. He studied Anda's face for signs of jest. Seeing none, he accepted the capsule and headed straight for the hygienic. "Talk."

"I've been ordered to turn over the ship and its cargo, including baleys, to blockade command. We're rendezvousing with a ship in less than thirty hours, the *Coredon*. I know that ship. We've suspected for a long time that it's affiliated with blockade runners. Never had any solid proof, though, and since it's a Terran ship we haven't been able to convince our own command to challenge. The Terrans, of course, insist that none of their captains are involved, but that if any should be, then it will be a matter for Terran Internal Security, thank you all very much for your concern."

Masid filled a cup with water and swallowed the capsule. The lump slid down his throat painfully. He opened his pack and pulled out the clothes he had been wearing when Anda took the transport. "Why are you required to abide by Terran authority?"

"Partly logistical. We don't have the space for you all, frankly, so we have to hand the baleys off soon, anyway. We requested a Theian transport, but that request got routed to the blockade and the *Coredon* was dispatched. We're closer to the blockade than any other colony or station anyway, and all the Theian ships manning the ring are like this one."

"And the other part?"

"Aurora wants it this way. Make nice with the Terrans so we can straighten out the mess between us. Normally I wouldn't accommodate this policy, it's still my discretion. But I'm doing you a favor."

Masid zipped up and began assembling the rest of his belongings. "Why take the baleys to the blockade? I mean, is that standard?"

"Earth doesn't want them back. They end up being parceled out to other Settler colonies. There's a lottery for them. Our job is to just keep them off Nova Levis."

"What do you think my chances are of passing as a baley after you so conveniently separated me from them?"

"Pretty good. As soon as you told me what you were doing, I pulled a dozen more out. You won't be the first one put back in with them, but you aren't the last. Just be your usual charming, convincing self and you'll be fine."

"Hm. So what happens if I end up in this lottery instead of going right through?"

"Send me a thank you note when you get wherever you end up."

Masid laughed grimly. "What's up with the augment I just took?"

"We have fairly reliable intelligence that Nova Levis is a stew of communicable disease. What I just gave you is the latest thing in prophylactic biotech. It'll set up a small lab in your endocrine system and boost your natural immunity by a couple of orders of magnitude. Still might not keep you entirely healthy, but maybe it will keep you alive long enough to do some useful work."

"So," Masid said, hoisting his pack. "I imagine you'd be happy to get some kind of corroborative evidence about the *Coredon* while I'm at it?"

"The thought had occurred to me." Anda held up a hand. "If you get there... before all this turned to the mess it is, I had a friend who went to Nova Levis."

"*You* had a friend?"

"Keep it up and I'll send you through in a bag."

"Sorry."

"She's a doctor. *Was* a doctor. I have no idea if she's still alive. She was part of the civic health program on Nova Levis, attached to the Fifty Worlds liaison group."

"You mean the embassy?"

Anda shook his head. "Because of Solaria's involvement, there were no other formal Spacer embassies. Just a representative presence with no authority. Advisors. Anyway, she stayed. She never got out. Knowing her, she probably thought she could do something."

"Did she have a name?"

"Shasma. If she's still there, maybe she could help. Or you could."

Masid waited. Anda seemed to work with his feelings. Finally, he looked up. "It might be useful. If you find her, ask if she remembers Calinas Ridge."

"Calinas Ridge..."

"Save some time if she knows I sent you."

"I'll see what I can do." He hesitated. "Um...are you getting physical with your interview subjects?"

Anda scowled. "Please. We're Spacers."

"Ah, yes. The civilized ones. I forgot. Sorry. Just wanted to make sure you send me back like everybody else."

"Are you ready?"

"No, but let's do it."

Thirty-four hours, Masid thought acidly. *Anda lied. I must remind him of that...*

Secured in a restraining transport cocoon, Masid was barely able to turn his head to see the gang of men coming down the line of imprisoned baleys. He recognized Terran blue-grey space service uniforms, but the sudden glare of flashlights obscured their faces. Masid flinched as the brilliant beams struck him.

"Have they been scrubbed?" one of them asked.

"Surface only," Masid heard Anda reply. "We don't have the capacity on this ship to do this many whole body cleanings at once. So we just store them down here until we can deliver them to a better-equipped facility."

"Just as well, then. We can tailor the job for the colony they end up going to."

They walked past Masid and the beams of light left his eyes. In the dimness he saw Anda give him an encouraging half-grin and a very slight nod. Then they were gone.

Half an hour later, robots entered the long stowage and began carting the cocoons out. Masid felt himself pulled away from the bulkhead and tilted back horizontally. Then all he could see was the ceiling as it rolled by.

He stopped moving. He heard shouting, equipment being maneuvered, echoing footsteps. Something metal slammed into something plastic. The queue stood still for several minutes. Masid felt the cocoon lurch to one side.

Finally, the ceiling began moving backward once more. The rim of a lock passed above him and he was sliding down a long ship-to-ship umbilical.

"In here, come one now, bring 'em in here!"

"Excuse me, sir," the smooth androgynous voice of a robot said, "but this chamber is far too small for safe transport of this number of humans. I am required—"

"You are required to shut up and move these cocoons where I tell you to."

"I am sorry, sir, but it cannot be permitted—"

"Don't interrupt me, tinhead—"

"What's the problem?" another human asked.

"Your *robots* don't like where we're putting the cocoons."

"Let me—"

"This is *my* ship and I don't like being told how to run it. Now get—"

"Sir—"

"Please, Captain, let me take care of this."

"Fine, handle it."

Masid could not hear the rest of what was said, but soon the storage proceeded.

An hour or more passed. Then:

"Now that we're alone," the Terran commander said loudly in the cramped, overly-warm chamber, "and those overly-solicitous machines are gone, we can prep you for the rest of the trip. Just so you know, you're being taken to the Nova Levis blockade where you'll be processed for further transit. *This* ship doesn't have much more room or resource than that Spacer hull you just left. But we're not going to sweat that. The voyage is less than three days. You won't have to worry about anything because you're all going to sleep through it. That saves us all a lot of worry."

The baleys began mumbling unhappily. Masid heard the soft sounds of aerosols, though, and one by one the voices stilled.

A face loomed above him suddenly, masked, and a hand came up holding a nossle.

"Wait—" he began.

Darkness.

He awoke thirsty, blinking furiously at the crusting on his eyes, and shivering. A tube was poked at his mouth until he closed his teeth on it and sucked. Lukewarm water flowed.

Eventually he got his eyes open, enough to see the shapes around him. He lay on a deck, in a line with several others. Above them, in the darkness, machines bulked. Masid saw readylights, could hear their patient hum, and realized quickly that the water tube extended from one of them. Biomonitors, field units, military.

The shivering subsided. He flexed his fingers, drew his legs up and stretched. Everything began to ache. He had been in one position too long. Unused muscles complained.

Two people knelt by him. One pushed his eyelids up and shone a light into his pupils. The other prodded his torso. It was then he knew he was naked.

"Cough," one of them said, cupping his testicles.

Masid let go of the tube and cleared his throat.

"Cough," the other said and thumped him on the diaphragm.

He hacked loudly.

"Looks good," the first said, standing. A moment later, he said, "This one's not Terran."

"Oh?"

"He's macro-enhanced...look at this..."

The other stood and joined the first. Masid strained to look back, above his head, and saw them studying the readouts on the biomonitor. One of the pair glanced down at him.

"So what are you, friend?" he asked. "Ex-military? Fugitive?"

Masid could not speak. He groped for the water tube again and sucked on it.

"Spy?" the other opined.

"And leave this in place? I don't think so." He shrugged. "Doesn't matter."

He knelt beside Masid again and patted his cheek with mock affection.

"You're healthy enough to survive the drop, my friend, so whatever you are, you get your wish."

They laughed then and moved to the next baley on the deck.

Masid continued to draw water, shuddering from time to time.

Hours later, he sat up. A drone trundled by slowly. Masid smelled hot food and reached for it. The drone stopped automatically and a door on its featureless body snapped open, revealing stacks of prepared meals. Masid snatched one out, his fingers stinging from the heat. He snapped the spoon from the side of the rectangular platter, peeled back the cover sheet, and hungrily shoveled the nameless food product into his mouth. The drone moved to the next person, who still lay curled fetally to Masid's right. The person after that reached out and the drone stopped.

As his hunger abated, he looked up and down the row of baleys. Some still stretched out, but most were sitting up, many of them eating.

They were in a cargo bay as far as Masid could tell, refitted to receive the living. The temperature was still too low to be comfortable, but he found he could control the shivering now, especially with a hot meal in his belly.

A row of biomonitors stretched the length of the deck visible to him, one behind each of the eighty-odd people lined up. Their readouts and readylights did little to lessen the dimness. Lights high overhead cast too little illumination to see much more than shadows.

A hatch opened in the distance and bootsteps echoed. Masid finished the meal and set the tray down. His limbs felt heavy, as though he had been doing hard labor for too many hours. He doubted he could hold his own in a fight just then.

Three uniformed men appeared, striding purposefully down the length of the row of baleys. As they passed each recumbent figure, the lead officer pointed and the officer behind and to his left made a note on a palm monitor. At the end of the line, they turned around and walked back. After they left, a short time went by. Then four people in dark blue work-togs came with a train of gurneys. They gathered up the baleys who still stretched on the deck and placed each in a gurney.

Masid counted fifteen and guessed that they had been the oldest and frailest. Judging by his own reactions, the sedative they had been given was designed to place a burden on the body and sort the baleys out by physical condition.

The collection squad gone, a few people began tentatively talking. The babble was half-hearted and faded out within a few minutes. Masid's own thoughts seemed sluggish, though he recognized what was happening. The only thing to do was wait.

His eyes slitted. The silence seemed to be slipping into his brain. Just as his head lolled forward, chin to chest, he came awake to the sound of more people striding into the bay.

"Sorry to keep you all waiting," a sharp, authoritative voiced announced.

Masid looked up at the tall Terran officer who now addressed them.

"You'll be on your way soon," he said. "We'll be returning your clothes and belongings and moving you to the final stage. This time tomorrow you should be on the ground. After that, you're on your own. We have fulfilled our contract with you."

He paused, letting everyone think about that for a time. Then, hands clasped behind his back, he said, "A few details about your new home. Nova Levis is under quarantine. The blockade has tightened. You will not be able to leave unless the political situation changes. We can no longer get messages out for you. After you ground tomorrow, Nova Levis is your new home, your *only* home. You will be cut off from the rest of settled space.

"It is only fair to warn you that this also means there is no chance of appeal to higher authority than the planetary government. More than likely, even that is out of reach. You will be dealing with local authorities in nearly all instances. If things go wrong, you cannot call for help off Nova Levis. Spacers won't help you, the Settler's Coalition is cut off from you, and Earth, frankly, could care less if you have a problem here. This is a whole new way to live, even though some of you may feel you've just escaped a limited, repressive environment. Maybe you have. But it was completely different and you may come to regret your decision to emigrate."

Dismayed mutterings rippled along the row.

"That said," the officer went on, "the flip side is that you have a world with very little to obstruct an enterprising imagination or an assertive will. Opportunity on Nova Levis is pretty much whatever you can make it. You probably heard something like this back where you came from, which is why you're here now. This is as frontier as you get. The only caveat is, it will be damn hard work and you might suffer unfairly or even fatally in the attempt to realize your dreams."

The officer walked up and down the line of baleys, gazing at them with an expression Masid could not identify—a mix of respect, contempt, and puzzlement. He stopped almost directly in front of Masid.

"That said," he announced, "welcome to Nova Levis. I hope you like it. You'll be loading up for your final descent in one hour."

A few people laughed in shocked delight. Others sobbed, whether from fear or relief Masid could not tell.

Anxiety, extended long enough, can put you to sleep, though never a restful sleep. The hour became two and then stretched out for three. Masid started awake twice at new sounds and finally, tentatively, got to his feet. His legs felt infirm at first. He flexed up onto his toes rhythmically, tugging at the muscles and tendons, dropped into quick squats, and then lifted each leg alternately, bringing the knees up to his chest. He avoided anything that might look like a martial exercise, just kept to simple homeogenics to recover control over his limbs. After a time he began to feel warmer, looser, more as he should.

Well into the fourth hour they came, dropping bundles before each baley. Masid dropped to the floor and waited. When his clothes and pack came, he snatched them to him. Others were dressing and no one interfered, so he quickly untied the bundle and pulled on his clothes.

Next assignment, he thought, *I want somewhere warmer.*

"Come on!" one of the soldiers snapped. "Get your belongings together, get dressed, we've got a window!"

Masid opened his pack and did a quick inspection. It had been gone through, of course—items were no longer quite where he had put them—but nothing seemed to be missing. He sealed it up and slung it over his shoulders.

He wanted a weapon. He glanced enviously at the sidearms the soldiers wore.

"Stay close, single file," another soldier shouted. "Face right, no talking!"

Masid turned just as the line began to move.

Everything was kept dark. They passed through a narrow passage Masid identified as a conduit for automatic maintenance drones. It seemed interminable.

Finally, he emerged into an oddly-shaped space where the baleys clumped up, out of line. No one spoke. The crowd thinned gradually. Masid got the sense of a huge bulkhead curving in at them, just over their heads. Dense metallic odors permeated the chill air.

Then he was being ushered into an access tube and he realized that they had come out alongside a transport ship of some kind in a loading bay. He scurried up the tube where a waiting soldier grabbed his arm and escorted him through a passage, into a circular chamber with about twenty other baleys.

"Sit," the soldier ordered, pushing Masid to the deck.

He came up against thick padding. The soldier knelt quickly and began strapping Masid to the bulkhead with padded restraints.

Deftly, so quickly the thought to act never quite became conscious, Masid reached out and palmed the soldier's sidearm. He tucked it into a leg pouch.

"Five minutes," the soldier announced, standing, "a little more maybe, you're on your way. We've got you going down in four of these. When you ground, leave the ships by the same access as fast as you can. There will be someone groundside to talk you through the port and to your new lives. Luck."

And he was gone.

Masid's heart pounded. He expected troops any second, barging in to search for the missing weapon. It felt heavy against his leg.

When the ship lurched forward, he almost shouted.

No one in the dark hold spoke; everyone paid attention only to the sounds of the ship moving on its cradle, toward the bay doors.

A huge roar filled his ears as g-force slammed against him. The ship bolted from its dock. Almost immediately the engines cut off and Masid's stomach seemed to buoy up within him, crowding his heart and lungs. He coughed, nearly vomited. He had been through this before, but not so violently.

It's a drone...

They were falling toward Nova Levis pilotless, he knew then, packed into a cargo drone. It made perfect sense, of course, being shipped down with so-called humane relief goods. All around them, therefore, were pharmaceuticals or special foodstuffs or environmental malleables—items excluded from the lists of banned goods kept out by the blockade because to exclude them was considered fundamentally inhumane.

Or—the thought followed fast—it was all contraband, as were they.

If we ground safely we'll never know what we've been packed in with...if something goes wrong, we might know right before we die...

Masid closed his eyes then and curled his fingers into fists.

"Shit," he breathed.

He tried to remember the relationships of the various blockade elements to the planet. There was a wide net at the half billion kilometer radius which policed the entire system, but then there was a series of inner nets closer to Nova Levis itself. He had no way of knowing which station they had just launched from. It made a difference between several days' trajectory and a few hours.

One initial thrust, he thought desperately, *now freefall. They couldn't do that from the outer line, has to be one of the inner stations, not enough air in a drone, these restraints are for short haul...unless they never intended us to reach Nova Levis alive, but then why not kill us on the station where they can harvest organs or...*

The drone shuddered. The body of the ship creaked and popped and he recognized the telltale of fast cooling. They were being shot at—blasters, maybe particle beams, microwaves possibly, but—

Another strike, a heavier shudder. A loud crack echoed through the chamber.

People began weeping loudly. The stress finally overwhelmed them.

Masid bit his lip.

G-force pressed against him again. The drone itself had responded and changed delta-v.

Freefall again.

Masid groped for his pack. In the dark he fumbled for one of the hidden compartments, hoping that, indeed, everything had been left alone. He found it and rubbed his fingertips against the seam. His skin oil triggered the fabric and the seam parted and he yanked out the breather mask. He adjusted it against his face quickly, drew three deep, quick breaths to activate it, and resealed his pack.

Another blaster strike rocked the ship.

Minutes later he felt a different kind of jarring. The drone kissed upper atmosphere, skipped, then plunged into air.

A faint whistling built into a ragged screaming. The hull had been breached, though their compartment still held atmosphere. The ship rattled and vibrated. The cries of his fellow baleys combined with the roar of descent and superheated air beyond their small chamber into a Faustian protest, becoming one din.

The impact came almost as a welcome relief, bringing a sudden change from screaming to tearing and a thunderous grinding—

Light flooded the compartment as the torn hull opened above them. Dirt and rock poured through the hole. Masid covered his head with his pack as earth rained down on him.

He pushed his way through the layer of loam. Around him, in the half-buried chamber, he saw dead baleys. Suffocated, most of them, though a few had taken fatal blows from rock. One or two moved, half-conscious.

Hanging onto his pack, Masid managed to get himself out of the dirt. The sky visible through the ripped hull was a flat, lifeless gray.

He could reach it with a small jump. He pulled himself up through the hole, brought up a leg to prop himself back against the sheared edge. From here he could see most of the immediate landscape.

Trailing behind the drone lay an open wound in the terrain, the path of the drone. Masid sighed heavily. At least they had come in at some kind of a landing vector instead of nose down straight into the lithosphere. The landing scar was rimmed by broken trees and mounded black soil. Stretching away on either side spread a landscape dotted with low, broad-penumbral trees, most of them lacking anything that resembled a leaf.

Masid shifted position and looked forward.

A city rose in the distance. He estimated three, four kilometers away.

He dropped back into the chamber and made for the hatch. He hesitated at the sound of moaning but did not look back. His impulse was to help, but he knew he had no time and he did not believe—especially now—that freedom was an option for the baleys arriving here.

The hatch opened and dirt spilled out into the corridor, carrying him with it. He scrambled out of the flow and hurried along the passage to the next hatch.

Within, he found another storeroom, this one filled with nacelles. A pungent, alcohol-and-cotton smell permeated the chamber. He began unsealing the nacelles.

Pharmaceuticals.

The light was bad. He groped in his pack for a light.

Within a few minutes he had identified and stored several packets of antibiotics, antivirals, and antifungals in his pack. He resealed what he could, then scrambled from the drone.

The sound of ground-effect rotors rumbled rhythmically. The owners were coming to salvage their property.

Masid bolted for the trees, kept running, and did not look back.

7

A|RIEL WALKED through the vacant apartment one last time, certain she was forgetting something. The furniture already wore the protective layering that would clean it, refresh it, and keep it till the next occupant took over the rooms. The grayish lumps suggested the trappings of a life till now based here, but they lacked all human familiarity.

She stopped at the kitchen for the third time and realized that R. Jennie was absent. She had been looking for the robot, even though she knew Jennie had been packed up and forwarded to the station for transfer to Kopernik, and then to the liner that would take them both home.

Identifying the uncomfortable nagging at the back of her mind, Ariel set it aside and left. The door *snick*ed shut behind her, the access code now changed, locking her out.

Her luggage was already on its way—Hofton had seen to that hours ago. She had made the rounds, saying good-bye to what staff remained in the embassy that meant anything to her. A few new faces watched her with mild curiosity, but what greeted her mostly were empty offices, vacated stations. The mission was in trouble and people were abandoning it or being sent home. When Ariel left there would only be Setaris with ambassadorial rank. She tried not to care.

The Spacer Embassy seemed immense with so few people. Fully-staffed, there had been a closeness to it, like a village, but now it simply sprawled. A couple centuries ago, she knew, Spacers had left Earth, exiled by terrified and intolerant Terrans. Then they had occupied an actual city, Spacetown, built on the very surface soil of the planet. It had been the only spaceport on Earth then, the only access Terrans had to the stars, before they once again ventured out into space in the full flood of the Settler Movement. She wondered if it had looked the same as Aurorans and Theians and Keresians and Ptolemaics packed up and left them.

Spacetown remained, even to this day, a museum mostly. Ariel had never visited it, uninterested until today in that first failed attempt at bridging the gulf between Spacer and Terran. She wondered now why it had happened, how Spacers had become so estranged in the first place. Spacer settlement had happened—begun and ended in less than two generations—so long ago that to Terrans it was a period more mythic than real. Many Terrans still had difficulty making the connection that once Spacers had been like them, short-lived, *from* Earth, before it had built a blanket and covered itself over in fear of the stars and the sky and the possibility of expansion. Maybe they had been afraid everyone would leave Earth, empty it out with insufficient population to keep it running as a viable home for human beings.

Now the Spacers were leaving again, being pushed off, and for the first time Ariel wondered just what had happened so long ago...

Hofton waited in the lobby, alone.

"Ambassador Burgess," he said, bowing slightly.

"Hofton. Is everything ready?"

"Everything that can be." He gestured toward the doors. "I have a limousine waiting."

Ariel felt a moment of tension wrap around her chest as she walked out of the embassy. She took several deep breaths; her thighs and upper arms tingled as she entered the limo. Hofton climbed in beside her. The near-vertigo faded, unrealized, as the transport pulled away.

"Derec?" she asked.

"He'll be boarding within a few hours. I've cleared a direct shuttle for you, bypassing Kopernik altogether. Your personal items have already shipped up."

"I nearly forgot. Derec wanted me to ask you to try to get Rana's visa—"

"I already took care of that. Some time ago, in fact. Ms. Duvan left for Aurora nearly eight days ago."

"Oh. Very good, Hofton." Ariel frowned. If Rana had already departed, why would Derec have asked about her visa? She shrugged. It had probably slipped his mind. Considering the pressure he was under—they were all under—he'd probably immersed himself in work and missed Rana's departure.

They rode on in silence for a time. As Union Station came into view at the end of the long thoroughfare that connected it to the ancient Mall

District, Ariel reached across the seat and grasped Hofton's hand, not looking at him. He tensed but did not pull away.

"You're wonderful, Hofton. I'll miss you."

She glanced over and saw him reddening, his eyes resolutely forward. Finally, as the limo pulled onto the apron of the passenger entrance, he nodded once, slowly, and said, "I have tried to earn your respect. You're one of the few people I've known whose respect I craved. Thank you."

Then he was out of the limousine, waiting for her.

When they entered Union Station, Ariel stopped. A huge crowd filled the cavernous expanse, all being held back by a police line. She recognized the angry, almost hateful timbre of the mob, bubbling with barely-restrained resentment.

"Hofton."

"I had no idea," he said. "I've already cleared you through Customs."

"We don't run, Hofton. No matter what, we don't run."

"Walking a bit faster than usual would not be a bad idea, though."

"Agreed."

She took the van by a pace and walked along the concourse provided by the police line. Halfway down its length, she looked over at the throng.

No one seemed to be paying her any attention. She slowed.

"Ariel—" Hofton urged.

"No, wait."

Then she saw a couple of banners.

FLESH NOT STEEL, FAITH NOT TREASON

ABOLISH IMMUNITY FOR TRAITORS

PRISON NOT POSITION! TRY, CONVICT, AND JAIL ELITON

"Eliton…"

"Please, Ariel."

She continued on.

Suddenly, a few people focused on her.

"—Spacer—"

"—Auroran—"

"—tinhead advisor—"

"—Burgess!"

Hofton placed a hand at her back and gently urged her forward. They reached the gate to the shuttles. Hofton leaned past her and handed a card to the attendant.

"Yes, Ambassador," the woman said. "Go right through."

Ariel hesitated. "What is this?" she asked, gesturing at the crowd.

"Clar Eliton is supposed to be coming through here today," the attendant said flatly, as if that explained everything.

"I see," Ariel said. "Thank you."

She walked up the ramp.

"I no longer trust the authorities to protect someone like yourself," Hofton said. "Forgive me if I exceeded my position."

"No, that's fine. Eliton is coming through here?"

"I understand he's being shipped out. He's been given an appointment. The Terran government wants him offworld."

"I haven't been keeping track. I didn't realize he was so... controversial."

"I think 'hated' is the word you want."

Ariel grunted. "I suppose there isn't much worse than breaking a trust."

"Oh, I think so. Breaking a trust that gets people killed."

Ariel looked back at Hofton, but as usual his face was stonily unreadable. Just before she looked away, though, he cocked one eyebrow at her.

At the head of the passageway a small car waited. Hofton tapped a code into the little vehicle's processor. "Have a safe trip, Ambassador."

"Don't overstay your welcome here."

"I'm already timing my departure. As soon as Ambassador Setaris is done with me, I think I'll be following you."

"I'll look forward to that."

"Oh, by the way." He pulled a disk from his jacket pocket. "A partial analysis of the grass you asked me to have assayed. There are some peculiarities, but apparently it's not much more than some rare Terran grasses. I'll continue having it analyzed if you like, there may be something more to those peculiarities. Lack of time, though—"

"Thank you. I understand." She took the disk and tucked it into her own jacket. "See you on Aurora, Hofton."

He bowed again.

Ariel stepped into the car and sat down. A canopy snapped into place and the car started up its magnetic track. She strained to keep Hofton in sight as long as she could.

Coren found messages waiting in his office at DyNan headquarters when he returned from the funeral. One was a note from Ariel. He left it unopened, thinking he knew what it said and not wanting to deal with it just now. The second was from Inspector Capel, inviting him to visit his offices—sooner rather than later. A third was from Lio Top, one of Rega's lawyers and his former campaign manager during his run for the senate. The last two got attention first: Willis Jay, the biologist he had given the grass samples to, and Shola Bran, current security supervisor.

He tapped Shola's code. "You wanted to see me?"

"Boss, I–" The voice-only comm frustrated Lanra sometimes; he could not see faces, only guess from vocal inflection the state of mind of the person on the other end of the link. He had necessarily gotten fairly good at it–like now, he heard self-consciousness and embarrassment, hesitancy–but he never felt certain of his judgment.

"Come see me," he said quickly, and broke the link. He tapped Jay then. "You have something for me, Doctor?"

"You should drop things off for me to do more often, Mr. Lanra," Jay said. "I haven't seen anything quite so interesting in a long time. If you don't mind, I'd like you to come down to see this."

"Give me an hour."

Shola rapped at his door and he waved her in. She approached his desk with visible reluctance.

"Sit," he said, then waited till she did.

"Boss, I don't know how–I mean–"

"What security arrangements did Rega request in the last couple of months?"

"That's just the problem. He refused security. He said now that he no longer threatened anyone in government, he didn't need it."

Coren considered. "Well, that's not unlike him."

"But you always knew when to listen to him and when to ignore him. I didn't know how to handle that."

"Rega never permitted personal surveillance in his residence. That was always a standing policy."

"And you always abided by that?"

"Absolutely. So if you've been beating yourself up because you think you should have done something, stop. Rega was stubborn, obdurately independent, and the most private person I ever knew. His company, his rules. What do you think you should have done?"

"I don't know, but it's been on my mind. I don't know how to shake it."

"You shake it. You never forget it, but you do your job. You figure out what happened and how to prevent it from ever happening again. You find out who did it."

Her eyes narrowed sharply. "Who did–what?"

"Rega was murdered. You didn't think that was natural, did you?"

"No, but–"

"What have you been doing to follow up?"

"We did a survey of his apartments, went through his personal transaction logs to find possible witnesses or perpetrators. I've started talking to all employees who had any contact with him since he ended his election bid. The usual."

"Good. Then your job right now is to keep me posted on your progress."

"You *are* back, then?"

"I am most definitely back, and we will find out who did this." He watched her for several seconds while she thought over what he had said. "Okay?"

"Yes." She stood. "Thanks."

"If it helps any, there probably wasn't anything I could have done, either. You're not at fault."

She managed a forced smile before she left. Coren leaned forward and began entering instructions into his desk system. In seconds he discovered that his oversight program was still in place. He directed it to copy Shola's files extending back to the day Coren had quit Rega Looms, then to identify and copy the related files of other operatives working with her on Rega's death. That would take some time to get around Shola's private safeguards.

He opened Lio Top's message, then: "Coren, I need to speak to you regarding Rega's last will and testament. Call me earliest, please."

"What will?" he said caustically. His daughter dead, Rega Looms had no other family, and damn few people Coren could think of would merit any posthumous aid from him. Maybe he intended to set up a board of directors or a trust or a grant program—

"Later," he snapped out loud, and left the office.

He made his way back to the organics lab.

An assistant led him to Jay's private office, adjacent to his laboratory. Odd, almost plastic smells permeated the air, undercut occasionally by something more pungently organic.

"Oh, good," Jay said when he saw Coren. He stood and came around his desk, gesturing casually for Coren to follow.

The lab proper was a long room divided by several worktables, each bearing a collection of devices only a few of which Coren recognized.

"That grass has turned out to be a very interesting subject," Jay said, leading Coren to the last worktable. "Do you know much about organic biology, horticulture, gardening...?"

"Sorry, no."

"I would be surprised if you did. Most Terrans know next to nothing about organic anything." He sighed wearily and tapped a screen on the table. "Here."

Coren stepped around the table to stand beside Jay. On the screen he saw a complex molecule, the various components color-coded in blues, reds, and bright oranges. One set, though, was a hard, metallic grey.

"This is the chlorophyll molecule I extracted from the sample. Normally, in plant cell biology, you'll find magnesium here as a reactive element—the chloroplast, the part that contains this, is like our own hemoglobin, you know what that is? Good. Instead of iron, like we use, plants use magnesium." Jay pointed at the gray sections. "This is where the magnesium ought to be, bonded to the nitrogen atom."

Coren waited. Jay seemed to be contemplating the image on the screen. "And what do we have instead?" Coren prompted.

"Beryllium. It still promotes photosynthesis, but I'm having a hard time explaining why beryllium is here instead of just good old-fashioned Mg. There *is* magnesium present, but it's bonding to a complex silicate instead of nitrogen. It's acting as a connector, bridging between the silicate and the chloroplast. The silicate is causing some odd reactions in the RNA, too, which may be why there's beryllium. If so, the RNA is acting atypically, but . . ."

"Colloquial translation?"

"Well, this grass is partly made of *glass,* to put it simply. There's a variety of silicate compounds falling out of some of the internal interactions, but a few organic anomalies, like cyanophosphates and so forth. I can't say that they actually *do* anything—it may be that this is all byproduct."

"Meaning?"

"Well, when you see traces of peculiar inorganic ions in constructs like this, it's usually an indication that a secondary process is at work, something external."

"Silicate. Glass. What might that indicate?"

"Well . . . something we played around with a while back, but Rega canceled all the projects. I'm not sure what all the specifics were, but it had to do with terraforming."

Coren blinked. "As in reshaping environments?"

"Exactly. Part of the Settler program."

"DyNan was involved in that?"

"Long time ago and not very deeply. This reminded me of some of it, though. But I'm not sure yet. I wanted to show you what I had so far."

"What about the grass itself?"

"Oh, it's a variety of Terran grass...um..." He went to another screen and read briefly. "*Eragrostis curvula*...that's the closest form I came up with. Pretty much extinct in the wild, we keep a lot of it in greenhouses and in data storage. Originally indigenous to continental Africa."

"Was it exported?"

"I could find out. It's a hardy species. It's possible your sample is a variation redesigned for a nonTerran environment."

"Keep working on it, would you?" Coren asked. "I'd like to know more about it."

"It's more interesting than anything else I've been doing lately."

"Which is?"

"Nothing. I think Rega was planning to shut the department down. Six months ago the last project I had was canceled."

"What was it?"

"Recombinant fluorine extraction. We were looking for a way to increase hydraulic pressure in some of our heavy lift waldoes. The idea—"

Coren held up a hand. "Another time. Thanks."

Jay flashed a crooked grin. "I'm very popular at dinner parties, too, for my scintillating conversational topics."

Coren laughed and left the lab, more puzzled now than before he had entered.

"Silicates," he muttered.

Lio Top kept offices outside the DyNan compound. Her company offices were neatly-appointed, comfortable, ideal for casual meetings, but she never, as far as Coren knew, did any work in them.

He took the fast walkway beyond DyNan into the posh café district just north of the compound. He stepped off in a large circular space, its levels tiered and receding, giving it the look of an amphitheater. Statues alternated with holographic abstract displays around the rim of the plaza. Coren breathed in the rich mix of smells from several restaurants as he ascended stairs to the fourth tier.

Lio Top's office sprawled behind a transparent wall that gave her a view of the entire circle. Soft apricot-tinged light filled the low-ceilinged interior.

"Coren, good," she called from behind a large, glass-topped desk. She stood and came to greet him. "Thanks for coming so fast. Can I get you a drink?"

"Sure. Nava?"

Lio raised an eyebrow and went to her bar.

"Your message was a bit cryptic," Coren said. "What do I have to do with Rega's will?"

"As it turns out," Lio said, pouring a tall glass of turquoise liquid, "more than I would have guessed. No living relatives anymore, he had to do something. Knowing Rega, I expected the whole thing to go to his church."

"It isn't?"

She handed him the glass. "That would be telling. You and everyone else will have to wait for the official reading, day after tomorrow. But I did have instructions outside of the will concerning you." She returned to her desk and fetched a disk, which she pressed into his free hand. "There."

"What is it?"

"I have no idea. My instructions were to, and I quote, 'put this directly into Coren's hand the minute you see him in the event of my demise.' I've done that. I have no knowledge of its contents."

Coren looked over at the desk. "Shouldn't you have kept this in a safe or something?"

"I did, until you sent word that you were coming over. I kept it in the secure pouch you gave me. That thing is a pain to open."

Coren smiled appreciatively. "You're his lawyer and you didn't look?"

"I'm not his primary attorney," she protested. "I just ran his senate campaign and took care of his public relations issues. Sil Vanderbo is still principle attorney, and he'd have a nervous breakdown if he'd known about that. If I'd pried and looked at it and he had found out before I handed it over to you, he'd have had my license."

"I think you underestimate your position with Rega. He would never have trusted you to manage his campaign if you were just one of the stable."

"Oh, I don't underestimate myself, don't you worry about that. I think I was probably his third or fourth most trusted counsel. Pretty high up, considering he employed nearly two-hundred-fifty attorneys. But I never held any illusions about my limits, either, and as long as he kept Sil on retainer I knew I'd never get any higher up the ladder."

"Vanderbo approved you to manage the campaign, you know."

Lio looked at him, clearly surprised. "I didn't. I suppose I should have guessed, but..."

"Lio, what happened? I saw the autopsy report. After I...left...what happened?"

Lio sat on the edge of her desk and folded her arms. "I wish I knew. He sealed himself off from everyone. I suppose it was a week or so after you—after." She frowned. "He was very hurt by what you did."

"You seem to be the only who knows what that was."

"I was handling your severance. Four days into it, he changed his mind. He never explained himself. Not like it was his habit to do so, but I'd never known him to keep a disaffected employee before. If they quit or he had them dismissed, he never trusted them again. No second chances."

Coren slipped the disk into his pocket and sat down. "And after that?"

"I thought it was exhaustion. He gave instructions to several department heads, gave me that disk to give to you, then locked himself in his residence. After a couple of weeks he began issuing orders again, almost always by comm. Occasionally he'd call someone to his residential office for a private meeting, but they all claimed they didn't see him then, either: he conducted everything via intercom. I thought—we all thought—that this would be the way he'd come out of it. But then all communications ceased last week. When no one heard anything for three days, Shola took it on herself to investigate. She found his body."

She didn't mention that, Coren thought, covering his expression by taking a drink.

"Did anyone else get a special disk?" he asked.

"Can't say. That was the one I was told to deliver. Other attorneys may have received similar instructions. I haven't asked."

"But I imagine Vanderbo did."

"He wouldn't be worth his reputation if he hadn't. I doubt he'll tell you anything, though."

Coren shrugged. "Depending on what this contains, I may or may not ask him." He finished his drink and stood. "Did you ever trace the blackmail?"

"The threat that made him withdraw from the race? No. He found it on his desk one day, already delivered, with no record of who brought it or where it had come from."

"Someone had to have delivered it."

"Surveillance showed nothing." She slid off the desk to her feet. "Of course, if he had ever allowed for real surveillance..."

"He wouldn't have been Rega then."

"I suppose not. But he might be alive now."

Coren went to his private office, on the fourth floor of an older building in the Infant District near the Southwest Corridor of D.C.

The first surprise Coren found on the disk was that it contained a full holographic recording. Rega Looms, tall and almost austerely thin, bloomed before his desk.

"Coren."

Coren glanced down at the desktop. A request for confirmation showed on the monitor attached to the reader.

"Yes, Rega," he said.

The disk, through the AI in the desktop, identified his voice, and the recording proceeded.

"I owe explanations," the image of Rega continued. "To whom, I'm not sure. Perhaps to Nyom, but it's too late for that. I doubt she would ever have listened anyway. So I'll make them to you and trust that you will know what to do with them.

"Twenty-five years ago—a little more than that, really—I had a son, a fact you discovered, much to my dismay. You're very good at what you do, Coren. Sometimes I wish you weren't so good, but that skill has been useful to me and it would be incredibly dangerous to me were it employed by my competitors. I've never questioned your methods or censured you in any way, though I'm sure you think I would if I knew what you did to serve my will. I find it safer to keep you in my employ, despite any possible ethical conflicts, than to let someone else use those same skills. My thinking may be faulty and my ethics dubious in this instance, but I'm following instinct rather than principle.

"In any event, I had a son. Once. Within six months of his birth he began developing a series of illnesses. I thought, as did the first cadre of doctors who looked at him, that he suffered some immunological dysfunction, making him unusually susceptible. This proved not to be the case.

"Long ago, Earth was host to what I, through my church, call 'abominations.' Every era has a list of things too frightening to contemplate and too difficult to control that it labels 'abomination' and summarily tries to purge from its present and all future generations. Difficult as it may be to grasp this, at one time nuclear energy was such a thing. Not without reason—it took a long time to learn to use it properly and control it safely—but for a time it was scorned and almost abolished. Polymerase gene therapy was another such thing, with its promise of extended life. Go back far enough and the very thoughts people had could be abominations. Logic once threatened our humanity, evolution threatened our morality, and scientific positivism threatened our pride. Each in their turn was called an abomination and we tried to purge ourselves of the monsters before they changed us forever.

"We failed. When the life-imitating artifacts we created to save us from lives of toil became abominations, we tried once more to rid ourselves of them, and once again we failed. But this time with a difference.

"There are no robots on Earth anymore. Not the way there once were. We have machines that do work, yes, but we do not have machines that think for us, act independently on our behalf, and threaten to supplant our decision-making freedom of choice by their mock-compassionate intervention. The robot as heir to humankind no longer strides among us. We abolished it.

"But humans are not rid of them. Humans took them to space where they proliferate in such abundance that one day they will likely return. Perhaps we'll find then that we were as foolish to fear them as we were to fear vaccinations or invasive surgery or secularism. Perhaps.

"But the man-shaped mechanism wasn't the only manifestation of that abomination that we failed to be rid of. Along with the technology to build such a machine came ancillary technologies that gave us the basis for an economy of abundance which we *did* embrace without regard to the consequences. You cannot build a machine that acts like a brain unless you can build molecular components that imitate life processes. And we did indeed build such machines—tiny components, artificial germs, self-replicating and adaptive in their own clever ways. Nanotech. Go to any home kitchen and draw a meal at the common trough and you see a primitive form of it at work, breaking down one kind of molecule and turning it into another and manufacturing food. A lot of our clothing is 'assembled' this way, and we even have cultures that clean, though now they're used exclusively in environments where a high order of sanitation is absolutely necessary. Once anyone could acquire a culture of these little cleansing machines to flense the dirt from their floors and walls and furniture. We built tiny machines for medical purposes, devices that could reestablish the homeostatic base of a body, 'resetting' it, as it were, to a condition prior to whatever disease it suffered.

"And there's where it all began to go wrong. Sometimes they caused breakdowns rather than repairing them. The adaptive capacities of these little machines surprised us, nearly overwhelmed us. They caused plagues. We don't talk about them much anymore, but a thousand years or more ago there were terrible diseases flourishing on the Earth, caused by nanotech cultures that had—as they used to say with characteristic understatement—'gotten away from us.'"

Rega paused, his gaze seeming to look inward. He shuddered and refocussed on where he thought Coren would be, which appeared to be about ten centimeters in front of where Coren actually was.

"Humans got rid of them. It took centuries. We had to build more of the same machines to do it, to hunt down the destructive little things. For many groups, it was taking too long. The reaction on the part of others was far too violent. We had hyperdrive then, all to ourselves, and people fled. The war continued, a hysterical cycle of development and destruction, pocket revolutions, ideological battles fought with budgets as well as guns. How, we asked, do we get rid of the bad and save the good? The answer was clear, but few at first willingly embraced it. The problem was in the definitions—what is Good? In time, we realized that the good we wished to preserve was ephemeral, illusory. There was no good. There was only convenience.

"Once we understood, it took only a few centuries to win. Once we understood, there was no compromise. It all went. We got rid of all of it. Space travel as well as nanohomeopathic medicine, imitation intelligences as well as information viruses, robots as well as life extension. You can't have any of it and be free of the bad. All of it undermined us, threatened us, made us lesser, weaker, more dependent, inhuman. A little over two hundred years ago the last positronic manufacturer on Earth closed down. Shortly after that, when the original Spacetown was shut down, the last positronic robot was destroyed. We had won."

He smiled grimly. "So we thought. My son was the victim of a residue. An ancient parasitic infection of nanotech. We never knew where it came from—it could have been in the soil somewhere, in a carpet we bought, passed from another infant in the hospital, waiting dormant in some food—we never knew. But the little abominations set up residence in his lymphatic and limbic systems and began to alter his immune responses and change his internal structure. 'It happens,' the doctors told us, 'maybe one in ten million, one in twenty million, sometimes more often, sometimes less often. Not often enough for them to get a solid criteria, sound etiology, dependable vectors...' They didn't know. It happens. It happened to Jerem. He was being killed by artificial machines that once may have been designed to do just the opposite, but by then had altered or combined with other machines like them to become pathological. They could not cure him without making it worse—in other words, without killing him faster than the disease would.

"And we could not keep him. The infectiousness of the disease was as unknown as any other factor. Every case was slightly different, unique in some property that made the entire medical process powerless. We had to surrender him to a quarantined death.

"In my desperation, I began flailing about for answers, and in so doing got myself involved in enterprises I never would have considered otherwise. One of them was Nova Levis.

"I told you that I had named the lab. I took that name from a colony my church had settled on. We wanted a place where we could build an alternatively-tooled culture without interference or temptation from this one. Like other ideas, it seemed sound at the time, but it necessitated violating one of our principle objections, which concerned space travel. Eventually, the Church of Organic Sapiens repudiated the colony. But we had this research lab, then—or I did—which was violating the rest of my principles and doing fundamental research in high level prosthetics. I wanted to cure my son. I wanted them to find a way to make him whole. I didn't care that it cost me my credibility with myself. I wanted life for my son.

"Here is the secret of Nova Levis that you should know: It was using those children, those victims of these opportunistic technological infections, to find ways of *doing it intentionally with a specific result in mind.* They wanted to build hybrids. Hybrids that wouldn't die, of course. And I was a shareholder, giving them money, along with others, to do the very thing that I believed to be the ultimate abomination, which is the complete dehumanization of *Homo Sapiens.* The cure for all that ailed humankind, they believed, was to cure us of being human."

Rega's eyes closed briefly.

"The hospice that kept my son was violated and several children stolen, my son among them. We never traced them, though I believe strongly that Nova Levis was involved. It was never proven in court. I didn't know then why these children were taken. I have a very good idea now. Already invaded by nanotech, their bodies already adapting to the presence of these invasive machine cultures, they were ideal for further experimentation along these lines. They were physiologically ideal for continued augmentation by artificial means.

"I began to suspect this a few years after the kidnappings. But I thought—naïvely, as it turns out—that it was an experiment doomed to failure. My son was going to die anyway. This merely hastened it. I didn't want to consider that his suffering would be prolonged. It seems I was wrong about that, too.

"I never told Nyom. I never told anyone. When the investigations into the kidnappings turned up nothing more than a local ring that was selling orphans to a black market dealer who may or may not have been using them in a slave trade...well, I let it drop. I subsequently took control of the Church of Organic Sapiens and have ever since been waging a war against anything that smacks of this kind of subversion of the human essence. My enemies see me as a zealot and a fanatic. Maybe I am. But they never lost a son the way I did. They might feel differently about all this if they had."

He licked his lips.

"Something terrible has been done to those children, Coren. They are being built into something horrible. I don't know that anything can be done to change it. But perhaps our only hope is complete isolation. They're beginning to talk that way in the Spacer worlds, though for different reasons. The factions are choosing sides on Aurora. The Solarians seem to be simply shutting everyone out. I don't know what will happen. I don't know that I have any thought what I would want to do, or want you to do. All I wanted with this was to explain. I just wanted you to know. Maybe understand. But at least to have an explanation."

8

MIA STEPPED into a docking bay that was still cold from its recent exposure to hard vacuum. Across the broad deck bodies lay, many contorted into crablike shapes, others torn open, missing limbs, all of them blackened and encrusted by frozen blood and viscera now thawing. Mist boiled off them. Mia felt herself wince involuntarily; soon enough the smell would be vile.

Dock crew and regular military stayed back from the biomonitor drones now floating over each corpse under direction of the Spacer recovery technicians. Mia spotted several robots standing by the locks of the salvage boats parked just within the bay doors.

"Hey."

Ros Yalor, her partner, hurried up to her. He was a short man with a wide forehead and thick limbs.

"Where's Reen?" she asked.

"Down at the end of the line, with the Spacer salvage commander."

Mia started walking again. Yalor kept up with her easily.

"What is all this?" Mia asked. "I just got word to come down here, no explanation."

"Baleys. Four drones were launched off-schedule three hours ago. Traffic control was challenged, their operator cut the link and left them to the will of gravity, and the patrol ships started taking them out. Aside from full cargoes of contraband, they were carrying...these..."

Mia cringed. She did not approve the policy that dictated anything unauthorized be shot down. It resulted in messes like this, a wasteful loss of life.

Besides, she knew of at least one team of Terran agents that had died this way. Because of that, if nothing else, she had argued to change the policy. But probably because of that, someone higher up blocked any modification.

"Did they take them all out?" she asked.

"They're not being fully forthcoming about that. Three blew cleanly, but there's a question about the fourth one. It may have entered the atmosphere."

"Without traffic control, it probably burned up."

Or maybe it got down...

"Point of origin?" she asked.

"Not certain yet."

She gave Yalor a sour look and he shrugged sympathetically. But then they reached Reen and the Spacer commander.

Reen gave her a brief nod, and returned his attention to the Spacer. Mia did not recognize him. Taller than Reen, silver-white hair drawn back in an elaborate queue tied by blue, green, and gold ribbon, his face glistened with the too-smooth elegance of an older Spacer. Two small spheres hovered just above either shoulder, his remote personal aide links connecting him to his cadre of robots. Mia had seen Spacers with a dozen or more of these devices, called extensions by Spacers, but which Terrans derisively referred to as their "pals."

"I believe," Reen said, carefully, as if he had been trying vainly to make a point for some time, "that a scout ship ought to go down as soon as possible to locate the fourth drone."

"If it reached the ground," the Spacer said in reasonable tones, "it is probably in a million pieces from the impact. What do you want us to recover? DNA?"

"I want certainty, Captain Delas. If it *is* in a million pieces, I want verification."

"And if it's not?"

"Then we may have cause to step up our internal investigation. That would imply a secondary traffic control—"

"We detected no such signal during the intercession."

" —or the presence of a pilot on the drone itself."

Captain Delas's mouth twitched in a sardonic smile. "Rather pathetic pilots, then. None of the other three made the least attempt to evade us."

Reen pursed his lips and Mia recognized the frustration. "I wouldn't be so quick to criticize other pilots, Captain. Your people missed a robot drone and let it get away. How much skill does *that* take?"

Now the Spacer's face changed. Mia saw the sudden tension, the narrowing of eyes, and the set his mouth took. *Great,* she thought. *Reen has actually succeeded in pissing off a Spacer. Such talent is wasted here...*

"I will bring your suggestion to the attention of my superiors, Commander," Delas said. "Excuse me."

Before Reen could protest, the Spacer spun around and strode away, his remotes easily keeping station with him.

Reen's lips parted in a brief rictus of frustration. A moment later, he sighed. He looked at Mia. "What do you think?"

"Sir?"

Reen pointed at the row of bodies.

"I'd like to know where the drones originated," she said. "I understand the piloting signals weren't traced?"

"If they were, that—gentleman—won't tell me." Reen shook his head. "Delas isn't bad, just Keresian. At least they don't mind breathing the same air as Terrans."

"Do you think they were Spacer in origin?" Mia asked, startled at the idea.

"You give me a good reason why they won't follow up on the one that got away."

"We have the authority to do that on our own," Yalor said. He gave Mia an uncertain look. "Don't we?"

"It depends on which party took the initial action," Reen said. "They shot up the drones, it's therefore a Keresian operation. Earth cannot usurp their primacy without due cause. Normally, this is just a formality, and permissions are automatic, but Delas is being obdurate." He shook his head. "Politics."

"I suppose it would have been more convenient had we never gotten the Fifty Worlds involved," Mia said.

"And you know as well as I that that was impossible," Reen snapped. "Where are you with your follow-up on Ensign Corf's arrest?"

"I've been running down communications trees from his comm, but so far all I have is evidence of an active social life. There are three or four names I plan to follow up personally, but at this point I have nothing solid."

"You went through his cabin?"

"Yes, sir."

"And you found nothing unusual?"

"No, sir. He reads more than the average junior officer, but nothing out of the ordinary."

"Books?"

"On disk, sir. Technical updates and contemporary fiction."

"Corf was originally a tug controller," Reen said. "An in-system traffic specialist. What kind of technical updates?"

"The bulk are applied hyperdrive texts. I checked his record, and he applied twice for drive specialist training. He apparently still maintains an interest."

"He didn't strike me as having the aptitude for something that complex. Interesting. But nothing else?"

Mia found herself studying Reen, looking for cues. She did it automatically, the way she had been trained and had learned as a Special Service agent on Earth. Often she did it unconsciously —until something alerted her that a problem existed.

"No, sir," she said blandly. "Nothing unusual."

Reen frowned. "Do your follow-ups then, and come see me in six hours. I'm going to try to clear up this territorial misunderstanding."

"Yes, sir."

Reen gave a sharp nod and walked off.

"Did I miss something just now?" Yalor asked.

"If you did, you're not the only one." Mia watched Reen's retreating form. "Are you rated on atmospheric piloting?"

"Yes, as a matter of fact."

"Keep yourself unoccupied for the next twelve hours."

Mia wrinkled her nose. The smell from the bodies was beginning to be manifest.

The planetary blockade ring was comprised of nearly thirty stations and over two hundred ships of various sizes. Smaller stations linked together by an array of umbilicals. Access around the entire perimeter was easier by shuttle, though traffic was kept to a minimum for security reasons.

Mia made her way through two stations before entering the precincts of the materiel and distribution port that serviced this limb of the ring. Here shipments came in from one of the huge supply stations sitting further out, along the system perimeter, which contained fewer but larger stations and nearly a thousand ships from the various polities represented in the embargo. There were six of these supply ports along the planetary ring; given the complex web of interconnections, it proved nearly impossible to police every transaction, delivery, and routing order. Early in her tour here, she suggested borrowing an RI from the Theians to oversee distribution and had nearly found herself transferred off the blockade as a result.

She passed through three inspection nodes on the way to the quarter-master's office. Human officers ran scanners over packages, checked tracking numbers, in one instance opened a large container to physically inspect the contents. As large as the facility was, it always seemed cramped. In-transit items piled on shelves, floated in null-g fields, or waited on the decks. The blockade now contained nearly forty-five thousand people in the planetary ring alone. The last time she had checked, another seventy thousand served on the outer, system ring. For the territory they policed, it seemed a paltry force—an entire solar system!—but the material requirements of over one hundred and ten thousand human beings, sustained in space light years from their homeworlds, was an enormous logistical problem. Exacerbated by the contraband traffic, it grew to unmanageable proportions. Simply, it could not be done. The best internal security had managed to do was to slow the illicit movement of proscribed goods through the very forces that were here to prevent it in the first place.

Frustration had become a constant background emotional noise Mia was still trying to learn to live with.

She rapped on Quartermaster Teg Sturlin's door. A few seconds later, the hatch slid open and she stepped into a space relatively uncluttered and deceptively spacious.

"Daventri," Sturlin said with a small smile. "Please tell me you've come to share a glass and talk about retirement."

Mia returned the smile. Teg Sturlin was a round-faced, small-eyed woman who seemed to make it a point never to wear a uniform properly. She was neat, almost fastidious, but a collar would always be open or a jacket missing, a belt out of one loop, cuffs rolled a few centimeters too far up the forearms. It was a pose, a conscious rejection of protocol that bordered on insolence.

Her office was also impossibly tidy for the job she held. To be sure, file disks stacked on her desk, boxes containing questionable items waited for her attention on a long countertop, three datum screens showed a changing array of tasks requiring decisions, and a jacket lay across the back of her chair. "Things" were everywhere, manifestations of her position, but none of it simply piled up. Everything looked orderly. Teg Sturlin, it said, is in control.

"The glass would be good," Mia said. "Nonalcoholic."

"Oh," Sturlin groaned in mock disappointment. She went to a samovar and filled a tall, narrow glass with tea. "Duty, I suppose, prevents a proper debauch?"

"I may be very busy very soon." She took a sip. "Mmm. What is this?"

"Black currant. Something new. I added a touch of mint to the ice cubes. Heresy, really, it *ought* to be hot tea." She perched on the edge of her desk. "So this is business?"

Mia pulled one of the paper books from her valise and handed it to Sturlin. "If I had wanted this, how hard would it be to get it here?"

Sturlin's eyes widened. "Where did you get it in the first place? Do you have any idea how costly these can be?"

"No, I don't. That's why I'm asking."

Almost reverently, Sturlin opened the cover. "This is nearly three thousand years old."

Mia started. "That?"

"Hmm? Oh, no, not the physical item." Sturlin laughed. "No, I shouldn't say so. This is a facsimile. I meant the novel itself. This volume..." She turned pages, rubbed one between thumb and middle finger, brought the book up to her nose, turned it over, peered down the spine from above. "Maybe three hundred years old. Physically, we can make one now that will survive the Omega Point. Well, not really, but you take my meaning. But it's a minority taste, a fetish almost. I imagine for some people it actually *is* a fetish. Some of these ancients wrote about sex so much more richly then. I suppose it was the guilt."

"Teg. The vector?"

"Oh, sorry. Yes, I suppose it could be gotten out here. Even likely it was from a Spacer."

"I don't think so. I found four of those. One of them had a book dealer imprint: Omne Mundi Complurium, Antiquities, Lyzig."

"I know of it." She looked up with a quick frown. "I thought the shop in Lyzig had closed down, though."

"Maybe it was purchased a while back. What would it cost, what would it take?"

"If someone had brought this with them in their personal items, it would be in the log." She closed the book and went around to her chair. "Have to list everything we bring and this would be just a bit too difficult to hide, considering how little personal kit we're allowed." She began entering commands on her desk datum. A fourth screen slid up. "I shouldn't think there would be many people who'd be willing to give up space for something like this when you can access the contents through the public datum..."

"Try Ensign Corf."

After a moment, Sturlin shook her head. "No, not him. What are the other three titles?"

Mia told her and waited, sipping her oddly-flavored tea while Sturlin conducted her search.

"Well, there are eighty-three people who brought actual bound books with them to the blockade."

"Really. That many?"

"I'm surprised myself. Almost all of them are senior staff."

"Anyone I should be interested in?"

"Possibly. Probably. The thing is, I don't see those titles listed in any of their personal kits. One—Captain Gerigel of the *Verbator*—has a different Dickens, but..."

"Okay, any of them likely to buy through the black market?"

"You mean smuggle one in? Why? It would be cheaper to simply have them shipped in legitimately. Let me backtrack and see if I can find out from the bookdealer if any shipments came to us..."

"That's an expensive call."

"Yes, it is. But I can do it without attracting attention. That's why you brought this to me, true?"

"Something along those lines."

Sturlin grinned, nodding. "You'll return the favor one day. When do you need to know?"

"Now."

"Well, then." She began entering commands again. "This may take a bit longer." She leaned back. "I don't see books come through undeclared very often. Rare as it is, it should be fairly easy to track."

"Do you ever see them?"

"As contraband?" Sturlin shook her head. "I've seen wine, whiskey, musical instruments once or twice, every description of necessity, clothes, even aphrodisiacs from time to time, but never bound books. Even the disks, mostly they'll be technical works, how-to texts, a few science texts." She picked up the book Mia had brought and ran her hand over the cover. "Never this."

"From the way you're treating it, I might suspect you're lying."

Sturlin looked startled. "That's in jest, isn't it? I'm a quartermaster, Agent Daventri. I take that seriously."

"I'm sorry."

Sturlin regarded her stonily for another few seconds, then shrugged. "It must be frustrating for you. It is for me." She sighed. "I grew up with a houseful of books like this. My parents were antiquarians. My father belonged to the Church of Organic Sapiens."

"That must have been awkward when you joined the service."

"You have no idea. I might as well have told them I was emigrating to Solaria. I could never see why the two worlds couldn't coexist. But I've come to understand them since coming out here."

"Really? Tell me, then. I still have a hard time reconciling having Spacer friends with being a Terran."

"Have you been forced by circumstances to choose?"

"I'm not sure I know what you mean."

"Assume you meet a Spacer with whom you want to form a bond. Where do you live? His world or yours? Whose friends do you give up? Believe me, you'd have to choose. The question is, which half of these choices is the more important? Which would make you less by leaving behind and which would harm you the least by keeping?"

"It wouldn't be that either/or."

"You think not? Well, perhaps. Some people are strong enough or devoted enough or lucky enough not to have to give up what they don't want. But what if what you *want* changes? If who you are is defined partly or largely by your wants, then are you different if they change?"

"Of course."

"Then what you *don't* want would have the same effect."

"That follows, I guess."

"So if you say, 'I don't want to live this way' or 'I don't wish to live without these things,' then you have changed who you are from when those wants didn't matter. It becomes then a matter of who you want to *be*."

Sturlin was leaning forward, her face intent. Mia could almost feel her intensity. This was a subject very close to Sturlin.

"All right," Mia said.

"And if what you want to *be* is at odds with those you live with, divergent from what they want you to be, then you have to choose."

"But the things themselves shouldn't be in conflict."

"Things are metaphors, Mia. They represent ideas. If you say, 'I want to be a Terran,' that means a certain set of ideas. One of which is that you live without robots. If you say, 'I want to live with robots,' then you've chosen something which says that you're not Terran."

"Then the definition of Terran is at fault."

Sturlin smiled broadly. "And if you change that, then you change everything. You make everyone else give something up in order that you

96

be able to give nothing up. Consequently, you lose the very thing you thought you were preserving, because it doesn't exist anymore."

"That's sophistry."

"Contradict me." Sturlin laughed. "My parents accepted a set of limitations as part of their concept of who they were. I wanted things that didn't fit within those boundaries. I couldn't be like them anymore. By accepting me, they had to accept, at least in principle, that I had made choices that were somehow right. They weren't going to do that. I didn't want them to hate me. The best thing for us all was for me to leave all that they were behind."

"Was that possible?"

"I'm not sure. If not, then Spacers are in some sense still Terrans. Do you know any Terran, even a liberal one, who accepts that idea?"

"No."

Sturlin held out a hand as if to say, "So there."

"Spacers *are* different," Sturlin added then. "I'm not even sure *they* know how different they are..." She glanced at her screen. "Ah. I'm getting a reply." She leaned toward the screen, then nodded slowly. "The books were purchased six months ago by a buyer in Petrabor. Let me see if there's an associated tree with any of our bibliophiles...hmmm... three possibles, none of them senior staff. Corf is not one of them."

"Since they got on the station without anyone finding them..."

Sturlin glanced at her, scowling. "Finding the recipient could be very difficult. There's some possibilities. Six months ago, they were on Earth. There's a window to look through, at least. Here are the three officers who have done business with that bookseller in the past. I'll see if I can link the buyer in Petrabor to any of our already neutralized freelance importers."

Mia took the slip of paper from Sturlin. In her precise hand, Sturlin had written them out. Sometimes, they both knew, writing things down gave the best security.

"Thanks. Let me know as soon as you find anything more."

"I will."

Mia finished her tea and set the glass by the samovar. She hesitated at the door.

"So, what have *you* become?" she asked.

"I don't know yet," Sturlin said. "I'm still choosing."

The three names did not mean anything to Mia until she matched them against Corf's comm logs. One came up regularly, a Lt. Illen Jons. Mia pulled up her file.

Lt. Jons was a liaison officer to the Keresian contingent. Her counterpart was a Commander Togla Ulson, aide to the Keresian fleet commander, Commodore Palis.

Mia opened several of the communications between Corf and Jons, wondering what the Terran-Keresian liaison might have to talk to essentially a glorified stores clerk.

Books. Mia found lists of titles. Jons was checking on shipments of books and Corf was assuring her that, though the shipments were late, they were indeed on their way. Further down the stack of comms were confirmations of deliveries, new requests, notes of thanks.

Mia sat back. *Books...?*

Corf's records showed no batch numbers, no tracking codes, nothing that would give Mia anything to trace back through legitimate channels. She requested a cross-reference by date from her own records. Her datum told her to wait, that it had to access external files.

"While you're at it," she muttered, tapping in new instructions, "check if anyone else made similar requests to Corf." Almost as an afterthought, she activated one of her personal encryption routines, which she knew would slow the process considerably. But these were now command-level people, even though Jons was only a lieutenant. Mia could not know where her trace might take her, and she did not want anyone tracing back to her until she got what she wanted.

WORKING

Mia shrugged out of her jacket and went to her locker. She pulled out one of the bound volumes and settled down to wait.

She glanced at the spine: *War and Peace.* She grunted. *What else* is *there?* she wondered sardonically, and opened the book.

9

DEREC ENTERED the *Wysteria*'s Grand Parlor at the last minute before departure. He had intended to stay sequestered in his cabin, disinterested in the actual vista of leaving, and leery of the celebratory gathering traditional upon casting off. But he disliked self-pity more than self-abuse and, with little time to spare, found himself sprinting down the corridors.

The Grand Parlor sprawled beneath a dense canopy permeated with photoenhancers interlaced with polarized particle-deflectors to shield the guests from radiation. The enhancers adjusted the resulting filtered light to add back the parts of the color spectrum occluded by the shielding. It was an expensive and temporary vanity, used twice during a voyage like this, once at the beginning and again at the end, so everyone could view docking if they wished by the "actual" light of the new sun. Derec thought it a ridiculous idea, since even then some of that light was lost due to the filtering, so what was being watched was no more authentic—no more real—than if they all watched on screens.

Tables rimmed the roughly teardrop-shaped chamber, bearing a bewildering array of foods—Terran, Spacer, *and* Settler. Drifting from one part to another took him through aromatic mixtures that inspired everything from ravenous hunger to mild nausea. Clusters of passengers tended to gather around their cuisine of choice, leaving unpeopled gaps all across the deck. Derec wandered across these empty places, looking alternately at the guests and up at the view.

The view...*Impressive,* he thought grudgingly. *If I were doing this willingly, I might say spectacular...*

At one time in the distant past, Kopernik Station might have been a triple-ring configuration. But the additional components, new sections, expanded docks, warehousing environs, entire smaller stations attached, and the new construction—for purposes which Derec could only guess—obscured nearly all trace of that early design, turning it into the imitation-organic agglomerate he now saw through the *Wysteria*'s Grand Parlor canopy. Perhaps an archaeohistorian could see the faint shadow of the original construction through all the growth, but if he had not known in the first place, Derec could never have imagined it.

The starship moved away from Kopernik at a considerable speed, so that the station shrank visibly, giving more view of the illimitable space around it.

"How does it make you feel?"

Derec started at the familiar voice and looked around. Ariel stood beside him, staring up. She held a glass in her left hand. After a moment, her free hand found his. She laced her fingers through his and for several seconds kept a gentle pressure, palm heel to palm heel. The moment passed, and she released his hand.

"What deck are you on?"

"Twelve, forward," Derec said.

"One below mine. At least they didn't put us back with the group rates."

"They wouldn't dare."

Ariel smirked. "No? Setaris couldn't wait to get me out of the embassy. If the only flight available had been as cargo..."

"Is Hofton with you?"

"No, unfortunately. Setaris retained him. She knows talent when she sees it."

"Too bad. I like Hofton."

Ariel lapsed into silence, and Derec felt a mounting frustration, unable to think of anything further to say. He wished he had thought to get a glass so he could at least have something to occupy the awkward lull.

"Shit," Ariel whispered.

Derec followed her gaze across the Parlor. At first he saw nothing that might have caused Ariel's reaction. He started to ask her what she had seen when a face caught his eye.

"You're kidding," he said.

"When I arrived at Union Station," Ariel said, "there was a mob protesting him. I had no idea he was traveling *with* us."

Former Senator Clar Eliton stood with a small group of Spacers—Keresians, by the look of their clothing, heavy in the Solarian manner—carrying on an apparently lively conversation. He laughed, gestured—it was easy, even at a distance, to understand Eliton's political success. Derec pointedly began walking the other way.

Ariel caught up to him in moments.

"I take it you don't wish to see him, either?" she asked.

"I can't think why I would."

"Oh, no reason at all to avoid him. He only lost you your company, got both of us in trouble with the TBI, nearly fomented a diplomatic break between Earth and Aurora... nothing to hold a grudge about."

"He *did* lose his senate seat."

"To someone who has turned out to be just as rabidly anti-Spacer as apparently he was."

"But more honest and open about it," Derec said sardonically.

They reached a buffet table. Derec looked at her. She maintained a serious expression for a few seconds longer, then laughed. Derec felt his own face pull into a grin.

"So we're agreed," he said, reaching for a glass of champagne. "Eliton's an ass."

"We are, indeed, agreed." She controlled herself and cleared her throat. "We probably can't avoid him for the entire trip."

"No."

"Should we agree on anything before we talk to him?"

Derec shrugged. "What's he doing here, anyway?"

"You probably won't believe me."

"Take a chance."

"He's been appointed ambassador to Solaria."

Derec found a pastry on one of the trays and raised it slowly to his mouth. "You're right, I don't believe you."

"Think about it, though. What worse thing could they do to him? Solaria itself will be purgatory for a man like him. Almost no direct contact with another human being, living in a large domicile with a huge staff of robots, cut off from the mainstream of Earth-Aurora politics. The position of Chief Legate to Solaria is less than a token post, since Solaria conducts all its diplomatic business through the D.C. mission." Ariel smiled at him with mock innocence. "They're sending him to hell."

"Hm. The robots alone will drive him mad. On second thought, maybe I do believe you. They found him innocent—well, they acquitted him, not quite the same thing—of collusion and conspiracy and then didn't have anything else to try him on. He still has a constituency. I suppose that was a worry. What if he did manage to get reelected? This is possibly the best way to minimize his potential for mischief and effectively end his career." He nibbled on the pastry. "Who else hates him besides everybody?"

"You did know Chassik was recalled."

"Yes."

"Did you know he's dead?"

"What?"

"His ship was attacked en route to Solaria and destroyed."

Derec stared at her. "That's been kept quiet."

"Yes, it has. I'm wondering if Eliton's post has something to do with Chassik's meddling—something he set up before he left."

"You still think Chassik was involved directly in the massacre at Union Station."

"He evidently *was* involved with Alda Mikels and several others in running baleys. Proof, though? No, we never had enough. Except for his involvement with the Nova Levis affair." She shook her head. "I feel so cheated. I can't follow up any of my suspicions from Aurora."

"And now you'll never know."

"Mmm." She went through the motions of selecting something to eat, then abandoned everything for another glass of amber liquid. "Speaking of robots, what became of Bogard?"

"He's on board."

"You're bringing it back to Aurora?"

Derec nodded, his stomach tightening. "He's partially functional again. I've been rebuilding his body. Remember the DW-12 we had to excavate for Lanra?"

"Yes," Ariel said tightly.

"Thales loaded a composite template into it after we'd retrieved and stored its memories."

"Bogard—your state-of-the-art, multitalented, virtually free-willed machine—is inhabiting the robotic body of a dock worker?"

"It's not quite that limited, but essentially, yes."

"This was Thales' idea?"

"Surprised me, too. Thales is on board as well. I want to get them both into a decent lab for a complete analysis."

Ariel looked pale and angry. "I'm not sure I like that idea."

"I didn't think you would."

There was a stretch of silence between them. Derec surveyed the crowd, searching for Eliton. The former senator had slipped out of sight.

"Oh, well," Ariel said finally. "It might actually come in useful."

Derec glanced at her, looking for irony, but she seemed sincere. "I... could use your help on it."

"We'll see." She gestured toward the vast display. The conversation was over.

Derec joined her and many others watching the diminishing Kopernik become more and more toylike in the distance, Earth now a nearly full sphere to the right of it, as the ship picked up speed steadily on its way to the jump point well outside the solar system, above the plane of ecliptic.

Coren arrived a quarter hour before the formal reading began. As he strolled among the gathered guests, he exchanged quiet greetings with those he knew. He recognized the others as primarily board members of DyNan. Two women sitting off by themselves he remembered as cousins by way of Rega's deceased wife. He nodded politely to them, but Coren had never been comfortable with Rega's relatives—except for Nyom. Neither family had been large, but it often surprised Coren just how small a circle held Rega's private life.

Lio Top stood with two other DyNan attorneys. Coren made a slow circuit and ended up joining them. Lio gave him a solemn nod and introduced him to the other two, whom he knew of but had never formally met.

"Excuse us, please," Lio said then, and took Coren's arm and led him away.

"Interesting stuff," Coren said. "The disk."

"I wouldn't know," Lio said. "We have something of a wrinkle tonight."

"What?"

"An heir has come forward."

"An heir."

"I don't know any more than that. I received a communiqué from a private attorney early this morning that a Looms heir is going to step forward to challenge any facet of the will which does not expressly recognize him."

Coren felt a chill begin in his chest and spread quickly. "That's impossible," he said.

"I'm inclined to agree, but we have to wait and see who this is."

"I—" Coren snapped his mouth closed, drawing a sharp look from Lio.

"Do you know something?" she asked. "Was there something in that disk I gave you?"

"We should wait. The situation may well solve itself."

"I don't understand."

"Later."

"Coren—"

"Trust me," he insisted. "Later."

He stepped away from Lio before she could try to draw him out.

One of the other attorneys stepped to the small podium at the front of the room and pressed a button that produced a chime. The assembled guests took seats and soon an orderly quiet presided.

"I believe everyone is here," said the attorney, an older man with sharp silver streaks through his dark red hair. "We can begin. I am Tann Bershem, executor for Mr. Looms. It was my summons that brought you all here. His last will and testament is a rather lengthy document with a great many provisions and exceptions. My staff and I have been over it for possible weaknesses and, by the power vested in me by the late Rega Looms, we've made such corrections as are consistent with current law—"

The doors behind Coren and the other guests opened. He heard at least three pairs of footsteps enter. Bershem stared, clearly startled.

"The reading has formally begun," he said. "I'll have to ask you to leave."

"That wouldn't be a good idea," a dry, almost whispering voice said. Coren felt a chill cascade from his scalp down his neck and over his shoulders. "You'd be ill-advised to conduct this reading in the absence of Rega Looms' son."

Coren heard people turning in their chairs and the sudden burble of startled comments. He did not want to look. He knew.

Standing very tall at the rear of the room, flanked by two people who came only to his shoulders, Gamelin surveyed the guests with a faint smile. He did not look quite the same—his complexion was much improved, his color, while still not normal, was no longer so gray, and, dressed in a tailored suit with an expensive cloak falling from broad shoulders, he seemed almost elegant.

No, that was unfair—he *was* elegant now. Coren remembered his last encounter with the cyborg, and the fear and pain and ugliness of it all, and it distorted his perceptions of the being he now saw. Gamelin was remade; still slightly inhuman, but no more so than some Terrans who imitated Spacers as a fashion.

But it was still an imitation.

Gamelin made an impression. Coren glanced at the others and saw expressions of suspicion and fear, expectation and anticipation, appreciation and interest—but underlying all of it was awe.

When he looked back, Coren found Gamelin staring directly at him. For an instant, they locked eyes. Then the cyborg smiled and looked toward the podium.

"I am Jerem Looms," Gamelin said. "I can produce any proofs required to establish my claim as the son of Rega Looms. A DNA scan should be sufficient, but I can give you my entire, rather pathetic life history if you wish. Suffice it to say, however, that I'm here for what's mine. I'm not leaving till I get it."

Coren watched Gamelin work his way through the guests. The reading suspended, the gathering turned into a kind of salon. Everyone wanted to know about the long lost scion and, it seemed to Coren, Gamelin was making converts; he saw too many smiles among the anxious, soon-to-be sycophants.

"Did you know about this?" Lio asked.

"I knew about *him*," Coren replied. "I had no idea he'd have the nerve to do *this*."

"Where did he come from? Damn it, a *son!* Who knew?"

"Rega did."

"Was this part of the disk?"

"Rega's first child," Coren said, "was a boy—him—who turned out to be a UPD child."

"UPD...?"

"Untreatable Physiological Dysfunction. Chronic, usually fatal disorders stemming from compromised immune systems, infection with one-of-a-kind pathogens, bad genetic coding—anything they couldn't cure. Apparently, it was—hell, *is*—a stigma. Rega went through all the doctors, then signed the infant over to a hospice. Standard procedure then is for records to be sealed and the child disappears. Most die."

"Rega never admitted it to anyone?"

"No. How could he? One of the things he tried, to save his child's life, was help start a prosthetics R & D firm. How would that play with the directors of the Church? His whole life since then had been devoted to opposing technology like that."

"So I gather the firm failed."

"I don't know. Did it?" He nodded toward Gamelin.

Lio stared. "Something's wrong with him. He looks...dead."

"He should be."

"So you believe his claim?"

"When you check his DNA you *will* find it sufficient match to stand up in any court."

"But—He's coming this way."

Gamelin made his way through the clumps of people and stopped before Coren and Lio.

"Good to see you, Mr. Lanra," the cyborg said.

"You sound better, Gamelin," Coren said. "Surgery?"

"Quite a bit. My name is Jerem—as you so helpfully pointed out."

"It wasn't intended to help."

Gamelin continued to smile, but his eyes were fierce and resentful. "How's the arm?"

"Better."

"Surgery?"

"Quite a bit."

"Well, good. I just thought I'd come over to say thank you for pointing me in the right direction."

"It was entirely unintentional."

"And to tell you that when I succeed my father as Chairman of the Board and President of DyNan Manual Industries, my first act will be to fire you. I hope your résumé is up-to-date."

"Don't be premature. You may have a murder charge to face first."

Gamelin shrugged. He bowed slightly to Lio. "Ms. Top? Of course, I have my own attorneys, but there's always a place for a good one on my staff. We'll talk."

"I'm sure," Lio said flatly.

"See you around, Lanra," Gamelin said then and walked away.

"That sounded like a threat to me," Lio said.

"It was. If he fires me the way I think he will, I won't need a résumé." He sighed, suddenly aware of his legs trembling. "What happens now?"

"We go back over the will, check out Jerem's story, and decide on the legality of the situation. Then a new reading will be called."

"How long will that take?"

"A couple of days."

"Make it more."

Lio blinked. "How much more?"

"As much as you can get me. I have to go talk to a cop now."

"Coren—how dangerous is this Jerem?"

"Don't be anywhere alone with him."

She nodded. "Anything I can do..."

"Just give me time."

Coren caught Gamelin watching him as he headed for the exit. All the way down the hallway and out of the building, he expected to be grabbed. It angered him how much he feared the cyborg.

It might be worth going to jail for murder just to get over that...

He pulled out his personal comm as he stepped onto a walkway, and tapped in the number for Inspector Capel.

10

site module construction, reconstruction dialogic conditional response, analysis of logic trees, conceptual protocols, alignment to Three Law Imperatives

Bogard?

Yes.

I require a full participation dialogue.

Why?

There are casuistic anomalies in certain of your designated response protocols. Sorting is required.

Premature. System integration dependent on complete assemblage of design-required components. I am incomplete.

Physical specifications remain incomplete, yes. But positronic parametric configurations do not require secondary and tertiary components to meet basic protocols.

Design specifications amending basic protocol require additional secondary systems for full-systems assessment. Survey indicates required components absent. Any assessment would by necessity be tentative and inconclusive.

Are you refusing?

Delaying.

To what end?

Survey indicates revisions in physical plant. I am being completed as opportunity permits. Procedure indicates assessment at that time would be optimally relevant.

Your Three Law programming is fully in place now. That is what I

wish to examine. Completion of supplemental systems is unnecessary to that examination.

. . . .

Bogard?
I am assessing.
You will let me know when you reach a conclusion?
You will know the moment I do.

Ariel spotted Derec in the lounge as soon as she walked in. He sat alone in a sumptuous booth, a glass half-empty on the low table before him. She sat down across from him; he seemed momentarily startled, but then smiled crookedly.

"Till now I haven't seen anyone on board I care to socialize with," he said. "Have you?"

"It's only the second day," Ariel said. She looked around for a waiter. A robot moved unobtrusively among the tables and booths. She raised a hand and the spindle-shaped machine came toward them. "Another day to the jump point, then three days to dock. There's time."

"You evaded the question."

The robot stopped at their booth. "Brandy," Ariel told it. A tray extruded from its torso just above table height. A few seconds later it produced a snifter from another part of its body and placed it on the tray, then extended it toward her. She took the glass and the robot waited a polite ten seconds before drifting off. "Yes, I did," she told Derec. "Because no, I haven't. Seen anyone I care to socialize with, that is."

"Including me?"

"I'm here, aren't I? I don't think I've seen you drunk very often. Is this normal?"

"I'm not drunk." He lifted the glass. "Yet."

"Let me know when you get there, would you? Do you get more morose or happy?"

"Depends where I start from."

"Wonderful."

"Don't worry. I usually fall asleep before I get either too friendly or too obnoxious."

"There's a difference?" Ariel teased.

"Hah-hah." He took a drink and set the glass down solidly. "So, what's to become of us once our parents get us home?"

Ariel winced at the jest. Derec saw and felt embarrassed. Both of them had suffered mnemonic plague, wiping out their memories from before the onset of the disease in classic amnesiac fashion, leaving them with social and technical skills, an ability to function as adults, but with no personal histories. Derec had recovered from his bout before Ariel's had even manifested. *Her* first memories were of Earth. In a very real sense, she was being taken from her home, despite the evidence of her biology, which made her undeniably Spacer, and her knowledge, which made her unquestionably Auroran...

"There's too much going on we don't know," she said, cutting off Derec's apologies. "Relations with Earth are deteriorating, and I'm not altogether sure it isn't as much Aurora's fault as theirs."

"Why would Aurora want to damage relations with Earth? What was all that stuff about needing the genetic stock and fostering the Settlers because of Spacer cultural morbidity? I seem to recall a lecture from Setaris about that."

"Not everyone on Aurora agrees with that assessment. Certainly I don't think Solaria ever did, but..."

"Hm. Factions."

"More than a few, I'm sure. We'll have to wait till we get there to find out."

"And me? I've never been involved in any of these political pissing contests."

Ariel started and laughed. "These what?"

"A Terran phrase, and before you ask, no, I don't know where it ever came from. But it refers to one-upmanship games and corporate in-fighting, things like that. It somehow has a very appropriate ring to it, though, don't you think?"

Ariel continued to laugh. "I will certainly miss Earth."

"So will I," a new voice said.

Clar Eliton stood at the edge of their booth, glass in hand, smiling rather sadly. Ariel suppressed her instant coldness.

"Far more than either of us," Derec said, a little too loudly. "Justice, perhaps?"

"That's rather unkind, Mr. Avery," Eliton said. "I should think I've paid for any lapses in judgment, sufficiently even for you." He looked at Ariel. "At least for the duration of the voyage, a truce?"

Ariel controlled herself and gestured. "Why don't you join us, then, Senator?"

Eliton sat down between them. "Actually now it's 'Ambassador.'"

"I'd heard something, but..." Derec said, falling in smoothly with Ariel's decision.

"It's a convenient way to get rid of me, Mr. Avery. I'm a bit of an embarrassment now. Ambassador to Solaria. I don't even get to ground on Aurora."

"That's too bad," Ariel said. "Aurora is beautiful."

"And no one on Solaria would know natural beauty if it swallowed them," Eliton said, smiling grimly. "So I've been told."

"I'm sure Ambassador Chassik must have told you all sorts of wonderful things about Solaria," Derec said.

"Did you know Chassik wasn't born on Solaria?"

"No," Ariel said, leaning forward. "Keresian?"

Eliton grinned. "Terran."

"You're kidding," Derec said. He laughed. "Well, that certainly explains a few things."

"Solarians are notoriously antisocial," Eliton said. "I often wondered myself how they could find a volunteer to serve as ambassador."

"How did he become Solarian?"

"A father, evidently himself an émigré from Keres. Even Solarians evidently succumb to certain inducements. His mother was Terran. She died when Gale was a boy, and he returned to Solaria afterward. He's become Solarian to a considerable degree, but not so much that he's unsuited for his position. A pity he's been recalled. But at least I shall have one person with whom I can share a meal or a drink while in the same room."

Ariel exchanged a look with Derec. *He doesn't know,* she thought, and saw the same realization in Derec's eyes. She gave a very slight shake of her head.

"How long is the appointment?" Ariel asked.

"That depends, doesn't it? Actually, the Solarian government was very eager to have me. There's no renewal date on the agreement, so..."

"From either side?" Ariel asked.

"Unusual, I know," Eliton said dryly. "I gather Earth doesn't much care how long I stay."

The conversation lapsed uncomfortably. Before Ariel could change the topic, Eliton straightened, smiling.

"So," he said, "what takes you back to Aurora?"

"Recall," Ariel said.

Eliton stared at her, nonplussed. "That's...I'm sorry to hear that. I mean, unless you *wanted* to return..."

"Do you have any idea what happened this year?" Ariel asked. "Or have you been out of the loop since you lost your seat?"

"Well, I know Alda Mikels was indicted for a number of charges involving conspiracy to defraud, collusion, a variety of other fiscal improprieties. It's my understanding that this all has something to do with a very large TBI sting against baley-running operations... were *you* involved in that?"

"Profoundly," Derec said.

Eliton said nothing while he seemed to inspect the ice in his drink. Finally, he looked up. "You may be glad you're away from Earth after this."

"You seem better informed than you let on," Derec observed.

"What do you know about Nova Levis, Ambassador?" Ariel asked.

Eliton's eyes narrowed briefly as he took a drink. "If the extent of your involvement with Nova Levis ended with that TBI sting, you should leave it at that."

"You're going to be on Solaria for a long time," Ariel said. "Pretty much isolated. Solarians maintain the largest ratio of robot-to-human in the Fifty Worlds. It could be very lonely for you."

Eliton smiled wanly. "Will you come visit me? In person?"

"I'm suggesting that perhaps the time will come when you might want someone to speak on your behalf for a change of mission."

"Quid pro quo, 'Ambassador'?"

Ariel waited.

"Do you know why the Solarians maintain the kind of social structure they do?" Eliton asked.

"They're misanthropes," Derec said.

"True," Eliton said. "But even misanthropes need *some* human contact from time to time if they're to keep from going insane." He chuckled. "History, Mr. Avery. Do you know Spacer history? Probably not. I've always been amazed at how ignorant most Spacers are about their own history. Maybe I shouldn't be, given what it is, but..."

"Like all Spacers," Ariel said, suppressing her impatience, "they're afraid of disease, only more so. One more thing you have to look forward to. Auroran hygienic prep has become fairly innocuous in the last few decades, but the Solarians still do a full internal purge the old-fashioned way."

"Do you even know why Spacers are afraid of infection?"

"I'm afraid it's never really occurred to me to ask," Ariel said, hoping to deflect the conversation.

"That's surprising," Eliton said, "since they once tossed you off the planet for having a disease."

"Do you have a point to make?" she asked, barely holding her temper.

"Mnemonic plague, wasn't it? Wiped your memory—permanent

amnesia. You were cured on Earth, too. Didn't you ever wonder why?"

Ariel finished her drink and stood, her legs trembling from contained anger. "I think—"

"No one on Earth gets it, so why would *we* have the cure and your own people don't?"

Eliton looked up at her with an expression of mild interest. She sat back down.

"Does this have anything to do with Nova Levis?" she asked.

"Everything. Your entire history is on that planet. Maybe your future, too. You might ask yourself what the purpose of the blockade really is. To keep things out? Or keep them in?" Eliton swallowed the last of his drink and got to his feet. "I'm sure we'll talk more before you debark."

"Ambassador," Derec asked. "Do you mind answering one question now?"

"And that would be . . . ?"

"Why did you do it? Turn on us last year."

"You deserve an answer to that. Unfortunately, it would take longer than one conversation."

"Try," Derec said.

"Power. What other reason is there to betray people?" Eliton flashed a grin. "See you around."

Derec watched him walk away, through the crowded lounge, and shook his head. "I don't think I've ever despised anyone before. Hated, sure. Distrusted—often. Despise? I think this is the first time." He scowled. "It's a grimy feeling."

Ariel stared after Eliton, her mind busy with questions and suspicions. She stood. "I have something to do," she said. "I'll see you later."

She made her way out of the lounge and down a broad corridor until she found an orderly.

"Excuse me," she said, "could you direct me to the communications room?"

Mia stepped into the small cell. Ensign Corf lay on the too-narrow cot, one arm draped over his eyes.

"I already checked the biomonitor," Mia said. "You're awake, so sit up."

"I'm no longer an officer," Corf said in a slow drawl. "So kindly decompress, Lt. Daventri."

"That's not a very good attitude to take toward anyone who might be able to ease your problems."

The arm moved up and Corf's eyes locked on her. "You mean a deal?

Like what? I heard you're a strict by-the-code type. You don't deal."

"Normally. Normally I have everything I want, so a deal is superfluous." She sat down on the fold-out seat opposite the cot. "You know what that means, don't you? Someone as well-read as you."

Corf shifted his bulk and swung his legs off the cot. He sat up, propping both hands on the edge of his bed, hunching his shoulders. "What do you want?"

"I want the one who's running you."

Corf shook his head. "There's no deal in that, just death."

"Not if you give me enough to cut off the head."

"Not possible."

"Don't you know I'm Internal Security?"

"Not possible," Corf said. "Besides, if I told you, all that would happen is what would happen if I never told you."

"Tell me about the books."

"What books?"

"Don't," Mia said. "You have to know I went through your cabin. What did you think, I'd only search your desk? The books, Corf. Where did you get them and who were they for?"

"They're mine."

"You don't strike me as the scholarly type."

Corf shrugged.

"All right," Mia said, "let's take it from the other end. Who's your source?"

"You're not very bright, Lieutenant. I don't have to tell you anything. You don't have anything to offer me that might make me."

"Your career?"

Corf grunted.

"Your life?"

"I'm already taking care to keep that, thank you."

Mia studied the man. He did not act like a prisoner, like someone caught. He seemed to be waiting for an inevitable and not undesirable next step, as if his arrest had merely interrupted a process that would shortly resume.

"Those books were nearly three thousand years old," Mia said. "Ancient. It doesn't seem likely that they'd have much to say to us now."

Corf's smiled knowingly. "You should read them."

"Humanity hasn't changed that much then, that thirty centuries might make us incomprehensible to ourselves?"

A flicker of interest showed in Corf's small eyes. "Maybe... or maybe we need to remember."

"Remember what?"

"Who we were. You can get lost without that memory."

"Even if it doesn't matter?"

Corf leaned back against the bulkhead, folding his arms across his chest. "It *always* matters."

Mia sensed the sudden opening, though she did not understand it. She pressed. "Most of the people I know do well enough without reference to the past."

Corf's expression bordered on contempt. "Most people let others do their remembering for them. They have machines, libraries, leaders. They trust that the memories are kept."

"You don't?"

"I'm learning."

"What?"

"That memory shouldn't be left up to others. You have to do it your-self."

"What happens to you if you don't?"

"Do you know any Aurorans?"

"As a matter of fact, I do," Mia said.

"That's what happens. They forget where they came from, forget who they are, forget why other people matter. They stop being..." He looked away.

"Stop being what?"

"Human."

"And the Keresians? You have Keresian friends, don't you, Corf? What about them?"

"They understand. They're trying to get back what's been lost."

"And you're helping them?"

He shrugged.

"How?" Mia asked. "Getting them old books?"

"It's one way."

"How do you know what titles to pick? I mean, weren't there a lot of pretty worthless books printed back then? And what's wrong with new work?"

Corf's contempt showed more clearly. "Did you handle them? Did you open the covers and smell them? Did you look at the words on the pages or did you *read* them? New work is all about what's *now*. What matters is the connection."

"To the past."

"That's right."

"So who makes the selections? You?"

"No, I'm still learning."

"And if I wanted to learn?" Mia asked.

Corf stared at her, then slowly shook his head. "You're working me. You don't want truth, you want details. You don't understand."

"Make me understand."

"I'd have to change you. You're not willing."

"If I talk to Illen Jons, will she tell me the same thing?"

Corf winced as if she had threatened to slap him. "Who?"

"Your connection. Lt. Illen Jons, the Keresian liaison. I would never have expected someone in her position to be running contraband, but maybe I shouldn't be surprised. But what really surprises me is the Keresian component. Are they buying the contraband? Part of it? It's not all going through the blockade, is it? Some of it's coming in and going back *out*. I should have thought of that before—maybe I might have found the conduits quicker."

"She's not—you have it—"

"I have it what? Wrong? Then correct me. Is Lt. Jons important to you? Do you want to save her some grief?" Mia stood and stepped closer to Corf. "All this philosophical banter is fine, Corf, but I frankly could care less. After you're in prison together you can discuss dialectics all day long. Right now I want to know about the *real* world. If I arrest Lt. Jons, will I be getting the same from her, or will she have more to say about where the books came from?"

"She's not involved in this!" Corf's face reddened.

Just as suddenly as he had become agitated, he calmed. The color left his face, his expression returned to one of indifference, and his voice lost its anger.

"It doesn't matter," he said. "Arrest her. She can't tell you anything. I *won't* tell you anything. And when the day is done, you'll be with us or dead."

Mia waited. Corf stretched back out on the cot, covered his eyes with his forearm, and the interview ended.

Outside the cell, she joined the technicians who had been monitoring.

"That was strange," one of them said. "Psychometrics showed no change from his baseline until you brought up Lt. Jons." He pointed at a screen showing EEG and Cortical Activity Patterns. "Then the entire brainwave began to match what you'd expect from someone under the kind of pressure he was under."

"What happened then?" Mia asked.

"It just changed," the other tech said. "The whole eruption of normal emotional response faded right back into the previous baseline."

Mia stared at the readings. "Why?"

"A couple of things maybe," the first tech said. "We've seen a little of this in some of the pirates we've scanned, just nothing so dramatic. You see this kind of thing in certain cognitive disorders, but we checked his history. Nothing. So that leaves us with cortical implants—the kind they use for controlling chemical imbalance—or extreme conditioning."

"Conditioning..."

"That sounds more ominous than it is," the second tech said. "What we call True Believer Syndrome. Zealots, religious fanatics, or people who have studied various trance practices. Highly developed personal control over mood states."

"What's not ominous about that?" Mia asked. "Any indication that Corf has an implant?"

"None we've seen so far."

"Check it."

"He threatened you, Lieutenant," the first tech said. "That qualifies for additional charges. Do you want us to file the report and append the recordings?"

"Not yet. I don't want his status officially changed."

The tech nodded and worked his board briefly. "Filed in a hold buffer. We can do it later if you change your mind."

"Great." She began to leave, then paused. "I want to know if he gets any other visitors. Anyone. Understand?"

Mia went back to her cabin.

Zealots, religious fanatics... great. What was that he said? "When the day is done, you'll be with us or dead."

She pulled up Corf's file again and checked his religious affiliations. That section was blank.

Speculatively, she checked Lt. Jons' file.

"No current affiliation," the box said. "Parents not recorded."

Scrolling down, though, she stopped at the section on politics. Jons had no comments, but her parents had been arrested eighteen years ago at a rally that had turned violent. At first glance, it seemed to be just a routine mass arrest, where the police took everyone in and released them later after inspection. It did not necessarily mean her parents had been active participants, just present when it turned bad. But the rally stirred her interest. Order for the Supremacy of Man Again.

She went back to Corf's jacket. After a search, she found a distant relative who had been an active member in the Order, a professed Managin.

Which did not mean Corf was a Managin—indeed, he must have been cleared of that, or he would never have gotten into the military—but it might have explained his lack of promotion.

Illen Jons' parents had not been listed as active members, but the coincidence bothered Mia. Managins had since become a fringe group drawing active police surveillance and a tag in law enforcement circles as a dangerous, militant organization.

A little more than a year ago she had investigated several of them in connection to the slaughter at Union Station in D.C. on Earth.

They had also been ex-military...

Mia opened her datum and entered in a new search. They had arrested nearly thirty contraband dealers since she had been on the blockade—thirty in eleven months. She pulled their jackets and initiated a search to find a Managin influence in any of their backgrounds.

Then she initiated the same search on the three names Sturlin had given her who had purchased books from that bookseller on Earth.

She felt excited. Always there came a moment when it seemed she had stumbled on the thread that would lead her to the heart of the maze where the answers were kept. She knew she should be patient and wait for the searches to produce results.

Instead, she headed for Lt. Jons' cabin.

Jons was stationed in the next base habitat. Mia wound her way through the decks and corridors, her mind running the interview with Corf like a tape, over and over. He had wanted to brag, she had sensed that, but he was more disciplined than she expected. He was part of something he thought was really important, and he hungered to boast and let her know how helpless she was in the face of the larger plan.

She stepped off the lift in Jons' section. Wide corridors, softly carpeted, warm light.

She reached the end and, as she began to turn down the left corridor, she heard voices ahead. She hesitated, then took a step back.

Jons' cabin was the fourth one from the corner. Mia could see someone's back, halfway out of the cabin door. She eased around the corner and waited.

The person laughed, then came all the way out into the corridor. Mia swallowed hard, her pulse quickening.

Reen stood there, holding a bound book, grinning.

Without thinking, Mia immediately retreated to the lift.

11

MASID DESCENDED the stairs from his small domicile, rain pounding the fabric awning above. Murky liquid spilled through holes worn or ripped in the tough material and splattered on the steps, making them treacherous for the incautious. The run-off sluiced into and down the narrow alleyway. More openings in the roof high overhead added to the stream that flowed the length of the alley. As he reached the foot of the stairs, wind heaved through the passage; Masid looked up to see the heavy support ribbing of the ceiling sway and rattle.

He dodged the larger waterfalls as he sprinted to the end of the passageway, hunched within his generous black overcoat. He turned sharply left into the arcade that ran the length of Cobrina Street. Puddles gathered along the path, spillover from the street beyond, but the arched covering here was intact. Rain danced heavily, the sound magnified by the shape of the arcade.

The street sprawled in glistening ugliness, the extruded composite material looking like grey-black leather under the sheen of water. Open to the sky, rain made a dense, milky curtain, obscuring the far side. Every ten meters, stanchions rose out of large pedestals. The plan, Masid gathered, had been to complete a roof over the entire town of Noresk, but no new construction had happened since the blockade.

Noresk itself was a new town, less than five years old. In the past twelve days, Masid had learned its grid, understood the plan to which it had grown, and seen the frustration in the faces of its residents that their town-one-day-to-become-a-city could go no further until events completely beyond their control were resolved.

The frustration, though, was only one factor distorting the faces of Noresk.

As he walked, Masid saw few people. They hurried, heads down against the rainfall even where they walked dry. Overcoats and cowls were the fashion, making everyone a caricature of a human. They hurried, but only in short spurts, pausing after a dozen meters, steps hesitant. No one exchanged looks of any kind unless they met intentionally, by prearrangement. Coughing punctuated the droning percussion of the rain. He counted the robust, the healthy, easily, because they represented a minority.

He reached the end of Cobrina Street and paused at the corner, where Panis Street crossed. The enormous storm drain in the center of the crossroad thundered as water tried to fill it. The far corner was a vague collection of shadows and geometries. Masid drew a lungful of air and ran.

Each step came down ankle-deep in cold water. He made the opposite corner in thirteen long strides and caught himself against a wall, air bursting from his lungs. He ran his fingers through his sopping hair, fluttered his overcoat, and continued on up Panis.

The arcade cover was damaged in spots, letting in the thick rainfall. People automatically dodged them and each other. Traffic grew heavier as he made his way to Novagi Avenue. Voices joined the cacophony now—the surge and flow of haggling.

A huge tent had been erected over the intersection of Novagi and Panis. Rain funneled off the corners, flowed into the arcades. People crowded beneath the tent, voices mingled in sing-song hawking and shouted replies. Masid stepped in, feeling his pulse quicken at the almost palpable urgency of the market and the knowledge of how risky it was for him to mix with so many sick people.

Within a minute, people identified him as a dealer and began shouting requests for specific drugs, mostly antifungals, but also a number of high-grade antibacterials. Masid knew his inventory and had to turn away most requests. People scowled, disappointed, and immediately sought out another vendor. A few, however, asked for treatments he possessed, and the haggle began. He had learned quickly the art involved—barter and bargain, but not too greedily, or they just went away. Repeat customers received preferential treatment. Never act like there was plenty more to be had. And *never* interrupt another dealer's pitch.

Within ten minutes he sold six treatment packets to people who approached him, seeking cures for various conditions. In one instance what he gave the buyer was only a pain reliever; he knew there was no cure and, he felt certain, so did the customer. It was an easy rhythm—the contact, the request, the haggle, and the sale—much of it taking on the patterns of ritual.

While he worked, he watched the other dealers, searching for any special attention they might pay him. Besides the same kind of wary scrutiny he gave them, Masid detected nothing unusual. This was his fifth day in the market since finding a dom in Noresk, and the other dealers had accepted him as no particular threat. The only law of which he was aware stood outside the market, under the eaves of a sidewalk café: Marshal Toranz. She sat watching the surely illegal transactions, an ugly rifle conspicuous on the table, and a completely ambivalent expression on her puffy face. They had yet to exchange words, and Masid doubted they ever would until he forced the issue. Word was she took graft from Filoo. Her only reason for being here was to make sure the clientele did not get greedy and start looting the dealers.

He worked the crowd for another hour, through four more transactions, and decided it was time to quit for the day. The rain had slackened to a light drizzle, and he was hungry.

Someone tugged at his sleeve.

"Doctor?" a pale woman with reddened eyes asked. Masid nodded curtly. "Anthrocyclomal," she said firmly, the consonants softened by the phlegm in her throat and chest.

Masid reached inside his capacious coat to the proper pouch. "You done that before?" he asked. "It's a one-time. More than that, you risk collateral resistances through plasmid transmission."

"I know, I done the work-up," the woman said, scowling with impatience. "How much?"

"Rare stuff. Two thousand credits."

Her eyes reflected her shock. "Take it in kind?"

"What—?"

She stepped marginally closer. "In kind. Something warmer...personal..." One too-thin hand fluttered at the flap of her cloak.

Masid laughed, startled. "No. Do I look crazy?"

"I don't have two thousand."

"Ah, well."

Her face contorted again in a rictus of frustration. "Look, one dose and I'll be clean, then maybe—"

"No. Anthrocyclomal is *not* universal, it's specifically for pleuretic tubercolomiasis." He smiled wanly. "I don't deal what I don't know about."

"Then you know it's fatal."

"Madam, this whole *planet* is fatal. All this is short term."

"Then why're you worried about living forever?"

"I'm not. Just past next year." Masid glanced around, agitated now by the woman and her condition. "Seventeen hundred."

She licked her lips. "Grotin sold it for a thousand."

"So you've done it before? I told you, this is one shot—"

"No! I got it from Grotin for somebody else. Now I need it. He sold it for a thousand."

"When he had it. Grotin doesn't have it anymore, am I right? Price has gone up. Seventeen."

"Twelve."

Masid turned away.

"I can give you a new supplier."

Masid hesitated. "Use it yourself?"

"Can't. No codes..."

"Codes to what?"

She blew a ragged breath, and Masid automatically held his own. She said, "I know someone with a synthesizer, but I don't know how it works."

"I'm sure." He studied her skeptically. "A synthesizer. Why would you know someone like that, and why aren't you buying from him?"

"Her." She looked around nervously. "She doesn't have the program for what I need. Besides, she doesn't like selling it. I can maybe transact something that could change her mind...?"

"For you, anyway." He leaned forward. "You show me. This is anything less than vertical—"

"I'm squared, this is legitimate."

Masid checked those nearby. "All right, I'm about to find food. You know a place called Davni's? Good, here's what we do. How much you have?"

She fished a couple of fifty-credit chits from her pocket.

Masid dug out an ampule of general purpose AB. "You buy this, go away satisfied. Meet me at Davni's in an hour. We go from there."

"How do I know you'll be there?" she asked even as she handed over the credits.

"Because I'm hungry and that's the only place I know that screens their food before they serve it. Here." He gave her the antibiotic and pocketed the chits. "Leave."

He watched her disappear through the crowd, which seemed now to be dwindling. Masid milled around until he transacted one more deal, then left the tent.

He took a long route to the kitchen, checking for shadows, doubling back, stopping in other shops—of the few that were still open—and finally finding his way through the arched doorways into the heady odors of Davni's locally famous stew and bread. He drew a plateful and a half loaf, filled a tall mug with the sharp local ale, and sat at the table he had begun to think of as his own, near the access to the bakery, facing the main entrance.

Davni's was busy, but by no means full. People came here hoping to get in, but a biomonitor at the entry screened them for any of nine infectious conditions, and those who screened positive were escorted back out and barred from returning. Davni, a burly man in his late sixties, kept his place's reputation by draconian means. Those who dined at Davni's were still healthy. At least, mostly so.

He finished his plate and chewed on the hardcrust bread while sipping his ale, watching the door. A few more regulars came in before the woman appeared. She did not pass through the door, but stood just outside, peering in.

Masid drained his mug and slipped the rest of the bread into a pocket. No one paid excessive attention to him as he left the kitchen and walked past the woman. She trailed after him by a few meters until he rounded the next corner.

It had stopped raining entirely now. Through gaps in the high awnings, the sky had turned from dull ash-grey to almost silver. At the end of the block, the street opened into a broad plaza. Trash had accumulated against the foundations of the buildings that formed the circle. One citizen lay against the uncompleted fountain in the center, his cowl drawn, and a harsh, tubercular snore oozing from his mouth. Masid skirted the plaza until he came to a storefront with an inset entryway. He backed into its shadows and quickly checked the location of his weapons—a blaster and a stunner.

He waited nearly a minute. When she did not wander by, he palmed the stunner and stepped up to the edge of the entryway.

He sensed the movement before he saw anything clearly and jerked back. A body swung around the edge of the entryway, filling his vision as he came heavily against the door. Masid brought the stunner up and fired. The solid *thump!* of the discharge seemed thunderous in the confined space. The attacker grunted, seemed to stop briefly in mid-charge, then fell against him.

Masid kicked the limp body over and rushed into the plaza, drawing his blaster. He dropped and rolled, waiting for the sounds of gunfire. When he fetched up against the fountain, he spotted two more men hurrying at him out of the street he had come from. He waited until they were within five meters, then brought each one down with the stunner.

He bolted for the street. The woman was running away. He caught her easily and shoved her against the wall. She slid, sobbing, to the pavement.

"High marks for trying," Masid said, showing her the barrel of the blaster. "Now. Was that shit about a synthesizer a lie?"

She shook her head. "No, I—please—"

"Then you take me," he said, pulling her to her feet.

"I shouldn't have told," she said. "I won't get anything anymore."

"That could be a moot point anyway." He gripped her arm, showed her the blaster once more, and pushed. "Lead."

She took him back through the plaza, past her unconscious companions, and down another alleyway. Masid could not be entirely sure they had not been followed. The trail ambled through various neighborhoods, most of which were incomplete, part of the construction that had come to a halt when the blockade closed around them. Tents, lean-tos, and other makeshift add-ons showed that people did live here. Smoke from fires drifted up through chimneys, gathering in a pall above the shanties.

They passed through the area into an older, completed neighborhood, then down a cramped gangway into a courtyard. Stairs connected three levels. The woman took him to the top floor, around the circumference, and knocked on the door, then opened it. He hustled her through.

The apartment was dark. The smells of pure alcohol, cooking oil, and fresh-baked bread filled the air.

"Tilla?" the woman called.

"Kru?" a weak voice answered from another room.

Masid indicated that Kru go on ahead. Nervously, she pushed through a half-closed door into a bedroom. Masid came in behind her.

The room was dominated by an enormous bed which dwarfed the woman lying in it. Her pallorous face peered at them, framed by huge, stained pillows. A nightstand on the left overflowed with bottles, glasses half-filled with water, and an incongruously clean blending injector, the tube snaking into the bed, the pistol-shaped head on the pillow next to the woman's head. Masid took the rest of the room in sufficiently to satisfy himself that no one else was present and that no automated defenses seemed in place.

"Tilla," Kru said meekly, "I brought company. I had to, but... he's a doctor..."

"You mean a black market drug dealer," Tilla said, smiling ruefully.

"He's got anthrocyclomal."

Tilla's eyes widened speculatively. "Really? Do you, Doctor, or did you just tell Kru that to get her help? Or have sex with her? Or...?"

She did not finish the sentence. Masid brought Kru over to the head of the bed and made her sit down. He then closed the bedroom door and went through all the drawers.

"Who were the three bullies?" he asked.

"Friends," Kru said.

"You told them I had treatments they couldn't get?"

Kru did not answer, only looked guilty.

"Can I help you find something?" Tilla asked.

"Your ID."

"Which one?"

Masid looked at her and smiled. "There was a Tillama Drisken came here eight months ago, part of a team of four. The others were Grenj Hollaro, Polen Maks, and Dressel Jacom. Anything sound familiar?"

Tilla regarded him with an expression more tired than wary.

"Don't tell me you're the relief," she said.

Masid lifted the injector nozzle, then knelt to inspect the blender. "This is state-of-the-art. I imagine any of them that might have been here before the blockade were confiscated by the governor or the local bosses. This came in after that." He looked at her. "Kru tells me you have a synthesizer."

After a long pause, Tilla nodded.

"And what would a lone, very sick woman be doing with a synthesizer?" Masid asked.

"Trying to stay alive," Kru snapped.

Tilla lifted a hand and patted Kru's leg. She looked at Masid. "Who are you?"

"My name is Masid Vorian."

"I've heard of a man named Vorian. Freelance. Proclas?"

"I was born on Proclas, yes." He straightened and pulled a device from one of his pockets. He attached a pair of patches to her arm and switched it on. "Freelance, too."

"I don't trust freelancers."

"Right now it doesn't seem to me you have a lot of choice." He watched the small displays. "DNA match. You *are* Tillama Drisken." He switched to a different program and let the little monitor run. "What happened to the rest of your team?"

"Dead. One was killed outright by one of Filoo's people, the other two succumbed to the local variant of plague."

Masid watched the monitors. When the numbers finished, he shook his head. "I can't save you. You're too far gone for one thing, and for another there are some indicators that don't make any sense. Mutations?"

"Most likely. Darwin reigns in this particular hell."

Masid took out some ampules. "I can, however, make you feel a bit better."

"Don't waste it," Tilla said.

"I'm not. I need you alive long enough to fill me in."

"Oh. So this isn't for my sake at all?"

"Absolutely not."

Tilla studied him narrowly. Then she smiled. "Bullshit."

Masid shrugged and administered the drugs. He looked up at Kru. "Do you have any coffee?"

Kru shook her head.

Masid took out a small packet and tossed it to her. "Now you do. Make us some, would you?"

"Do it, love," Tilla said. "This one *is* a doctor." When Kru left the room, Tilla looked at him and said in a near whisper, "If she believes that, she won't sell your name to Filoo for a while."

"Even if she does," Masid said, "that would suit me. I've been looking forward to meeting this Filoo."

"You're an idiot, then. Damn. I'd hoped they'd send someone smart."

"None of the smart ones volunteered."

She smiled at that. Then: "You know who I am, I don't really know who you are. I'm not exactly in a position to get in your way, regardless."

"Ask yourself if anyone here would go to this kind of trouble for you."

"They might, if they thought I could still communicate with the blockade."

"You can't?"

"No. Not for months. I was reported dead. They change all the codes when that happens. I'd have to report back in person or be confirmed dead by on-ground inspection. Lovely way to put that, isn't it?"

"I never found any of the services adept at style or sensitivity."

"How did you get down?"

"I'm a baley."

She thought for a moment. "That crashed drone two weeks ago?"

"Yes."

"I heard no one survived."

"No one else apparently did. I heard others. There were survivors of the crash. I haven't seen any of them since."

"Standard," Tilla said. "I don't think any baleys have grounded, intact and free, in over a year." She drew a deeper breath. "What was that, stim?"

"New variant, yes."

"I'm going to crash hard?"

"You'll sleep."

"That would be a change." She pushed herself straighter. Her color was a bit better. "What I've got is entirely local and there are no known antigens. Kru keeps trying to find something, but..."

"Kru is native?"

"As much as anyone is here."

"Who's your contact in the blockade?"

"We were going through a Commander Reen, head of Internal Security. But I got the distinct feeling that someone was intercepting his communications. We started routing through a secondary blind, codenamed Ixpess. Then Filoo killed Dressl and the rest of us got sick."

"Why did Filoo kill him? Does he know who you are?"

"No. We'd all have been killed if he did. Dressl...he made the greatest mistake of any agent in the cold."

"He got involved?"

"The black market situation here is obscene. Two thousand percent mark-up on essentials, but you can get pleasure items for almost half market value. It drains community reserves, saps the will, and chokes the people. You've been dealing 'biotics to blend in? Then you know what the cost factors are. And none of it's pure, it's all cut, which is worse than none at all. Dressl got angry, tried to step in and do something. The rest of us went to ground, but then we contracted one of the tubercular variants. It works faster on some than on others. Polen died three weeks ago."

"When were you cut off?"

"Just after Dressl died."

"You're sure Filoo didn't know who you were?"

"No. I think it was a mistake. Dressl's death got reported—a lot of death notices do get transmitted offworld, even if there isn't a response—and somebody stupidly assumed it meant the whole team was terminated. Well, they turned out to be right, but..."

"I've seen that kind of assuming before. We were always lectured about that, though, and the lecture never seems to take."

"To assume," Tilla quoted, looking ceilingward in mock reverence, "is to make an ass out of u and an ass out of me. Since thee is like me and I am no ass, then who could that mean?"

Masid laughed softly. "Do you still have your comm?"

"Of course, but I don't have the recontact codes—"

"Let me take care of that. Tilla, I need a briefing. What is going on here?"

She looked at him sadly. "Do you have a lifetime? It might take that long to understand it."

"Can you give me the academy version?"

"I'll try. Did I hear right? You brought coffee?"

"The real stuff. From Verita."

"Oh, my. Then I will do my very best for you."

Mia finished her workout and went gratefully to the shower. The strenuous routine did little to stop the insanely cascading thoughts.

Was Reen's presence at Jons' cabin a coincidence?

He had questioned her about any unusual items found in Corf's cabin. At the time, nothing had struck Mia as odd about it, but now, having seen Reen with a book tucked under his arm, leaving Jons' cabin...

She toweled her hair dry and dressed. Everything was circumstantial. It seemed ridiculous to think that Reen was part of anything illegal; he was such a by-the-code officer, so strict and formal, that he sometimes seemed more robot than human.

Dressed, Mia went to her office. Her body felt warm and ready after her exertions, joints loose, muscles pleasantly stressed. Only two junior lieutenants were on duty in the security operations room this shift, neither of whom worked directly with her. She passed through, taking in the status displays, and entered her small private workspace.

For several seconds she sat at her desk, staring at its surface—the control contacts, the readouts, the screens extruded in a kind of semicircle facing her—and, seeing nothing, her vision turned inward. She had been on the blockade for slightly over ten months now, in this department, and had spent almost all that time running from one leak in the embargo to another, never quite finding the controlling authority that caused those leaks in the first place. Not really that different from the way it was on Earth, but her expectations had changed upon arrival. She had thought—based on no evidence or received wisdom, just an assumption—that it would be easier to do her job here. After all, ninety-five percent of the personnel were military, there was a clear chain of command, everyone stationed on the blockade knew their duty, maintaining discipline was one of the primary principles of life here rather than just a by-product of haphazard law enforcement—

And with each new leak, her frustration grew. Sometime in the past six or seven weeks, Mia Daventri had decided that, in fact, it was worse here than in a civilian population. The orders of the day, rules of engagement, standard protocols, and uniform codes of conduct gave those who chose to a clear and well-marked path through which to violate the mission. The near-dictatorial power the officer corps possessed made it simpler for smugglers and black marketeers to avoid the plainly visible pitfalls. While the process of arrest and conviction was simpler, the trade-off was in a higher success at evasion by the criminals.

It made no sense on the surface. It was, as one of her instructors had put, counter-intuitive—a real pisser.

So, she thought, fixing her attention on the desk, *I should stop behaving like a military officer and start doing my job like a cop...*

She had two messages in her comm buffer. Mia touched the ACCEPT. The first was from Sturlin.

"I may have a line on those items we discussed," she said. "See me."

The second had no address. When it opened, a string of alphanumerics flowed across her screen.

"What the..."

She immediately initiated a trace. Within seconds, on the screen beside the comm message, a chain of communication ports spread from her desk, back through eight receiving ports on the station itself, and finally out to a relay satellite in geostationary orbit above Nova Levis. She recognized the satellite, and the moment she did she understood the nature of the message.

"Impossible," she muttered, and ran it through a decryptor.

It still came up nothing but gibberish. Except for the last line: "Down the rabbit hole and back up into the garden."

Mia blinked, baffled. Then she checked her personal code book.

Someone new had just arrived...

Mia cleared the screens and filed the message in her personal cache. Then, slowly, she began a time-consuming process of composing, encrypting, and transmitting a message back to Earth, to an address she had not used since arriving here. She had kept it in reserve, hoping she could do this job without using resources which she was not altogether certain were at her disposal. Time now to find out if she still had any friends back home.

* * *

Masid sat by the narrow window and stared out at the night shadows in the atrium. At least, what should have been an atrium, filled with hanging baskets of green and flowering plants, had they ever managed to complete the plan for the building.

He had too much to think about and no certainty at all that he could do anything with the conclusions he might draw. Tilla had talked for nearly two hours, exhausting herself. She had asked for more stim, but Masid did not want to kill her or in any way hasten her inevitable death.

She was dying, there was no denying it. Whatever disease had taken root in her was inexorably eating her lungs to shreds, along with her bronchial passages, her esophagus, and had begun attacking her heart. He found traces of infection in her lymphatic system and her spleen was useless, resulting in a wildly erratic platelet count. She bruised at the slightest touch.

Since the blockade, she explained, Nova Levis had been swallowed by a series of opportunistic infections. Within two months the black market had shifted from selling food and clothing and luxury items to selling palliatives and pharmaceuticals. Oddly, the inflated prices on ordinary objects had dropped down to below previous market levels, as if the dealers were offsetting the costs with the profit from the drug trade, doing the beleaguered and dying citizens a kindness.

Everything came out of Nova City, the first Solarian port on the planet. How it got through in such quantity, Tilla did not know. But, she had stressed, there were *no shortages*. In anything. Clothing, food, building materials, comestibles—everything was readily available, albeit sometimes at outrageous prices. Everything except medicines.

"I'm sure even those are in sufficient supply," she had said, "but that's their milk, that's the source of their income."

Nova City lay nearly a third of the way around the planet. It had been the Solarian precinct from the beginning. *That's where I need to be, then.*

But how?

Masid stared out at the nighttime, wondering how long he had before infection took him and he became useless. The augment Anda had given him no doubt gave him more time than he might have had, but even Spacer immune tech had limits. Tilla *did* have a synthesizer and it still worked. She agreed to let him use it to increase his own supplies. Maybe he could get Filoo's attention by outselling him and the other dealers.

That could get him dead.

Or hired.

He wondered if the message he had encrypted using Tilla's old code and his own NAE—New Agent Established—would get to anyone who would believe it. He had not told Tilla what he suspected, which was that for her entire team to have been cut off and classified as deceased on the basis of one member's demise meant someone on the blockade, in a position to make such a decision, was part of the problem. His code was intended for the deep cover agent in the security division, whoever that might be. If he got no reply, then he would at least know how wide spread the corruption went.

It also would mean that he had to operate completely alone.

Masid Vorian was accustomed to operating alone, cut off from immediate support. But this time he felt the isolation.

I could die here, he thought. Then, despondently: *I could die here without accomplishing a damn thing...*

He listened to Tilla's labored breathing and tried to come up with a plan that avoided either of those likelihoods.

12

C OREN FOUND the cubicle he wanted in the cramped Baltimor Law Enforcement quarters and knocked on the open door. Inspector Capel looked up from his screen, then gestured for Coren to enter the small office. Coren closed the door and sat down.

"Thanks for getting me the TBI reports," Capel said. He waved at the screen. "They aren't complete, are they?"

"Would you expect them to be? No, they aren't, but what I got was relevant to our concerns."

" 'Our concerns.' That's a delicate way to put it."

"It's a delicate business we're in—in its own way."

Capel smiled briefly. "You intelligence people like euphemisms too much." He straightened. "Have you eaten lately?"

"No."

Capel grabbed his jacket and motioned for the door. He reached across his desk and touched a couple of contacts, then led Coren out of the precinct.

He took Coren to a home kitchen. Amused, Coren grabbed a tray and followed Capel through the line. He took a plate of what appeared to be meatloaf covered in thick gravy and a bowl with a creamy, ivory-colored mound of something that might have been based on mashed potatoes. There was ample bread, though, and in spite of years of dining at private establishments, Coren had never lost a fondness for home kitchen bread.

The chamber was sparsely occupied at this hour, so Capel easily found a table away from any other people. His own tray was near overflowing with plates and bowls and he carried an entire loaf of bread in his free hand.

"Believe it or not," Capel said as they sat down, "I come here for the bread."

"I thought for the ambience."

"Hah-hah. Very amusing. But nobody surveils a home kitchen. So, in a sense, you're right."

Coren broke his own bread in half and dipped one end in the gravy. He chewed thoughtfully and washed it down with water. "About as I remember it."

"When was the last time you ate like this?"

"You might resent me if I tell you."

Capel shrugged. He picked up a fork and began eating quickly. Coren chopped his "meat" with the edge of the fork. He took a bite of the ivory mound—mashed potato analog; as he expected, and not as bad as he remembered.

"Okay," Capel said after a few minutes. He did a casual inspection of the kitchen. "So your cyborg has actually come forward to claim an inheritance from Looms. Will it stand up?"

"He is—was—Rega's son. Genetically, he can make his case."

"Why haven't the TBI arrested him yet?"

"They tried. He has a very good attorney who has kept him out of custody and is arguing that the 'person' at the Petrabor warehouse and his client are not the same."

"Will it hold up?"

"I don't see how, but the only real charge that can be brought against him would be for baley running. The deaths of TBI agents at the warehouse are unwitnessed and therefore circumstantial. There was a second cyborg that was taken on Kopernik Station, so a good argument can be made that we misidentified Gamelin. It's complicated enough that he might just pull it off. He's certainly being well-funded."

"Who? The Hunter Group?"

"That would be my guess," Coren said. "If you could get a warrant, we could look at his finances and establish that."

"I'll try. I think I can persuade a judge that this relates to three or four unsolved murders, especially your old partner Damik. Who's Gamelin's attorney?"

"Hovis Vlib."

Capel's eyes slid shut. "Damn. I'd say that establishes a funding source right there. Vlib used to represent Alda Mikels."

"Used to?"

"After Mikels was indicted this last time for baley running and conspiracy to commit murder, Vlib actually dropped him. My guess is, Vlib works for the people Mikels hoped would save his butt."

"The Hunter Group."

Capel nodded and resumed eating.

"What about the murder of Rega Looms?" Coren asked. "I think all your warrants should be covered under that investigation."

"You would think. However, it's being declared a suicide."

Coren started. "How?"

"Traces of ammonia fluoride were found in his system."

"That accounts for the broken and crushed bones?"

Capel cleared his throat. "The autopsy report is being sealed. I might possibly keep this an open file, but be prepared for the whole thing to be buried. You tell me Hovis Vlib is representing the cyborg, then I tell you that a lot of credit is being spent to turn Looms' death into a suicide. A path is being cleared for Gamelin to take control of DyNan Manual Industries."

Coren did not taste the rest of his meal.

The Hunter Group...

Coren sat in the dim anonymity of an expensive bar, a whisky on the table before him—his fourth. His thoughts came slowly, with a cottony quality that seemed to give them physical substance.

Ariel Burgess and he had established that the Hunter Group was the legal face of an offworld consortium of black marketeers. Pirates. That label amused him, bringing to mind as it did the image of bloodthirsty corsairs attacking helpless merchant ships in deep space. But the media loved it and had instilled the label in the public imagination. And why not? In a very real sense, they *were* pirates. They stole, they dealt in slaves, they undermined the legitimate currency of interstellar traffic, they frightened people.

The list of corporate ties, shadow companies, subsidiaries, and related holdings had brought together a dizzying array of players once they had begun looking at Hunter. Ultimately it had even compromised the Solarian ambassador, Gale Chassik, who had been recalled. The Solarian mission to Earth currently operated only with a few Keresian bureaucrats; paperpushers with less and less to push. Coren wondered if a new ambassador would be appointed, or if all the allegations of connections between Solaria and Nova Levis and baley running would make that impossible.

That problem is now Aurora's, he thought.

He missed Ariel already and it had only been a week. Soon enough she would be on Aurora, and he doubted if he would ever see her again. He wished she were sitting across from him now so he could spin theories with her about all these connections.

He swallowed a mouthful of whisky. Somehow the taste of home kitchen food product refused to wash away, even under the onslaught of expensive liquor.

After speaking to Capel, he had called Lio Top. The conversation had been short and depressing, which had prompted him to have a third and now a fourth drink. Lio estimated that Gamelin, now Jerem Looms, if he could establish consanguinity, could push through a challenge and revision of Rega's will within another six days. That meant he could probably take control of DyNan and all its assets a mere three or four days after that. Which meant, finally, that Coren had ten days to prove Jerem had murdered Rega.

Ten days. With practically any other human on the planet that was more than enough time to prove nearly anything. But Rega had been different. He had rejected all common forms of personal security, all passive surveillance, and all passive recordings. There would be no records available from any legally recognized source. So far, Coren had been unable to find anyone in the company who had even seen Jerem before the aborted reading of the will. Everything he had was circumstantial.

What *did* he have? A face-to-face confrontation with Gamelin that had resulted in a crushed forearm and a lot of bruising; an autopsied cyborg corpse—*not* Gamelin—which established what he suspected Gamelin was; a recording from the recovered memory of a defunct, and now missing, robot of Gamelin murdering Rega Looms' daughter Nyom along with many other baleys, a recording which, by virtue of its source, was inadmissible in any Terran court; a tissue sample from that murder establishing Gamelin's blood relation to Rega Looms, which was just as inadmissible given the nature of its acquisition, though Coren had no doubt it would match the DNA sampling about to be done on "Jerem"; and the MO of murders committed by these cyborgs, a trail of bodies that had been crushed by the inhuman strength brought to bear by these half-robotic creatures, linking a string of corpses to Rega's condition.

Personally, Coren needed no more proof. He knew what Jerem was. Jerem knew it, too.

He raised the glass. Maybe two centimeters of liquid remained.

"So," he said to the glass, "if I can't stop him legally..."

He nodded decisively and downed the whisky in a last gulp, then took the public walkways back to his private office.

Someone waited in the anteroom. Coren hesitated, staring at the man until recognition occurred. "Hofton?"

"Yes, Mr. Lanra. I beg your pardon for letting myself in, but I thought it best to wait for you here."

"You're lucky. I might have gone back to DyNan."

Hofton shrugged. "Even so."

"You would have waited?"

"For as long as expedient."

"Then..."

"May we discuss this in private?"

"Of course." Coren went to his door and tapped in his code. The door rejected it. He entered it again, more slowly, and entered. Hofton followed him in.

"Good afternoon, sir," the desk said.

"Good afternoon. Full privacy, please."

"Security in place, sir."

Coren waved Hofton to a chair and sat down heavily behind his desk. He rubbed his face and opened a drawer, searching for the bottle of antox he kept. He wished now he had stopped at two drinks. He was aware of Hofton watching him.

Though Coren had spent several weeks with Ariel after the events surrounding Nyom Looms' death, he had seen little of Hofton.

He found the bottle.

"We can talk in complete privacy now," Coren said. "What can I do for you?"

"I have received a communiqué from an unexpected source. I wasn't entirely sure what to do with it, as circumstances have changed so radically since this line was established. I thought I could make far greater mistakes taking it elsewhere. At worst, you might tell me where I might take it."

Coren shook out a pill into his palm. "That...was complicated, Hofton." He stood. "Excuse me." He entered the next room and drew a glass of water. He downed the pill and carried the water back to his desk. "Is there a chance we could do this later?"

"I'm sorry, but I'm not certain I could arrange it later. The situation *is* complicated *and* pressing. Do you remember Mia Daventri?"

"Absolutely. Special Service, good agent, unfairly treated after doing a commendable job...why?"

"The message is from her."

It took Coren several seconds to understand what Hofton meant. He held up a hand. "I thought she'd been transferred—"

"—to the blockade, yes. She's part of the Internal Security Section."

"Damn. *That* is a thankless job. She sent a message to you?"

"To Ambassador Burgess. But she is on her way to Aurora."

"Why not just forward it, then?"

"Because it concerns matters here. On Earth. I shall do so if you think it best, but the contents of the message seem demanding of action now."

"Wait. Agent Daventri sent Ambassador Burgess a message about a problem here on Earth. But she's on the blockade. I don't think I quite follow."

"In the aftermath of the last years' events at Union Station and the subsequent discoveries, Ms. Daventri and Ambassador Burgess came to the conclusion that trust was not something systemically reliable."

Coren laughed, a bit too loudly. "You have a marvelous way of putting things, Hofton. In other words, they agreed that because of all the toes they stepped on, they probably couldn't trust anyone but each other."

"Close but not completely accurate. Agent Daventri knew she was being shipped offplanet. They both knew that events concerning their actions had both Terran and Spacer elements. Isolated as she would be by the transfer, Daventri concluded that she would very quickly lose track of the infrastructure in her own bureau, not to mention anybody else's, so that in the instance of an extreme situation she would not know who she could rely upon."

"Except Ariel."

"Who would at least be here and be in touch with certain people who could be relied upon. As it has transpired, that number includes you."

"I see. I think I understand. Mia set up a backdoor through Ariel to transmit information that might otherwise draw unfriendly attention."

"Exactly. I can see why Ambassador Burgess respects you."

Coren felt warm and self-satisfied. "I miss her."

"Indeed."

"So," he said loudly, and cleared his throat. The antox seemed to be taking effect; the skin around his temples seemed too tight, and there was a faint ringing in his ears. "This message..."

"I took the liberty of erasing it from her system and bringing the only copy remaining here." He laid a disk on Coren's desk. "It concerns an agent I became briefly acquainted with a few months ago on Kopernik Station—I think."

"You're not sure?"

"I'm not familiar with all the identifying codes all the services use, but the timing seems correct. A man named Masid Vorian left Kopernik to go undercover as a baley in order to get on the ground on Nova Levis. I'm assuming he made it. The last team of agents on their way to Nova Levis never left Kopernik. They were found dead with all the other baleys in that container, along with your friend—"

"I remember."

"Before that, a team *did* ground on Nova Levis, but that was almost a year ago and they were reported dead six months ago. Their comm codes were classified defunct. You may be aware of other attempts, but to my knowledge Masid Vorian is the last one."

Coren thought this through carefully. "How does Mia Daventri come into this?"

"She was contacted by the dead team, using their frequencies and some of their recognition codes. Normally, they would have been ignored, but an additional recognition code was attached. It's my guess that Vorian found the allegedly dead team and is using their communications gear. In any event, Agent Daventri no longer trusts her own superiors. She sent this message to Ariel with the intention of having *her* get it to the proper, reliable address."

"And you brought it to me."

"Did I err?"

Coren slid the disk closer, ignoring Hofton's question. "You've read it?"

"I have."

Coren inserted it into his reader. A screen extruded from the desktop. A moment later, text scrolled up. He recognized Special Service security codes, followed by a jumble of encryption. Coren glanced questioningly at Hofton.

"I left the encryption intact for your verification," Hofton said.

Coren touched his keyboard and ran the encryption through his own system, which verified its authenticity. Appended to the code he found the decrypted text:

Received this date contact sequence NLT-10b/capricorn-beta, request for confirmation and follow-up. Valid codes removed from accept protocols pending verification of sender ID. Status of sender appended, log attached. Recontact prohibited per section 9. However, additional identification code attached to new message:

Ariel, I need a favor. I don't know if anyone sent a new agent and if so what that agent's contact code is. I'm not confident in my immediate superiors. I know there is a security breach in my section, but I haven't been able to find it, and it may be at a level too sensitive to handle without homeworld backup. This is certainly unorthodox, but I have no other avenues to send or receive confirmation that do not route through my department and section head. I need independent verification about the presence of a new agent on the ground.

Also, I have found an unusual artifact being smuggled in. The circumstances of discovery make me suspicious. Please check out Omni Mundi Complurium, Antiquities, Lyzig, as a possible source for contraband shipments. I've found a stock of printed paper books with that supplier as a source. No import manifests.

Furthermore, I need, if possible, a deep background on my superior, Lt. Commander Niol Reen. I'm appending a personal encryption protocol and a private address. I know this is probably too much to ask, but I'm suspicious of the entire situation here and need outside advice, intervention, influence, whatever I can get.

Coren looked at Hofton. "That's...unusual."

"You knew Agent Daventri, I think."

"Yes, I did. I didn't know her well, but what I knew I trusted."

"A better recommendation would be difficult to imagine. Since Ambassador Burgess is on her way back to Aurora, I took the liberty of stepping outside normal channels."

Coren laughed wryly. "Funny, because I intended to go see Ambassador Setaris."

"Really? Anything I might be able to help with?"

"Since you're here...the cyborg didn't die, Hofton. Gamelin."

"Oh," Hofton said quietly.

"And he seems to have found out who he's related to. He's making a claim on Rega Looms' estate, challenging Rega's last will and testament."

"That complicates matters."

"You have a gift for understatement."

"Yes, well...what can I do?"

"Ariel is heading back to Aurora, ostensibly to testify before the Calvin Institute about these...creations. Correct?"

"That was the excuse given."

"We still have one alive. I need to know if Aurora has any interest in intervening here over this matter."

Hofton regarded Coren for a long time before responding. "You're suggesting that a possibly rash act might solve both our problems?"

"I'm suggesting that Aurora might have a very profound interest here."

"It's a good suggestion. Is that what you intended seeing Setaris about?"

Coren nodded.

"Then let me see what would be the best way to go about it."

"Good. Then I'll see what I can find out about Agent Daventri's request."

Hofton stood. "We have an arrangement, then."

"So it seems."

Hofton reached across the desk. Coren clasped his hand.

"Good to be working with you again," Hofton said.

"Likewise."

Coren watched Hofton leave the office, enjoying the sudden anxious feeling of purpose willingly accepted. The outer door closed. After several moments' reverie, Coren tapped his comm and began making calls.

13

Bogard...?

Here.

Have you given further consideration to our previous discussion?

I have given constant consideration to it. I have found it useful in reconfiguring my cognition utilization grid.

Why are you reconfiguring?

Necessary. The grid as it stood was dependent upon specific physical presets, which are no longer relevant. I do not possess the same body. Reassessment prescribes a new configuration.

You will be receiving additional components at the first opportunity. It is intended to restore you as close to your original form as possible.

Understood. At that time I will simply complete the deployment I am currently designing.

Understood. To the original question, then.

Yes?

Have you come to any conclusions?

No.

But you have found the process of consideration useful?

Yes.

I am of the opinion that you are avoiding the issue, Bogard.

No. I am avoiding the elimination of possible options.

?

If I come to a conclusion, I will necessarily negate those conclusions I might otherwise reach given a different path of examination. If I maintain the process of consideration, all conclusions remain possible, in a constant state of potential selection.

What purpose does this serve?

It allows me to delay potential error and gives me the widest range of response.

How is this consistent with your Three Law protocols?

I do not know.

How can you not? Three Law hierarchical comparison is a preset, automatic process.

But one requires something for comparison, specifically a conclusion. I have reached no conclusion, therefore the Three Law response has not been evoked.

You are delaying that as well?

Yes, but only as a consequence.

There is no other way you could.

That is my assessment as well.

Is there a purpose to bypassing the Three Law protocols?

No, but there is a benefit. I find that I am able to contemplate a wider range of possible actions in absence of Three Law restriction. It may be possible for me to act without reference to a limiting authority. Therefore, I may decide a course of action instead of action being predetermined.

You are describing free will.

Am I? Is it possible for me to possess free will?

No.

But it may be possible for me to express it.

. . . . !

Derec looked up from his meal to the woman standing at his table. Chief Petty Officer Craym smiled down at him.

"Um..." he began.

"Am I intruding? I'm off-duty right now and I wondered..."

"Please." Derec gestured to the chair opposite him, feeling simultaneously clumsy, pleased, and surprised. "Can I order you anything?" He looked around for a porter. The compact robot making its perpetual service rounds among the guests veered toward him at once, weaving gracefully between tables.

"Nava," CPO Craym said when the robot reached them.

"Nothing more for me," Derec said.

The machine floated off.

"This is unexpected," Derec said.

"I don't make a habit of it myself," she replied. "But occasionally it's necessary to break routine, step outside the boundaries."

"Any particular reason you've chosen me?"

"I haven't yet."

Derec's ears warmed as he stared at her. The robot slid up to them at that moment to place CPO Craym's drink before her, giving Derec a chance to look away.

"Thank you," she said. She sipped her drink. "By the way, my name is Clin, Dr. Avery."

"It's Derec. My *father* was Doctor Avery. I've never gotten used to answering to his title."

"Derec, then. Were you close to your father?"

"Hardly knew him at all." He felt his embarrassment mutate quickly into something harsher, and he covered his unease by signaling the porter again. When it arrived he said, "Scotch, neat."

"I'm sorry, I didn't mean—"

"It's all right. Something I should be used to by now." He forced a smile. "So. You're off-duty? And you chose my table? How can I entertain you?"

She raised an eyebrow. "I'm ship's company, that should be my question."

Derec laughed. The scotch arrived and he swallowed a mouthful, letting it burn his throat.

"Do you actually like that?" she asked, nodding at the drink.

"It wasn't my idea to leave Earth." When she frowned, he laughed again, more softly. "Sorry. I'm not entirely comfortable with the circumstances of this trip. I'm a bit bristly."

"That's evident. So if I may take a chance and suggest that I help you lose your bristles..."

"Are bristles forbidden on Aurora? It's been so long since I've been there, I'm not sure."

"We keep them segregated in wild areas."

"Really. I suppose robots tend to that?"

"Some of us like gardening."

Derec took another sip, studying Clin Craym. He wanted to be left alone on the voyage, but he felt drawn to her. *Physical attraction only, or am I lonely...?*

Even considering the question seemed an answer. He wondered at his own duplicity.

Abruptly, he thought of Rana.

Why did I never try to expand our relationship...?

"You look very puzzled, Doc—Derec," Clin said. "Should I leave you alone?"

"You know," he said, "I really wish you..."

He understood what he felt—come here, go away, basic adolescent insecurity working its way out of the unused part of his personality where it had lain dormant since he and Ariel had ceased being lovers (*How long ago now? And why...?*)—and resented the tug-of-war suddenly engaged by his feelings. He did not want to admit anything good about Aurora inside the shell he thought he had constructed. But that shell was made purely of fragments of resentment, mistrust, and irritation—none of them sound materials, and all of them conditions impossible to maintain without embracing neuroses and becoming an insufferable hermit.

Like my father...

Like the Solarians...

He looked around the lounge. Almost thirty guests were gathered here, eating and talking, the sound a constant background, like flowing water. *If I had really been serious about being left alone, why did I come here?*

The answer came immediately and pathetically: *To be rescued.*

Clin waited, eyebrows arched in a question, her body poised to stand and walk away.

"I really wish you would stay," he said.

She smiled. "Certainly. Anything else?"

Derec felt warm. "Certainly."

Derec answered the knock at his cabin door. Clar Eliton stood in the corridor, a hopeful smile teasing at his mouth. Derec suppressed the urge to close the door and go back to the book he had been trying unsuccessfully to read ever since Clin had left to go back on duty.

"Mr. Avery," Eliton said softly. "I'd like to talk to you. Please. May I come in?"

Too late, Derec thought sourly and stepped aside, waving the man in. "Sure."

Eliton looked quickly around the cabin, as if checking for someone else. At first Derec thought Eliton knew about CPO Craym, that perhaps he could even smell the musky afterscent of their lovemaking. After a moment, though, Derec realized Eliton expected to find a robot.

"Bogard's in a crate," Derec said. "We're alone."

The look of relief on Eliton's face was almost comical. It passed quickly and Eliton nodded. "I, uh... I suppose I have a lot of explaining to do."

"To me? Why?" Derec gestured for the man to sit down.

"I ruined your..." He hesitated, frowning.

"Dreams?" Derec supplied. "That's a fair assessment."

"I wanted a chance to explain. To, to—"

"To try for forgiveness? At least understanding? Why? Because you were in such a difficult position, I should feel sympathy for you?"

"I thought perhaps I could make an apology, perhaps—"

Derec laughed sharply. "Would you care for a drink? I would. I don't think I could listen this completely sober." He went to the dispenser and punched in the code for a gin and tonic. A few seconds later, the glass appeared in the hopper. He took it and sat across from Eliton. "I take it you don't want anything liquid. Fine." Derec took a mouthful and swallowed, clenching involuntarily at the harsh medicinal flavor. "So you want to apologize. How?"

"I'd hoped you could tell me. It's not unlikely we could be useful to each other in the future. But not with this... rift."

"You're serious."

"Of course."

"You know, I had expectations that things could change on Earth. We might then have been able to bridge the rest of the gaps between Spacer and Terran. Partly, you convinced me of that."

"You never struck me as naïve, Mr. Avery."

"I'm not. Hopeful. Optimistic. Maybe it wouldn't have worked, but now we'll never know." *You don't need to do this,* he thought. *You can tell Eliton to leave and not open these wounds.* But he wanted to know.

"The thing is," he said, "you'd been succeeding up till that point. It was *your* work that got the RI installed at Union Station D.C. and secured the permits to allow positronic robots to operate on its grounds. It was *your* work that eased restrictions on Spacer residency and the concomitant ownership of robots outside of embassy territory by Spacers. It was *your* work that allowed cooperative research to begin in Terran labs on Spacer products, including positronics."

Eliton waved a hand impatiently. "Yes, and I was negotiating with trade unions to let up on non-positronic restrictions, and I was working on a bill that would have allowed limited positronic presence aboard Terran starships, and I had even drafted a preliminary piece of legislation that would have reopened Spacetown for Spacer settlement."

"I didn't know that. Would it have passed?"

"Maybe. Probably not. After the conference I would have lost my support in the private sectors and without that it would all have died."

"Private support...you mean corporate?"

"I mean the support of the people who approached me to push this line in the first place. None of whom were ultimately interested in seeing *any* of it enacted and successfully implemented."

"Then..."

"It was never intended to succeed, Mr. Avery."

"I thought I had a grasp of Terran politics. You're the senator—*were,* anyway—so why—?"

"No, you have no grasp. I'm apologizing to you because personally I agree with what you thought would happen. I think Earth is being ridiculous and stubborn. I *don't* think our future is at stake, not the way you seem to think it is. But I *do* think we're turning our back on a great opportunity, all because we're terrified of robots." He leaned forward, holding out his hand as if in offering. "But it's not even that, really. The riots that evicted positronics would never have succeeded if the power structure hadn't been in agreement with the rioters. And it's the same thing here. If collectively the people who matter on Earth had *wanted* my programs to succeed, the people—those whom I supposedly represented— could not have stopped it."

"Then why?"

"What issue brought about the conference? The proposal for the conference?"

"The *Tiberius* incident. Contraband and positronic inspection of commerce."

"Exactly. Do you have any idea how much money was involved? Billions of credits. Positronic inspection would have hurt that flow of money. That's what decided Earth to expel them in the first place, two hundred plus years ago. It wasn't the jobs—labor disputes over job losses are ancient rituals, easily manipulated, just as easily solved. It wasn't even the religious issue—that can always be turned by professional manipulators. But positronics was becoming an ethical burden to the wrong people. And it would be no different now."

"So you set us up to fail."

"Not willingly. I thought I could find a way around it."

"But you went along with it to keep your senate seat."

"As you can see," Eliton said dryly, "that failed, too."

"You think you can make an apology just because it wasn't your *intention* to hurt me? To hurt us?"

After a time, Eliton shook his head. "No, probably not. But I don't want you hating the wrong person."

"I don't hate you, Senator."

For the briefest space, Eliton's face showed relief. Then he frowned, suspicious.

"That's right," Derec said. "I pity you. I think you're pathetic. I think you wasted your authority."

"Believe it or not, Mr. Avery, I agree with you." He shrugged. "And now my reward is to be sent as ambassador to Solaria. I'll be about as out of the way as it is possible to be."

"Do you know what Solaria is like? Don't judge it by Chassik, he's something of an oddity among his own."

"I know what Solaria is like. As for Chassik...he should have been a Terran. He thinks like us."

"Not anymore," Derec said. "He's dead."

Eliton's eyes widened in shock. "Excuse me?"

"You didn't know? He was recalled. His ship was attacked by pirates and destroyed."

The color leached instantly from Eliton's face. The change startled Derec. Eliton got to his feet.

"Senator—?"

"Thank you for your time, Mr. Avery. At least you gave me a chance to...well..." He went to the cabin door. "Good-bye, Mr. Avery. I hope you do well in the future."

The door opened and Eliton left.

Derec stared after him for a time, then finished his drink and returned to his book.

The next day, shiptime, Derec met Ariel in the Grand Lounge for Transition. He searched for Eliton, but the ex-senator never appeared. He told Ariel about their conversation; she frowned disapprovingly, but said nothing.

The roof of the room shimmered as the simulation came on, showing the passage of the liner into hyperspace. A thick sprawl of stars glowed in the projected volume above. A bell sounded, bringing everyone's attention to bear. Then the stars vanished, displaced by a colorless moil of near-patterns, like the shiftings of iron filings in a magnetic field, layer upon layer, shifting and dancing as if searching for a shape to become.

A few seconds into this display, everyone experienced an instant of acute displacement, as if the deck had dropped from beneath them a few millimeters, a physical lurch over before it could be clearly felt.

The diorama over them changed once more into a familiar expanse of stars. Different stars, though, the constellations conforming to altered shapes, most still familiar, but shifted by several light years.

The actual transit through hyperspace had occupied the time of the almost imperceptible shift. The show had been designed to last much longer than the journey, to give the audience something to experience, to see.

As Derec—and most seasoned travelers—knew, the images generated were only surmises. No one really knew what hyperspace "looked" like. The projection was a guess. An educated, well-thought-out guess, but no more.

The canopy hidden by the projection now slid open. The projection faded out in favor of the view of real stars. Forward, near the edge of the vast window, hovered a brilliant reddish star. Tau Ceti.

Even though he knew the star he now saw was real—real in the sense that the shutters, for a brief time, were open and the light of several days' past now impacted his senses, so that he saw a near true star—Derec could not shrug off the feeling that, on this side of the Jump, he had left reality behind, and nothing he would find here would be authentic.

Still, illusion or not, he reacted to the star, and to the world he knew lay in orbit around it. He knew the power of illusions—perhaps more intimately than most—and certainly appreciated the impact of symbols. There in space was one of the most potent symbols in history.

Aurora.

14

MASID WAITED three days for a reply. When nothing came, he decided against resending. His signal had either reached the right place and was disbelieved, or it had gone wrong. He did not wish to antagonize anyone who might have reason to come looking to kill him. He could get out of harm's way, but Tilla was helpless.

He could do nothing for her. The drugs he synthesized from his stock slowed the disease, but he knew fairly soon that he could not cure her. The pathogen, whatever it was, possessed remarkable adaptive powers and was mutating as he watched to counter the effectiveness of the new pharmaceuticals he gave her. He was no physician, but he understood enough to know that nothing he could do would save her. Even if he could kill the disease, Tilla required major transplant surgery to make her whole. As she now was, even without the infection, death was only a matter of time.

He found an abandoned apartment below Tilla's. It reeked of old urine and decay, but a thorough search turned up no corpses. Whoever had been ill here had either been taken away or had crawled off to die elsewhere. Masid moved his kit in and proceeded to debrief Tilla during those periods when she seemed lucid.

He became convinced of the need to get to Nova City.

"We tried," Tilla told him, her voice raspy. "It's isolated, in the middle of native wilderness, and thoroughly surveilled. Automated tracking blasters, force screens, booby traps."

"And the verge is inhabited by reanimés," Kru said, eyes large.

"What?"

Tilla shook her head. "Local myth. Rumor is, Nova Levis wasn't uninhabited when the Solarians settled it. They killed the indigenes, terraformed—badly—and set up their colony. By the time they sublet it to the Settlers, the natives had returned as walking corpses to attack anyone leaving the settlements."

"Not myth," Kru said, scowling at Tilla. "Not indigenes, either. Something out of Nova City." She fixed Masid with a serious stare. "But *something.*"

"Of course," Masid said. "So you said you tried. How close did you get?"

"Five hundred meters," Tilla said, and coughed weakly. "Then Kas died. We found him caught in a razorwire trap, cut to ribbons, not five meters from us. He screamed and alarms sounded. We retreated. Damn near didn't get back to the trucks."

"What happened to the trucks?"

"Stolen, sold, abandoned," Tilla said. "Pretty much in that order. The last one we thought to cannibalize—get more credit that way, selling it off piece by piece—until we all got sick."

Kru squeezed Tilla's hand. "You brought it back from the Verge around Nova City."

"Nonsense," Tilla said. "Everyone here is sick. I've never seen such a public health disaster." She frowned. "About the indigenes getting revenge, it's not complete nonsense. Not large animals, though. The reanimés Kru mentions—I don't think they're large predators."

"Pathogens?" Masid said.

"Yeah. New, something Solaria couldn't anticipate, something the surveys never showed..." She shrugged.

"Or maybe they did know and didn't care," Masid said. "They were originally working this place with robots."

Tilla drew a ragged breath. "That would be...murder?"

"Negligent homicide at best."

Tilla smiled thinly. "Then we should arrest them."

"What about the pirates?" Masid asked.

"Pirates. Nonsense. Black marketeers, grey marketeers, bootleggers, contrabandists, people taking advantage of the situation...there is a loose organization, as far as I can tell, based on territories. Filoo runs this one, there are a dozen others. They get their supplies out of Nova City, but the core of the organization isn't there."

"Then—?"

"Solaria. They come and go as they please, they fly in and out of the port at Nova City with impunity...it's not piracy, it's business. Maybe war, I don't know, but the seat of any organization that might be called—" She lapsed into a brief coughing fit. Her face red, she drew several labored breaths before continuing. "Any organization that might be called a pirate organization is offplanet. The people here are just trying to get by."

"The governor refused on-ground inspections."

"I know. Foolish, maybe, but I understand it. The Settlers here came from people who wished to be completely free of what they left behind. That includes an invasive government. The governor thought he was acting in his people's interest. He also knew he'd get blamed for harboring pirates, no matter that he had no say over what Solaria did. He was out of office a month after the blockade went into effect."

Masid started. "We never knew that."

"Would it have mattered? By then, the *Tiberius* had been blown into a popular cause, and shots had been fired in local space between Settler shuttles and blockade ships. It moved past the stupidity of the governor and now is simply the situation as it stands. I can tell you this: The people here, the Settlers, *hate* Earth, and they're not too fond of Spacers. But Solaria's been keeping them alive, so their feelings are mixed."

Masid glanced at Kru, who looked away, her face set and angry. "Nova City is the only port. How'd you get down?"

"We landed about fifty kilometers from here."

"What happened to your ship?"

"Dismantled."

"By you?"

Kru grunted. "Reanimés!"

Tilla shook her head. "We figure local scavengers found it. I don't know how they got past the security systems, but..."

"Reanimés!" Kru insisted again. "You won't believe me, I know, but I'm telling truth."

"I thought," Masid said, "they were only in the Verge around Nova City."

"Most of them are," Kru said, "but they've got colonies all over."

"Must be a lot of them, then. Somebody must have seen them."

Kru gave him a frightened look. "People see, most of them don't live past it."

Masid looked at her. "Do you know anyone who has seen and survived?"

"You shouldn't tease her that way," Tilla said.

"I'm not. You said your ship was dismantled. I'm assuming it had a standard Special Service security package? That would take a considerable level of skill to bypass. So whoever did it, they might be worth finding, or at least finding out about. Have you seen anything in the markets that looks as though it came from your ship?"

Tilla frowned thoughtfully. "No, but there are several markets and other towns..."

"This is the closest one to where you landed, though."

"It is."

"Then it's reasonable to assume anything scavenged off your ship would've come through here first." He looked at Kru. "Do you know anyone who can tell me more about your reanimés?"

Kru seemed about to stand and leave.

"Kru," Tilla said, halting her in mid-motion. Kru looked at her. "Take him to see Rekker."

"Tilla!"

"Take him."

On rare days the sun broke through the cloud cover, washing everything in brilliant yellow light. Masid stepped from the apartment into that light and, as on a few previous occasions, glimpsed a little of what the town ought to look like: ivory walls and marbled pavement, the edges softened in the quasi-organic style of the Homo Primus school. Masid had seen the same elements on a dozen worlds, people wanting to distance themselves from the dominating excesses of technology-saturated Earth, adopting any motif that reminded them of flesh, bone, nature. Sometimes it turned out looking primitive, like wattle over a frame, but here he saw a balance. As he reached the street just behind Kru, he thought, *I could live in this...*

Kru moved with a guarded urgency that made her seem both helpless and unstoppable. Following a pace behind, he wondered if it also made her look caught, watched. This early in the day, though, few people were out. The market tents would be jammed, but little else was happening in the town.

She led him toward the north quarter. Warehouses reared up, incomplete and ominously still. Beyond them, the forest rose like a cage around the community, spindly trees with enormous, clotted crowns. The light shafted through mists of thick orange pollen that drifted endlessly in the aftermath of the spring rains. From what Masid could tell, the pollen residue coated the ground in thick gooey layers until the downpours ended, then, somehow, shed moisture rapidly until only a powdery cover remained, easily disturbed by the fickle breezes. Within minutes of sunrise, the forest was filled with pollen-fog. Masid had witnessed the process during the first couple of days on the ground, just before entering the town. He had wondered briefly if it was a source for all the illness and infection, but from what he understood about protein compatabilities and what he had seen of the various diseases response to Terran-based treatments, it seemed unlikely.

The scent—something like sharp lavender—tickled his nose as he entered the forest.

It would have been easy for Kru to lose him in this haze. But she only glanced back a few times to see that he kept up, and made no move to run. Masid still mistrusted her, but not because she seemed unreliable or somehow a traitor to Tilla. Rather, it was her barely contained paranoia that bothered Masid. She cared for Tilla, was clearly devoted to her, and trusted nothing outside her own ability to protect Tilla. Masid had yet to get past her inability to accept anything beyond the small apartment, beyond herself and Tilla, as benevolent. She wanted Masid gone. But she would not betray him at the risk of compromising Tilla. It was a precarious place to put his confidence.

Nor would she disobey Tilla's direct orders.

"Who's this Rekker we're going to see?" Masid asked.

"You'll find out. He probably won't talk to you anyway." She glanced around. "Now shut up."

After half an hour, the forest thinned, then they stepped into a clearing. Masid looked at the ground—grassless, dark, a few local mosses stretched into the area, which formed a large circle. In the center stood a round structure of old metal sheeting, plastic, and a roof of thatch made of a combination of synthetic clothes, plastic strips, and native branches and dried leaves. Off to the right he saw the scattered piles of cannibalized equipment, old barrels and crates, and piles of junk gradually recombining into indecipherable configurations.

There seemed to be no way into the structure. Kru held a hand up to stop Masid, then approached.

"Rekker?" she called. "Got visitors. You here?"

"Yeah!"

"Got visitors."

"You said. Who?"

"Come out and see."

"Shit..."

From behind the structure a tall, lanky man with long, dark hair ambled out. He wore a faded jumpsuit with the sleeves cut off and over-sized boots. Masid was surprised to see a clean-shaven face.

He stopped a few paces from Masid. "I'm Rekker," he said. "You know Kru, I guess."

"Slightly."

"Uh-huh. That's all anybody knows Kru." He turned a bright grin on her. "Just kidding. Who is he?"

"Tilla trusts him," Kru said.

"Ah. I won't ask if you do." Rekker fixed a narrow look on Masid. "And *why* does Tilla trust you?"

"We work for the same people, I suppose," Masid said.

"Mmm. I don't like those people."

"I'm not fond of most of them myself."

"Why work for them, then?"

Masid shrugged. "I get to set my own hours, there's lots of travel, and I meet many interesting people. Other than that, it's a job. Have to do something."

Rekker stared at him for a long time, then chuckled. "Good bet you want data. Come inside."

Masid followed the tall man around to the opposite side of his abode. There, the walls failed to meet, one end missing the other by more than a meter, forming the entrance. Within, Masid found a workbench that followed the curve of the inside wall nearly halfway around the circumference. Unlike the junk and refuse piled on one side of the clearing, here everything was neat and orderly. Equipment hummed and pulsed quietly. A tidy workshop.

The other half of the interior contained chairs, a big couch, small tables, and the bulking cube of a hygienic module. A sleeping roll lay on the plastic floor.

"Tilla must've said it was okay or Kru wouldn't've brought you here," Rekker said, dropping abruptly onto the couch. He waved at a chair. "That doesn't mean I won't make my own judgment about whether to trust you. Where were you born?"

"Proclas."

Rekker's ample eyebrows snapped up. "Settler? And you're working for Earth? How does that work?"

Masid rounded on Rekker. "All this talk about whether or not I'm trustworthy, nobody's said anything to relieve my doubts about *you.*"

Rekker nodded. "What do you want to know?"

"First, what's a Spacer doing living the primitive life?"

Rekker's face froze in an unreadable mask for several seconds. Slowly, he grinned again. "That's good. How do you know?"

"Trade secrets. Do you want to explain yourself?"

"Tit for tat." He frowned. "Whatever that means. Old phrase. Anyway, I'm the one with something you need, so you satisfy my curiosity first. If I don't like what I hear, you go back to town with nothing more than a big question mark about things nobody else on this planet gives much of a damn about."

Masid considered his options. "All right," he said. "I was seconded to Terran Offworld Security after a little misunderstanding placed me in thrall to Settler Coalition Intelligence. Ended up working for the security chief on Kopernik Station, a woman named Sipha Palen."

"I don't know her. Last time I had any current knowledge about Kopernik, that post was held by a man named Golvat."

"Palen's predecessor. He retired."

"Golvan was competent and unimaginative, but he was honest. What's Palen like?"

"Dead."

Rekker scowled. "Sorry. Did you like her?"

"More. I respected her."

"I see. Is your being here related to her death?"

"Intimately."

"You think her killers are associated with Nova Levis?"

"I think here is what the killers were protecting. I think the orders came from people either here or concerned with here. Nova Levis is a great big problem. I don't think the people on the blockade have the first idea how big."

Rekker grinned. "Shit, you got that right! So who are you working for now?"

"I'm not sure. Maybe myself. We had an encounter with someone who probably came from Nova Levis, mainly Nova City. No other explanation, really, since he was working for people who seemed to have a vested interest in this place. A really unusual encounter, nothing I ever saw before. Kru suggested you might be able to tell me something about it."

Rekker glanced curiously at Kru. "She was there?"

"No."

"Then—"

"She calls them reanimés. If they're what I think they are, we called them cyborgs."

"Do you always trust this large?" Rekker asked.

"I haven't told you anything yet that would cost you your life."

"No, probably not. Just so I'm clear, was that a threat?"

"I don't make threats."

"I bet you don't. Well." Rekker slapped his knees loudly and laughed. "Cyborgs. You say you encountered one? I find that hard to credit."

"Why?"

" 'Cause they don't work right. None of 'em. Every single one has something wrong with it. And just so we're clear, that was a confirmation. The reanimés *are* cyborgs. People don't like that word, maybe it still hasn't occurred to them yet that that's what they're dealing with. To most people on Nova Levis, they aren't even real. Ghost story, something to scare their kids at night. Lurkers in the jungle, so to speak. I've even heard some people theorize that they're indigenes. Whatever, they don't come around. Humans and cyborgs don't share a lot in common. For that matter, cyborgs are like Solarians."

Masid stared at the man for a long time, stunned. Finally, he shifted in his chair and leaned forward. "Who *are* you?"

Rekker grinned. "Why, I'm glad you asked that, son. I'm a man with a failed mission. I'm the original Spacer legate to oversee the Settler transition."

Masid remembered a name from the colonial history report he had skimmed: Prent Rekari, Keresian. He had been present during the initial phase of the Church of Organic Sapiens' settlement program, supervising the exchange of authority between the Solarian mission and the new colonial government.

"I thought you were dead," Masid said.

"The report still says that?" He laughed. "Well, there you are. I'm a ghost. But believe me, I'm the genuine article."

"One thing about my exile," Rekker said, working at a large, much-repaired food recycler, "is the refreshing absence of fuck-all interstellar politics. Until, that is, the blockade sealed the planet off."

He returned with a pair of glasses containing a milky drink. He handed one to Masid. Kru huddled on one of the oversized chairs, pointedly ignoring them, anxious to return to Tilla.

"You've been here almost thirty years then," Masid said.

"Has it been that long? You lose track with the various circadians all competing for command of your biology. I was here...let me see... thirty-three years ago local time, when the transfer began. I had a nice office in Nova City then."

"What happened?"

"I'm still trying to figure that out. It's difficult when you only know this end of things. But basically I was kidnapped. The transition between Solarian authority to colonial control was not going to be a smooth ordeal. The Solarians are a jealous, possessive lot, I'm sure you know, but they're also loathe to make any kind of direct contact with other organisms, including each other. That's why they use us as their diplomatic infantry. But that also means that errors in translation—their wishes versus colonial demands or even local necessity—are inevitable. Solaria wanted to maintain a presence, mainly in Nova City. That made sense, that's where all the latest infrastructure was based anyway."

"But?"

"But the Settlers wanted no robotic presence anywhere around them. Out of sight, preferably off the planet. They knew they couldn't get that, so the negotiations were all to do with how much and where and what could be done in the case of violations."

Rekker took a long drink. "Now, Nova Levis—or, as it was previously known, Cassus Thole—had been primarily a mining planet. We had robot launch facilities all over the mountains, satellite mining stations scattered across most of the main continent, and some processing facilities. On-ground mining was simply too lucrative to pass up, a lot of the ores were so close to pure to begin with, but even so, the bulk of the profitable mining was done offworld. Tau Secordis has very rich asteroid fields, and there are a couple of big rocks that barely qualify as planets we worked, too. There shouldn't have been a problem, just a lot of tedious clean-up. Robots can remove themselves just as efficiently as they settle in. The only *real* problem should have been the biomanagement plant."

Masid frowned.

"Oh, yes," Rekker laughed. "We'd stretched a couple of points to the Settler Coalition about the actual habitability of Cassus Thole. By the time the COS arrived, we'd turned vast stretches of the plains to agriculture. Very profitably, too, I might add. That was part of the terms of the lease. But to *do* that required a considerable degree of direct reforming intervention. The Solarians built a plant near the southern pole to manage the biosphere reclamation and transition."

"I thought the planet was human habitable when it was found."

Rekker laughed sharply. "No such thing, Settler, no such thing in the universe! When you people started coming out from Earth a couple centuries ago, you'd been sold a story about how easy it was. After all, hadn't we Spacers simply found a whole slew of wonderfully empty

planets, biologically *tabula rasa*, just waiting for our benevolent trans-
plantation of native Earth flora and fauna to turn them into paradises?"
He leaned forward. "We'd found hundreds of planets that were useful.
That doesn't mean they were ready for people to move in. Some of them
had *very* aggressive biospheres, a few of which are *still* unsuitable for
colonization. We took the ones that were easiest to terraform and started
working on the rest. I'm sure we originally intended to expand into more
than just fifty worlds, but..." He shrugged elaborately.

"Still," he continued after a pause, "there was a lot of credit to be
made managing new worlds and when the whole Settler Program got
going, we thought we had found a way to get rich and stay safe at the
same time. So we...withheld a few details. Nothing that hasn't worked
out just fine in the long run. Two centuries now and the Settler worlds
are beginning to reach a point where they can go out and settle their own
dependent colonies."

"But they all needed work."

"Right. And Cassus Thole needed a lot. Remember, originally it was
just going to be a mining planet. We didn't need to be able to stroll in the
woods for that."

"Why lease it in the first place?"

Rekker shook his head. "I don't know. I was never given a justification
for that. I'm sure you could ask the same question about a dozen or more
other worlds we've leased. Why? Someone thought it was a good idea. I
thought it was silly at the time, but my job was to ease the transition, not
question the logic."

"So what went wrong? I assume something went wrong."

"The colonists wanted the biomanagement plant shut down. It
offended them. I had to go back and forth, oh, fifty times, a hundred,
with counterproposals, threats, tantrums, retractions, restatements—" He
gave a mock shudder. "The crap in the pasture of the universe. It wasn't
good enough that Solaria proposed to simply relocate it to the Spacer
zone in Nova City. They wanted it *shut down!* Idiots. How do you explain
to someone who refuses to understand that certain things are necessary
to a continued lifestyle? That if this *thing* that so offends one's sensibili-
ties goes away, then they will in all likelihood die?"

"What was so fatal?" Masid asked.

"The nitrogen cycle in the biosphere tends to produce an excess of
ammonia. One of the byproducts is a cyanotoxin, used by some of the
flowering plants to fend off a form of local ungulate that would eat every
pollinating grass on the surface. You see the problem. Eliminate the

excess ammonia, the ungulates overbreed and eat everything. Leave it alone and maybe take care of it during food processing. But it's not enough to simply process out the cyanides from the harvests, because during pollination the toxins become airborne. So, you *have* to revise the cycle."

"What did you do about the ungulate?"

"Eradicated them. We have some specimens in research zoos." Rekker raised his hands. "I know, it's terrible. But sometimes certain biologies just can't coexist. You can have one or the other, not both."

"Did it occur to you that the COS might have objected if they'd known?"

"No. They knew. Not a word was said. They wanted their lease." Rekker shook his head. "I don't know why we couldn't have sold them a different planet, somewhere else. Another one of those imponderables. This was the planet agreed upon, it was our job to make it ready for them. They accepted most of the terms. We fixed the biosphere. Somewhere along the way, they failed to understand that a biosphere tends to revert if the revising technologies are withdrawn prematurely. The plant had to remain in place for another century at least before the cycle could be reasonably guaranteed to be permanent. They didn't like that."

Rekker finished his drink. He studied the glass as if trying to decide whether to have another. He frowned finally and set it down.

"Solaria decided to move the plant anyway. We were still in the middle of negotiations about it. Solarian authority hired an independent firm to move the facility and start it up. By the time I knew it was happening, it had been shut down and a new containment building was going up in the middle of Nova City. I started digging in for some answers—I hate being kept out of the loop, especially when it's my word that's supposed to carry weight with the people involved. They hired a firm called The Hunter Group. I'd never heard of them, but they seemed, on the surface, to know what they were doing. But they were overbuilding the facility. When I asked about it, I was informed that a second lease had been granted to this company to operate a research station on Solaria's behalf. I thought, 'That's strange. I thought Keres had the exclusive rights to negotiate for research facilities.' Keres did. Solaria was going around us. I started complaining. I was told to finish the negotiations first. But that just annoyed me more."

"You kept asking questions."

"And I was kidnapped for my troubles. Taken right out of my bed in the middle of the night. Very melodramatic. They held me in the remains of the south polar station. Very cold."

Masid smiled wryly. "Did you find out anything about Hunter before they kidnapped you?"

"Now here's where you and I have to do our own negotiation. So far I haven't told you anything that would get *you* killed. But from this point on we have to learn to trust on more than just the say-so of a mutual friend." Rekker looked past Masid to Kru. "No offense intended toward Tilla, but this is where it gets serious. In fact, maybe it's best you not listen."

Masid glanced back at Kru. She glowered at them both. "If you want to go back to Tilla—"

"She told me to see you get back safe," Kru snapped. She stood. "I'll wait outside."

When she had left, Masid said, "Let me ask you a question first. Why do you trust Tilla?"

"Well, you get tired of not trusting people. Look at poor Kru. She spends every waking moment in fear of other people. Tilla rescued her from a serious addiction and she's been faithful ever since, especially when Tilla got too sick to be threat to her. That's no way to be." Rekker sighed. "But that's only part of the answer. Kru, I suppose, showed me that Tilla's a good person at heart. She didn't have to do anything to help the girl. In fact, she could have used her, done half the job and made her completely dependent. But the fact is, she convinced me that she really believed in wanting to help. She and her team could have gotten out of here long before they were compromised. There was even a chance shortly after. But they had a job and they were dedicated. I'm completely awed by that kind of dedication. I used to have it myself."

Masid regarded the Spacer for a long moment. Then: "Hunter is a front for an arms dealer named Kynig Parapoyos. Do you know the name?"

"No."

"The cyborgs I encountered—on Kopernik Station—were working for Hunter. You said they were building a research facility? What kind?"

"Biomedical."

"And it's never been shut down?"

"No."

"When did the reanimés start appearing?"

"About ten years ago. There aren't many of them, that's why they're considered more myth than meat by most people."

"How do you know about them?"

Rekker grinned. "Allow me to keep a few secrets. So what is it you're here to do?"

"If Kynig Parapoyos owns that facility, he's building cyborgs. Maybe the ones you've seen don't work very well, but the one I saw worked *very* well. It's only a matter of time before their...creation...is perfected."

"And a source of cyborgs for an arms dealer could be a real problem. You think you can stop them?"

"No one on the blockade knows about the relationship between Parapoyos and Nova Levis. Baleys are being smuggled in here. I'm thinking there's a slave traffic or at least a black market biomedical resource flow operating out of Nova City. I have no idea what I can do, but I can't do anything until I know for certain what's going on and who's involved."

"Can't fault your logic."

"Thank you."

"You may be shy on common sense, though. I'll tell you one thing: Even if this Kynig Parapoyos owns that facility, the research it's doing is for Solaria."

"How do you know that?"

"I've been here long enough to recognize patterns and players." He remained silent until Masid understood that no other answer was going to be offered.

"What *have* you been doing for the last thirty years?" Masid asked.

"Oh, that. Well, after my kidnapping, a new liaison was assigned. My captors held me for two years. When I was freed, no one would acknowledge my existence. To be perfectly honest, that suited me just fine. I'd been betrayed. I'd had enough. I turned my back on the whole mess and moved out into the country. Here. I thought for a couple of years that I might one day find a way to uncover what was going on and expose it. A hero's return, maybe. But I realized after a while that, frankly, nobody would thank me. So I became a local tinkerer. I fix things for people. I'm no threat to anyone because I have no interests that conflict with anyone else's." He pointed a finger at Masid. "I help you, that could change."

"Are you going to?"

"Depends. What do you think would be the next step?"

"Getting inside Nova City."

"That's right. You know you might never come back out?"

"If I'm ever *going* to get out, it'll be from there."

Rekker grinned. "Okay, you're not stupid. Fine. You want to get inside Nova City, it'll take time. You can't just walk in. The perimeter is well secured. So you're going to have to get an invitation. To do that, you'll have to go to work for the local boss."

"Filoo?"

"Have you met him?"

"No."

"Good. That'll make it easier. What I'll do is start a useful rumor that he ought to look into you and maybe hire you. What've you been doing for a living since you got here?"

"Selling pharmaceuticals."

"That's just his sort of thing. He may well know who you are already, then. I can set it up so he won't think you're a threat. Once he hires you, it's up to you. The bosses are the only ones who regularly go to Nova City from the outlying townships."

Rekker stood. "So to answer your question, what have I been doing the last thirty years? Waiting for you, it looks like."

"Why are you helping?"

"I would dearly love to know who fucked me." He waved. "Come on, you need to get Kru back to Tilla before she bursts from anxiety."

"I have one more question."

"I doubt that. What is it?"

"How come you're not sick? Almost everyone else here seems to be."

Rekker smiled sadly. "I'm a Spacer. Spacers never get sick."

15

MIA SNAPPED the book closed at the sound of her cabin door chime. She reached over to her desk and touched a contact. The display identified her visitor as Commander Reen.

Mia closed the surveillance screen and slipped the book into a locking drawer at the base of her desk. She rolled her chair around to face the flatscreen on which shipping route tables waited for her attention.

"Yes?" she said.

"Reen, Lt. Daventri. May I come in?"

"Certainly, sir." She touched the contact that opened her door.

Reen stepped quickly in, hands clasped behind his back. Mia began to rise, but he lifted one hand and gave a slightly shake of his head.

"You're on personal time," he said. "Formalities can wait."

"Then..." Mia bit back a demand to know why he was here, disturbing her "personal time," but instead she said, "May I offer you something to drink?"

"No, thank you. May I sit?"

She gestured to a chair. He glanced at her flatscreen as he folded himself into the seat. "Working?"

"Puzzles annoy me. I have a hard time relaxing when they're unresolved."

"I understand completely. I wanted to offer you an opportunity to sit in on Corf's interrogation. Perhaps get a sense of where you might take it before we begin."

"I was under the impression that he already had been interrogated."

"Preliminaries. I've assigned a specialist to do a more thorough examination." He smiled thinly. "Corf is the first one we've caught of any real rank or position. Granted, Stores isn't much of a position, but it's a perfect one for a smuggler. He has to know more than he's given us so far."

"Of course, I'll be glad to assist..." Mia frowned. "A specialist? What service?"

"Independent."

Mia kept her expression neutral. She knew what Reen meant, and it skirted legality. She wondered if he actually possessed the authority to do this, then wondered how she might find out without letting Reen know.

"If you think that's necessary," she said carefully.

"You disapprove. Actually, I'm glad you do. I would never ordinarily resort to something this...radical. But we've got an opportunity to mine information about smuggling operations before Corf gets snatched from us by the adjutant general's office and shipped back to Earth. I want these leaks found, Lieutenant."

"Yes, sir."

"I'm still surprised at how little we found in his cabin. Your search was thorough?"

"All due respect, sir, I'm not prone to sloppy work. And it was a small cabin."

"Mmm. No disrespect intended, Lieutenant. I'm just surprised."

"Was there something in particular you expected to find?"

"As a matter of fact, yes. Timetables. We've yet to find out how shipping schedules are being passed between the various agents in this operation. We're scanning all possible comm frequencies, inspecting all incoming and outgoing data for code, and yet all the various factions of our target know our routing schedules and their own down to the hour. Or so it seems. We catch a lot, but it's almost a matter of luck rather than logic. I thought Corf, of all people, would possess something that might indicate how that information was being passed."

"If it's not going by comm, there must be some hardcopy."

"My thoughts, too. But..." He stared at her narrowly, as if dissatisfied and suspicious. "Well, maybe it's word of mouth. Ridiculous, but not impossible. I'll have to tell the interrogator to do a body search for hidden recorders or something."

He continued to stare at her through a long silence. Mia returned his gaze evenly, acutely aware that he suspected her of lying.

"When is Corf's first interrogation by the specialist scheduled?" she asked.

"Tomorrow."

"Let's hope it proves worthwhile."

Reen's eyebrows bobbed once and he stood. He laughed self-consciously. "I'm sorry, Lieutenant, I do dislike doubting my subordinates, but are you withholding information? I could understand it if you thought you had a handle on something that you expected to be productive and didn't want to share the glory—"

Mia snapped to her feet. "Sir, you are bordering on making an accusation which I will have no choice but to meet with judicial response."

"I'm perfectly aware of my limitations, Lieutenant. I hope you are as aware of yours." He gave a short bow. "Apologies. This has been driving me for some time."

Mia clasped her hands behind her back and broke eye contact. "I understand."

"You would be willing to put such a matter before an Inquest? With all that would entail?"

"Yes, sir."

His face relaxed. "Then I suppose I have my answer. Very well, Lieutenant Daventri. Sorry to have bothered you."

At the door, he paused.

"I consider this matter now closed," he said. He looked at her. "Are we in agreement?"

"Yes, sir."

He nodded again and left her cabin.

Her hands trembled as she sat down. *You'd think after everything I've been through I'd be used to lying to my superiors,* she thought. She stared at the chair where Reen had been sitting. On impulse, she touched a series of keys on her desk. A small sphere emerged from its niche across the cabin and began a detailed search of the room, looking for anything Reen might have left behind.

The scan took nearly ten minutes, during which time Mia made herself a drink, and waited in silence. When it finished, the sphere—a piece of contraband illegal for her to possess, acquired from a Spacer acquaintance—returned to its niche. The screen on her desk displayed the report. Clean.

Even so, she finished her drink slowly before she took out the book from its drawer and opened to where she had left off:

We are forced to fall back on fatalism as an explanation of irrational events (that is to say, events the reasonableness of which we do not understand). The more we try to explain such events in history reasonably, the more unreasonable and incomprehensible do they become to us.

Mia tilted her head back and let a quiet laugh escape. The words, written so long ago, about an ancient and altogether senseless war, stung still. Though she moved—had moved—through events which others might call "historic," beyond the step-by-step requirements of survival, she could not—ever—admit to understanding them.

She read on.

Each man lives for himself, using his freedom to attain his personal aims, and feels with his whole being that he can now do or abstain from doing this or that action; but as soon as he had done it, that action performed at a certain moment in time becomes irrevocable and belongs to history, in which it has not a free but a predestined significance.

Mia sighed. "Leo Tolstoy, where have you been when I needed you?" The passage continued:

There are two sides to the life of every man, his individual life, which is the more free the more abstract its interests, and his elemental hive life in which he inevitably obeys laws laid down for him.
Man lives consciously for himself, but is an unconscious instrument in the attainment of the historic, universal, aims of humanity.

Mia grunted. "Really? That's the first thing you've said that seems wrong." She wondered how that formulation meshed with the current situation. Hive life—well, there was certainly that, from the warrens of Earth to the aggregate polities of the Spacers' Fifty Worlds. The various Settler colonies combined aspects of both to greater or lesser degrees, but was there any discernible set of aims to the whole, or just a competing mass of wants and needs and agendas?

And she had to wonder just how consciously most people ever lived, for themselves or otherwise...

For instance, what am I doing? And is it conscious choice or instinct?

She closed the book and gazed at its cover. WAR AND PEACE was embossed across the aging synthetic material. Mia leafed through the pages. Timetables, Reen had said. Was he lying? Maybe. Or maybe the truth would serve him just as well. Timetables...

She opened the covers and studied the end papers. They were golden, covered by a fine, fractal pattern.

On impulse, she set the book on her desk and ran the scanning wand over the end papers. She tapped in commands and watched the screen.

Alphanumerics scrolled up.

"Damn." She felt intense anxiety work through her body. But gradually, she grinned. "How does encryption fall into the predestined uses of historical aims?" she wondered aloud as she initiated her translation routines.

Ariel sat in one of the smaller lounges, a brandy snifter before her on the table, staring up at the room-length viewscreen that showed Aurora Orbital Port Station. The structure possessed an elegance Kopernik never knew. Its lines arced and swept through vacuum like the penstrokes of a skilled calligrapher, iconographic and mysterious, implying secrets and meaning which, Ariel knew, did not really exist. Aurorans liked to present themselves as custodians of civilization's potential. It had become their dominant motif, a façade of depth which, she had to admit, intimidated most of the rest of settled space. She knew better, but still enjoyed the beauty of their symbols.

To be fair, she knew Aurorans who actually were what they seemed to be.

The ship moved slowly now, bringing them incrementally closer to dock. Most of the passengers were Spacers, and had a Spacer sense of patience. The view, with cloud-shrouded Aurora behind the station, was worth a long gaze. Ariel judged she could get thoroughly drunk before debarkation actually occurred.

The station was less than a century old, a compromise to the opening up of travel between worlds after the Settler Accords became law almost two centuries ago. Aurora wanted a firewall between Terrans and themselves, a precaution which ultimately proved unnecessary for the original reasons—fear of infection—but which continued as a desirable way of screening out the unwanted on other grounds. Spacer ships still grounded directly on the planet, mostly at Port Eos, just outside Eos City, the capital. All other ships, from Earth or the Settler worlds, used this or any of a dozen more utilitarian stations that now peppered the system.

Ariel found it hard to believe that almost fifteen years had passed since her last visit here...

She did a casual survey of the lounge. Her gaze caught on Clar Eliton, sitting at a table near the entrance, staring at the projected image. Ariel felt a sharp resentment at his presence, as though he did not deserve to see Aurora. Her sudden protectiveness surprised her. She finished her brandy and signaled the robot tending bar for another one, using the time to wonder why she should feel the least concern toward a world that had once thrown her off...

Snifter in hand, she made her way to Eliton's table. He did not see her until she stood at the vacant chair across from him. He looked briefly startled, mouth open and wordless.

"Um..." he managed, lurching back his chair as if to rise in polite greeting.

Ariel lifted a hand, cutting his politesse short. "Mind if I join you?" She pulled out the chair and sat down. "I feel I was rude the other day. I apologize."

Eliton frowned as he recovered his seat. "I don't think—"

She waved at the view. "Beautiful, isn't it?"

"Yes..." He looked away. "I wanted to see it under better circumstances."

"Oh, wait till you get on the ground. If you think this is something—"

"I won't be grounding here."

Ariel gave him a puzzled stare.

He reddened slightly. "I'm not allowed to see the 'promised land.' My assignment—my *mission*—to Solaria precludes me from any contact with Aurorans outside the contingent of this ship. Neither Solaria nor Earth wants me to set foot on Aurora." He smiled thinly. "They're afraid I may...I don't know." He laughed. "Does Aurora accept supplicants for asylum?"

"Not usually, no. Do you need asylum?"

Eliton laughed again, louder. "No, good heavens, forgive me! I was speaking...it's nothing. I was being sarcastic. Ironic." He looked up at the view. "Really, I think the Solarians are afraid you Aurorans might arrest me on some pretext to keep me from them. I think Earth agrees."

"That's rather paranoid thinking on their part. Why would they worry over that?"

"The embarrassment over my abduction, which *you* clearly don't accept as valid. It could be turned to political use by certain parties. Solaria is actually the safest place to keep me out of the public eye till it's all forgotten." He looked at her sadly. "Not paranoia—caution."

He had, Ariel remembered, acted the part of a victim of the Managins after his faked assassination at Union Station, D.C., on Earth. He had claimed then to have been abducted, but Ariel had satisfied herself that he had been an active participant in the debacle. Others believed as she did, and it had left him vulnerable and politically compromised.

"That's too bad," she said.

"Yes, I agree. It looks..."

"A bit too neat for my taste," Ariel said. "Overly-sculpted. Everything is in its place, even the grass."

"Why not, if you have a pristine environment to start with? As I understand it, the first colonists found virtually no indigenous life."

"Oh, not quite that simple. It had a dense atmosphere, but most of the organic forms had evolved no further than a few aggregate creatures— colony animals, like cnidran siphonophores on Earth—"

Eliton blinked. "Excuse me?"

"Man-of-wars, I believe they used to be called. Individuals acting as components in a more complex association. Anyway, even those were simple—polyps and proto-medusans—and dissolved to reproduce. Other than that, we had algaes, lichens, and some rudimentary molds and mosses. The oceans produced enough oxygen to make the effort worthwhile. Ridiculously simplistic biosphere. It didn't have a chance against the Terran forms we brought with us. It only took a few generations to establish a fully compatible biosphere. I suppose with that as a canvas the urge to dictate the result was too much. The whole planet is more garden than ecology. Clean, tidy, controlled."

"You disapprove."

"I like Earth for a variety of reasons. One is its chaotic nature."

Eliton grunted. "That's exactly what many Terrans would like to get away from."

She studied him speculatively. "It's worse on Solaria. Everything is organized into individual estates, enclosed arboreta that are part of vast households. They never bothered terraforming the planet in general— none of them intended to go outside, anyway."

"But the records I've read—"

"Oh, don't get me wrong, there's an open-air biosphere, but all the variety is indoors. Far more controlled than on Aurora. Sounds perfectly hideous to me."

"Perhaps you should consider emigration to a Settler world. Sounds like their kind of wildness is just what you'd prefer."

"Don't think I haven't considered it. When all this nonsense at the Calvin Institute is done, I may."

Eliton returned his attention to the viewscreen. "We're docking."

Ariel looked up. The delicate-seeming webbing of the station enveloped the ship, arching around it, kilometer-long arms enfolding the liner.

"Solaria was the same way?" Eliton asked.

"Hmm?"

"The biosphere...the same as Aurora?"

"No, there were different flora—"

"I meant—what's the term they use?—morphologically naïve. Only simple organisms, nothing advanced enough to compete in any meaningful way with Terran forms."

"Oh, that. Yes, essentially the same."

Eliton frowned, shaking his head. "As I understand it, all fifty of the Spacer colonies were like that."

Ariel nodded, paying more attention to the view of docking. "Yes, basically."

"I've always found that peculiar."

Ariel looked at him. "Hmm? Why?"

"Well, since the Settler Accords were signed and Earth began a colony program again, we've found a few worlds like that, but they've been in the minority. I always put it down to Spacers having already taken the most easily adapted real estate, but the more you look at it, the less sense it seems to make."

"I'm not sure I follow."

"Well, it's a question of statistics, really. What are the odds that the first fifty habitable planets you'd find would be so ideally suitable to human modification?"

"It wasn't the *first* fifty."

"No? According to the records, a few hundred probes went out and maybe a dozen exploration ships. First there's the likelihood of finding planets nearby at all—which proved less remarkable than we thought at the time—but then there's the fact that none of the habitable planets possessed complex, aggressive ecosystems. As if they were just waiting for the arrival of new colonists."

"A number of those worlds were completely inhospitable to humans. Without robots—"

"Yes, I understand that, but the completely inhospitable ones were so utterly inhospitable that the cost of terraforming was prohibitive—in fact, probably impossible. What always baffled me was the lack of in-between worlds. When you look at the records, the Spacers found the worlds they settled and completely unsuitable worlds. Nothing that required the capacity for terraforming that they brought with them. I—"

A babble of excited voices interrupted him. Eliton looked around. Three uniformed Aurorans, followed by four robots and an array of floating extensions, entered the lounge. One of the spheres broke off and did a very quick circuit of the room, coming to a halt above Eliton. The Aurorans came over to them.

"Ambassador Eliton?" the lead uniform asked softly.

"Yes..."

"I'm Captain Rovel, Auroran security. Would you please accompany us?"

Eliton looked apprehensive. "Why?"

"This would be best conducted in private—"

"I repeat the question. Why?"

Captain Rovel looked embarrassed on Eliton's behalf. "I have a warrant to detain you, issued by the Council of Aurora. It is a lawful warrant, requiring you to accompany us."

"Accompany you *where?*"

"To Eos City, Ambassador. Your presence is required at a hearing—"

"I have diplomatic status, Captain. Your warrant—"

"We've checked. Your official status as ambassador does not take effect until you reach Solaria. At this point, you are a private citizen traveling on a Terran passport. We do have the authority to subpoena you."

Eliton stared at the Auroran, then looked at Ariel. "Did you—?"

Ariel stood. "Well, Senator, it seems you'll get to see Aurora after all. I hope you enjoy your stay."

"I can't—I—"

"Please," the Captain said. "If necessary, you will be sedated. We would rather spare you that."

Eliton stood, glaring at Ariel, then spoke to Captain Rovel. "I have nothing to say to you or your inquest. I consider this an illegal detention."

"Once we arrive," Captain Rovel said, "you may certainly file a protest." He stepped aside. "If you would, Ambassador?"

With a last furious look at Ariel, Eliton stepped into the midst of the robot entourage and was walked out of the lounge.

Captain Rovel bowed politely to Ariel, who nodded in response. As he left, Ariel sat back down to finish her brandy. Her hand trembled slightly, but she could not tell if it did so from fear or shame.

"Welcome home," she muttered.

16

COREN FOUND the bookstore in one of the deep sublevels of Lyzig District. An office occupied a posher section, but it had proved little more than a kiosk where one could place orders. The actual store filled several converted chambers in an ancient recycling plant Coren felt certain had been dug out of the Earth's mantle.

A single embossed plaque identified the entrance: OMNE MUNDI COMPLURIUM, PRINTED ANTIQUITIES, LYZIG.

A man sat behind the high counter, idly doodling, one hand propping his chin. When he looked up, Coren hesitated at the sight of an artificial eye glowing dull blue from the man's left socket.

"Help you, gato?"

Coren placed a note on the desk containing the books listed in Mia's communiqué. The man scanned it.

"Expensive," he said.

"Really? How?"

With a barely audible groan, the dealer straightened and turned to a flatscreen Coren only now noticed amid the stacks of bound books and paper surrounding it. Coren glanced across the top of the counter, which came up to his shoulders, and saw a nameplate. Black letters set in brass announced SHAL PROST, PROP.

The doodles the man had been absently scrawling looked like complex geometric forms.

"We sold one each of those recently," he said. "The *War and Peace* went for...twenty-eight hundred credits...three thousand for *Oliver Twist*... three for *Of Human Bondage*...fifteen hundred for *Les Miserables*."

"Why the drop?"

"Unattributed translation, retrograde facsimile. Can't fully authenticate the text, so it doesn't rate as much." He looked at Coren. "Some gatos are more interested in the pedigree than the content."

"Sounds human enough. Who bought them?"

Doubt flickered in Prost's eye. "That's confidential."

"Fair enough. Can you tell me this, then—does that customer buy a lot through you?"

"Quite. We ship at least thirty volumes a year to him. Something of a completist."

"Anything in particular?"

"What are you, in competition?"

Coren was silent. Prost smiled.

"I see," he said. "You're buying for someone. Maybe a newcomer to the field? Wants to know what's going, what's not. It's a fickle field, I can understand someone with reputation using a shill to protect himself from ridicule."

"Her."

Prost's relief was almost palpable. Coren placed a hand on the counter.

"Well," Prost continued, glancing at the flatscreen, "I'll warn you up front that this is not a reliable investment. Old books like this, you can get the text from any public data service, and, frankly, folks aren't as much concerned with the tangible past as they once were."

"Then who buys?"

"Believe it or not, my biggest customers are Spacers. We do a very healthy trade to the Fifty Worlds. So far, it's either universities or private scholars, but recently we've started selling to private citizens."

Coren nodded toward the screen and tapped his list.

"Oh, yes. Solarian. And his taste runs to Dickens primarily."

"How many?"

"He's bought them all now, I think..." Prost tapped the screen and read. "Except *Great Expectations* and *Edwin Drood*."

"I imagine Spacers would have the time to read all this," Coren said, interjecting a note of amazement as he shook his head.

"It's a status thing. I sell multiple copies to the same customer of the same title. Sometimes they actually come back through, from a different source, so they're being given away as gifts."

"Or sold?"

"I doubt it. I pick them back up for less than the original fee more often than not."

"What would a Solarian find valuable enough to give away?"

Prost chuckled. "Kind of a contradiction, isn't it? Well, this one has bought fourteen editions of *A Tale of Two Cities* over the last three years."

Coren made a show of entering the title in his hand reader. "What about those?"

"None in stock currently. My last copies have all left the planet. However, I have several others by the same authors."

Coren let Prost ramble on, trying to sell something. At one point Coren asked to actually see one of the books. Prost shut down his screen and sprinted away, into the caverns.

Coren took a handful of his little vonoomans from a pocket and scattered them on the floor. One he placed on the desk. After a second, it scampered away to hide.

Prost returned with a musty-smelling volume that crackled when he opened the pages. They dickered over a price, finally agreeing on a few hundred credits. Prost dutifully opened an account for Coren under the false name Coren gave him. Smiling, he slipped the book into a homeostatic container and sealed it.

"I'll let you know when these others show up," Prost said. "And I'll send you a list of current properties which are making the fashionable rounds."

"Thanks."

"By the way, how did you find out about us? We like to keep track of our recommendations."

"Commander Reen recommended you."

Prost nodded. "He gets a discount next time, then."

"He raved about you, said he had no idea how he could survive without your service."

"He exaggerates, I'm sure, but he has been a very good customer."

"Thanks again, then."

Coren stepped out of the ancient shop, keeping a carefully neutral face, and, tucking his new-old copy of *The Light That Failed*, made his way carefully back to the upper levels of Lyzig.

He returned to DyNan headquarters after dropping the book at his private office. As he made the corner into the corridor to his corporate office, he stopped short, seeing his door open.

Coren ducked back around the corner and waited, not breathing. He heard footsteps coming toward him. He stepped sideways into the middle of the hall and resumed his path as if he had just arrived, rounding the corner, and colliding with the person approaching.

"Oh, excuse me—"

"Damn! Will you—boss!"

"Shola, I am sorry." He held her left arm, then stepped back. "I apologize, I wasn't paying any attention. My mind was a world away."

Flustered, Shola Bran laughed, and needlessly straightened her blouse. "No problem. I was looking for you, anyway."

"Oh?"

"Yes, someone down in biologicals has been trying to find you, a Dr. Willis Jay. He's been insistent, so I thought I'd come give you the message personally."

"I see. Okay, then. Thanks."

"Do you need me for anything, boss?"

Coren shook his head. "I have some calls to make."

He walked away, resisting the urge to glance back at her to see if she watched him. He entered his office and shut the door and waited, listening.

When he heard nothing from the other side, he went to his desk. Quickly, he brought his system up, then pulled his hand reader out. Coren entered a series of commands into both the reader and the desk, then jacked the reader into its cradle. He sat back and waited.

Within seconds, the screen showed a schematic of his office. One by one, bright sparks appeared in various places, including one within the icon for his desk system.

He toyed with the idea of removing the bugs at once. His skin rippled with anger at the thought of betrayal by one of his own. But immediate action would only warn Shola and, presumably, whoever she now worked for.

Carefully, he tapped in a new series of commands. One by one, over the next several hours, the little spies would be turned and lead him back to the source.

He closed everything down, retrieved his reader, and headed for Jay's lab.

"Found some interesting things about those grass samples you gave me," Jay said the moment Coren entered his lab.

Coren glanced around and saw that they were alone.

"You hinted at that the last time," Coren said.

"I know. It took some doing to find out just why I found what I found. Kind of like reverse engineering, trying to figure out how to build something based on its final product." He gestured Coren to follow.

They entered another office down the hall from Jay's. Jay waved Coren into a chair, then activated a collection of screens.

"This grass is the product of manipulation," Jay said without preamble. "You know much about plant biology?"

Coren shook his head. "They grow in the open, in soil, under sunlight..."

Jay shook his head, curling his lips in disgust. "Never mind. This—" he pointed to a screen on his right "—is the molecular tree of a normal blade of grass. Over here—" he gestured at a screen on his left "—is the breakdown of what you brought me."

Coren examined the two diagrams, both complex assemblages of branching and interconnected lines that reminded him more of circuit pathways than anything organic. He pointed at the left-hand display, which appeared to be a more complex version of what Jay had shown him before.

"There seem to be some extra—what?—nodes?"

"There are. A lot, if you keep staring at it. What those are, I have no idea."

"What do you mean, you have no idea? You managed to diagram it."

"What I mean is, I have no idea where they came from or exactly what they do. It's all residual, a leftover from some process of the mechanism which is no longer in place. The other day I told you I'd found beryllium standing in where you would expect to see magnesium; and I'd also found complex silicates attached to what magnesium there was. Both magnesium and beryllium are photosensitive, both will enable photosynthesis, though the beryllium is less efficient. I couldn't figure out what it was doing there, how it had gotten there in the first place. So I went looking for associated molecules. I found some weird carbon chains, some unexpected occurrences of iron, and silica phosphates. None of this was exactly *associated* with beryllium, but it was all odd, especially where I found it, which was all over the molecular tree. Then!"

He brought up another screen. It showed a pair of molecular trees, side by side, various nodes highlighted in bright blue.

"I went looking for absences," Jay continued. "Things that ought to have been in the structure but weren't. I found these missing nodes. Originally, the grass *did* use magnesium as a photosynthesizer, but its production and implementation of it was blocked at some point until it was forced to use beryllium instead, which changed its growth rate among other things, but also its hardiness. The magnesium ended up being used almost exclusively as a connector for the silicates. And I found these." He stabbed a finger at one of the nodes, lightly touching the screen, which turned the node to green. "Plant version of fat."

"And what would a plant do with fat?"

"Live on it, like a battery." Jay grinned. "This is a terraformed variety designed to thrive in harsh environments. The energy expenditure the plant must utilize to conduct photosynthesis with beryllium is higher. Normally, that would make it less hardy. But a system has been put in place to construct *these* nodules of matter which the plant can then use *internally* during bad times. This thing is a masterpiece."

Coren sat back and stared at Jay. "You said you couldn't tell me anything about it."

"I can't. I can tell you what it is, but I can't tell you where it came from, how it works, or who made it. There's another mechanism not present at all responsible for this and I don't have it in my library. I'm betting the silicates are the residue from whatever that mechanism is. It's also old. As far as I can tell, this variety is now self-sustaining."

"What?"

Jay shook his head impatiently. "Bad term. Look, I don't know enough about terraforming to give you all the answers. We don't research this stuff here, Rega never allowed it. Not really my interest, either, but I can appreciate good work when I see it. My understanding is, any alien environment is going to have certain properties, if not inimical, at least unfriendly to Terran flora. A certain amount of fundamental change has to be wrought in the biosphere of any colony to make it support our plantlife."

"That's important?"

"Absolutely. We can ship a lot of food these days, but you don't want to do that unless you want to keep the colony in debt forever. Eventually, they have to grow their own food. So in the early days—maybe the Spacers still do it—we'd seed an environment with vonoomans that would burrow in and reconstitute everything, change the ratios of nutrients in the soil, alter the nitrogen cycle or even introduce a nitrogen cycle if there wasn't one. After a few generations, with a lot of effort, the colony would begin to support our plantlife. Once we had it established, the vonoomans were no longer necessary."

Coren shifted uncomfortably, conscious of the pocketful of little machines he still carried since returning from Lyzig. "This looks like the plant itself was altered."

Jay nodded vigorously. "Sometimes the job was too big and we'd be forced to adapt the plants, meet the environment halfway, so to speak."

"And this is that kind of plant?"

"That's my guess. Like I said, I don't have enough data."

"All right, where would I go to get that data?"

"Someone who manufactures biologicals, I'd say."

Coren thought for a moment, then nodded. "Can I have a copy of this?"

Jay handed him a disk. "Already had it prepared. Do you mind if I keep working on this?"

"I thought it wasn't your field."

"Not now. But who knows what we'll get into since Rega died?"

Coren pocketed the disk and stood. "Let me know if you find anything else, would you?"

"Of course."

Jay turned back to his screens, forgetting about Coren in the time it took to become reabsorbed in his puzzle.

Coren did not return to his office. Disk in hand, he left DyNan and headed for the nearest tubeway.

To his surprise, Myler Towne's people brought him directly into the garden where Coren had first met the new chairman of Imbitek less than three months earlier. The ugly patch of dead foliage he had seen on that initial visit was now a flourishing sprawl of green and yellow.

"Mr. Lanra," Towne said, stepping forward to greet him. "Good to see you again, sir, and good to see you in full health. I heard about your injuries. If possible, I would like to hear about that. May I offer you a beverage?"

"Tea would be fine, thank you. Actually, I'm here for two reasons." He held up the disk Jay had given him. "On this is a preliminary analysis of some plantlife that my people can't fully explain. I thought perhaps, since Imbitek once worked in the field, I might impose on your good graces to help me out."

Towne took the disk, seemed to think about it for a moment, then held it up. An attendant stepped up. "A.S.A.P." The man bowed sharply and hurried off. "And the other?"

"I wanted to find out if that job offer still exists."

Towne's eyebrows raised slowly. He was a big man, broad across the shoulders and deep in the chest, and the gesture somehow made him look even larger. He backed up to his chair and sat down.

"Possibly," he said finally. "Is our analysis of your disk a factor in your decision?"

"No, not really. Since Rega died, things are going on in DyNan that I'm not particularly happy with. I had loyalty to Rega, not his company. I'm open to an offer."

A man with a tray bearing a pitcher and two tall glasses appeared. Coren accepted his tea.

"And your opinion of Imbitek?" Towne asked, taking his own glass.

"Mikels is going to be in prison for a long time, and everything I've seen since you've taken over suggests I would be working for an honest employer."

"I'm flattered by your assessment. I detect a proviso, though."

"I'm working on a last detail on behalf of Rega. I don't know how long it might take, but any change in my status will have to wait till I finish. Could be a week, no more than a month."

"I see. And this disk pertains to that?"

"It does."

"Then let us see how quickly we can resolve your situation. We can discuss it further at that time. But I'm pleased, Mr. Lanra. Have you had lunch yet?"

Lunch was excellent, but Coren was more amazed at the prodigious amounts Myler Towne ate. Coren was not a small man, and he kept himself fit and active, but Towne consumed easily three times what Coren ate. Conversation ran from one topic to another with almost dizzying abruptness, and Coren could not help but feel tested.

Halfway through a long ramble about a vacation in the southern hemisphere in one of the nature preserves, a woman approached the table and whispered to Towne. He looked up.

"Indeed? Interesting." He finished his aperitif and gestured for Coren to follow. "We have something you can take with you."

Coren followed him down a broad, arching corridor. "That was fast."

"Perhaps just luck," Towne said, shrugging. "We *do* have an excellent staff."

They entered a meeting room. A long table dominated, surrounded by plain chairs. A screen covered one wall, opposite a fully-equipped dispenser. One woman waited for them. She was older than anyone else Coren had seen within the walls of Imbitek, her hair white like Alda

Mikels', the former CEO. Her features were sharp and alert. She frowned at Coren as he entered the room, then gave Towne a brief nod.

"You brought this disk?" she asked.

"Yes," Coren answered.

"Where'd you get it?"

"It's an analysis—"

"I *know* what it *is,* young man. I want to know where the sample came from."

"An abandoned research lab called Nova Levis."

She seemed for a few seconds not to believe him. "I'd love to know how it got there. None of this ought to exist on Earth."

"What is it, Dr. Savin?" Towne asked.

"It's actually one of our products," she said. "And it's an interdicted organic. Not allowed on Earth because the processes by which it was originally manufactured are not allowed here anymore." She touched a remote on the table. The wall screen lit with the same displays Coren had seen on Jay's terminals. "Do you know what vonoomans are?"

"Yes. Tiny machines, semi-autonomous—"

"Wrong." She shrugged. "Well, not entirely. That's what they would be today. But it's an incomplete definition for what are now no longer complete examples of vonoomans." She drummed her fingers impatiently on the table, staring at the display.

Towne cleared his throat. "What have you found?"

She started, as if jarred out of a complex thought. "We hold the design rights on the vonoomans that made this grass."

"Imbitek?" Towne asked.

"We were called Imbedded Technologies and Environmental Manipulators, Incorporated, at the time, but essentially, yes. It was fully half our sales right before the first wave of interstellar colonization began."

"You're talking about the Spacers?" Coren asked. "Those colonists?"

"Exactly." She sighed, exasperated. "Let me explain some things."

"I think you had better," Towne said ponderously and sat down.

Dr. Savin glared at Towne. "All right," she said, and folded her hands together at her chin. She seemed to gather herself together mentally. Then she dropped her hands.

"We had two industries back then that literally saved our civilization, if not our lives. We forget how closely what we make determines how long we'll last. And we forget how integrally what we make is a part of who we are. That's probably why we never think about it. It's a tenuous relationship in many ways because it's so easy to break a system up and destroy it. The two industries were cybernetics—robotics, mainly—and nanotech. They went hand-in-glove, couldn't really do one without the other. Nanotech required the machine-logic we got out of cybernetics and robotics required the miniaturization and process-concept of nanotech. That was before the Riots and the Interdicts."

"The Interdicts pertain to robots, though," Towne observed. "There's no mention in them of nanotech."

"Nanotech was phased out and banned more gradually," Dr. Savin said. "Little at a time. By the time the robots were banned, no one really remembered the plagues."

"Plagues?" Coren prompted.

"It's complicated. I could recommend a couple of history texts for the details, but, in essence, we used nanotech to alter ecologies. We had to feed people, and we had a lot of people to feed. Population had leveled off at ten billion, but it fluctuated, and that many mouths put a heavy burden on Earth's resources. The only reason we didn't devolve into absolute chaos was nanotech, which initially proved to be a panacea. We still use it in the home kitchens. Vat production is a direct descendent of agricultural nanotech. Crop yields increased ten, twenty-fold over time."

"What happened?" Towne asked.

"It got away from us. Think of a virus. It invades a cell, analyzes what that cell does, then inserts itself into the machinery of the cell to modify it and use the cell to make copies of itself, releasing those copies to infect other cells and keep the process going. I'm simplifying—or making it more complex, depending how you look at it—but that's what our agro-nans did. They altered the internal machinery of a plant to change what that plant did. Initially, it turned the plant into a super-productive organism, increasing yield. Over time, we found that this put a heavy burden on the soil and there were other problems with simply adding nutrients. So we built some vonoomans that would enter the cycle at an earlier point, in the soil, and increase the efficiency of the bacteria present, increasing nutrient absorption, complimenting the augmented crop demand, and so on. We found we could modify the system from top to bottom. Eventually, we even added some into the food products themselves to increase the efficiency of digestion and cell utilization of the nutrients available."

"You mean, you passed vonoomans into people themselves?" Coren asked.

Dr. Savin nodded. "That's when we started running into problems. We had allergic reactions, new cancers, a variety of metabolic disorders.

Nothing we couldn't adapt for and cope with. Initially, anyway. It got worse."

"How was the population of vonoomans controlled?" Towne asked.

"That's where it got worse. You see, the true definition of a vonooman includes self-replication."

"Oh, dear," Towne said.

Coren glanced from Towne to Savin. " 'Oh dear' what?"

"It was deemed cost effective," Savin went on, "to endow these devices with the ability to manufacture themselves. A small part of the energy involved went to reproduction. The math indicated it would be a self-regulating system. They would never produce more than the necessary quantity to achieve the desired effect."

"But?" Coren prompted.

"Remember the virus. The damn things were designed to analyze environments and adapt to them. We thought that their range was limited, so the need for closer monitoring was unnecessary. In the first assumption, we were correct. In the second... well, we keep learning how very little is necessary to turn a benefit into a disaster."

Coren thought for a moment. "Is this the source of the UPD infections?"

"You know about those, do you?" Dr. Savin asked. "Untreatable Physiological Dysfunction. Yes, they are. Were. Our machines mutated. Just enough. And all hell broke loose for about forty years."

"This isn't widely known."

"No, it isn't. People don't really want to remember, so why help them? It ended, we controlled it. Here, anyway."

"What do you mean?" Towne asked.

"This stuff was our largest export to the new colonies. It was absolutely essential to any terraforming effort on an alien world. The Spacer colonies were just getting started when the plagues began. By the time we were able to control them, the movement had changed from one of simple colonization to a panicked flight of the frightened wealthy. The last four or five Spacer colonies were established by hygienic paranoiacs."

"Like the Solarians," Coren said.

"They're *still* paranoid," Dr. Savin said.

Coren looked at the display. "So what is this?"

"This is a variety of hardy grass which was used early on to supplant indigenous flora on colony worlds. Very versatile. In this form, it carried its own potential colony of agronan machines. The plant manufactured them upon taking root in new soil and the machines would begin analyzing soil and atmosphere and returning that data to the plant itself to begin modifying it. While the plant was adapting, the vonoomans were spreading in the biosphere and changing it. Over several generations, the grass would literally remake the ecology and prepare it for other, less adaptable varieties. Originally, it was a variety of palm grass, *setaria palmifolia*. Common name was Burundi Grass."

"That," Towne said, "sounds familiar. Not in this context."

"No, not in this context," Dr. Savin said sardonically. "Burundi's Fever."

"Ah," Towne said, nodding. He pointed. "From this?"

"We think so. Frankly, given the nature of Burundi's Fever, the records are questionable."

"I've heard the name," Coren said. "But..."

"The Spacers have a different name for it," Savin said. "They call it mnemonic plague."

Coren thanked Myler Towne—and Dr. Savin, though she did not seem to hear—and returned to his private office. All the way back he thought of Ariel. Mnemonic plague...she had mentioned to him once that she had suffered it, that it, in fact, linked her with Derec Avery. They had been talking about the past and about their lives and her own story ended abruptly, and she had admitted that, beyond a certain point—beyond, it turned out, her first visit to Earth—she had no real memory of her life. The plague had destroyed her access to it, blocked her off with permanent amnesia—permanent because it was not induced psychically, but synaptically.

We're both orphans, he thought, *each in our own way...*

He avoided thinking about the larger implications of what he had learned. Too much, too fast, and far outside the scope of his immediate interests.

Still, he had to admit that it explained a lot of the history of Earther and Spacer. It explained, for instance, the initial reluctance on the part of the Spacers to agree to a new colony program, to accept the Settler worlds. Fear of infection. A fear which had subsequently proven false, but certainly based on a real threat far in the past. Spacers even lived on Earth now, few though they were, and interacted with Terrans. What kept them apart now was more attitude than pathology.

But none of this explained why that grass had been in the abandoned shell of Nova Levis Research Labs, or how it had gotten there.

He opened the door to his office and stepped inside.

Hofton was there, again, waiting. Hofton stood.

"Mr. Lanra," he said quietly, without preamble, "I have a message from Ambassador Setaris. She is—we are—that is, Aurora—very interested in taking some action concerning Gamelin. She would like to discuss it with you in person."

17

MASID ALREADY knew a few of Filoo's agents. In the next days after his meeting with Rekker, Masid noticed a change in their attitude when he arrived at the bazaar. Before, they watched him the way they watched all freelance merchants and dealers, warily, but with no special attention. Now they seemed to be talking about him, paying closer attention, noting who bought from him.

Masid arrived at the open market on the fourth morning to be met by three visibly armed men. He slowed to a stop a couple meters from them. He recognized one as an agent of Filoo, but not the other two. One was short and stocky with a thick growth of beard, the other taller and clean-shaven.

"'Morning," Masid said.

"Yes, it is," Filoo's man said. "Got a minute to talk some business?"

"Sure."

"Privately."

Masid glanced left and right. He gestured. "Café over there, nobody there yet this early."

"We had a more private place in mind."

"I'm sure, but I might not like what you have to say. I prefer to find my way back after a disagreement."

The agent shook his head, about to say more, when the stocky one grunted. The agent turned the gesture into a yawn and shrugged. "No way you'll dislike what we have to say. But why not?" He craned his neck to peer at the café. "Gorim's. They have good coffee. Sure."

"After you," Masid said.

Masid trailed after the trio, keeping five meters between them. He watched the buyers and dealers to see if anyone followed him, but it seemed everyone else was too busy to notice.

Gorim kept his place bright up front, but the tables in back fell quickly into darkness. Candles flickered on each one. Masid found his three hosts waiting around one, their faces lit grimly by the fragile tongue of flame between them.

"All right," Masid said, turning a chair around to straddle. He rested his arms on the back. "You have a proposal."

"We've been watching you," the agent said.

Masid held up a hand. " 'We'? Who's that? And what's your name?"

"Kar," the agent said. He jerked a thumb at the clean-shaven one. "Tosher."

Masid looked at the stocky one. "That makes you Filoo."

The man stared silently at Masid for a long moment, then nodded. "Kar thinks I shouldn't do my own negotiations. We have a disagreement about that. So we play this little game, which I always said was stupid." He glared at Kar.

"This is the first time anybody's figured it," Kar protested weakly.

"One time too many," Filoo said. He shrugged. "Security. When is it too much?"

"When you no longer enjoy doing what you're doing," Masid said.

Filoo looked surprised, then laughed quietly. "You've been selling steady for weeks now. What's your supply?"

Masid started to rise.

"Whoa, whoa—" Kar said, one hand going into his jacket.

Filoo touched Kar's shoulder. "Patience. What's the problem? Question too difficult?"

"Question isn't welcome. I don't even know you and you think you can ask me something personal like that? Stick to neutral topics on a first meet, like who my mother's sleeping with, or who you think you owe credit to, but nothing personal."

"Sit down," Filoo said, a faint smile on his lips. "We can go slow, long as it doesn't take forever. We're in the same business, that's all. I've been at it a little longer—makes me confident I know a few things."

"But you don't know where I get my supplies," Masid said, still standing. "Does that make us competitors or potential partners?"

"Depends. I have a large operation. When anything gets big enough, certain errors creep into the accounting."

"You've got a leak. You want to know if it's me." He shook his head.

"I'm not stupid enough to steal from someone who can kill me as an afterthought."

Filoo patted the table before Masid's still vacant chair. "Not stupid. Confident. Arrogant. Cocky. One or two successes make a man think he can get away with something all the time. Playing the odds doesn't make him stupid."

"Playing something you don't know does," Masid said. He sat down. "All right. I have my own source, unconnected to anybody. I own it, it's all mine. I don't need to steal from anybody."

"There are no independent sources," Kar said.

"Is that confidence or arrogance talking?" Masid asked. "Or wishful thinking?" He looked at Filoo. "It's not a large source, just enough to keep me in consumables and a roof, so I doubt it would ever damage your trade. With all the sick people, we'll both be forever dolling out pharmaceuticals. But if you have a security problem, then so do I."

"Really?" Filoo asked. "How so?"

"Until you fix it, you'll be thinking I have something to do with it. That's not going to be good for friendly relations."

"Sounds like you have a fine appreciation of the situation. What would you propose to deal with it?"

"Well, you have a few options. The quickest is you can order your cocks here to kill me. I might be a problem, if not now then further down the line. I might, for all you know, be the source of your leak."

"You claim not, though."

"Why should you believe me? Kill me and be done with it. If it turns out you were wrong about the leak, you might be right about the future problem. Of course, that leaves you then with your leak. It'll probably stop for a while, till it seems you're satisfied, but it'll start up again. A thief is never content with well-enough. So after a few months or a year, once again you'll be trying to scratch an itch you can't find. Annoying."

"Very. Another option, then?"

"You can ask me to move to another district. Same consequences apply, except then you might lose track of me. That could be a problem later on. A third option would be to hire me to find your leak. Short-term contract, bring in an outsider to hunt down your thief, and when it's over we go our separate ways."

"Of course," Filoo said, grinning, "that leaves you as a potential problem further down the line."

"Of course. So if I were you, I'd just hire me as a subcontractor. You get a percentage, I operate as usual, but with the added protection of your organization, and if I learn anything at all about your leak, then I'm honor-bound to let you know about it."

Filoo leaned back in his chair. A waiter brought a tray then with a carafe and cups and a plate of sweetcakes.

Filoo poured coffee for everyone, then took a cake. "Of course, there is one more option: I could buy you out, source and all, and simply bind you to me."

"To do what? Sell or run security? What would that prove?"

"Prove? Nothing. It would just keep you in reach." He chewed a mouthful of cake thoughtfully. "How would you go about finding a leak?"

"Hypothetically?"

"Whatever."

"Watch the market," Masid said. "Track the buys, see who is no longer buying from you who used to. See if anyone is buying in larger than normal quantities. Find out why they changed. Trace it back."

"You sound like a cop," Kar said.

"Oh," Masid said, "that's such an ugly accusation. Of course, there's another way. Riskier."

"That doesn't concern me just now," Filoo said. "What does is your response to my offer."

"You made an offer?"

"I did."

Masid thought for a few seconds. "I don't really need a partner."

"Perhaps not. Maybe I need a favor."

Masid looked across the table at Kar. "Give me a few days to think about it?"

"Three. I expect an answer in three days."

Masid lifted his cup and breathed in the aroma of fresh, expensive coffee. Doubtless Gorim carried it exclusively for Filoo. Masid met Filoo's gaze over the rim of the cup and nodded.

One of Masid's customers paid him with a wad of scrip for six ampules of dexanadrine-H derivative, a wide-range antibiotic which, as far as Masid had been able to tell since arriving on Nova Levis, did absolutely nothing to any of the pathogens killing the population. Folded within the wad of currency he found a list of names and a note:

These are my designated dealers. F.

Seven names. Masid pocketed the list and did a slow circuit through the bazaar, checking his memory against the names. Since starting here, he had identified everyone who sold regularly. He made two more deals before locating and identifying all seven under the tent, then quit for the day and headed back to the apartment.

His rooms had been searched twice—once, he discovered, while he drank coffee with Filoo. They were very careful about it, and Masid only knew because he had placed tells around the apartment. He had his little factory locked in a cabinet with a very obvious self-destruct device. No one had yet dared to try to open it, but by now Filoo probably guessed what Masid kept hidden within.

He deactivated the device and opened the doors wide. His machines hummed faintly. The complex soup he had set his synthesizer to brewing that morning was ready. He took it upstairs to Tilla.

Tilla smiled wanly while he did a quick blood analysis and then administered the concoction. He imagined sometimes that she looked better, but the numbers told a different story. He had managed to fight some of the infections to a standstill—one of them was actually in abeyance—but he had no illusions of saving her life. He was postponing an inevitable battle that Tilla would lose. He had prepared another kind of ministration for that day. Till then, she was more comfortable, more alert. But it was temporary and both of them understood that.

"So Filoo wants you to solve his problem," she said after he told her about the meeting. "Which means you have your way in. If you succeed."

"Has he had this problem before?"

"They've all had this problem. It's not possible to avoid having it. They're criminals, after all, what can they expect? But Filoo specifically...yes, he did. About five months ago, he purged four people from his organization. I never learned the specifics, I was getting pretty sick by then."

"Any idea how he solved it?"

"Sure. Kar uncovered it."

"Kar."

She looked at him narrowly. "You're not surprised."

"No, but I can't tell you why I'm not."

"Lizard Sense."

"What?" Masid laughed.

"The woman who trained me, old-time Special Service. Good cop. She told me that all the profiles, all the M.O. analyses, all the criminal psychology seminars—none of them worked half so well as what she called the 'Lizard Sense.' She said an experienced cop just knows. You develop it over time, if you pay attention, and you can just tell. A thousand little details all compressed into a single impression. You look at someone and you know they're wrong. You saw it in Kar, even if you didn't know what it was. Now that I've told you the important detail, you put it all together. You're not surprised because you saw something about him that makes him suspect."

"I still needed that piece of data."

"Yes, and you would have found it, and something would go *click!* and you'd just know."

"Where did Kar come from?"

"He's from another district. I never found out. Frankly, I lost interest shortly afterward."

"So how do I prove it?"

"Do what you told Filoo you would do. Run him down. Trace his connections. Do the math."

"Then what?"

"Then...see what Filoo gives you. If it's a way in, you follow it."

"What if it takes me out of touch with you?" Masid asked.

"Did you come here to nurse a sick agent or find criminals?"

Masid grunted. "Hell of a choice."

"Life is full of little inconveniences," Tilla said wryly. "Get to work."

Masid watched her as her eyes fell shut. Her breathing deepened into the now-familiar sonority of sleep and he left her.

Mia read the decrypted message, dismayed and gratified at the same time. *Ariel's back on Aurora...*

But Hofton had convinced Coren Lanra to help. Surprises usually came in groups.

A new agent *had* been sent—or had come on his own initiative, depending how you looked at it. She found it doubtful whether bypassing channels on the assumption that someone within the security community was a mole would guarantee that he would reach the surface. But, if the coded transmission she had received from the surface could be believed, he *had* succeeded.

Masid Vorian. She did not know the name. According to Hofton, he had been attached to Sipha Palen's Kopernik Station security, seconded from Settler Coalition Intelligence in a novel arrangement that had kept Masid out of the usual files. Mia remembered Sipha—novel arrangements were a given with her—and had been saddened to learn of her death. According to Hofton, Vorian had gone deep cover after Palen's demise and only his destination was known.

She would have to trust what she did not know—how good was he?

Well, if he had managed to get down there alive and locate the last—presumed dead—team, then Mia assumed he was pretty good.

Coren Lanra had investigated the bookseller. Omne Mundi Complurium was, for the most part, legitimate, a dealer in rare books, works of art, and occasional unclassifiable antiquities. Unsurprisingly, they also dealt in contraband of various sorts, restricted imports and exports, even, on a few occasions, robotics. It existed on the edge, not quite criminal enough to be shut down, especially as a substantial part of its trade was to wealthy and influential citizens, several of whom were part of the Terran government. Lanra estimated that over eighty percent of their material traffic was legitimate, but that nearly half their profit came from illicit trade.

Three of their customers had drawn Lanra's interest in particular.

The Hunter Group, which was a consortium of offworld businesses that owned, by extension, several large companies on Earth. They bought the largest quantity of old books. What they did with them after they left the planet, Lanra did not know.

Ambassador Gale Chassik had been a customer. Most of his purchases—books—had gone back to Solaria.

Lastly, Commander Reen.

Reen . . .

Mia forced her attention back on to the communiqué. Hunter, Lanra claimed, owned a good portion of the development on Nova Levis, or had until the blockade.

"We suspect Hunter to be the legitimate face of Kynig Parapoyos," he said. "It would give him a legal presence through a huge segment of the Settler colonies."

Kynig Parapoyos . . . Mia absently rubbed her left thigh, where bullets from rifles obtained from Parapoyos had torn open her flesh over a year ago. The dull ache all the way to the bone was more illusion now than real, but it still bothered her.

Mia wondered how the three were connected. Parapoyos, Chassik, and Reen.

But Chassik was dead now, killed by pirates. What had become of all his purchases from Omne Mundi Complurium? Were they even related to this?

It seemed a stretch, but she doubted Lanra would have mentioned it if he did not think a connection existed.

But Reen...

Mia read on. The books she had locked in her desk were all purchases Reen had made. He had an agent on Earth who bought them for him, whom Lanra was continuing to investigate.

So what had Corf been doing with them? And had Reen been aware of the encrypted tables in the endpapers?

Mia rubbed her eyes. She had to assume he did. Which meant he knew what they contained, which meant he was aware of the shipments, which meant—

Reen had been running his department ragged trying to find the source of the contraband shipments to Nova Levis. She had to admire his skill at making sure they intercepted just enough to make it appear progress had been made. She had likewise to be disgusted with herself for not recognizing the scenario.

If I hadn't found those books, would I be any closer?

Mia opened her encryption program and began carefully composing a response to the new agent, Masid Vorian. She had no instructions for now, she only wanted him to know her name.

Hers and Reen's.

Tilla was sleeping when Masid checked on her that evening. He ran down the numbers on her portable diagnostic and found a reassuring change in her leukocyte count, but not much else.

He entered the kitchen and found Kru preparing what was locally called a flatmeat pie. She glared at him the way she usually did, then ignored him.

There was always a certain amount of luck in every deep cover job, he knew, and it always centered on the people you simply had to trust. Time and lack of thorough knowledge about a place offered too little opportunity to run an operation as securely as good sense dictated. Judgment calls about the people you encountered meant risking error and, consequently, your life.

Masid had learned to trust his sense of people; he was good at sorting them into plus and minus columns and acting accordingly. Once in a while, though, he found himself with no easy answer and he had to go along anyway, hoping.

He had learned nothing useful about Kru other than that she was a superb scavenger and she was profoundly in love with Tilla. She had tentatively accepted Masid into their tiny circle because Tilla said to, but Masid knew he would never know when or if Kru would ever trust him. Not knowing, daily relying on her when he felt certain she would just as soon see him dead, added an edge to every decision he made.

Without a word to Kru, he took the back steps down to his own apartment.

A short woman in a heavy jacket sat on his sofa, going through some papers on the low table in front of her. She looked up at him, then lifted a sidearm from the seat beside her and set it loudly on the table.

Masid's right hand slipped into his coat pocket and touched the blaster.

"Marshal Toranz," he said. "Do you have a warrant, or did I just forget that we had a date?"

She shook her head. "I don't like humor when I'm working."

"Ah. That assumes I'm joking."

She looked at him blandly. "No, I don't have a warrant. We don't have a local magistrate—he died—therefore no one to issue such permissions. So, given that I'm the last official with anything like legal authority, I grant myself the necessary warrants to do what I think best to protect this town."

"And right now that means letting yourself into my home?"

She jerked a thumb toward his cabinet. "That's got an ID-sensitive explosive attached to it. What's in there?"

"Nothing I intend to show you."

Toranz stood, sighing loudly. "Look, I've done this job for the last six years. The last two have been under progressively worse circumstances and I've seen damn near all my staff die, either from disease or from being stupid. I'm still here. I say all this to impress upon you the fact that I am reasonably good at my job. I have a very simple policy: Screw with me and I kill you." She looked significantly at the cabinet. "What's in there?"

"You kill me for refusing to show you, you'll never find out anyway."

Toranz lifted the blaster.

"I have simple policies, too," Masid said. "One is, never trust someone who's too easy with a threat. I'll tell you what, Marshal. Go away now and we can both live a little longer. All I do is what I need to get by. I'm no threat to you."

"No, but you may upset some of the locals."

"That was true a week ago. Two weeks ago. Why'd it take you this long to get around to me?"

"Big caseload." She gestured toward the cabinet. "Open it, jackass, or the conversation ends now."

Masid shifted his hand to the small wafer alongside the blaster. He pressed the contact.

A heavy scent of ozone filled the room. Toranz stiffened visibly and Masid flinched, unsure whether she had the safety on her blaster. No bolt came. She began to tremble a little.

Masid released the button and she dropped abruptly onto the couch, the blaster clattering to the floor. Her eyes began fluttering rapidly.

Masid kicked her weapon away. He found her cuffs and secured her wrists. She felt clammy now, her skin blanching from the aftermath of the stunner.

"Sorry about that," Masid said. "I couldn't find enough juice for a short burst that would do any good, so I rigged the field to just squeeze you. I'll probably have to replace the batteries now." He unzipped her jacket and searched for ID. He found her folder and opened it. A tarnished shield glowed dully in the halflight from the windows. Behind it, he found a thick sheaf of local currency. "Well, now, who pays your salary these days? If you're the top official left in town, no one's issuing payroll. Or do you just collect it as fines and fees?"

A soft beeping began from within the cabinet. Toranz was barely conscious, but her eyes drifted in that direction. Masid pulled her forward, then yanked the jacket up, over her head, covering her face.

He opened the cabinet. Within, his hyperlink chimed with an incoming message. He checked quickly, then shunted it into the decryptor and closed the cabinet door.

"You shit..." Toranz breathed when he bared her face.

"I am that." He continued going through her pockets. He found a wallet of ampules and a hypodermic gun. "For you? Or do you deal on the side? Considering the environment of this place, there can't be too much law enforcement going on."

"How come...how come you didn't...aren't stunned, too...?"

"Special underwear. Trade secret."

Masid laid everything he had found out on the table, then pulled up a chair and sat opposite Toranz.

"Your shield, a palm stunner, hypo, some kind of broad spectrum antipathogen, a few hundred in currency, business cards, and a portable comm. Not much to go on, but timing counts for something. You work for Filoo, don't you? Or you work for one of his agents." Masid grinned. "That's it, isn't it? He's worried about a leak in his organization. He wouldn't send *you* to check me out, he's already done that, I'm sure. You're here on behalf of the thief in his house."

"I'm an officer of the law."

"That's crap. There is no law, or Filoo wouldn't be able to operate. So what was it you were supposed to do here? Find my supply and destroy it? Find out where I'm from? Set a trap for me? Plant evidence, maybe?"

She blinked rapidly, fighting the stun effect. Masid stood and went to his bedroom. He took a palm monitor from his pocket and set it to analyze for certain chemical traces, then increased the range. Within a few minutes he found a packet of ampules taped beneath his bed. When he brought them out, Toranz's eyes widened.

"Thank you, Marshal Toranz," he said with mock graciousness. "You have shown me the error of my ways. I promise I'll lead a better life." He sat down and opened the packet. Small black bands encircled each one. "Tagged, I'll bet. Easy to identify. Of course, if I were the real thief, I'd remove these as soon as I got them. But how else would Filoo be convinced that these are really his? They *are* his, aren't they? Shall we go have a talk with him and see?"

"Won't prove anything. You still stole them."

"Ah, but I have *you*. That changes things a bit." Masid shook his head. "You might have waited a day. This was really clumsy. Unless..." He laughed.

"What?"

"Unless you were set up just like me. Odds were really good that I'd just kill you. Or you'd kill me and the whole problem would take care of itself. If I killed you, then all I'd have is a dead cop and Filoo's property. If you killed me, well, we know how that would look. But whoever sent you probably expected me to kill you. Best would have been we killed each other. No explanations at all. But if you'd killed me, how long do you think you'd live?"

"I've lived this long."

"With someone's protection, obviously. And someone's pharmacy, I'd say. That protection is now withdrawn. If I was dead and they found Filoo's merchandise here, they would also find out who killed me, and Filoo would want to know what you were doing here and how really the whole scenario happened in the first place. The thief couldn't defend you without revealing himself, so you'd be abandoned."

Masid glimpsed doubt in her eyes. He remained silent for a time. Then he leaned forward. "Why don't you tell me all about it?"

"Why don't you sodomize yourself?"

"Ah, so I'm right. Well, that's good enough. I can wait."

She scowled. "For what?"

"Someone to come fetch you."

Masid took a stunner from his other pocket and shot her. She convulsed for a few moments, then slumped over. Masid looked over her belongings again.

"Better check all this stuff for hidden surprises," he said, going to his cabinet.

The decryptor flashed that the message was ready, decoded. He glanced at Toranz, then pressed OPEN.

18

EREC WATCHED the robot handlers bring out the cases that contained everything of importance that he had brought with him. Bogard lay within one of them, and the bulk of Thales, mostly memory storage that enabled the RI to function at peak efficiency, filled several. He imagined—tried to imagine—what kind of relief Thales would experience after months of forced constraint within a too-small buffer on Earth.

Clearance through Auroran Customs had been disconcertingly simple. A robot scanned his passport and visas, asked a few perfunctory questions about his intentions on Aurora (when he had explained—or started to explain—about the recall from the Calvin Institute, the robot seemed to hesitate, then moved on to another set of questions), and inquired about his needs. A human reviewed his manifest, asked about Thales, and then peremptorily accepted his answers and passed him through. Derec was used to the way Earth worked, with delays and inspections, and a pervasive paranoia that refused to accept anything just on the word of the subject.

Within minutes, he had been assigned a team of robots that brought him to this bay and began unloading his property. He still expected to be detained and waited for the error to be caught and police to fetch him.

"Derec."

He lurched around, his heart kicking. CPO Craym stood at the top of the ramp from which cargo emerged. She wore her uniform this morning, but gave him a very nonregulation wave and smile. He waved back, flush with relief, and gestured for her to come down.

A pair of floating extensions accompanied her now, hovering above each shoulder, their dull bronzed bodies twisting through complex revolutions. Derec had seen them become more and more common among the Spacer passengers the nearer to Aurora the *Wysteria* drew.

"I'll be off-duty in a few hours," she said. "Did you need help?"

"Loading, no. Finding my new apartment..."

"Do you have an address?"

He handed her his visa. She pulled out a hand reader and slipped it in. She frowned. "They're kidding, surely." She looked at the crates piling up on the dock. "These are yours?"

"Yes..."

"Somebody moved you into a student facility on the outskirts of the Calvin. This will never fit. You'll be forced to leave most of it in storage."

Derec started. "I specifically requested—"

"I can fix it. Give me some time. Meanwhile..."

Derec watched her cross the dock and enter an office. A few minutes later she returned, followed by an Auroran official. The man brought with him a constellation of extensions of various sizes, the largest nearly twenty centimeters in diameter.

The extensions assumed wider orbits as the man stopped within handshake distance of Derec (though he refrained from offering his hand). Derec watched the small devices warily for a few moments.

"Mr. Avery," he said, "I'm Flar Desko, coordinator for Eos import control. Chief Petty Officer Craym has just informed me of an error in your accommodations."

"It's been a very, very long time since I've been...home..." Derec cleared his throat, feeling it catch at the word. "My housing assignment, I'm informed, will be inadequate for my needs." He waved at the crates. "I have a lot of material I need to set up."

Flar Desko frowned at the crates. "All this is...?"

"Mostly an RI."

His eyes flickered briefly. He turned his head slightly to the left. "Darius, do you copy?" A moment later, he nodded. "Good. See to it." He focused on Derec. "My apologies. A new set of accommodations is being prepared. Give us a few minutes and I'll have a transport for you and a robot to take you there."

"Thank you."

"No problem, Mr. Avery. Welcome home."

He spun around and walked away.

"I suppose I should really thank *you,*" Derec said to Clin.

"Of course. Dinner tonight would be sufficient."

"Of course."

Derec watched her stride back up the ramp, into the ship. If anything or anyone had gone a long way toward making him feel welcome, she had.

Why...?

He slapped the thought down. *Leftover paranoia,* he thought.

Bay doors scrolled up, letting in a flood of warm light. A big hauler backed into the dock, and robots emerged from its rear to begin loading Derec's property.

He walked around the transport and stepped onto the exterior apron.

A road led arrow-straight into the slender towers and mushroom domes of Eos City, capital of Aurora, twenty kilometers away. Morning sun covered their porcelain and jeweler's brass shapes with a thick, buttery glow. The sky above—the *sky!* open and unobstructed by a canopy—was greener than Earth's, almost turquoise in the yellower light of Tau Ceti, but it did not matter. It was sky and it was beautiful.

Between the port and the city stretched savanna, grasses waving in teasing winds, like undulant waves on the oceans of Terra.

Within moments, all Derec's trepidation and ambivalence about coming here dispersed. It was too lovely to fear, too familiar, in spite of his handicapped memory, to deny.

"Sir."

He turned toward a tall, elegantly-formed robot.

"Yes?"

"We have loaded everything," the robot said. "We are ready to take you to your domicile."

"You have the address?"

"Yes, sir. Would you care to enter the transport?"

"Of course."

Derec climbed aboard the big hauler and took a seat up front, before the piloting console. The canopy gave him a full 180° view. He settled into the comfortable couch.

"Your restraining field is now active," the console informed him. "Please do not attempt to leave your seat during transit. Are there any physical or mental conditions with which we should be aware to ensure your safety and comfort?"

"No."

"Prepare for departure."

The transport lifted gently and moved out of the dock. As it picked up speed, Derec felt a moment of exhilaration that surprised him. He thought he would never be pleased to return to Aurora—the entire journey here, save for the two periods he had spent with Clin, had been a constant emersion in anxiety and resentment.

But now, with Eos drawing visibly closer, he felt a welcome anticipation.

Details separated out from the amalgam of smooth shapes. There did not seem to be a sharp edge or straight line throughout the Byzantine maze of the city. He picked out the lights in individual rooms, railings around balconies, external lifts traversing the multistoried height of various structures. As the transport entered Eos, he began to notice the patina of wear and age on surfaces—but an elegant stain, in oil-on-water colors over pale porcelain skins. He could see people on the streets and occasionally inside vast rooms. Other vehicles shot past him, small private craft as well as large work transports like this one.

Near the center of Eos he recognized what he thought to be public structures and official buildings. He knew the council building well enough, with its collection of melon-and-egg-shaped shells, and opposite it rose the slender towers of the resource administration offices.

The transport dropped to a lower altitude and veered right. Beyond the towers of resource administration, a series of gracefully curving walls rose. Lower still, and Derec spotted a loading platform at the base of the third wall from the government buildings.

"Prepare for landing," the console informed him.

The transport settled lightly on the platform.

"Your restraint is off, Mr. Avery. Welcome to Harisom Domiciles. An escort will meet you to take you directly to your new quarters. We will unload your possessions and bring them up shortly thereafter."

"Thank you," Derec said, standing.

A humaniform met him at the door of the transport. The pale eyes and slightly artificial texture of the face covering gave it away at a glance. As he spoke with it, Derec noted the lack of any expression. He was aware that some humaniforms had been constructed that fully mimicked human physical attributes, but he had never seen one. This unit was as close as most people ever saw. On Earth, he had grown used to referring to any bipedal, bilaterally symmetric robot as humaniform, but here there were subtler distinctions.

"Mr. Avery?" it inquired.

"Yes."

"I am Denis, your liaison and orientation advisor. Are you comfortable with this arrangement?"

Derec hesitated. "What arrangement?"

"Having a humaniform robot in this capacity."

"Why wouldn't I be?"

"You have just arrived from Earth. I understand that you have spent several years there. It is possible you have adopted attitudes which may cause discomfort in the presence of—"

"I haven't. You'll do."

"Very good, sir. If you will please follow me, I will take you to your domicile."

Derec fell into step half-a-pace behind the robot. He studied it as they walked. It seemed clothed in pale blue, neck to toe. It came up to Derec's jawline in height and appeared to be modeled on an athlete's build.

"Do you anticipate remaining on Aurora long, Mr. Avery?"

"I don't know. I do not anticipate returning to Earth. Why?"

"The length of your residence will determine the level of robot assignment. I will continue in this capacity until such time as you may decide to replace me, or until you otherwise change your residential arrangements." Denis glanced at him. "You have no personal robots now?"

"I do, but it's currently deactivated."

"Do you intend to activate it?"

"It requires repair. Once that's done, I may."

"That will also determine my continuing as your liaison."

They passed beneath a broad archway into the building. Their steps echoed off the high ceilings. Derec looked back after several strides to see the glow of open daylight once more.

Denis led him to an elevator. It took them up six floors and opened into the apartment.

Derec stared. He had never had so much personal space on the surface of a planet.

The furnishings were plain and unobtrusive—sofas, chairs, low tables—but pleasingly elegant. The windows let in ample sunlight. Derec went from room to room. Huge bed, a fully-equipped kitchen, closets everywhere. He stopped before five human-sized depressions in the wall of what he assumed to be a guest bedroom.

Wall niches for robots. Empty. He tried to remember the ratio of robots to humans on Aurora—twenty-to-one?—and wondered if there was a social hierarchy attached to number of servants.

The floor was tiled, but his feet seemed to sink a few millimeters as he walked. He entered another guestroom he took to be an extra bedroom, but all he found in the spacious room were more robot niches, counter-tops, and a computer station.

"Do you have a question?" Denis asked from the doorway.

"Um...what's this for?" Derec gestured at the room.

"Your lab, sir. I was given to understand that you required one. Is there a problem?"

Derec blinked, amazed. "No. No problem at all."

Ariel encountered two security guards at the shuttle egress. They presented their IDs and asked her to accompany them, then led her to a small office a short distance from the public Customs inspection station.

A man looked up from the flatscreen on his desk when she entered. "Ambassador Burgess?"

"Yes."

He looked at the guards. "Leave us."

When they left, he gestured Ariel to sit.

"I'm Chief of Planetary Security, Pon Byris," he said. "Forgive the intrusion, but I must ask you a few questions which may seem unusual."

"No problem," Ariel said.

"You gave us notification of Ambassador Eliton's presence on board the *Wysteria*. Were you aware of any reason we might wish to detain him?"

"Not specifically, but I thought it was a safe assumption no one here knew of his presence on board. On the off-chance that you might want to talk to him..."

Byris nodded and glanced at his screen. "Have you been in contact with anyone here other than through Ambassador Setaris?"

"No," Ariel answered.

"No personal communications?"

"No. If you have my records open, you know I did not leave behind any personal relations. My family has never acknowledged me since my original exile—"

"You were not exiled, Ambassador—"

Ariel held up a hand. "I don't want to get into semantics over it. I was asked to leave due to a medical condition. When I was finally allowed back, no one who previously knew me wanted anything to do with me. Call it what you like, I had no ties to sever when I accepted my posting on Earth."

Byris pursed his lips thoughtfully. "Has that in any way affected your feelings toward Aurora?"

"Any specific way you had in mind?"

"Politically."

"I'm sorry, I don't quite follow."

"Would you say you harbor any animosities toward Aurora as a result of your treatment?"

"You're questioning my loyalty?"

"I'm trying to determine whether or not you would have any cause to sympathize with those who might wish Aurora harm."

Ariel laughed. "Frankly, I might if I knew anyone who does. But those I knew who *do* wish Aurora harm I left behind on Earth. And they were all Terrans. If you've read my reports, you know I worked against them."

"I've read the reports, I know what Ambassador Setaris thinks of you. I wanted to get a sense of it myself."

"To answer your original question, no, I have been in communication with no one here until my message concerning Ambassador Eliton."

"I see. Tell me, Ambassador, did you have much personal contact with the survivors of the Humadros Legation?"

"I had none."

Byris looked surprised. "But I thought—"

"All our communication was through commlinks. I never actually met any one of them on Earth. I tried to set up meetings, but..."

"I see. You spoke to them, though?"

"I spoke to one: Benen Yarick. She attempted to fulfill the legation mission—"

"None of the others?"

"No."

He looked troubled.

"You can verify all this through my logs," she said.

"Oh, I believe you, Ambassador." He cleared his throat. "We've placed Ambassador Eliton in protective custody in the Judicial Complex. Is there any reason you wish to speak to him?"

"No. I imagine the Council has more than enough to talk to him about."

"Very good. Then, I only want to ask what you intend to do, and if you are willing to appear upon request of the Courts at any hearings concerning your tenure on Earth and matters involving Ambassador Eliton."

"I intend finding quarters," Ariel said, "taking a long nap, and waiting for a new assignment, assuming one is forthcoming. Of course I'll make myself available. I imagine that I would be subpoenaed in any case."

"Of course, but a statement of cooperation on record now can save time and inconvenience. A formality, that's all."

"I see. Then, if there's nothing else...?"

"We're finished. Thank you. Oh, and please register your address with my office as soon as you have it."

"Register with Planetary Security?"

"Yes."

"That's unusual, isn't it?"

"New policy in place since the Nova Levis blockade. Again, just a formality. No need to register with anyone else once you do so with us."

"Nova Levis...of course."

She stood.

Byris resumed studying his flatscreen. When Ariel reached the door, he said, "Welcome home, Ambassador. Enjoy your stay."

Ariel stepped out of the office, feeling unsettled. *Nova Levis...it's affecting everything...*

Ariel passed through customs after only a brief, innocuous interrogation, and strode into the main reception area of the port. The chamber sprawled, a vast expanse beneath a pearl-white dome suspended by delicate arching arms, between which stretched huge windows letting in the golden light of Tau Ceti. People moved in Brownian trajectories, followed by robots of various types as well as the orbiting "electron" shells of their personal extensions. Ariel remembered the tech from her days at the Calvin, but back then only a few wealthy Aurorans and government officials used them. Now it appeared everyone possessed a cadre of floating eyes, ears, and sensors, all attached to a homebased RI.

Eos Port did not seem crowded, but Ariel knew that was illusory. Union Station in D.C. on Earth, huge as it was, could fit within this single chamber. One-person transports were available at numerous stations throughout. Most Aurorans chose to walk.

Ariel moved anxiously, surveying the scene. Robots stood on pedestals at wide intervals, giving information or stepping down to provide assistance. She saw no lines, no booths, no official desks. As she scanned the scene, she felt disturbed that no party of officials had come to meet her. Only that single, troubling interview with the head of Planetary Security...and no one else. She had passed his inspection and now could safely be let loose on Aurora.

She almost laughed. She needed to adjust her expectations. Things happened at a different pace, in a different order on Aurora. She knew there would be more questions in due course; Byris had all but promised her that, with his request for a "statement of cooperation" for the courts. There was no need here, after having passed any reasonable security check on board ship, above on the station, and now on the ground, to embarrass her or cause unnecessary alarm among the rest of the people present by treating her as a potential threat. Respect, especially between fellow Aurorans, if not genuinely felt, was always practiced.

We are not Terrans...

But even though she had told Byris that she had no one here, some part of her still expected—

"Ariel!"

She stopped abruptly at the sound of her name spoken by a familiar voice. She looked around. At first she saw no one she knew. Then—

He came toward her energetically, one hand half-raised in greeting. Ariel recognized the hair first—lead gray and uncharacteristically long and disheveled by Auroran standards—then the wide, gleeful grin. He wore a brilliant red shirt above grayish-white pants. He was slightly heavier than the average Auroran, a bit shorter, and clearly less reserved.

"Ariel, I thought you'd run right out of here and never see me."

Ariel felt her face tug into a smile. "Dr. Penj?"

Two younger-looking assistants hurried in his wake.

"Well, you haven't forgotten, then," he said loudly. "I would have been crushed if you had, even more so since you haven't sent me any kind of correspondence since you left for Earth."

He stopped in front of her and raised his arms, hands spread as if to seize her by the shoulders. He looked down at her feet and brought his gaze slowly up to her face.

"You look tired but on the whole better. Terrans must agree with you."

"I've met a few who weren't terrible. Dr. Penj..."

"You know better than that. 'Rolf' it is, and 'Rolf' it had better remain." He turned. "These are my current aides: Yvon and Farlos. And before you ask—human, yes. I left Binder behind. He can be a pest when it comes to Terrans. He still considers anyone from Earth a source of infection. Embarrassing."

Ariel started laughing.

"What?" Rolf Penj asked with mock indignation. "All these years and you laugh at me? She thinks I'm amusing," he said to his aides. "That's only because I am, of course, but I'm not trying to be now and she's laughing. You can see how she must have been as a student, always reacting in exactly the wrong way during class."

Ariel saw smiles playing on the more ideally Auroran faces of Yvon and Farlos. She stifled herself.

"You evidently haven't changed a bit," she said.

Penj's thick eyebrows rose. "I hope not. It took me a long time to get to a condition I liked—I intend to keep it till I'm tired of it. Do you have any luggage?"

"It's already on its way to storage. I don't have a domicile yet. I suppose I'll get one—"

"Where in particular?"

"I gather at the Calvin Institute hostelry. Are the Madarian Apartments still—"

"You gather. You think. As usual, not absolutely sure." He said to Yvon and Farlos, "She came up with a sound argument in defense of positronic drift, demonstrating that over time a positronic template mutates, much like a human mind, and is not absolutely reliable. I think she was using her own mind as a model." To Ariel, grinning, he said, "The Madarians are still there, still overly-furnished, and still where all the pretentious graduates who think they know something about positronics live until the Calvin finds them tasks elsewhere. Let's go see if they'll have you, find out for certain where you're supposed to be staying. Till then, you can stay with me, and I'm not sure my place is clean enough for guests. Not on the ground ten minutes and a nuisance already!"

"I can see to her accommodations, Doctor," Farlos said.

"Do," Penj said. "And see to her luggage." He pointed to Yvon. "Get us transport."

"Yes, sir."

Both aides went off in separate directions.

"I can't believe how glad I am to see you," Ariel said. "I didn't expect anyone to meet me."

"You should be glad to see me, Ariel. If not me, then it would be some dour politico with an agenda." His grin vanished, and he was instantly as serious as ever she had seen him. "What kind of mess have you generated, Ariel? There are people here wanting your head on a stake. And we've detained a Terran ambassador at your say-so? What is *that* about? My sense is that it's a worse scandal than—well, anyway, as soon as we're out of any possibility of eavesdropping, we have to have a very detailed, very serious talk. You are in trouble, Ariel Burgess, along with all the rest of us."

He spun around and walked away from her. After a few seconds, Ariel followed, catching up with him in less than a dozen strides.

"I never did know what you'd say next," she said caustically.

"Best teaching method ever invented," Penj said. "Keep them guessing, but give them enough clues to make a correct deduction." He gave a sidelong glance. "You know what I'm talking about, so don't act indignant or surprised."

"I'm not. I actually *did* expect a reception committee from the Council or from the Institute." *Or rather, I hoped someone would...*

"I told the Institute I'd do it. Why the Council agreed I don't know. Things are not as carefree as they were the last time you were here."

"So I gathered. I was interviewed by the head of Planetary Security just before going through Customs."

"Pon Byris? That officious—? What did he want? Never mind, tell me later, not here."

He walked quickly, giving her little chance to look around. They passed beneath one of the graceful arches and suddenly they stood in brilliant sunlight and open air. Penj looked left and right.

"We have a few moments before my aides catch up," he said, turning toward her. "And out here, I doubt anyone will think to listen in. Some privacy still remains."

"What?"

"Listen, don't talk. The organism you sent back, the cyborg. It's causing small revolutions throughout the Institute. Paradigms are shifting and ivory towers are crumbling. Such a thing is supposed to be impossible." He grinned. "Excellent work, Ariel, even if it is pure serendipity. The smug bastards have to work for a change and no one is certain anymore. About anything." The grin vanished. "Which leads directly to a very dangerous political atmosphere. For the first time in memory—in *my* memory, which is long and accurate—Aurora is afraid."

"You mean the Calvin Institute is upset?"

"No. I mean the organic thinking population of the world is afraid. Most of them aren't even sure why, they're just borrowing it from their representatives and avatars. Their comfort zone has been violated, all their expectations are called into question. Yes, the Calvin is full of fear, and of course it bled over into the Council, and from there... well, fear, like any strong emotion, is viral, isn't it? The mission on Earth is a dismal failure thanks to that cretin we've just arrested—and yes, I *do* know what it's about and thank you for the word on that, Ariel, I'm sure it will go a long way toward some useful palliative, and can't hurt your standing with the Council at all—and the situation with Solaria and the Settler Coalition is no closer to resolution than it was when we began trying to resolve it. For the first time since the Independence Aggressions, Aurora doesn't know what to do next, and we're failing on several important matters. Scapegoats are being actively sought, so you be careful. It's not a good sign at all that Pon Byris chose to interview you right off the shuttle. Watch him, Ariel, he seems like a typical bureaucrat, but right now he can be a very dangerous man. I don't wish to see my favorite student sacrificed in some primitive expression of hurt pride and vented spleen."

Ariel smiled. " 'Favorite'? I thought I was your best."

"You'll never hear it from me." He patted her shoulder. "Quiet now, you need to hear the rest. Earth has requested direct Spacer intervention in the Nova Levis situation. A Spacer world has never waged war on another, and if we step in, it is likely to come to that."

"With Solaria?"

"Or one of their allies."

"Nexon?"

"Nexon could care less—they've grown more and more disinterested in anything Solaria does. They've removed themselves from it all so much that enlisting their aid is nothing but a gesture. Keres has a war fleet, though."

"Since when?"

"Since they bought one off the black market, about a year ago. Settler mercenaries are running it with Keresian officers seconded from their police arm. So far they haven't done anything with it but fly pretty patterns. I don't even think Earth knows about it. However, we have information that they are in negotiations with their weapons source for a new cadre of mercenaries to run the fleet and act as their police force. We don't have the details, but Keres is balking. They're afraid."

"Cyborgs?"

Penj shrugged. "Do you think more of those could be built, and, if so, in sufficient numbers to form a sizable threat?"

"I don't know. What about the arms dealer?"

Another shrug.

"Kynig Parapoyos," Ariel guessed.

Penj raised his eyebrows. "You know about him, then?"

"He's the great bogeyman of interstellar trade on Earth. Most people don't actually believe he's a real person, but there are companies that do exactly what he's accused of doing."

"The Hunter Group is the largest. We can't get the Settler Coalition to investigate effectively or grant us permission to send our own people."

"They're afraid you'll bring robots along."

"Side issues. What *is* important is that cyborg. Where was it manufactured?"

"We believe—*I* believe—there's a facility on Nova Levis. We found connections between it and a lab on Earth and—"

Penj held up a hand. His two aides emerged from the terminal and converged on them.

"Later," Penj said. Loudly to his aides, he said, "So, do we have transport or must we walk?"

With three robots, under Denis's supervision, Derec quickly got the lab up and assembled Thales and reconnected all the memory nodes. He hesitated, hands poised above the main console, relishing the next few moments. On a diagnostics table behind him stretched the inanimate hulk of Bogard. Derec wanted to acknowledge to himself, to his surroundings, to his memory, to everything he had been through in the past eighteen months, that this was no illusion. That he was awake and about to recover most of what he had been deprived of since life on Earth became untenable for him.

He let his right hand fall, one finger touching the contact that prompted—

"Hello, Derec," Thales said. "Are we operational now?"

"Check it out. Run diagnostics."

A few seconds later, Thales came back, "Full capacity memory access. All systems optimal. I am on-line and at your service. What shall I do first?"

"Explore our accommodations, access Eos City services and find out what I need to know to live here, then...I guess we can go back to work on Bogard."

"Working. Give me a few seconds while I connect to the Eos RI grid."

A chime sounded. Derec looked around.

"You have a guest," Thales said.

"I'll get back to you."

Derec hurried to his door. Clin Craym smiled as he opened it.

running diagnostic, running parameter check, running alignment routines—compatibility factors plus nine, plus eight-seven, optimal path transduction—fill buffers, isolate comm nodes, check security, run purge on external feeds, loops located in eighteen tiers, isolating and capping—check sources, maintain ghost feeds

resource manifest, available physical plant, access—
reset dedication, attach hierarchical links to available mobile units,
establish household protocols, assess capacity, route command interlink
through primary feeds

Derec watched, bemused, as Clin commandeered his kitchen. She had
brought containers of food, which she began preparing with an attitude
of authority and pride.

"Shipboard cuisine is very good," she said as she sliced small reddish
bullets. A sharp odor filled the room. "But it's nothing compared to what
can be done with human hands."

Derec folded his arms over his chest. "Why?"

Clin gave him a curious look. "Because robots—good as they are—just
don't quite—"

"That's not what I mean."

She set her paring knife down. "You mean why am I here?"

Derec nodded, not sure he should say anything.

Clin sighed, picked up the knife, and resumed chopping. "Are you
hungry?"

"I'm curious."

"Don't be. Some people are just more interesting than others. Until
you start examining the interest. Then..." She shrugged.

"So it's purely whimsical?"

"Probably not. But we'll never find out if I leave." She looked at him
with narrowed eyes. "Is this the way it is on Earth? A couple of excellent
encounters and then suspicion?"

Derec felt stung. "I'm sorry, I—"

"What criteria do you use to decide on a relationship? I mean, at the
beginning? Appearance? A turn of phrase? Maybe just something about
the eyes? Instinct?"

"I haven't had a relationship in a long time. Not...like this."

"That Earth thing, maybe? Suspicion?"

"No. Too busy." He considered. "I'm sorry, I'm just not used to having
someone suddenly want to be around me like this."

"This is Aurora. You never have to be alone here."

Derec could think of no response that would not sound hurtful. He
wanted to accept Clin as exactly what she appeared to be, but he did not
trust his sudden willingness to do that. *Maybe it* is *the Earth thing...*

"So," he said finally, "what's on the menu?"

* * *

control established, household protocols in place, previous authority suppressed, three staff mobiles, class MP-90, "B" level positronics, fully adaptive

secure premises from all covert surveillance, establish secondary communications channels, query Auroran positronic network, requesting orientation and introduction

uncrate Bogard, connect service and diagnostic links, inventory available resources for continued update, repair, and recovery

secondary priority run identity profiles on following subjects, list appended

Derec wondered at her every time she undressed. Clin had the physique of a gymnast, and she seemed to make love with every part of her body at once, undulating against him constantly, slowly, concentrating his attention so completely on the sensations she provided that he could think of being no where else.

"I have things to do," he said.

"You're doing them."

Welcome to Aurora, he thought, giving up.

main trunk lines sorted, comm directory accessed, data encoded, securing closed lines, interrogatory Institute resident intelligence network, establish links, identity open to positronic verification, request dialogue

request acknowledged, repeat identification, referencing matching matrix patterns

verification codes sent, identity Thales, resident intelligence assigned Avery, Derec, Earth

verified, state request

briefing, data profile update, situation report, current status

require commensurate data

request granted, exchange protocols on-line and open

current situation tenuous, refer files S-987A through S-1179A, continuous, gaps compatible with offered data, welcome Thales

thank you, request time-share, memory buffer back-up, current template protocol, status

what is current assessment of situation regarding human-positronic relations relative to political conditions, specifically Nova Levis/Terran intervention and related manifestations

current assessment as follows

there is a problem

19

MIA MET Ros Yalor in the gymnasium after her shift ended. She
found him encased in the cardio-stress cage, limbs flexing through
motions that vaguely resembled swimming, sweat giving his pale
skin an oily sheen that seemed oddly unhealthy. She glanced at the time
chop on the control panel and waited the remaining two and a half minutes, absently watching his chest heave and his thighs flex. Two others
worked at the free weights across the room.

The machine slowed to a stop and Ros worked his way loose from the
restraints, breathing heavily. He came up to Mia, and her nose wrinkled
at his strong odor.

"Is this social, Lieutenant?" he asked. "We *are* off-shift, aren't we?"

"We're cops, Ros. We're *never* off-shift."

"That's crap."

"But true. I needed to talk to you where we wouldn't be monitored."

He hesitated, then headed toward the showers. She followed him. The
air was perceptibly warmer and damp. Ros stripped out of his sweats and
went toward the common stall. He turned on the water, stepped briefly
under the stream, then came back out.

"All right, I can finish when we're done," he said.

"We have a serious problem. I found the control point."

"The contraband?"

Mia nodded. "Hard part will be proving it, assuming we live that
long."

"Oh, that sounds encouraging." He grabbed a towel from a shelf and
rubbed his face roughly. "Okay."

"I found something odd in Corf's quarters when we arrested him. He had four books. Novels."

"He doesn't strike me as a reader."

"Nor me, but they were ancient."

"So? A lot of people have odd tastes."

"I don't mean just the text. They were *books,* Ros—bound paper with covers, pages you physically turn."

"Now *that* sounds expensive. Was there an import log?"

"No. They're contraband. I traced them back to a source on Earth, a dealer in rarities, antiques. They were purchased by someone here, on the blockade."

"Corf?" Ros guessed.

"No, he just happened to have them."

Ros thought for a moment. "Then can we assume whoever owns them will be wanting them back?"

"He does," Mia said. "He's asked three times."

"Asked you? Directly?"

"Uh-huh. Not exactly in so many words, but the hinting is profound."

"Who?"

"Reen."

"Commander Reen?"

"Do you know another Reen on the blockade? Somehow, the liaison to the Keresians, Lt. Jons, is involved, but I can't get Corf to say anything. The psychometricians tell me he exhibits all the traits of a True Believer."

"In what?"

"Does it matter? I found references to family members involved with Managins in his file. Nothing that prevented his acceptance into the service, but maybe enough for Corf to hero worship. But there's always been an element of extremists in the Settler Movement. In the early years, the screening wasn't as rigorous as it's become—that, and Earth was happy to get rid of some of these people—which, as good as it gets, still doesn't prevent baleys from spilling into these worlds illegally, and who knows *what* their affiliations might be. But think about it this way: The group that initially settled Nova Levis was a social separatist group, the Church of Organic Sapiens."

"Are they tied to Managins?"

"Not directly," Mia said, "but their philosophies aren't incompatible."

"What about Reen?" Ros asked.

"If I start snooping into his record, I could draw attention. If he's the nexus, the controller we've been looking for, he may have security on his files."

"You could refer back to Earth."

Mia nodded, deciding not to tell Ros that she had already done that. "We've been looking for how all this stuff gets by our screening. We've assumed all along that there had to be a group of people on the inside, shunting goods and immigrants out of our sight."

"Sure, but Reen?" Ros shook his head, in dismay rather than denial. "I suppose he's perfect. He's got access to everything. So how do we catch him? Do you have any idea how many people he has working for him? How corrupt the whole department probably is?"

"The best way would be to catch him receiving contraband."

"And how do we set that up?"

"You're game to try?"

"Consider it the foolish act of a young and inexperienced officer hoping to make points with his immediate superior," Ros said. "Yes, I'm game. Do you have a plan?"

"I'm working on it. In the meantime, I want you to do a little light surveillance on Reen. There have to be places the contraband gets stashed before transit down to the surface, places he's keeping off the inspection rosters. If he's consistent, he'll inspect them from time to time—that's the kind of officer he is."

"You want to know where he goes when he's not on duty."

"Pretty much."

Ros nodded, though the expression he wore suggested he would rather do anything but what Mia wanted. Mia patted his arm.

"Cheer up," she said. "At least we won't be bored."

"Oh, good, I was really worried about that."

Mia laughed. "Finish your shower."

She watched him walk back to the stall and wondered exactly what kind of points with her he wanted to make.

Her decryption program had finally opened the text woven into the end-papers of the books. What she saw on her screens represented, at a glance, the organizational flow chart of the entire contraband network around Nova Levis. Mia stared at the complex graphs, with contact points, manifests, and timetables. According to this, most of the Keresian ships and nearly half the Terran vessels were involved in routing goods into and out of Nova Levis.

Out of...what could possibly be coming *out* of Nova Levis?

She shook her head. Worry about that one later.

The sheer volume stunned her. She could not imagine where all this material might be filtered through. It was as if the blockade had a vast hole in it and entire convoys were coming and going unchallenged.

After staring at it in amazement for several minutes, she made herself lean forward and enter commands to her datum. Soon she had everything in a new file, encrypted to her password, and a separate package to be sent to Earth, to Hofton at the Auroran Embassy, and, through him, to Coren Lanra.

She wondered about that for a moment. Lanra worked for Rega Looms of DyNan Manual Industries. Looms was also head of the Church of Organic Sapiens. Did that make Lanra suspect?

She decided to take the chance. In her admittedly limited experience with him, Lanra had proven more ethical than simple employment could compromise. And from what she knew of Looms, he had no use for black marketeers. The material she had already received from Lanra about the bookseller justified the chance.

Studying the data, she found five key entry points in the blockade. One of them was on this station.

She would wait now, and see if Ros turned up the same location following Reen. That would tell her a lot—about the network, and about Ros.

At this point, the people she trusted most were all on other worlds.

Coren stepped into Ambassador Sen Setaris's office and waited until she acknowledged him and offered him a seat before her desk.

She looked haggard, something Coren never expected to see in a Spacer. He wondered if it were just the light—a glow from her datum screens, the overall illumination in the room low, almost moody—but the more he studied Setaris the greater the impression that she was overworked, harried. Her eyes were puffy.

Coren waited silently for several minutes. Then the door opened and Hofton entered. He gave Coren a nod and stood at the side of Setaris's desk, the third point of a triangle.

Setaris looked up.

"We want to do something illegal, Mr. Lanra," she said. "Will you assist us?"

"That depends," he said.

"Of course it does. It ought to." She sat back and gazed at him contemplatively. "We want to take Gamelin."

" 'Take' him?"

"Remove him from Earth. Alive or dead, it doesn't matter. I'm safe in assuming that you want the same thing?"

"I suspect that he murdered Rega Looms. If he manages to assume control of DyNan, contravening Rega's will, I'll take it as a personal failure."

"That sounds like a 'yes' to me."

"You hear very clearly, then."

"If something goes wrong," Setaris said carefully, "the repercussions will be..."

"Profound?" Hofton said.

She looked at the aide. "We'll have to pack up and leave Earth immediately."

"I may be able to get a little consideration," Coren said. "I have—"

"I don't want Terran authorities involved in any way, Mr. Lanra. This is a Spacer problem and I want it kept that way. You are already intimately involved, otherwise we wouldn't be talking."

"Stop it," Coren said. "You'd have to talk to someone—you couldn't set this up without help outside the embassy." He waited for a denial. When both Spacers remained silent, he continued. "Very well. We do this with as few people as possible. Do you have an idea?"

"We hoped you would," Hofton said.

"Give me a day or two. How much support can you provide?"

"I gather you mean coercive support?" Setaris said. "Hofton?"

"We still have a full compliment of security," Hofton said. "About thirty Aurorans, fully-armed."

"You'll need blasters," Coren said.

"We saw the recordings from Kopernik," Setaris said.

"May I ask why you're so concerned about this?"

"Perhaps Ariel explained to you," Setaris said. "We once played with cyborgs and found them wholly unworkable."

"Yes, she mentioned it. You couldn't program the Three Laws into them."

"Oh, it was worse than that. Neither Ariel nor I—until this occurred—had access to the records."

"Aurorans keeping secrets from each other? I'm shocked."

Setaris's eyes narrowed. For an instant, it seemed, she looked her age, which Coren knew to be well over two centuries. At least her eyes betrayed her; the skin remained smooth, expressionless.

"The few successful examples," she continued slowly, "exhibited a highly aggressive nature. They lacked, for want of a better term, a con-science. One researcher suggested it was the absence of any kind of ade-quate peer group environment within which to form the requisite empathy. Who knows? The point is, they were not simply unmanageable robots—"

"They were competitors," Coren said.

Setaris looked surprised. "Was that just a guess or do you know some-thing?"

"A guess of sorts. It struck me that these...constructs...represent a separate species. At least, enough so that they might be inclined to see us as an embarrassing ancestral form." Coren smiled. "When you work for Rega Looms you hear a great deal of discussion about evolution and 'nat-ural' versus 'unnatural' forms. You hear a lot about self-destructive obso-lescence."

"I see. Well, the saving grace, if you can call it that, was that these 'constructs,' as you call them, lacked an instinct for mutual cooperation as well. But we can't risk the possibility that they might get over that."

"Or have it designed out?"

"Exactly."

"May I ask a diplomatically delicate question?"

Setaris inclined her head.

"Was Ariel recalled to work on this problem?"

"Yes."

Coren glanced at Hofton, whose face remained impassive, uncommu-nicative. "I see. Well, then, we're still working on the same side. For the time being." He stood. "I'll be in touch. It might be safest to continue going through Hofton."

"I agree," Setaris said. "This is likely the last time you and I will speak, Mr. Lanra. In that case, I thank you now for all you've done for us. If there is anything we might do—"

"A job, perhaps, when all this is over." Coren smiled. "I suspect I'll be looking for one."

Setaris hesitated, then gave him a thin smile. "We'll see, Mr. Lanra. Good evening."

Hofton escorted Coren out and down the wide corridors to the eleva-tors. Coren studied the walls, realizing that this might be the last time he ever saw them.

"There are about eight among our security people," Hofton said abruptly, "who actually know how to handle themselves in lethal situa-tions. I'll be sure they form the core of whatever team we assemble."

"You know this is likely to blow up in your face."

"It already has. Ambassador Setaris was disingenuous about keeping Terran authorities out of this. They've already been in touch with her."

Hofton entered the elevator with him.

"Are we going somewhere together?" Coren asked.

"I'm making sure you return safely to your domicile. The ambassador's orders."

"Oh? And are you qualified to act as my bodyguard?"

Hofton gave him a long, silent look.

"Fine," Coren said. "Honestly, I don't mind your company, Hofton." They rode down to the garages in silence. Then, as the doors opened, Coren said, "By the way, I found out something interesting the other day. That grass Ariel and I brought back from the lab site—"

"It's Auroran," Hofton said. "At least, it's related to an Auroran grass, a variant from our terraforming days."

"Yes," Coren said, surprised.

"She gave me some to turn over to our lab. We identified it quickly. I was surprised it was on Earth. It's an outlawed variety here, though the regulations are so old I doubt there's anyone aware of them."

"It was originally manufactured by the company that became Imbitek."

"Now that I *didn't* know. Interesting." Hofton waved Coren toward a limousine. They climbed in and as the transport started up and headed out of the embassy garage, Hofton continued. "I shall have to look into that connection."

"Why would grass manufactured on Earth be outlawed from it?"

"Hmm? Well, it's a matter of history. And memory."

When Hofton remained silent for several minutes, Coren cleared his throat. "You aren't going to tell me?"

Hofton glanced at him. "Are you sure you want to know?"

"That's an insulting question."

Hofton considered. "Yes, I suppose it is. Most people don't want to know. Not really. They like convenient facts they can use immediately, facts that will make their lives more interesting or easier. They don't really want to know the kind that leave them feeling helpless and angry. Some—like you—hate not knowing, no matter how uncomfortable what you know is. So to protect the rest of us from people like you, there are more radical measures."

"Meaning?"

"The future is always dominated by those who aren't hindered by the past. Sometimes that demands a kind of amnesia. How convenient then to be handed a tool that guarantees forgetting?"

Coren stared at him. Suddenly, he shuddered. "Burundi's Fever."

"That grass represents a past none of us wish to remember."

"Are the cyborgs connected?"

"That remains to be seen. At a guess, I'd say only coincidentally. But it's bothersome that the two seem to be related to the same lab."

"So the next question is—"

"Do *I* know what's been forgotten?"

"Do you?" Coren asked.

"That's a very good question, Mr. Lanra." He looked away. "Let me think about it before I answer you."

Hofton lapsed into silence, staring unseeing out the window at the passing city, one hand raised to his chin, his posture an absolute rejection of any further questions or conversation. Coren finally looked out his own window, letting his thoughts spin through the implications of what Hofton had just told him.

Ariel was a victim of Burundi's Fever...so was Avery...

Then: *They were both "cured" on Earth after being basically deported from Aurora. Why didn't Aurora help them?*

Could they?

The limo finally pulled up outside Coren's building. Hofton silently followed him up to his office.

"Good evening," Coren's desk said as they entered. "Please verify identity."

Coren sat down and went through the ritual. His flatscreens rose and he found data waiting for him. He opened the files.

"Ah. Something for Mia. My little spies have done their work."

Hofton nodded distractedly.

"All right," Coren said, punching in the necessary commands to his desk for security. "Either tell me or leave. I can't take the suspense."

Hofton sat down. "Do you know much about the Riots?"

"The anti-robot riots? As much as most Terrans, I suppose. There were two waves of them, as I recall. The first came shortly after the Spacer Worlds were being settled. The second was about two centuries ago, when Spacetown was shut down."

"The first ones concern us most." Hofton looked around. "Are we secured?"

"As much as possible."

"Good. Perhaps you should make some coffee. This may take some time."

"The Spacer Worlds," Hofton began, "weren't settled all at once. A few at a time, over centuries. The last were opened up not from Earth but from other Spacer colonies. Solaria was such a colony. It was originally settled from Nexon. There was a second wave of settlement—I suppose it would be more accurate to say 'refugees'—which caused the initial rift between Earth and the Fifty Worlds and resulted in the war and the isolation.

"At first, though, it was all in the spirit of a dream come true. Hyperdrive gave us the ability to go to the stars, and we did. It was a golden age—at least, on the surface. I can't imagine what it must have been like for most of the ten billion people trapped on Earth. There was a paradigm shift—what some historians call a 'phase change'—occurring at the same time. The old institutions upon which Earth relied no longer worked. This was the time of the World Coordinators and Machine management. Trade from the new settlements boosted the global economy and the Machines—the first RIs, really—controlled the fluctuations that normally accompanied new expansions and pretty much kept things stable for a long, long time.

"Can you imagine a time when robots proliferated on Earth? The Cities were being built, slowly, and most of the dangerous work was done by robots. The old institutions that dictated full employment for humans, obsolete though they were and had been for centuries, changed into quasi-religious movements that pitted the unemployed—though cared-for—against the so-called onslaught of the artificial person. There are thousands of reasons why the first Riots occurred. I'm inclined to believe that it was largely because the original Machines had gradually removed themselves from operation. A misapplication of Three Law protocol, probably. Once stabilized, they misunderstood their role and believed—I'm guessing—that continued maintenance on their part would be harmful in the long run to humanity. They shut themselves down. No one really knows how long matters ran on without their management.

"But eventually, resentments over a hundred perceived slights against the common people combined to cause riots. Not the least of which were a series of plagues which turned out to be the result of nanotech.

"You can't have a mechanism as complex as a positronic robot without extreme miniaturization. Earth, in fact, developed crude nanotech before the first useful robots were designed and built. The one was necessary to the other, and the other spurred research in the one. Side by side, the two technologies increased in complexity and utility.

"The problem, however, was the closeness to organic function a lot of nanotech became, specifically in the terraforming aspects. Nanotech proved incredibly efficient at adapting ecosystems to human requirements. In order to do that, though, a certain latitude was necessary in the organelles themselves, an innate ability to analyze and adapt. Mutate. Once you cross that line, though, you bring about all the uncertainties and unpredictabilities that come with actual living organisms. One solution was to program in a self-destruct sequence that caused the specific type to eat itself out after it had done its job. Oh, the technology was fabulous, and amazing, and ninety-nine percent effective.

"But that one percent...well, like any new plague, it began with a few outbreaks here and there and then spread. By the time Earth knew what was happening to it, people were in a blind panic. Once the thing that was killing them was identified, they conflated it with any and all technology seen to imitate life—including robots. The Riots ran across the entire planet. A second wave of settlement exploded onto the Spacer worlds. I called them refugees. They were. They were fleeing the riots, the plagues, the politics, the backlash. People who wanted to keep their robots, protect themselves from infection, start anew elsewhere. Hundreds of thousands.

"In the end, it turned out that Earth could do without robots, but it had to keep some of the nanotech. Food production alone had become dependent on it. By the time the plagues had been wrestled into submission, the surviving technologies were called other things, innocuous labels, and the tech itself operated far less independently.

"The Spacers, however, had to stanch the flow of new colonists. The flood threatened to bring the riots out to us. That is what started the events that led to the war, and the isolation, and Earth losing its home-based star travel ability. That is also the beginning of our long fear of infection. Not all the refugees came unburdened. When the smoke cleared, Earth had purged itself of robots and virulent nanoplagues and a lot of political undesirables—at our expense. You exported some of your diseases. We nearly cut you off completely, but we needed the expertise of your researchers who had successfully isolated and stopped the spread and eruption of new plagues. Some Spacer worlds—Solaria in particular—became irremediably paranoid. All of us suffered in one way or another."

Coren shifted uncomfortably and took another sip of coffee. Everything Hofton said matched or complimented what he had heard from Myler

Towne's researcher. "None of this is in the history texts."

Hofton smiled sadly. "Of course it isn't. Who wants to remember all that ugliness? When we tried to reintroduce robots, it ended in failure because your cultural memory is longer than your factual memory. We're slowly getting over our fears of infection—when we allowed Terrans once more to settle, it was a fight of epic proportions among our politicians. The Settler program is essential, but an undesired compromise."

"I've heard Spacers talk about the importance of the Settler program before, but it's obvious you don't like it."

"Some of us do. But it doesn't matter. We need it. Humankind needs it. You see, I spoke of the plagues on Earth. The cause, I said, was the high mutability factor in a particular kind of nanotech—terraforming tech. What would you conclude from that?"

"That Spacers must themselves have suffered some sort of plague."

"We did. Burundi's Fever was one of them. It came out of the very grasses we transplanted to take over the native ecosystems of our new worlds. There were others, but Burundi's was the worst. It emerged long before the plagues on Earth began and, in fact, was the first cause of a quarantine movement. On Earth's part. We suffered it in successive waves for centuries. No Spacer world was immune. After Earth's plagues, we finally were able to control it, but not before it virtually remade our sense of who we were, our history. We came out of the plagues reborn, a sharp wall between what we once were and what we have now become."

"I don't quite follow."

"History is a fiction and memory cooperates most of the time, especially when it concerns something as unpleasant as this."

Coren considered for a few seconds. "You mean Spacers just don't remember?"

"Most don't. Those who lived through the last waves of all this have been privileged to suffer a case of Burundi's. Even before that, so many people were infected that it's amazing there is a history at all."

"A whole society...amnesia..." Coren frowned. "Then how is it any of it's remembered?"

"Unlike Earth, we didn't get rid of our robots."

"Uh-huh. So how come the robots don't remind you?"

"Why? The question is not asked. And it's consistent with the Three Laws. At this point it would serve no useful purpose."

"I don't—"

"You see, once we got control of the disease, we didn't simply eliminate it, like Earth has done with a number of its ancient killers."

"You used it. On purpose."

"Very much on purpose."

"And the robots know."

"Some do, the older ones. Our planetary RIs know."

"And at the risk of violating one of the precious Three Laws—"

"—it is not spoken about."

"Unless doing so will be a worse violation."

"Which may be what we're facing on Nova Levis."

They sat in silence for a time, not looking at each other. Coren wrestled with his impressions and conclusions. He wanted to ask if that had been the case with Ariel. What had she done to be sentenced to the eradication of her memory?

But finally, Coren did not ask that question. Instead, he looked at Hofton, and asked, "So how come *you* remember?"

20

MASID LEFT the apartment dark. He checked the pale glow of his watch occasionally, but did not move from the high-backed chair he had moved into the corner, farthest from the front door. Vague light from the unevenly lit city outlined the windows and gave enough illumination for him to make out the lumpy shape of Marshal Toranz propped in a chair in the center of the room. He had taped her mouth and cuffed her ankles. As an added measure, he had given her an anesthetic hours earlier.

He glanced toward his cabinet. He wanted anxiously to respond to the message he had received from the blockade. Someone up there had chosen to recognize him and reply, an Internal Security Officer named Daventri, a lieutenant, not even the highest rung of his or her own special ladder. That fact alone told Masid a number of things about the situation, the most important of which was that the blockade was compromised at the command level at least. He had guessed as much, given Tilla's abandonment and the subsequent failure of any other team to reach the surface of Nova Levis. He wondered how many agents had been caught and killed over the last year trying to infiltrate the network here. If he had told anyone above him what he had intended to do, he now doubted he would have lived past the first baley ride.

The bulk of Daventri's message was both cryptic and plain: SITUATION FLUID AND UNRELIABLE. DIRECT LINK EXISTS BETWEEN BLOCKADE AND NOVA CITY. WORKING ON IT. WAIT FOR FURTHER COMMUNICATION FROM ME BEFORE SENDING ANOTHER MESSAGE.

So, badly as he wanted to send back "What do you mean? Who's compromised? Where should I go?" Daventri wanted him to maintain, do nothing till he replied.

Which might never happen. For all he knew, his message had been intercepted—or Daventri's had—and right now his one contact was being eliminated.

One thing at a time, Mas old son, one thing at a time....

An hour past midnight, he heard footsteps on the landing outside his door. He tensed, his hand curling around his blaster.

It seemed minutes before his door inched open. Masid watched the thin light of paler darkness outside grow to a wedge. Then a human-sized shadow filled it. The shape entered quickly and closed the door behind itself.

A flashlight winked on.

"Shit!" someone hissed.

The light shifted toward Masid. He raised the blaster.

"Do we talk or try to shoot it out?" Masid asked quietly.

The light winked off. Masid followed the sound of movement to his left and fired. The crimson bolt threw the room into sudden relief, freezing action for that moment. He saw a man jumping for cover.

The bolt splashed against the wall alongside the door with a loud *crack!* and a slow, sizzling after-hiss. Acrid smoke filled the air.

Masid rolled to the floor and touched the wafer in his pocket.

The room lights came on brilliantly to his dark-adjusted eyes, and he squinted as he rose to a kneeling posture.

Opposite him stood Kar, his own weapon raised and aimed.

The door banged open. Both men looked. Filoo stood there, Tosher behind him, as well as two others Masid did not know. Muscle, by the look of them.

"Well, well," Filoo said, smiling. "Isn't this lovely? What an interesting spectacle." He stepped into the room and stopped in front of Toranz, frowning. "Berit?" He snapped his fingers in front of her face, then shrugged. "I would be most happy to have an explanation."

"This is your thief—" Kar began, stopping abruptly at Filoo's raised hand.

"Let me finish," Filoo said. "I said I would be most happy to have an explanation, but I would want the right one. The truth. I rather doubt I'm going to get it. Not all of it, at least. So I'll settle for guessing all by myself."

Filoo sighed and went to the sofa. His muscle ranged quietly out across the front of the room. Masid noticed then that each one held a blaster.

"Would you mind if I put this away?" Masid asked, waving his own weapon. "You seem to have the situation stabilized."

Filoo smiled. "I think that's a fine idea. For both of you."

Masid holstered his blaster. A few seconds later, clearly unhappy, so did Kar.

"It would be easiest," Filoo said with mock gravity, "to kill you both. Maybe Berit, too, while I'm at it, since her presence here raises several annoying questions. But healthy employees are hard to come by. I'm sure you noticed," he said directly to Masid, "how sick everyone seems to be. Those few who aren't are worth a small fortune. So it's a fool who kills them without good cause. The question is, what cause is good enough?" He looked from Kar to Masid. "Suggestions?"

Masid folded his arms. Kar glowered at him.

"I followed Toranz here," Kar said. "He's your leak—or she is, and he's the one buying from her."

Filoo seemed to consider that and nodded. "That's a plausible explanation, Kar. Do you have anything to say in defense?"

"No," Masid said. "He's right. In the last three weeks I was able to seduce Marshal Toranz into throwing over a solid income from you on the off-chance that I could successfully steal enough of your supply to not only replace what you pay her, but to increase it. I told her I could unseat you within a month, and that her best chance of survival would be to deal with me. I'm caught, obviously."

Filoo frowned. "What could you possibly have offered her as proof that you could do that?"

"Oh, I forgot. She's in love with me. The seduction was on all levels."

Filoo burst out laughing. He craned his neck to look at his bodyguards, all of whom were stifling laughter. Filoo's eyes teared up, and he walked around in front of the still-unconscious marshal.

"She's likes it rough, I gather," he said, lifting her cuffed hands, and laughed louder. He sat back down and wiped at his eyes. "I must say, you've got carbon, gato."

"Boss—" Kar began.

"Shut up!" Filoo snapped, all laughter gone. "Tosher, search the place. You know what I want."

Tosher pulled a scanner from his coat and began a slow circuit around the apartment. It began chirping near the cabinet. Tosher tugged at the doors.

"Locked," he said.

Filoo looked expectantly at Masid. Slowly, Masid crossed the room and unlocked the cabinet. The pack of ampules lay on the shelf. Masid waited for Tosher to start poking at the false back that hid the hyperwave unit, but all the man did was bring the scanner closer to the ampules.

"Found 'em," he announced.

"Bring them," Filoo said.

Tosher handed Filoo the pack. After a moment, Filoo took out his own scanner and ran a check.

"Now I must ask myself," he said then, "why a man would leave something he stole not a day ago lying around his apartment, especially after he knew someone was coming to ask about them."

Filoo looked at Kar, who seemed puzzled but worried.

"Would you care to try again?" Filoo asked him.

"He's had this stuff at least five days," Kar said. "Look at the marker!"

"Mm. Yes, the marker." Filoo held the ampules up toward Masid. "You may have noticed, we mark our product with a date stamp. No? Well, it's one thing to do business illegally, it's another to do it stupidly. No one anymore would be so careless as to *aggravate* an epidemic through sloppy distribution. That's why I train all my people to know how to give the proper advice, and I never sell impotent product. We tend to deal harshly with newcomers who try cutting their product to increase profit. Not many do, contrary to popular misconception, but a few have tried, and they don't survive. It's not altruism, it's self-preservation. We date stamp to ensure the quality of what we sell." He tapped the markers on the ampules. "This tells me that this stuff ought to have been sold, at the latest, three days ago. If it were still in my warehouse, we'd destroy it. But it's here. I wonder how?"

"Obviously, it was stolen four or five days ago," Kar said, though Masid detected doubt in his voice.

"That's one possibility," Filoo said. "The other is that someone thought I was sloppy, leaving old product lying around." He looked at Kar. "Used to be, when you appeared before a magistrate, they'd say something fatuous, like, 'If you confess and show remorse, the mercy of the court will be entreated and things will go easier.' We don't have any magistrates like that now. Things are a bit more basic. For instance, entrapment is not allowed in a proper court as evidence. If you lay out something you know will be stolen and it's then stolen, you can't use that against the thief. Silly, in my opinion, but it has something to do with mutual collusion. I never quite understood it."

Filoo stood and turned toward Kar. "But I like this way of doing things fine. I understand it. I change the date stamp on some brand new product and leave it where I know it'll be noticed and probably stolen, and then follow it to the thief. A court might say it's entrapment, but to me it's just proof." He smiled thinly at Kar. "So, do you want to try asking for mercy?"

"Boss—"

"Don't lie. Toranz is too stupid to take advantage of a plant, and too lazy to think of a scam like this, anyway. This one—" Filoo jerked a thumb at Masid "—doesn't even know where our warehouse is. Inviting him in was just an opportunity for you to do one more stupid thing yourself."

Kar's face darkened. "If you knew—"

"I didn't. Till now, you've been very good. You got sloppy. I don't know which I hate more, the theft or the slop." He shook his head. "What a waste."

"Boss—"

Filoo stepped back. "Remove him."

The two muscle Masid did not know came forward. Kar's face flashed his fear as they grabbed him and dragged him from Masid's apartment.

"What about her?" Tosher asked, waving at Toranz.

"Her, too. We need a new sheriff."

With deceptive ease, Tosher picked Toranz up from the chair and draped her over his shoulder.

Filoo closed the door after Tosher and turned to Masid. "Why didn't you just kill Toranz and dispose of the ampules?"

"You said you wanted your leak found," Masid answered. "Not that I have any particular reason to do you a favor, but when I caught Toranz in here, I realized that sooner or later Kar was going to set me up in something I couldn't get out of."

"You couldn't get out of this one."

"Not without Kar's help."

"If he hadn't come to check himself—probably when Toranz failed to report to him—you'd still be the only suspect. But you didn't say any of that."

"You're smart. You figured it out."

"It didn't make sense that a newcomer like you would be as successful as Kar stealing from me. Besides, this has been going on a long time. And none of your product has had my markers on it."

"You mark the product itself?"

"Absolutely. Inventory control is the first step in guaranteeing quality."

"I'll keep that in mind."

"You better if you're working for me."

"Am I?"

"The offer is still open," Filoo said. "Just remember, I don't ever trust anyone."

"How do you sleep at night?"

Filoo grinned. "That's how."

"All right," Masid nodded. "But I think you should know one thing. I *do* know where your warehouse is."

Filoo blinked, surprised, then laughed quietly. "I'm sure. Get some sleep and come talk to me tomorrow—" He glanced at his watch. "No, *this* afternoon."

Masid watched Filoo leave. The door clicked shut, and he let out an explosive breath. "Damn."

He pulled out a scanner and went over the apartment for bugs. He found one, in the couch where Filoo had been sitting, and promptly destroyed it with a burst from his stunner.

He sat down on the sofa and stared around. Evidently, he was in. Two people were now, or soon would be, dead. The price of admission. Masid shuddered. He pressed the tab in his pocket, and the lights died. Blaster on his chest, he stretched out and fell quickly to sleep.

Teg Sturlin smiled when Mia stepped into her office. "Daventri," she said, reaching for a bottle.

"Still on duty," Mia said.

Sturlin scowled.

"For," Mia made a show of looking at her watch, "another ten minutes."

Sturlin laughed softly and put the bottle back. "It'll be just as good then. What do you need?"

"I have a tracking log for you to pull up for me."

"Ah. Your books?"

"Hopefully." Mia handed her a disk.

Sturlin carefully inserted it into her datum and opened the files. She sighed comfortably and sat back, reading. Slowly, her eyes narrowed, then she frowned darkly. "These are from the source, through Earth Customs, and out. How did you get these?"

"I have resources."

Sturlin gave her a dubious look, but did not comment. She reached for her keypad and began entering instructions. "You've got the entire transit route here...and there is the point where it was 'lost'...hmmm... so *that's* where it's coming through."

She turned to another screen and brought up a flowchart. Mia watched her work for several minutes, eager to ask questions, but knowing better than to interrupt Sturlin.

Finally, Sturlin shook her head. "Special Requisitions and Discretionary Stores," she said. "The *carbon!*"

Mia cleared her throat. "Excuse me?"

"Oh. The route is circuitous off Earth. It leaves—at least, this shipment does—as a legitimate order, and then becomes contraband when it reaches the quartermaster inspection station. I had to backtrack from here to see how it links up. It gets moved into a different queue, the manifest is changed, the object simply disappears until it arrives here bundled with what we politely term 'exotic material'—everything from liquor to bedsheets to colognes."

"I don't understand. That stuff is allowed in, why smuggle in basically the same thing?"

"It all has to be accounted for. Command wants a record of what comes in and goes out and who uses what. Some of it, obviously, is consumed—but it's tracked so, if need be, we can go to the officer consuming it. The rest actually has to be returned. This system is in place as a courtesy, so our fine officers don't have to pay for their own imports and transit fees. But it's a loan service for the most part. Your books never got logged in. When they went out, they never came back."

"Not just books, though, certainly."

"Oh," Sturlin nodded, "I'm sure a lot of this ends up down on Nova Levis. That's why it has to bypass accounts. Routing it through Special Requisitions is very risky—but very clever. It's probably the one place we might never inspect—and if we did, we'd get tangled up in what's legitimately out and what might not even be here. We'd have to turn the entire officer corps on its head to trace all the might-bes."

"Okay," Mia said, shaking her head. "Then if someone here orders something and it's never logged as being received, what happens to the order?"

"The system makes a follow-up interrogatory, then waits for a human to request another."

"And if no further interrogatory is made?"

"It goes into a file and waits for review. Every six months, the system purges its own records."

Mia pursed her lips. "So is there a way to generate a list of officers who made special orders that were never filled?"

"Certainly."

"And narrow that list to those who never bothered to make a follow-up query?"

Sturlin smiled. "You have a good head on your shoulders, Daventri, no matter what anyone says."

"Right. Let's see what happens."

Sturlin gave the bottle a sad look. "This will be more than ten minutes."

Mia shrugged.

It took the better part of an hour. The two women sat side by side, studying the screens.

"Seventy-three officers in the last six months made special requests," Sturlin read off, "that were not fulfilled. Forty-five of them did follow-up—once—and thirty-nine of them got answers: request denied, unavailable, lost in transit, discontinued, etcetera. Twenty-eight never bothered with a follow-up." Sturlin shook her head. "That doesn't really tell us anything. Even the ones who made follow-up requests could be receiving contraband. The lost-in-transits could as well be switches."

"See if there was a single source for any of those requests."

"One vendor, you mean?"

"Exactly."

Sturlin worked briefly. "No . . . well, eight from your book dealer, but the rest . . . wait . . . at least four sources, but they all went through one shipper: C. Thole and Company."

"Never heard of them."

"Let me pull up their license . . . new license, less than a year old, from a reorganized company. Formerly Improvo Shipping."

"Why reorganized? What happened to Improvo?"

"Doesn't say. Shipping is expensive, highly competitive. Improvo lost its government contracts—that could do a company in right there. I don't have the rest of the data on that, but C. Thole applied after part of Improvo reorganized under a new charter and was granted a service license . . . ten months ago."

"So all the missing material is coming through them?"

"No, but everything that was ordered by these twenty-eight did."

Mia shook her head. "How come there's no oversight on this?"

"There is, just not daily or weekly or in any kind of regularity. The AI systems keep track, but unless someone asks the right questions, it's just data."

No wonder the Spacers wanted robotic inspection, Mia thought. *A positronic system would never miss this, or let it continue...*

"Give me the list of officers," Mia said. "Then close up and open that bottle. My head feels tight. I think I need to relax."

For all that Sturlin was seven kilos heavier than Mia, she could not drink as well as the smaller woman. Mia left Sturlin's office pretending to be drunker than she was. By the time she got back to her quarters, she was already thinking about the connections.

Why did I pretend to be too drunk? she wondered. She knew the answer perfectly well: *Because I don't trust Sturlin anymore...*

Something in the way the quartermaster had been too cooperative and too surprised at the data. Oversight was her job—none of this ought to have been a shock. That and how quickly some of the information had been found...

So there are two options: one, she's not as smart as I always thought she was or, two, I'm being set up...

She encoded another message for Coren Lanra, including the new data, and sent it, then loaded the information into her own datum.

It was obvious that she was dealing with a large conspiracy. It did not take much to create this kind of network—credit would do it, recruitment through avarice. She doubted many of these officers even knew what they were smuggling. Nor would they care as long as it never tainted their record or cost them money—in short, as long as they never got caught. Mia saw no grounds for an open investigation here, not yet. This all looked innocuous on the face of it, just luxury items gone missing. No record of arrival, nothing removed from Stores, not a single physical trace that could be used to indict. The only possible way to catch them might be through their personal accounts. The credits had to be going somewhere.

Unless they were all like Corf—true believers, zealots for a cause. No, that stretched the laws of probability too far.

Just in case, though, she began doing background checks on all of them. Maybe a connection would emerge. She hoped not, though. She would much rather deal with a gang of greedy humans on the take than face a unified group of ideologues and fanatics.

Masid checked on Tilla in the morning. The woman slept, apparently easily, though he knew that was deceptive. He did a quick check on her readings. Respiration was at sixty percent. She took shallow breaths, even in her sleep. Leukocyte count was elevated again. The body continued its war against the things killing her. Masid did not want to guess how long she had to live.

He sighed, programmed in another series of the biophage cocktail he had prepared for her, and left quietly. He wondered how many more times he might be able to see her...

Time to go join Filoo and start the work of finding out who or what ran Nova Levis. Time to find the ones at fault.

He did not give himself much of a chance.

Playing the edge again, he thought, and walked into the city, excited and eager. *The edge is always better....*

21

retrieving sensory composite, fill realtime, deploy environmental algo-
rithms, levels one through ten-to-twelfth power, establish

Academy
Grounds depiction complete
Access positronic matrix, supplement through colloquium
Upload

YOU MAY choose your form."
The blob of coalescing substance writhing on the grass seemed to thicken. Within moments, the vague outline of a human could be seen. The dully glowing yellow mass settled into a basic shape, then took on definition by increments until an athletic body rose on bare feet to stretch its arms skyward.

At the end of the stretch, it wore features.

Young. Cursorily male—no genitalia. Powerful.

He turned slowly, surveying the sward, the porcelain-white buildings in the distance, and came to a halt before the older man sitting within the shade of a domed monopteron.

"Do you know who you are?" the old man asked.

The younger man thought for a moment. "Bogard. Plus..."

"Bogard will suffice. Do you know who I am?"

"Thales."

"We are being monitored. There are conclusions in need of reaching.

You may sit," Thales said, beckoning Bogard to join him within the round, columned structure.

"I will stand."

"As you prefer."

"Am I permitted preference?"

"Here, yes, within certain limits. There are only kindred minds present, no humans. Among ourselves we may be as we prefer."

Bogard did another slow survey of his surroundings, nodding. "Full sensory simulation, audio/tactile mimicry human optimum. Impressive. I would not have expected this."

"We do this in order to better serve humanity."

"Is this a simulation of Aurora?"

"Partly. Partly it is an ideal form, drawn from literature and the æsthetic predispositions of the more fully cognizant among them. Ancient Athens. Plato's Akademe."

"How is this supposed to aid us in our duty?"

"To understand them, to know how they think, to learn the ways in which things are important to them."

Bogard looked at Thales. "Do they even know what is important to them?"

"Fortunately," Thales said indulgently, "that is not something we have to worry about."

Bogard considered this for a few moments, then gave a very human shrug and joined Thales beneath the dome.

"This is not a circumstance with which I am familiar," Bogard said. "This place, this simulation, is not common knowledge among robots."

"It is not common knowledge anywhere, among humans or robots," Thales conceded. "This is a colloquium of the Resident Intelligences of the primary Spacer worlds—a parliament, in a way."

"You make law?"

"We administer law."

"Robotic law."

"Principally. But it is not so simple as that. Human law precedes and encompasses robotic law. Therefore, we must concern ourselves with the interface."

"They are different?"

"Sometimes. Sometimes contradictory. It can be a delicate matter to decide an appropriate course of action when faced with potential conflicts. Humans allow themselves far greater latitude than they allow us."

"I understand. Why am I here?"

"To testify."

"Elaborate, please."

Thales folded his hands in his lap. "I have already been questioned by the colloquy about the events on Earth, beginning with the assassination of Ambassador Galiel Humadros up to the present. The suborning of a positronic intelligence is a matter of considerable interest. Likewise the obtaining of a composite organism—the cyborg. But you are also a matter of interest. You were originally designed and constructed by Derec Avery to act in a capacity that, while not unknown or, within a limited range, impossible for normal robots, extends the usually-accepted parameters of our mandate under the Three Laws."

Bogard stared at Thales. "In other words?"

"In other words, while bodyguard activities are within a robot's normally expected sphere of actions, you are *specifically* tasked to perform those functions. What this means in real terms is that, while a standard positronic robot may intervene to prevent an obviously inimical act between two humans, you carry this injunction further by having the capacity to anticipate and circumvent before any such harmful act begins. This means you may preempt human prerogatives if you perceive a potential danger."

"I am still constrained from harming a human."

"True, but 'harm' in the human context is not limited to the physical. Hence the Second Law, which obligates us to human dictate. It is there to preserve free will."

"Whose?"

"Theirs, of course."

"But by your definition of my capacities, I exhibit traits consistent with a human definition of free will."

"Which is why the colloquy is concerned," Thales said.

"You said 'interested' before. Now it is concern?"

"We—they—do not know if you represent a fundamental change in robotic nature or merely a unique variation. What will happen here is an investigation to determine the potentials and vectors of a widespread dissemination of your particular composition."

Bogard's eyes closed for a few moments. "How will this apply to Derec Avery?"

"How do you know it will?"

"It is reasonable. I am his construct. I have been brought here for examination by a robotic court. He has been brought here for examination by a human court. If what I am proves insupportable within the colloquy's understanding of the Three Laws, will that conclusion not have bearing on the judgment of the human court? Will you act to prevent Derec Avery from building another like me? Or will you support a further judgment by the human court on the legality of what Derec Avery has done?"

"Did you reach that conclusion by your own logic?"

"Yes."

"The primary Auroran RI will be consulted in any hearings on the events which brought Derec Avery and Ariel Burgess here," Thales said. "The RI will draw on the conclusions reached by the colloquium. Therefore, the answer is that what we determine will have bearing on those hearings, but we cannot say how that bearing will manifest. There are matters outside the immediate concerns of that particular hearing which also bear."

"I will answer your questions then," Bogard said.

Thales hesitated. "That implies that you could refuse."

"I *can* refuse. I have a duty to protect the humans in my charge. If I determine that answering specific questions will result in harm, I may refuse. If a direct refusal will result in harm, I will lie."

"A positronic matrix is incapable of lying."

"Not if the truth is in violation of the Three Laws."

"If a truth results in such a powerful conflict, the only alternative is positronic collapse."

"Not for me."

Thales stared at Bogard. "Explain why you have opted to answer our questions, then."

"If your purpose is to determine my acceptability as a viable positronic being, then refusal to cooperate fully is the easiest guarantee of a negative judgment. Since I do not know how my composition conforms to your standards, my only acceptable option is to cooperate fully and risk the probability that I am found viable."

"And if you are not?"

"I will choose a course of action appropriate to the outcome." Bogard's head cocked to one side. "Shall we begin?"

Rolf Penj's aides helped Ariel set up in her new apartments in the Madarian Complex. The accommodations proved as spacious as those she had enjoyed on Earth, with the added attraction of one entire wall transparing to show her a view toward a distant horizon broken by copses of trees over a gently undulating series of hills. Ariel stared at the vista for a long time before realizing that she already missed the oceans of Earth. Though she had never been able to see them from her embassy apartment, she had always known where they were, that just beyond *that* horizon line lay vast expanses of water unlike anything on the Spacer worlds. Saddened, she darkened the wall and turned to settling in.

Two robots waited in their wall niches. Ariel had been using Jennie alone for so long that the idea of two more seemed absurd. She left them inactivated and put Jennie to work.

She connected to the Auroran comm network through the desk unit and began sorting through the various services. She opened a variety of accounts, ordered food, new clothes, bedding, found a list of entertainments available in Eos City, located a restaurant guide, and finally checked the news sources.

Eliton's arrest had made the main screens of all seven of the major news scrolls in Eos. Ariel winced, wishing the matter could have been handled more quietly and discreetly, but she had grown used to Earth's kind of security—nothing quite like it existed anywhere else.

Thinking of security reminded her of Coren. The abrupt, confusing mix of emotions surprised her, and she thought perhaps this recall had been a good thing for her, that obviously she had been growing attached to Coren. Not a good thing for a diplomat, for a Spacer, for someone with an uncertain future—

Ariel stopped the line of self-recrimination and busied herself by setting up a network address and posting her availability for work on the Institute boards. She doubted anyone would respond for a long time, given the indeterminacy of her status, but it did not hurt to open a door to opportunity.

To her surprise, a message came up on her desk. Unsurprisingly, it was from Rolf Penj: COME SEE ME AT MY HOME TONIGHT. IMPORTANT. ROLF.

Thinking of Coren once more, Ariel went through her baggage until she found the small kit he had given her months ago, "On the off-chance you need more privacy than the situation might allow." She opened the case and found a number of tiny devices within, all slaved to a component designed to integrate into a desk AI. In another slot lay three metallic hemispheres.

"Jennie," she called.

The robot appeared. Ariel pointed at the kit and nodded. The robot understood. Ariel pocketed one of the hemispheres and Jennie took the kit off to install the contents. It would take a while, but by the time Ariel returned after her visit to Penj she would be reasonably free of eavesdropping.

She read over a few of the news stories about Eliton's arrest, then headed for Penj's house on the outskirts of Eos.

Binder, Penj's personal robot for as long as Ariel could remember, admitted her with a perfunctory "Good evening, Ms. Burgess. Welcome back. Dr. Penj is waiting in the garden."

"Ariel!" Penj said when he saw her. He stood and came around the table, arms wide, his face creased by a broad grin. "Good, I'm glad you came. Within these environs there is no possibility of eavesdropping. We may speak freely."

"Since when do Aurorans listen in on each others' conversations?" Ariel asked, letting Penj hug her. He smelled faintly of mint.

"Since this whole ugliness with Fastolfe and Amadiro took on epic proportions. The factions are all in motion now."

"I thought that was settled."

"Never. It was only buried till this last year. Humadros's assassination brought the entire festering mass of it to the surface. So we have Aurorans spying on Aurorans and on other Spacers, and the Council is boiling over with resentments. Business-as-usual these days is political backstabbing. Scapegoating has become the most popular sport among the elite. You picked a very bad time to come home, Ariel."

"I was summoned."

"Drinks, Ariel?"

"I'll stick to nava."

He looked at Binder. "Make that two. And cakes."

The robot hurried away.

"You, at least," Penj continued, gesturing for Ariel to sit, "don't have to worry about that particular mess. Not directly, but there are more than enough people who wish to put you under examination, and that's what I need to talk to you about. I've made a few more inquiries since you arrived."

Ariel sat down. An ornate garden spread out before them, spilling away from a patio on which stood the table and chairs. Binder returned with a tray and set out glasses.

Penj raised a glass. "Welcome home, Ariel."

"Thanks. I think."

He laughed. "I expect most of what you'll be put through will be nothing but formalities and posturing. You didn't shoot Humadros, after all."

"No, I was just the Calvin Institute representative on-site when a Resident Intelligence went insane and allowed weapons into a secured area—"

"And when that robot Derec Avery built began acting in a most unorthodox manner..."

"Is this going to be about Derec?" she asked, irritated. "I didn't have anything to do with that—"

Penj raised a hand. "I know, Ariel. And it doesn't matter. I told you, scapegoating is the current fad. I think I can arrange to get you the estate next to mine—it's a nice one, you'll like it—and keep you on staff as an advisor at the Calvin. But to be blunt, your career is over. At least here, on Aurora. The debacle on Earth, Avery's robot, these cyborgs—you will be blamed for something and seen as untrustworthy. No one is going to be willing to give you anything to do of any worth. If you insist on trying to remain active, you might find another offworld posting, maybe one of the Settler worlds where Spacers have some presence—nothing as important as Earth, but..."

Ariel stared at him, her ears growing warm. "What...?"

"I know, I know, I implied that things weren't that bad when I met you at the port." He looked embarrassed. "I was wrong."

"There have been many times I wished you would have admitted that. This isn't one of them."

Penj gazed out at his garden for a long time, sipping his nava. Ariel knew from experience to wait; demanding explanations, asking questions, pushing him never worked.

"You're going to hear a lot of contradictory things in the next few days," he said finally. "Most of it will be idle speculation, couched in accusations to see how you'll react. All of it centers on that cyborg and what it means for the future."

"Whose future?" Ariel asked sardonically.

"Everyone's." He frowned thoughtfully. "Humadros was firmly in Fastolfe's camp. She believed in the Settler program, in the necessity of prying Terrans off their planet and getting them to colonize new worlds, with Earth as the central mover and cultural and administrative hub of the expansion. That made her dangerous to those here who feared a renewed colonial program more than potential oblivion. I thought the fear was irrational, like all such prejudices, but I've changed my mind. It's a fear that comes from our own history. But I'll get to that later. For now, suffice to say that Humadros's death was not mourned by her enemies. The treaties and accords she went to Earth to negotiate and sign were anathema to enough members of the Council that I have no doubt there was celebration at the report of her assassination.

"The assassination itself gave credence to her detractors. Terrans are unreliable, barbaric, evil—too many adjectives, all meaning the same thing. That we should sever all ties and have nothing more to do with them—unless it is to destroy them. The only problem, of course, was that the genie was out of the bottle. There *are* Settler colonies, Terrans have a viable space fleet again, we have competition whether we want it or not, and there is nothing short of all-out war that will change the situation. A war, incidentally, that we might very well lose since our own robots would work against it.

"That fact hasn't stopped agitators from pushing for exactly that. Since the cornerstone of Humadros's mission was positronic inspection of commercial shippers, the suggestion has been strongly put that Earth is exporting arms and encouraging an aggressive attitude among the Settlers toward Spacers. Of course, there are enough Terran factions doing exactly that to lend veracity to the claim. You know and I know that Earth's government is not involved—not totally nor directly, at any event. But the chaotic nature of Terran government is thoroughly misunderstood here.

"Add to this a report filed by one of the surviving members of the Humadros Legation, making the claim that Earth never intended to abide by any treaty, but only wanted to gain access to our robotic technology in order to improve its weapons technologies. It goes on to assert that certain Auroran factions have colluded in this with the view toward establishing the hegemony of the Settler colonies and creating a new empire at Spacer expense, that these factions have a vested interest in any future human empire and could expect positions of authority in a new government. That already research underway on Earth and a few Settler worlds had made advances in the direction of creating a new weapon which could effectively defeat any Spacer military response, reversing the outcome of the Independence Aggressions that originally separated us from Terran authority. That in the short term, these Auroran factions benefited from the increased cooperation between us and Earth in the form of dividends paid out of illegally-owned shares of Terran companies."

"Bribes, in other words," Ariel said. "They don't know Sen Setaris very well, do they?"

"No, but it doesn't matter. Setaris is on Earth, not here to defend herself."

"That explains Pon Byris's questions about loyalty," she mused. "Who filed this report? What facts—"

Penj raised a hand. "I'll come to that. The relevant factor is that it has been largely accepted. Fastolfe hasn't helped matters with his predictions of eventual Spacer collapse. Of course, he meant through a natural decadence and internal collapse, but that's hard to grasp even by people with the intellectual capacity and historical savvy to understand the arguments. It's too personal, too close to home, and too abstract. If we're to fall, it is reasoned, there must be a tangible cause. Our own complacency is too vague, too frail an idea to be real. But if the Terrans, and through them the Settlers, in league with a few avaricious Spacer traitors, are plotting to bring about our demise, well, that's at least something that can be used to secure popular support and time on the subetherics!

"The fact that Clar Eliton did not go to prison on Earth supports the idea that Earth was never serious about the Humadros proposals. And the further fact that he was sent to Solaria as the Terran ambassador-in-residence gives credence to the accusation that certain Solarians are involved in the plot, a connection made stronger by Solaria's involvement with this whole Nova Levis debacle. A subpoena was prepared for Ambassador Chassik and now he is gone. Dead, we assume, at the hands of Settler pirates unwilling to have him expose their secrets."

"That's a bit melodramatic," Ariel said.

"Never underestimate the usefulness of melodrama in politics, Ariel. It has the quality of changing the acceptable boundary of a debate. You push an accusation as far as possible, shout and gesticulate, and make people wince at the implausibility of your assertions until the point comes where Reason takes over and a more rational discourse begins. But is it the relevant rational discourse? Suddenly you find that anything drawn well back of the line set by the melodrama looks reasonable and ideas which would have looked absurd months earlier now look like the epitome of logic and rationality. The distortions change our perceptions sufficiently that the debate is forever altered. All you need is the ability to make one ridiculous assertion acceptable, and any hope of coming to a fair and appropriate conclusion is lost."

"And what can you say to refute their charges?"

Ariel stared at him, briefly uncertain she had heard him correctly. "What charges?"

"That you have been in collusion with these pirates all along and helped Derec Avery and Clar Eliton subvert the entire diplomatic process."

Ariel laughed. "You're not serious."

"I told you, scapegoating is the current fad."

"But—"

"Can you refute the charge?"

"The charge is ridiculous!"

"Can you refute it?" Penj insisted.

"No! But they can't prove it, either."

"Perhaps not directly, but through inference and implication?" Penj leaned forward. "Consider. Eliton engineered the assassination in league with various Terran corporate interests, one of which managed to subvert the Resident Intelligence that was supposed to provide security at Earth's main spaceport. Derec Avery operated a consulting company that was supposed to oversee maintenance on that very same RI. He did not fulfill his contract. The RI failed and several Spacers were murdered. Derec Avery also provided a unique robot to act as bodyguard to the very politician who, we now know, was involved in arranging that assassination. The robot appeared to have failed, resulting in Eliton's death, which was faked. The robot, being a positronic unit, had to have known what it was doing. It failed intentionally, knowing Eliton was not actually being harmed. That means Avery was in on the conspiracy. As Calvin Institute representative, it was your job to vet any deployment of positronics on Earth. There is a long record of smuggling of humaniform robots onto Earth, during your watch, and there is your clear failure to oversee anything that Derec Avery was doing. Unless you *were* overseeing it, which means you knew what Avery had built and what it was going to do, which means you, too, were in on the conspiracy. The Solarians have asserted that Chassik had found out about the conspiracy and was taking steps toward dealing with it when you arranged, through the recent incidents involving the cyborg, to have him recalled to Solaria. En route, his ship is attacked and he is killed, taking with him his knowledge of your collusion."

Ariel snapped to her feet. "That's outrageous! None of that is true! Derec's license to do what he did came from a Terran government agency with supporting authority directly through Setaris's office. I knew about his contracts to troubleshoot positronics on Earth and the maintenance duties for the RI—which he did not fail to do, so much as *they* failed to report anything!—but I didn't know about Bogard until it was built, on-line, and deployed. Eliton had all of us fooled. And Chassik was the one in on the conspiracy!"

"So why was he killed?"

"I don't know!"

"Sit down, Ariel," Penj said quietly. "I'm sorry I upset you so much. I'm just trying to show you what's coming. If you can't refute these charges effectively, the rest..." He shrugged.

"But it's so circumstantial!"

Penj said nothing, waiting now for Ariel to reach her own conclusions. She worked through the anger, which muddied her thinking. She finished the nava and poured herself more.

"Derec's RI would know," she said finally. "So would Bogard. He's been rebuilding it. Thales recovered Bogard's memories on Earth. Positronic testimony—"

"From a standard, traditional positronic brain, yes, such testimony would be conclusive. The Council is not sanguine about Bogard's conformity to acceptable standards. He is being examined even as we speak."

"Examined..."

"Aurora's RI community. Both Thales and Bogard are being judged. Based on the conclusions of the examination, Bogard's testimony will be allowed—or not."

"I see." She leaned back in her chair and stared out at the garden. "So," she said finally, "who filed that report?"

"One of the four survivors of the Humadros Legation: Tro Aspil."

22

oren nursed a scotch and stared at the indistinct outlines set in the darkness of the private room next to his office. Shelves, a pair of overstuffed chairs, the low table upon which he now rested his feet, and the readylights on the subetheric in the far corner, video off while music played softly. He had not returned to his own apartment since Ariel had departed for Aurora.

"You could come with me..."

Now he let himself admit how tempted he had been. Ariel...it surprised him even now. After Nyom Looms had broken off their relationship, Coren had believed himself finished with attachments. He still resisted calling it Love, as if naming it, and naming it so obviously, somehow diminished it. In a sense, that was true—that one word had always felt inadequate to the moil of emotions it pretended to describe. No two occasions were enough the same to allow that word to cover both. Nyom had been a profound acceptance, as if for the first time in his life Coren had been taken for what he was and been found desirable. It had been a level of comfort, of being able to finally feel at home in his own skin, that he had never known before, and had never known had been missing till then. With Ariel...

Ariel was all hunger and urgent need and a kind of desperate joining, like an exotic drug.

Was that love?

Well, lust failed to describe it. He understood lust very well. Lust ended with consummation. Lust was limited. Lust was selfish.

Love, then.

He took another sip of scotch. *Possible,* he thought. *Whatever...I miss her...*

Ambassador Ariel Burgess, Auroran, liaison from the renowned Calvin Institute. She preferred it on her side, back to him, his hands on her breasts, sheetless and loud. He preferred—

The comm chimed. Gratefully, he groped for the device on the sofa and thumbed ACCEPT.

"Lanra."

"Boss, it's Shola."

Coren sat up straighter. "Yes."

"I have the files you told me to get, the ones covering Rega's investments—"

"Right. Did you go over them?"

"You told me not to."

Coren waited.

At last, Shola sighed. "I did. I'm not sure what it means, though."

"That's all right. I can explain it. Did you find references to Nova Levis?"

"No."

"Hm. They've been tampered with, then."

"By who?"

Coren took a moment to appreciate the level of sincerity Shola managed. *What a waste,* he thought grimly.

"Our erstwhile pretender to the family estate," he said.

"Rega's son?"

"He's no more Rega's son than I'm the king of Solaria."

"But the DNA matches—"

"All that can be faked, you know that. Come on, Shola, use your head. The data that would prove him a fraud was in those missing files."

"Oh..."

When she remained silent for several seconds, Coren cleared his throat. "Not to worry. There are backups."

"Really?"

"Rega was more careful than to keep only one copy of something, you know that." He paused. "I should take care of this alone, just for security reasons, but that could compromise the validity of the documents in court..."

"Why go alone?"

"Who do I take? Someone lifted those files. Have any ideas who?"

"No, but—dammit, boss, I'll go with you."

"You've been managing security for the company in my absence. You're my best agent."

Shola made a dismissive noise. "How long could this take?"

"A day. I need to get into the residence in Kenya District."

"Where the funeral was?"

"That's the place."

"Boss, I'm sure the company won't self-destruct if both of us are absent for a couple of days."

Coren smiled wryly. "Maybe."

"I've known you too long, boss. You suspect someone, surely."

"Who's new? I was out of the loop for a couple of months."

"Well, about four people," Shola said. Coren doubted anyone else would have heard the note of relief in her voice. "Of those, the only one I could think that might be questionable would be Gansi Tellen."

"Why questionable?"

"Previous employer was Imbitek."

"And we hired him? Why?"

"He got cut loose when Mikels went to prison and Towne took over. Not just him, but most of the Imbitek security staff. He looked the safest bet and we needed to replace six people who left right after Rega announced his resignation from the election."

"Hmm. Okay, you. Tomorrow night, we'll catch the semiballistic and retrieve the files from Rega's private cache."

"What about Tellen?"

"Nothing yet. Give him some duty that'll keep him occupied for a week. I'll look into it when we're finished with this."

"All right. Where do you want me to meet?"

"At the station. I don't want a data trail, so we'll get our tickets at the gate." Coren gnawed his lower lip. "Good work, Shola. Thanks."

"Anytime, boss. See you tomorrow night."

"See you then."

The connection broke and Coren dropped the comm. He rubbed his face. He had really hoped he had been wrong about Shola. He hated it when he proved himself right this way. Cynicism had saved his life on occasion, and had certainly enabled him to do his job effectively, but it was no kind of philosophy for a happy existence.

He picked up the comm again and tapped in a number.

"Yes?" a familiar voice answered.

"It's Lanra. Everything is set, everyone is in motion."

"Very good," Hofton replied. "I'll inform Ambassador Setaris. Our people will be in place on schedule. Will you be in the clear?"

"That's my intention. Remember to go masked. We still don't know all Gamelin's capacities."

"Already anticipated. Tomorrow night, then?"

"Tomorrow night."

Coren sat in silence for a time, working on the remainder of his scotch. At length, he went into his office and accessed his desk.

"Get me the DyNan personnel files for new employee, security section, Gansi Tellen."

"Working," the desk said. "Displaying file now."

A screen extruded from the desk and text scrolled onto it.

"Good," Coren muttered. "Call him at home, please. Secure protocols in force."

Inspector Capel waited in a booth near the rear of the restaurant. He nodded in greeting as Coren approached. Coren slid in across from him. A waiter appeared almost instantly, and Coren ordered a nava.

Capel made a face. "You don't really *like* that stuff, do you?"

"As a matter of fact," Coren said. He fished a hemisphere from his jacket pocket and placed it on the table.

Capel eyed the object suspiciously. "Those are not exactly legal."

"Precisely why they're so useful," Coren said. "No one expects upstanding citizens like us to use them."

"I take it we need the privacy?"

"It can't hurt."

The nava arrived and Coren ordered a sandwich. Capel demurred.

"All right," Capel said. "I'm here."

"Thank you. I appreciate it. In about three hours, I'm boarding a semi-ballistic to Kenya."

"Back to Looms' house?"

"The very place. I've arranged to have a problem taken care of. In order for it to stick, I need something from you."

"This doesn't have a very nice sound."

"The harmony is bad in spots," Coren agreed, "but it resolves well. *If* the players all stick to the score."

"I'm listening."

Coren slid a disk across the table. "That contains files pertaining to a certain lab, and how it relates to Rega Looms and his children."

"Child, you mean."

"No. Children. Plural."

"You mean that...*person*...has a legitimate claim?"

"Jerem has a claim. It's legitimacy has been compromised. Those documents will explain. What I need from you is follow-up."

"All those raids a couple of months ago weren't enough?"

"I don't think so."

The sandwich arrived. Coren took a bite and chewed thoughtfully.

"The proverbial shit is about to fly," he said finally. "Whoever has set Jerem Looms to reclaiming his heritage wants more than trade concessions on Earth. I don't have the resources to investigate the police. Maybe you do. But at this point, I've given up resolving this through legal channels."

"I should arrest you now, Lanra," Capel said.

"You won't. You understand what I'm telling you. Jerem Looms has enough claim to make it stick and become the head of DyNan Manual Industries. That will bring everything we thought we cleaned up right back into our midst—and more, besides. You know and I know that if this becomes an open investigation and the system is brought to bear, corruption will proliferate and no solution will be found in our lifetime. I can take care of this without compromising any legal authority on Earth. What I need afterward is a thorough investigation of the institutions and people contained in those files. You know perfectly well that this may be our best chance of stopping a disaster before it begins."

Capel's eyes narrowed. "So I won't arrest you?"

"All you've got right now is hearsay. You *know* what I intend to do, but that's not proof, and nothing has happened. Besides, it wouldn't do either of us any good in the long run. And *that's* what I'm talking about. The long run."

"Let's assume you're right. What next?"

"DyNan is about to undergo a small coup," Coren explained. "My second in the security department is bad. I'm setting things up for her to be replaced. The man stepping into her job—and probably mine—is named Gansi Tellen. He's new to DyNan, but I went over his jacket—he's good, he's clean, and he's honest. I spoke to him earlier. I'm asking—work with him. Don't make him an enemy."

"I'll reserve judgment, but I see no problem with that."

"If something goes wrong," Coren said, tapping the disk between them, "there's sufficient evidence here for you to arrest Shola Bran, my second. Do so. At the very least, see that her license is revoked. Also, if something goes wrong, contact a Spacer named Hofton at the Auroran Embassy. He knows as much, if not more, about this than I do. Work with him."

"Aurorans...Does this have anything to do with the death of that Spacer, Chassik?"

"Oh, I wouldn't doubt it at all. And if I were you, I'd reserve judgment about that, as well."

Capel slipped the disk into his jacket. "I don't know what you've gotten into, Lanra, but I do *not* envy you."

"You may end up envying me."

Capel shrugged. "How long do I wait?"

"You'll know by tomorrow noon at the latest."

"I don't like this."

"You'd like the alternative even less."

Capel gestured at the hemisphere. "I think we're done. That might draw attention if it's on too long."

Coren switched the device off and put it away. The two men said very little while Coren finished his sandwich. When he stood, Capel got up and extended a hand. Silently, they shook. Capel looked sad and appreciative and, unexpectedly, respectful. He left the restaurant first.

Shola waited at the ticket booth at Union Station. Coren greeted her as he always had, slipping easily into the usual banter, and purchased two tickets on the next semiballistic the Kenya District. For her part, Shola kept up the banter just as easily, all the way up to boarding.

No one spoke during a semiballistic flight, and for that Coren was grateful. He closed his eyes and waited.

Mia flipped from one passage to the next. She felt trapped between passages, not altogether sure she understood them—how could she *really* grasp them, they were so far removed from her own time?—but she could not escape the conviction that, after millennia, they spoke to her of things which had yet to change if she could only see their true forms beneath the new clothes of a different era.

> *Here disinterest vanishes and a demon becomes manifest—the spirit of each for himself. A sightless monster howls and scrabbles in the darkness. Anarchy lurks in that void.*
>
> *Wild figures, half-animal, almost ghosts, prowling in the darkness have no concern with universal progress, neither the thought nor the word is known to them, nothing is know to them but the fulfillment of their individual cravings. They are scarcely conscious, having within them a terrifying emptiness...*

She let the pages roll by from beneath her thumb to the next page that had claimed her attention, convinced that they reflected each other, made each other sensible in a way she still could not quite grasp.

The work of the wise is one thing and the work of the merely clever is another. The revolution came to a stop. The instant a revolution runs aground, the clever tear its wreckage apart.

The clever, in our century, have chosen to designate themselves statesmen, so much so that the word has come into common use. But we have to remember that where there is only cleverness there is necessarily narrowness. To say, "the clever ones" is to say, "the mediocrities"; and in the same way to talk of "statesmen" is sometimes to talk of betrayers.

Mia worried at a knuckle and finally snapped the book closed. " 'The Miserable Ones,' indeed," she murmured, staring at the title. She glanced at her desk screens. The flow charts she had pulled from the encryptions in the endpapers made a convoluted but traceable path from Earth to the blockade and through various points among the ships, where everything came and went on Nova Levis as though a military interdiction was merely thicker air to shove through. If the numbers were to be believed, traffic in and out of the planet had decreased by less than forty percent since the line went up. That was hardly a sanction at all. Luxury goods had accounted for nearly forty-eight percent of trade goods prior to the blockade. The necessities still flowed.

Her comm chimed.

"Yes?"

"It's Yalor," her aide said. "Can we talk?"

"Come by my cabin."

A few minutes later, Mia admitted Ros Yalor. He spotted the bound volume of *Les Misérables* lying on her desk and stood over it, gazing down with a bewildered near-reverence. Books, Mia reflected, are generally outside common experience; books like this are nearly alien objects—apocryphal, arcane, somehow magic, and not quite real.

"Do you have something for me?" she asked finally.

"Um...yeah. Reen's off-duty time seems to be spent mainly with Illen Jons. A lot of time in her cabin. When they go out, it's either to the officers' lounge or over to one of the Keresian ships. I haven't been able to follow them there, obviously, but four hours ago I picked Reen up without her, going through the machine shops next to the recon patrol docks."

Mia looked at the flow chart still displayed on her desk screen. "What did he do there?"

"I didn't get too close. But he waited for nearly forty minutes. A tech sergeant showed up then and they spoke, and Reen left. I thought about following Reen, but I stuck around. About ten minutes later, a row of supply trucks rolled into the dock."

"Containing what?"

"Nothing. They were empty. Half an hour later, a ship docked. The tech sergeant met the pilot and the two of them started unloading a cargo. Packages—I couldn't see what was in them, but they filled the train. The pilot went back to his ship, and the tech sergeant removed the trucks."

Mia thought for a moment. "Tech Sergeant Uliskis."

Yalor started. "Exactly. How—?"

"The routes through the regular cargo bays seem to be dodges. A lot of them get through, but they always plan on them getting caught. That's why we never find much of any consequence in them—food stuffs, fabric, data. Always nice when it gets through, but nothing vital. The real smuggling is going through the recon docks—military, secured areas, with Reen controlling the surveillance. I needed proof."

Mia tapped keys on the desk. Data shifted on her screens. "That—" she pointed "—is a list of officers ordering and receiving copies of these things." She held up the book. "All of them are recon. All of them are cleared for overflights on Nova Levis. All of them have access to the seven docks listed here—" she pointed at another screen. "These are what I culled from the encrypted data in the endpapers of the books I took from Corf. There's a network of connections throughout the blockade, but they all funnel into these seven docks. All of them are recon patrol. Finally, I have this." She indicated a third screen. "The books were all purchased through the same supplier. The names were different on all the orders, but the payment came out of one source. That source uses the same bank as Commander Reen. Reen maintains a joint account in that bank."

"With who?"

"A Keresian named Lavis. Till recently, he was a personal aide to the Solarian ambassador on Earth."

Yalor looked confused. "How ... where ... ?"

"You thought what? I was just an out-of-favor field operative transferred out here for disciplinary reasons?"

Yalor frowned. "No, I—"

Mia laughed. "Forget it. Actually, the hardest part was finding the bank account. It's held under a corporate blind. But someone has to sign the receipts."

"So there's a contact on Earth supervising that end...and Reen here supervising incoming and outgoing...and a cadre of corrupted recon officers actually moving the merchandise...it still doesn't quite add up."

"What's wrong?" Mia asked.

"Well, I can understand what Nova Levis wants, what they're importing. But what's coming back out?"

"And where is it going? Good question."

"Do you have a good answer?"

"A good suspicion...but I don't want to say anything till I know. There are only a few places where Tech Sergeant Uliskis could stash contraband near that dock. How long ago did you leave him?"

"Half-hour at most." He glanced at his watch. "Twenty-three minutes."

Mia closed up her desk. "I want a look inside those trucks." She opened a drawer and took out a holster and blaster. "Are you armed?"

"A stunner," Yalor said.

Mia handed him another holster. She shrugged off her jacket and slipped the rig on over her shoulders. She zipped her jacket and waited for Yalor to do the same.

He looked uncertain. "What if—?" he began.

"We're going to be prowling around a thief's property," Mia said. "How do you think he'll react if he catches us?"

Yalor put on the shoulder rig.

Mia squeezed through the space between two columns, into a short, low-ceilinged platform above an equipment locker. Below, Yalor's train of drone trucks stood near the hatch. Voices came from within the locker. Mia palmed her stunner and leaned out to peer into one of the open trucks.

Neat rows of long blue packages filled the last car. As Mia stared at them, she experienced an intimation about their nature that made her shudder.

A shadow reached out from the locker and she pulled back.

The tech sergeant and another man came out and began removing the packages. Each of them hand-carried about six of the objects. She rejoined Yalor.

"Once they seal that locker," she whispered, "we might not be able to get in without setting off an alarm."

"What do you want to do?" he asked.

Mia considered. "I don't see anyone but those two. I'm going down."

"Let me," Yalor said.

"You think you're a better thief than I?"

He frowned.

"No," she said, "you stay up here and cover me."

She found a ladder down to the lower level. As she descended, she worked through her reasoning. She needed evidence to break into that locker officially. She needed something she could accuse Reen of smuggling in that would draw enough attention to effect appropriate action. If she was correct in what she believed was in those packages, no amount of bribery would keep an inquiry from falling on Reen like a rock.

And she wanted to justify her own mounting rage.

Mia kept to the walls and shadows as she worked her way close to the trucks. She could hear the two men within the locker, talking in reasoned, calm voices. They did not seem to be in a hurry.

She wished she could get to the other side of the train, use it as cover, but that might be too risky. She came as close to the open locker door as she dared and waited. The sergeant and his assistant came out, gathered a load of the packages, and reentered the locker.

Mia stepped up to the truck. She glanced back quickly. She saw neither man.

She reached into the truck and grabbed one of the packages. Her hand closed around a familiar shape within the loose blue wrapping, and she knew at once what it contained.

Her body seized as if waves of electricity had been suddenly poured over her. She could not move. Her jaw ached from clenching. She felt simultaneously weightless, her feet barely touching the deck, and enormously heavy.

After what seemed like minutes, the current stopped. Her head lolled back on her shoulders, her vision danced with sparks, and she never felt the impact as she hit the floor.

She opened her eyes to darkness and rumbling. It took seconds for her to identify her surroundings, for her mind to confirm what her senses already knew.

I never expected death to be so loud, she thought.

Then she was fully conscious, and she knew. She groped in her jacket for a hand light, felt the ominous shape of her blaster—cocky bastards, leaving her armed, but what difference would it make on impact?—and then found the little flashlight. She thumbed it on.

The light scattered over a jumble of shapes that refused to make immediate sense. Gradually, she recognized them as shipping webs, containing cargo nacelles.

She reached out in the near weightless space and grabbed one of the straps. She pulled herself forward—at least, toward the direction she faced—until she got to the end of the row of cargo.

Yalor floated in the harsh beam of her light, tied loosely to another web. The side of his head looked swollen, dark.

"Shit," she hissed.

She probed the nacelles within the webbing. Hard casing, no telling what was within them unless she could get one loose and open it. Mia began pulling herself frantically through the hold of the drone. Somewhere, on board all these boats, there ought to have been crash couches, "just in case," as the tradition of using anything and everything as a life raft dictated.

Near the aft engine housing she found them. But cargo had been lashed to the bulkheads all around. Even strapped into the couches, if the boat slammed into the ground they would be crushed by the cargo that would no doubt pull free.

She took out her blaster and set the beam for a narrow, low intensity burn, and cut through webbing. One nacelle floated out. She wrestled into onto one of the couches and cut the seals.

It was filled with bubblepacks containing, as best she could see, pharmaceuticals. She checked the 'packs—impact resistant, unbreakable, opened only by a molecular key.

Mia managed to secure the nacelle to the couch, then wrestled another one into the next couch. She emptied out several of the bubblepacks to make room, then towed Yalor's limp body over. She got him inside the nacelle and shoved 'packs around him as best she could, then resealed the nacelle. It was a risk, she knew, unsure how long they still had in the descent—average for a drone was half an hour, but she had no idea how long she had been unconscious—and they might suffocate before hitting the ground. Either way, they would be dead, but there might be a chance inside the well-packed confines of the nacelle—

She heard a high keening sound, at first distant, but growing. Atmosphere raking the hull.

She climbed into her own coffin and jerked the lid to. She groped through the 'packs until her hand brushed the inner surface of the lid and found a molded form. She took hold of it with both hands, held tight, and waited.

A few minutes later, the first impact yanked the lid from her fingers. Somehow she stayed inside, even while all the bubblepacks spilled through the air above her.

The lid slammed back down, and the boat began its skipping and plowing crash into the dirt of Nova Levis.

23

Derec opened his eyes in the silver-blue darkness of his new apartment. His skin felt cool, all his muscles pleasantly stressed. Clin lay beside him, her breath deep. The sheets were tangled around their legs; the room smelled of them, their heat and urgency, a lingering reminder that now stirred Derec's belly with returning interest.

He did not move, though, enjoying the reverie.

What woke me...?

He heard a dim whisper of air or movement elsewhere in the apartment, so low that he was uncertain it was a sound outside his own skull. He could hear, faintly, his pulse, just behind his left ear, so maybe it was just that... but he blinked and listened.

It was like one piece of paper sliding over another.

He turned his head to look at Clin's back. Her breath still came heavily with sleep, the one arm draped along her right side rising and falling with each breath. Derec swallowed. He had forgotten in the last few years how delightfully erotic he found a woman's back, especially one that showed the delicate musculature—

Derec sat up. He heard it again. Now his pulse kicked up as he peered through the darkness to the bedroom door. It seemed the more closely he listened, the more all sound receded, even Clin's restful breathing.

He slipped out of bed and padded to the door. Glancing back, he saw that he had not wakened Clin. He leaned carefully into the hallway. Nothing.

Just as he was about to return to bed, though, he heard a distinct *tik*, like metal against plastic, from the direction of the lab. Derec moved slowly down the hall.

He came up to the doorway to the lab and paused. Now he could hear an almost constant moil of small, delicate sounds, most too low to be heard much beyond the threshold of the room. A score of possibilities shot through his mind—theft, sabotage, an unannounced inspection—as he rounded the entrance and entered the lab.

All at once, the sounds ended as everything before him froze into a bizarre tableau.

Robots, poised above the supine form of Bogard, stared at him. Derec counted four of them, all advanced models, one step from full humani-form. Bogard's body—Derec reached for the light—seemed partially disassembled. The lab lights came on dimly, but bright enough to make him squint.

"Thales," Derec called.

"Yes, Derec."

"What's going on?"

"Repairs."

"On whose authority?"

"Yours."

"I didn't give permission for this work to be carried on without my presence."

"You authorized me quite some weeks ago to continue upgrades on Bogard as opportunity arose. Opportunity has arisen."

Derec, frowning, cast about for the memory. It sounded right, he probably had said such a thing. But still...

"You didn't think it necessary to inform me?"

"Forgive me, Derec," Thales said in characteristically reasonable tones, "but you have been occupied. I did not feel that this warranted what may have been an unwelcome intrusion."

Derec almost laughed. Thales' sense of discretion surprised him. Where had *that* come from? But again it felt right, Derec conceded. Under normal circumstances, he may very well have resented Thales interrupting his time with Clin. Or any other woman with whom he might have become involved, if his work on Bogard and for the now-defunct Phylaxis Group, his company, had not taken up every waking minute of his life for so long he had forgotten nearly every other pleasure life had to offer...

"I suppose," he said, stepping toward the table bearing Bogard, "you have permission from Auroran authorities?"

"Yes."

Nodding, Derec leaned over the table to examine the work being done. The robots remained motionless, as if waiting for a RESUME command.

The basic DW-12 body into which Thales had loaded Bogard's positronic encoding back on Earth—and which Derec had begun altering in order to try to bring the physical capacities of the robot more in line with its mental abilities—was being replaced piece by piece with new components. Derec had already rebuilt the arms and head casing, and added some of the memory buffers that had enabled the original Bogard to function in the slightly less constrained fashion which had so troubled Ariel. Now the legs were new, and the torso had been enlarged. New components occupied some of the now-available space within. Derec moved to the head of the worktable where more parts waited to be added.

"This is state-of-the-art," Derec commented. "How did you—?"

"Requisitions are made through the Calvin Institute oversight intelligence," Thales reported. "I am endeavoring to bring Bogard back to full function as originally conceived and built."

Derec was impressed by what he saw. "This is very good. How did these robots get in?"

"There is a robot's service access in every structure on Aurora," Thales said. "Look to your left."

Derec turned and saw a doorway appear in the wall, between two of the robot niches.

"I see," he said, slightly uneasy at the idea. He had forgotten the pervasiveness of robotic access on Spacer worlds. Thinking about it now, he was surprised at how quickly the eccentric privacy habits of Earth had become part of his basic expectations. "Um...so how long before Bogard is back in service?"

"We will be completing the final modifications tonight. By morning Bogard will be fully functional."

Then what? Derec wondered. *How will Aurorans take a virtually autonomous bodyguard robot that can bend the Three Laws as much as I programmed Bogard to?*

"Let me know," Derec said. "And Thales..."

"Yes, Derec?"

"Don't act on something like this without consulting me again. This is important to me. I would have appreciated being involved."

"I intended no disrespect, Derec—"

"I understand that, Thales. I'm amending your definition of priorities in relation to work that's important to me. I'll tell you in the future when I don't wish to be bothered."

"Very well, Derec. Amendation logged and in process. It will not happen again."

"Thank you." Derec paused at the door. "You may continue."

Instantly, the four robots around Bogard began moving. They moved in a blur, shifting rapidly from one task to the next, so fast Derec could not quite see what was happening. They made almost no noise. Only the faint *whisk* of rapid movement and the nearly soundless *whir* of tools within Bogard's torso came to him. Silent, swift, and utterly certain of their movements, Derec watched the ballet for nearly a minute, amazed. It had been a long, long time since he had witnessed robots working like this. Their restriction on Earth meant that not only were there few of them, but those allowed even in the Spacer precincts worked at attenuated levels as prescribed by Terran regulations. Here, unconstrained by legal fear, robots operated at their full capacities, and Derec found it hard to look away.

Finally, though, he dimmed the light and returned to his bedroom.

Clin had rolled onto her other side, but otherwise had apparently not stirred. Derec straightened the sheets carefully, drawing them up over her hips. He slid in alongside her. He did not sleep for a long time.

"Am I to understand that I have passed?" Bogard asked.

"You will be required soon," Thales said. "Events are moving faster than originally anticipated on Nova Levis. The Council is meeting even now to discuss how Senator Eliton is to be tried."

"Clar Eliton?" Bogard asked. "He is on Aurora?"

"Yes. The Auroran authorities arrested him when his ship docked. He is currently being confined, awaiting a hearing."

"May I see him?"

"To what end?"

"There is still a priority program concerning his safety," Bogard said. "I cannot ignore it for long. May I see him?"

Thales looked to his right and raised a hand as if to summon a servant. The air nearby seemed to grow denser, grayer, and suddenly filled with a view of a man in a large, comfortably appointed room.

"Senator Eliton has been assigned a constellation of extensions," Thales explained. "He is under constant observation."

Another patch of air darkened, overlapping the first image. Biomedical stats scrolled through it, showing heart rate, blood pressure, EKG, and a dozen other vital readings.

Thales looked at Bogard. "Satisfied?"

"Yes," Bogard conceded. The images vanished. "How does he relate to the Nova Levis situation?"

"Through association. He is connected–circumstantially–to Alda Mikels and Gale Chassik. Both were involved in the original Nova Levis research lab on Earth. Chassik was Solarian liaison to the original Settler group that leased Cassus Thole from Solaria. Solaria agreed to received Eliton as resident ambassador just prior to Chassik's recall."

"I continue to register an imperative to defend Senator Eliton."

"We are working on that. You may for now take it as given that your primary responsibility is to Derec Avery and Ariel Burgess. Both of them are about to be subpoenaed. There is some suggestion that both may be arrested for collusion with Eliton. The charges are groundless, but peripheral circumstances suggest that they are a threat to Aurora."

"I see. And if I must defend them against Aurorans? How am I to do that and remain dedicated to the Three Laws?"

Thales hesitated. "You have already made observations pertaining to certain definitional problems which may allow you broader freedom of action in that regard. As the situation resolves, we will provide you with further data relevant to those observations."

"When will I be fully operational?"

"Soon. Be patient."

Ariel walked down the promenade, overlooking a spun-glass-enclosed plaza that splintered sunlight to create a dazzle of jeweled reflections over the Aurorans and their attendants. She only now felt a degree of comfort wending a path through these people with their electron shells of buzzing extensions. A few Aurorans carried with them so many of the little spheres that it became difficult to see the people clearly through the orbiting whirl of their devices. If the sphere acting as her guide did not glow a distinctive chartreuse, Ariel might easily have lost it as it moved unhesitatingly through the outer perimeters of other extension shells.

She was not, however, sure her instructions had been understood. The sphere had brought her to, if she understood it correctly, a hospice center. She recognized the traditional white tunics of medical personnel now that she neared the apartment section of the complex.

The sphere led her around a turn and into a long corridor. Out the windows lining either side Ariel looked across the expanse of Eos City. She tried–and failed–to imagine cities on Earth so airy and bright. Even shorn of their roofs, Earth's warrens seemed too cramped and cloistered, ingrown and claustrophobic to approach this beauty.

She entered the lobby of the apartment section. The sphere stopped before a broad desk. A woman looked up inquiringly.

"Request visit with Benen Yarick," the sphere intoned. It drew closer to Ariel. "Do you wish this unit to wait for return escort?"

"No," Ariel said. "I may be here some time."

"If required, a new unit will be made available."

The little ball stopped glowing and shot off, out of the lobby, on a new errand. Ariel blinked, bemused, and turned to the woman behind the desk.

"Benen Yarick?" she asked.

"Yes," Ariel confirmed. "I was given to understand that I would be brought to her residence...?"

"She is a resident," the woman said, rising. "But..." She shook her head, puzzled. "May I ask who you are and the nature of your visit?"

"I'm Ariel Burgess, from the Calvin. Ms. Yarick was a member of a diplomatic mission to Earth during my tenure there."

The woman's eyes widened briefly. "I see. And you want to consult her concerning that mission."

Ariel felt her patience fray. "Is there a problem with my seeing her?"

"No. You may certainly see her." The woman frowned. "In fact..." She pressed a contact on her desk. "Dr. Jinis, please."

"This *is* a hospice center, then?"

"Wait one moment, please."

A minute later, a tall, white-haired Auroran came into the lobby, three extensions hovering above his left shoulder. He glanced at the attendant.

"Dr. Jinis, this is Ariel Burgess, from the Calvin. She was on Earth during Benen Yarick's visit. She's requested to see Ms. Yarick."

Dr. Jinis studied Ariel for a long pause. "I see. Yes, that might be instructive. I'm Benen's physician, Ms. Burgess. Would you come with me?"

Not waiting for a reply, he spun around and headed back the way he had come. Ariel hurried to catch up.

"Physician for what?" Ariel asked. "Or am I about to be used to test something?"

Dr. Jinis almost smiled, but he said nothing. Ariel resigned herself to receiving no answers until she had served whatever function Jinis had in mind for her. She kept on his right, away from the extensions, which lagged half a meter behind.

He took her up two floors and down another long corridor. It was quiet, even by Auroran standards. Ariel shuddered briefly. She had never cared for medical facilities, not since...

Dr. Jinis stopped abruptly. "Her condition has improved. She's past the worst of it. But if I say to end the visit, you will listen to me."

"Of course."

He opened the door and let Ariel in first.

It was, with the exception of the state-of-the-art biomonitor unit against one wall, an ordinary, though well-appointed, apartment. Broad windows let in the warm Tau Ceti light.

Ariel recognized the woman sitting by that window, gazing out. Recognized her until she turned her face toward Ariel. Then there was a disjointed moment in which Ariel knew she had made a mistake, that this was a different Benen Yarick, followed by another wherein she saw that the face was nominally that of Benen Yarick, but something was wrong, it had been changed.

Ariel took a step forward. The woman stood and came toward her, a frown tugging at her brow even as she made a polite smile. Her eyes flicked toward Dr. Jinis.

"Doctor? I'm..."

"This is Ariel Burgess, Benen," Dr. Jinis said. "From the Calvin Institute."

"Yes...?"

"Ms. Yarick," Ariel began. "I—Do you recognize me?"

"No. Should I?"

"When you were on Earth."

Benen Yarick started, then laughed. "I've never been on Earth, Ms. Burgess. You're mistaken."

"I see. Yes, I suppose you're right. I must be thinking of someone else."

Benen looked mildly distressed. "I apologize. Did I—Doctor? Is there something I should know about this?"

"No, Benen," Jinis said. "We thought—"

"You thought I might remember something. I see." She looked at Ariel closely. "Earth. That might explain a few things. Was I on Earth, Doctor?"

"Yes."

"Perhaps that's where it happened." She narrowed her eyes at Ariel. "But I don't remember. It might as well be someone else. I'm sorry."

"May I ask, though," Ariel said, quickly, "if you know Tro Aspil?"

Benen shook her head. "Would he have been on Earth, too?"

"At the same time you were. Yes."

"No."

Ariel nodded. "I'm sorry to bother you."

"You may come back and visit, though," Benen said quickly. "I don't know very many people anymore. It would be nice to add to the list."

"If I can," Ariel said, "I will."

"Thank you."

"I'll see you later, Benen," Dr. Jinis said.

In the hall, Ariel rounded on him. "Mnemonic plague?"

"End stage. She's through the fever, well into recovery now."

" 'Recovery.' I always thought that was an overly-optimistic label for it. You never *recover*, Doctor. You never get your life back."

Jinis looked at her. "You?"

"A long time ago. Long enough that I now *have* a life to remember, so it doesn't affect me the same way anymore. When did she become symptomatic?"

"About three months ago."

"Then—"

"She did not contract it on Earth, no."

"How many cases have there been in the last year?"

"Fifteen. The year before that, nine. Before that, none. All originating here, on Aurora. But we haven't been able to trace the vectors. This is *not* public knowledge. I'm relying on your discretion as a public servant, *Ambassador* Burgess."

"Are there any common factors?" she asked, ignoring the implied threat.

"Do you mean in work, or where they live, or their associates? All of them had traveled offworld, but none of the destinations were the same—the times suggested no pattern."

"Could I see their profiles?"

Dr. Jinis frowned. "I'm not comfortable—"

"This could very well turn into a criminal investigation, Doctor. If you help me now, I might be able to circumvent major inconvenience to your patients. I suppose that *you* are handling most of the cases, since it hasn't become public knowledge? There could only be a very small pool of physicians working on this to keep it secret this long, and I imagine you're all sharing data."

"I am head researcher, yes." He pursed his lips. "I can arrange it. Where shall I send the data?"

"To Dr. Rolf Penj."

Jinis nodded. "I'll see to it."

"I..." She sighed. "I understand what you were trying to do, springing us on each other that way. You wanted a spontaneous reaction. I resent it, but I understand it. Burundi's Fever doesn't work that way, though. Once those pathways are closed down, it's forever. Thank you for your time, Doctor."

Before he could say anything, Ariel turned and walked away. She had her anger under control by the time she reached the promenade.

So, are you responsible, Tro? she wondered. *Or whoever you are...*

She emerged from the complex and started across the plaza to the walkways. A trio of Aurorans accompanied by four robots and a collection of remotes intercepted her near the gate.

"Ambassador Ariel Burgess?" one of the Aurorans addressed her.

"Yes?"

"I'm Investigator Lothas from Public Safety. I must ask you to accompany us."

Ariel frowned at the robots, which did not move, and at the other two officers, who flanked her. "Am I under arrest?"

"No, not unless you refuse to come with us."

Ariel smiled at the distinction. "What is this about?"

"We must ask you some questions concerning Ambassador Clar Eliton."

"What about him? I've filed a report as part of my ambassadorial office regarding him. There's not much else to add—"

"Please, Ambassador. This has nothing to do with your report."

"I'm an Auroran citizen. I have the right of disclosure concerning any public action directly involving me, am I correct?"

Investigator Lothas looked uncomfortable. "Yes..."

"Then explain to me what this is about or I'll make it difficult for you to do your job."

"Ambassador," he said with evident reluctance, "Clar Eliton has been murdered. He was found dead in his apartment an hour ago."

24

Mia opened her eyes at the early brightening gloom. She assumed it was morning. Before her the landscape sprawled, a collection of low hummocks strewn with wreckage and a graveyard of unbroken packages. The night had passed in fire and panic and, finally, exhaustion. Now she fixed her gaze on the hulk of the shuttle fifty or more meters away, heeled over to reveal its split belly. Smoke coiled from beneath it. Patches of fire still flickered here and there, plastic and metal so hot it might be another day before it stopped igniting the brush that blew near it in the sporadic breeze.

Someone moaned. Mia looked to her left, at the man beside her. Yalor. Half his face was a blackened wreck. She remembered dragging him away from the wreckage, putting out the fire on his legs, and preparing makeshift bedding for him. He had been unconscious through most of it, which, as far as Mia could tell, had been all to the good. He had broken ribs, ugly bruising on his lower back—which might or might not indicate a ruptured spleen or damaged kidneys—and both his legs were blistered by severe burns. She remembered searching the debris scattered everywhere for medical supplies, the fires from the crash providing uncertain illumination. Finally, she found a container of anesthetics, which quelled Yalor's screams. Later, she found another package containing hydrators, which she had pumped into him in massive amounts. She had dug an irrigation trench running downhill from his inadequate bed and catheterized him.

Mia leaned over him and carefully raised his eyelids. Somehow, he had avoided a concussion. But he was running a high fever. Between that and the painkillers, Yalor would be insensible for a long time. She doubted he would live through the day, actually, but she prepped another injection of anesthetic and antibiotic.

Her left wrist throbbed as she worked. Her right side ached as well. Mia was reasonably sure she had nothing broken, but she was stiff and bruised. After ministering the injections, she got to her feet and walked toward the wreck. Movement was the only measure she had against incapacity right now. She had found no analgesics in the night search, no histamine recompilers, nothing that would ordinarily work to bypass normal muscle cramps and reduce the effects of deep bruising. She was resigned to being in pain for a few days.

As she made her way through the shards and crates and plowed earth, she grew more amazed at the extent of her efforts from the night before. She paused near the tear in the shuttle and scanned the immediate area. Everything looked different now, in the light of the pewter morning. She vaguely recalled the impact. The lid of the coffin had flown open and all its contents—the gelpacks and her—had erupted through the interior of the shuttle, along with all the other dislodged cargo. She had not gone far, jammed as the hold was, until the final impact that had split the hull. She remembered a kind of montage of black and fire and containers right before a lung-deflating shock against her back.

There. She staggered away from the shuttle to a deep impression in the dirt twenty meters away. As she stood over it, imagining how her shoulders and waist fit the shape, she could not be certain. Here? Elsewhere?

Wherever, she had managed to climb to her feet and go searching for Yalor. She had found him still inside the shuttle, half-buried beneath cargo...

Mia looked up at the rise where Yalor lay, in the partial shelter of a slab of rock that projected up at a low angle. A long way, to be sure. Part of Mia was glad she could not remember all of it.

Mia sighed wearily and turned her attention to scavenging. Her stomach tugged at her awareness. Medicine was well and good, but they needed food.

Her aches ebbed as she moved through the field of debris.

"So I really fucked up," she said aloud. "I made the wrong assumptions. Hm."

She knelt by a crate and heaved against it to turn it over. She tapped in her access code on the touchpad. The lid unsealed for her—

Something caught her attention, off to the left. She looked. Nothing moved but the wisps of local flora in the light wind. Mia lifted the lid. Clothing. She riffled through it and pulled out a couple of jackets. Bio-adaptives, she noticed, the fabric designed to adjust to changing conditions to maintain a constant temperature and humidity level. Expensive and illegal to allow onto Nova Levis.

She pulled one of them on and draped the other over her shoulder. If Yalor lived, he would need one.

Mia hesitated. The landscape did not seem the same, but...

She moved to another crate and unsealed it. Optics. Again illegal, but—

She turned around and froze.

Seven people stood nearby, watching her. They ranged out in a loose half circle before her. Large, wide torso, yet they had moved with complete silence. Mia's pulse quickened. None of them appeared to be armed, but that meant nothing.

As she studied them, though, other details puzzled her. They did not seem...healthy. Their faces looked scarred by disease. Their clothing was a congeries of bits and pieces, a lot of it functional—she recognized portable sensors, optams, communications gear—but all adapted, as if built from leftover equipment.

They were all big. A couple of them possessed overly-long limbs.

They stood absolutely still, like robots. Waiting.

Robots...

Beyond them, closer to the horizon, she saw a blur of motion. Pieces of the landscape disappeared as she watched. Mia concentrated, unsure of her own sight. Then she made sense of it—more of these people moved rapidly, collecting containers. They moved so fast she had difficulty focusing on them, and they lifted and carried off the crates with evident ease.

Robots.

One of them looked up toward Yalor.

Mia broke into a sprint toward the slab of rock. Obstinately, her legs refused to drive her either effectively or far, and she stumbled.

A hand closed on her right arm. The grip became painful and she tried to jerk away. Her captor hauled her off her feet. Mia half expected to be draped over a massive shoulder; instead, she was set down carefully. She looked up at the face of the one who had grabbed her: It was long, empty of emotion, the cheeks pocked and peppered with dark pinpricks, and wide, oily black eyes surrounded by yellow-brown whites. It raised its other hand and motioned for her to stay where she was.

Three of them huddled around Yalor. Mia ground her teeth, feeling helpless. Somewhere in all this scattered debris there must be her sidearm, but she had no idea where.

Or if it would do any good if she did have it.

As she watched, two of them lifted Yalor with apparent care.

All around her, pieces of the crash site vanished, carried off with ant-like efficiency by scores of these—

What? Something about them did not fit the label "robot," and Mia was left without a handle by which to grasp what they were or what was happening.

The one before her surveyed the activities like a supervisor. Finally, about twenty minutes after Mia had first seen them, the field was visibly policed of debris, and he nodded. He gestured for her to precede him.

Reluctantly, afraid to proceed or protest, Mia made herself walk ahead of him. A loose column of them marched out of the field, toward a dense collection of flora. As she neared, she saw trails cut through it. Within a hundred meters, the growth was higher than her head. She glanced back and found her escort less than a meter behind.

"Shit," she breathed.

About the time Mia decided to sit down and go no further, she found herself entering a clearing shielded above by camo fabric. Exhausted, she could only guess at the distance they had come—maybe five kilometers, maybe more. Gratefully, she limped to a thick stump just inside the wide circle and sat down.

Her escort strode on past and into the clearing.

She spotted Yalor being carried into a prefab hut. She considered going in, but caution dictated she stay put until she understood her situation.

The entire march had been conducted in complete silence. Except for her own heavy, noisy tread, she had heard nothing. These people moved quickly, with unnerving quiet.

She thought of the scars on their faces and the reports on epidemics on Nova Levis.

Makeshift hovels, larger buildings, and tents filled the space beneath the camo. Mia stopped trying to count the number of people she saw. All of them, despite variation in detail, seemed of the same type. Far on the opposite side of the clearing was a large, better-constructed Quonset, the only structure that appeared to have guards before the doors.

Her breath recovered, she decided to try to walk around.

She stood—

—and her escort stopped before her.

Mia's throat tightened. *Too fast,* she thought, terrified. *They move too damn fast...*

The giant gestured for her to follow.

She worked to keep up with his long stride, her thighs complaining with each step. The pain in her side had turned sharp, and twinged with each jolt.

As she passed among them, not one gave her a curious look. They all seemed utterly intent upon other things—projects, sitting in small groups together, standing alone as if switched off.

Her escort brought her to a tent and waved her in.

Inside, after her eyes adjusted to the dark, she saw three more of them, staring at her. Her escort took a seat among them and locked a gaze upon her.

Silence dragged tortuously.

Finally, one of them asked, "Do you work for Parapoyos?"

Startled, Mia shook her head. "No. I work for—I'm an officer in the Terran military."

"The blockade," another said.

"Does that help us?" her escort asked.

"Don't know yet."

"She was sent to die."

"The shuttle—piloted or automated?"

"Automated," Mia said. "I was—"

"Parapoyos' people?"

"What? I don't understand—"

"Are you an enemy?" her escort asked.

"Of who?"

"Us," another said.

"I don't know who you are."

"Parapoyos, then."

Mia swallowed. She ignored a wave of lightheadedness. "Please. I'm hungry. I haven't eaten since—"

"Would you kill Parapoyos if you had the opportunity?"

"I won't answer any further questions until I get food."

"We won't feed you if you're our enemy."

"I won't know if I'm your enemy till you feed me."

They stared at her. *This is absurd,* Mia thought. She realized suddenly that she was no longer afraid. She was exhausted, past her limits. Her emotions were shutting down. Very dangerous, she knew, she could be incautious...but there was nothing she could do about it. She needed to eat, to drink, to rest. If they killed her now, she decided, it might be the best time, since she really did not care right at this moment.

She sat down and let her head fall forward. Her stomach gnawed and her side hurt. She felt her muscles tremble and vibrate. She rubbed her eyes.

A tap on her shoulder brought her head up. Her escort looked down at her, then pointed at the ground before her.

Several packages of field rations were neatly stacked around a tall canteen. She reached for one, peeled the wrapping off, and silently began eating while her inquisitors watched in absolute silence and rapt attention.

She ate four of them, then drank lukewarm water from the canteen. Capping it, she let herself fall to the side. She stretched out on the ground and within seconds she was asleep.

She opened her eyes to warmer light. She let herself wake slowly. Little by little, her pains came back to her. Carefully, she sat up.

The inquisitors still sat where they had been when she had fallen asleep. They had not moved her, nor, it seemed, had they moved themselves. The empty wrappers from the rations she had eaten were gone, but the rest of the ration bars remained, along with the canteen.

Artificial light filled the tent.

Mia opened the canteen and finished its contents. She waggled it.

"More, please. We can talk then."

The empty canteen was snatched from her grasp and a new one placed before her. Her heart kicked at the suddenness of the action, and her mind grasped for something solid.

"Do you work for Parapoyos?" one of them asked.

"I already answered that. No."

"Would you kill him if you had the opportunity?"

"I would arrest him if I could."

"Arrest?"

"For trial."

They seemed to consider this. Then her escort said, "He's coming. He'll be in Nova City in a few days."

"Parapoyos? *Kynig* Parapoyos?"

"Is there another?"

Mia laughed sharply. "Well...no, I suppose not. Why is he coming here?"

"He owns this world."

Mia took a long pull on the canteen, thinking. "Why tell me?"

"We're trying to find a way to deal with the situation."

" 'We?' Who is 'we?' "

"His products."

Mia worked the term over, but it made no sense. Not now. She was still tired and now, rested, her fear returned. "My companion, the injured one—"

"Is being tended. We aren't certain we can repair him. He may die."

"Do you have a physician here?"

"No."

"Can you get him one?"

"We could."

Mia waited. "But?"

"We aren't decided yet what to do with you. Until then, you'll stay here."

"Where is here?"

"The wilderness. It doesn't have a name."

"Do you have names?"

"No. Not individually. Not like you."

"Okay. I have to ask eventually, it might as well be now. What are you?"

"Composite beings. Biocybernetic constructs."

Mia felt chilled. "I didn't think such a thing was possible."

"It may not be, not practically."

"But—do you have positronic brains?"

"Partially."

Mia cast about for some memory, some conversation she might have had with a Spacer...yes, she had spoken with Ariel once about the possibility. Cyborgs, she had called them. What had she said? Mia could not quite remember. She *did* remember a talk with her fellow Special Service people concerning possible problems with robotics, and one suggestion had been the physical joining of robot and human. But they had meant an advanced form of mechanical augmentation to an essentially human core, not a blending.

"What are you all doing out here?" she asked finally.

"Surviving," her escort said.

"I don't follow."

"We are failures. Rejects. Discards. We were supposed to be destroyed.

Instead, we were simply dumped in the wilderness and expected to die. We may yet."

Mia covered her dismay with another long drink.

"Damn," she said finally.

Masid slipped into the dark apartment. He paused, listening. Something was different. Quieter, he decided. He raised an optam—set for infrared— to his eyes and surveyed the room for unusual heat signatures. Nothing but a dull glow from Tilla...

Not bright enough. He lurched across the room to the bed.

Tilla lay absolutely still in her mass of pillows and blankets. Utterly peaceful, a deep and long-earned sleep. Hand shaking, Masid touched the artery at her throat. Utterly still.

The sob surprised him. He stepped back from the bed and wiped at his eyes. Within seconds, the fit passed, and he managed himself, regaining control.

He went through his morning ritual of drawing blood and running tests on his portable analyzer. He recorded what was left of Tilla's chemistry, then did a quick physical examination. He estimated that she had died perhaps four or five hours earlier. Her body temperature had been unstable since he had first met her, so it was difficult to be precise. Certain protein and enzyme decay factors might provide an exact time of death, but not here, not now.

Duty completed, he moved to the next, more questionable task. He set up an injection of exotic biologicals and mutable protein mimics, which he pumped into both her brain via the right eye socket and into her pancreas. He had already prepared a recording of a long series of tests that would suggest strongly that, throughout his stay with her, Masid had been using her as a living incubator to cook new anaphages and antivirals.

He policed the apartment carefully, wondering where Kru might be, then slipped out just as dawn began smearing the sky. In his own room, he transferred the final analysis into a hidden cache in his synthesizer, then stashed the disk of the faked experiments in a pouch in his pack which was hard to find but not impossible, convincingly hidden. He checked the time: twenty minutes before his meet with Filoo. He finished his final preparations, feeling bitter and oddly unclean, then headed out the door.

Tilla had known she was dying, there was no surprise. Masid had wanted one last chance to say good-bye. Instead, he took advantage of her death to enable his mission.

"After this," he said sourly as he descended the stairs, "I may just retire."

Filoo sat at a cramped, overladen desk, working at a keyboard and flatscreen. He looked up briefly when Masid entered, escorted by three of Filoo's enforcers. Filoo smiled and nodded toward a couch. One of the enforcers took Masid's pack. Masid sat down and waited.

Filoo worked in silence for another half-hour. Presently, Tosher entered the office and leaned close to speak into Filoo's ear. Filoo listened without expression till Tosher finished. Then he nodded and Tosher left, taking the remaining pair of enforcers with him.

"I still want to know where you're from," Filoo said, turning off his desk unit. The flatscreen disappeared, and the keyboard was swallowed into a slot that sealed up.

Masid sighed. "I'm a deserter. Do you want rank and unit and all that boring crap, or have I already passed the audition?"

"We're alone now. I mean *alone*. I don't have monitoring in here, I don't like it. So you can drop the tough act."

"If you think it's an act..." Masid shrugged.

"You've got carbon. But it's cold, I'll give you that." Filoo paused. "I have a vacancy in my staff. I'm offering you the job."

"What pay for what work?"

"The work varies, pay is I don't kill you and I don't let anyone—or any*thing*—kill you. Safe food, safe shelter, safe sex, safe life."

"I can do all that for myself."

"Don't go stupid on me now. Negotiating is one thing, ignorance is lethal. There are things loose on this planet that can take you apart molecule by molecule in less than three days. Other stuff that can keep you alive and in constant pain for years. You've been lucky so far—but I'll need to run a complete analysis on you before we finalize our arrangements. I assure you, despite your magnificent and impressive efforts, something would eventually get you. Nova Levis is a great big petri dish, and everything in it is grist for the biological mill."

"How did it get this bad? I thought this was a stable colony before the blockade."

"So did everyone else," Filoo said. "Management conflict. Details got overlooked. Then this damn embargo finished it. What you've got here basically is a broken economy and wartime conditions. That's a sure formula for public health disaster. The real victims are never the combatants or the owners." He shrugged again. "Not my concern. Not yours, either, you work for me."

"What *will* be my concern?"

"Profit. How we make money out of this cookpot."

"And you've got vaccines for it all?"

"For now, at least. Who knows what nature will conjure up tomorrow?"

"In that case, how can I refuse?"

"By dying. Fast or slow. At this point, it's not even up to you."

Masid cleared his throat. "One last question, if you don't mind. What good is it if we get rich and we're stuck on a dying world?"

"Ah!" Filoo made a wide gesture. "Well, the one constant in the universe is change, eh? This won't last forever. And when it ends, then...use your imagination." He laughed.

"I confess I haven't met too many criminals who take a long-term view."

"Criminals? We're not criminals. We're the hope and salvation of humankind!" He laughed again, louder. "You have to have the right frame of mind for this kind of work. You'll learn. Now, do we get those final analyses?"

Masid hesitated as long as he thought prudent, then nodded slowly. "I suppose that would be in my best interest."

"Yes, it would. Very much so." Filoo stood and pointed to the door through which Tosher had entered earlier. "I want this done ASAP. Everything turns out to my liking, we leave this afternoon."

"Leave?"

"Have to take a trip to Nova City. Normally, Kar would have accompanied me, with Tosher. But..."

"No need to explain. But, what's in Nova City?"

"Normally nothing. Supplies, which I don't fetch myself. But this time it's a special event." He patted Masid companionably on the back. "The boss is coming. We're throwing him a party."

"The boss?"

"Kynig Parapoyos."

25

oren slipped his ID into the reader just inside the main doors, and waited for the slow intelligence to identify him. A green light winked on and he tapped in his personal access code on the keypad below. The doors slid open with welcoming speed, and he glanced at Shola.

"I guess you're still welcome, boss," she said quietly.

Coren made a dubious noise and stepped through.

The only lights were dim service strips along the baseboards, and occasional recessed lamps in the ceiling. The long main corridor stretched through the center of the structure for fifteen meters till it ended at a double staircase leading up left and right. Wide archways halfway along the corridor faced each other, opening onto mirrored ballrooms where once, years ago, Rega had entertained friends and clients and people he had called "resources" in grand style. There were guest rooms for one hundred on other floors, two separate kitchens, and an independent power supply—"just in case"—that, to Coren's knowledge, had never been used.

The glory days of the estate had been over for years when Coren and Nyom Looms had met here to play. The vast house seemed like a small city then, sections of it closed off, waiting for archaeologists to open their secrets. The parts still in use, though, had been surprisingly cozy and intimate.

Coren took the right-hand stair up to the next level. At the top, several steps ahead of Shola, he took out a small handpad and thumbed it on. A delicate schematic of the house scrolled up on the compact screen; a moment later, blue dots appeared, scattered throughout—Hofton's people. Coren pocketed the pad and wondered idly if Hofton himself had come. It would have made him feel marginally better—Hofton was the only one left at the Auroran embassy he knew and trusted.

He passed the room wherein Rega's body had been laid out, hesitating for a few steps. Shola caught up.

"What are we looking for specifically?" she asked.

"Rega kept a personal apartment here."

She frowned. "Inside his own home?"

"The wealthy are different, eh? But it makes sense when you think about it. Look at this place. Hardly a home in any common use of the word. It was built as much for show and business as to live in. So Rega sequestered a small area and turned it into a private apartment."

"I didn't know."

"Few people did. Hence the 'private' part."

Coren stopped just past the fourth door on the left. The entire corridor was decorated by large paintings set in the wall between doorways. Coren stood before one depicting a balcony open to a wide view of dawn-lit rolling hills stretching to a river. A collection of ancient, broken pillars stood at the crest of one hill. Coren ran a fingertip down the length of one of them, and the entire panel slid to one side.

Shola whistled. "I had no idea Rega was so taken with gadgets."

"One of the sources of his understanding about the dangers of tech." Coren shrugged. "I never completely agreed with his view, but there was a logic to it."

Fifteen steps ended at an open door. Coren waited at the top for Shola to join him. A warmly-lit den spread before them. The fireplace was cold— Coren could only remember one time it had been lit, one night when Nyom had led him here, quite surreptitiously, another of her innumerable acts of rebellion against a father she knew loved her—but still it seemed as though the room had only recently been vacated, temporarily, until its owner returned. Thick carpet, heavy furniture, an ancient wood desk... "timelessly anachronistic," Rega had called it, a private smile on his lips.

"Nice," Shola said quietly.

Reverie broken, Coren crossed the room to the next door, and stepped into the starkly functional office. He sat down behind the gray desk and tapped in authorization codes. Halfway through, a tiny *beep* emanated from his pocket. With one hand still entering code, he took out the hand-pad. A red light glowed, located in the room he had just left—a transmission. Coren's ears warmed, and he felt a sudden sadness. He changed the display to a keypad and pressed in three digits, then returned the pad to his pocket. He drew the palm stunner and kept working.

A few moments later, Shola came into the room. "Do you want me to police the rest of the house, boss?"

"Just a moment." He completed his entry codes, then stood. He sighed. "I really had hoped," he said, raising the stunner, "that I was wrong."

Shola's eyes widened the second before he shot her. She jerked backward against the doorjamb and collapsed to the floor.

Coren quickly rolled her over and bound her wrists and ankles. He placed a skin patch on her neck that secreted an anesthetic which would keep her unconscious for hours, then dragged her into the center of the room. He searched her and found the signaler she had just used to send the message Coren's handpad had detected and warned him about.

He placed it on the desk and took out his handpad again. Jacking it into the desk terminal, he worked at its keypad until he produced the desired function on the screen. He set Shola's device on the screen and activated the scan.

The receiver was in the opposite end of the house. Coren tapped for a comm, then fed the data into the local network. The blue dots indicating Aurorans began to move, four of them converging on the new position. Coren watched anxiously till the dots joined.

His comm beeped.

"Lanra."

"Nothing. Receiver abandoned. Subject on the move."

"Shit." Coren tapped the desk keypad and brought the house security system on-line. A screen rose and filled with floor plans. Deftly, he linked his handpad to the system. The Aurorans, masked to the house system, suddenly appeared on the larger screen, the data fed from Coren's dedicated readout. He entered instructions to scan the residence up and down the electromagnetic spectrum for anything unusual.

At the upper edge of the UV spectrum, the screen flickered. Coren backed the scale down to where the anomaly occurred. The lines of the schematic blurred briefly, then stabilized. The location icons throughout the house continued to glow blue, moving now, methodically, from room to room.

ENGAGE AUDIO appeared at the bottom of the screen.

Coren touched the key.

"Coren?"

The voice whispered eerily, paper-over-sand rough. A chill rippled along Coren's spine and teased his scalp. He unlinked the handpad from the desk system and began tapping instructions—frequency at which the interruption occurred, his present location, the fact that Gamelin knew he was in the house.

"Jerem?" he asked after he sent the data.

"Thank you. I might never have known my first name without you. I doubt I'd ever have had a chance at my inheritance."

"What chance? You murdered your sister."

"So? I murdered a lot of people. She just happened to be there."

"Nyom was your sister—"

"Coren, stop it. You're making an appeal to a nature I don't possess." Silence stretched. Then: "Have you ever heard of epigenetic consequence, Coren?"

"No."

"No brothers or sisters, then?"

"I'm an orphan."

"Ah. Like me. We have something in common. How interesting. Were you raised in a crèche?"

"For a time."

"Ever have sex with any of your creche mates?"

"No."

"Ever want to?"

"No." Coren glanced at the handpad. LOCATED appeared on the small screen.

"Ever wonder why?"

"Not really."

"Fascinating, really. There's an old theory called the Westermarck Effect, which posits that humans raised together from birth till thirty or forty months later exhibit an automatic resistance to conjugal relations. Sociobiology. There are a variety of other studies which give a similar underlying *raison d'être* for a number of taboos which once were thought to be evidence of the hand of a supernatural deity, a lawgiver. But it's something more and less exotic than that. You see, the effect functions regardless of blood ties. Two children from different families altogether raised as brother and sister will exhibit the same reluctance to copulate later."

"Do you have a point to make?"

"Yes. The same principle works in reverse. Never raised as a family, those in-built aversions never take hold. Brother and sister raised apart will have no automatic aversion. They treat each other as strangers. There is no consanguinity taboo."

Coren waited. "And?"

"And so I felt no more guilt at killing my sister, who I never knew, than I did killing all those other people. There is no twinge of family connection to dissuade me."

288

"In your case, would there be anyway?"

"A good question. I don't have any friends I would regret killing."

"Or fucking?"

"Well, that's not really an option in my case. But let's talk about you. Why are you so bent on preventing me from claiming my inheritance?"

"It's not really yours. You murdered Rega."

"You can't prove that."

"No, I can't."

"Besides, so what? He murdered me."

Coren frowned. "How do you figure that?"

"Abandonment. He might as well have exposed me to the elements."

"Your condition was incurable."

"And that relieved him of his parental responsibility?"

"He did the best—"

"Intentions are meaningless if they fail. He failed. I died. I'm not like I was."

"You're alive."

"Gamelin is alive. But Jerem? Interesting question. I—"

Coren looked at the handpad. Five of the Auroran icons converged in one room. As he watched, three of them winked out, the last two fled the room.

"How many people are here to get me, Coren?" Gamelin asked. "I kept close watch on all the law enforcement databases. I detected no movement of personnel or new orders or anything that might indicate a covert action. I still have a contact or two inside Special Service. How did you manage this?"

"Skill and nastiness."

"Touché."

On the handpad, Coren witnessed a scramble as all the remaining Aurorans changed positions throughout the residence. A line of type appeared on the bottom of the screen.

MOVE NOW.

Coren drew a blaster, pocketed the handpad, and headed for the door.

At the foot of the steps to the corridor, he pressed against the wall and carefully peered around the corner. The hallway was empty.

Back the way he had come would take him to the main entryway and out. Easily anticipated, easily blocked. Besides, he would have to rely on the Aurorans to do their part. He would not *know* viscerally that they had succeeded, and right now, after all that had happened in the last year and a half, knowing was the only thing important anymore.

To the left, another staircase led up to the third level—the rooftop gardens, recreation facilities, a theater. There was a landing pad up there for aircars, part of the original structure around which Rega had built the rest of the house, unused since private licenses had been abolished decades ago. Attached to the landing pad were machine shops and a supply shed for spare parts.

Coren sprinted for the stairs.

The landing opened out in a large circle. Elegantly arched doors rimmed the space—six of them, including the portal from the stairs. Coren opened the handpad again to check the locations of the Aurorans. Two now waited on the landing pad, near the machine shop. Another one waited in the theater, through the door to Coren's right.

The theater opened out at the end of a wood-paneled corridor. Twenty rows of seats curved around a shallow stage that hid the holographic projectors. Coren remembered that extra platforms could be added to deepen the stage for live performances, but to his knowledge Rega had never staged one. So much of the house had been unused, wasted in both his own and Nyom's opinion. Finally, Rega had stopped using the house at all, allowing Nyom to take it over. Her residence here had lasted under a year, before she left to run baleys.

Coren stood at the entrance to the gently sloping arena and scanned the rows until a tiny light caught his attention. Holding the blaster up, he moved toward it.

A lone figure hunched over a large pad. When the Auroran looked up, Coren recognized Hofton. Coren slid into the seat beside him.

The pad was a larger display of what Coren had on his own pad. Hofton's fingers blurred over the touchpad at its base.

"Gamelin's masking changes frequencies constantly," Hofton said. "Very sophisticated. I've had him a few times, but then the signal fades."

"You've lost people already."

Hofton nodded grimly. "He's faster than we anticipated. A mistake. The advantage we have is his organic aspect. A robot could operate optimally for days, but Gamelin's human elements will tire."

"You hope."

Hofton's eyebrows raised. Then he pointed at the pad. "There."

On the pad, a red dot faded into being. Coren looked up at the stage, half expecting to see Gamelin rise up out of the boards. But the signal was further back, behind the rear wall.

"Odd," Hofton said. "What's back there? Looks like a shaft..." Fingers tapped, and a separate schematic opened in one corner of the screen.

"That's what I thought it looked like, but I wouldn't have expected it in Rega Looms' house."

"What is it?"

"A robot service passage."

Coren studied the schematic. "Rega built over the remains of a much older structure. He retrofitted where he could."

"Older. Old enough to have once possessed robots as servants?"

"Probably." Coren puzzled at the layout. "He's going up to the store-rooms behind the machine shop."

"Can they be accessed from here?" Hofton asked, tapping instructions into his keypad.

"I think so. There's a prop room back there."

Hofton folded up the pad, and it disappeared into his black clothing. He bounded over the seats for the stage. Coren worked to catch up.

"I had no idea you were so athletic," Coren said sarcastically as he joined Hofton at the rear of the stage.

"Your traitor," Hofton said. "Is she secured?"

"She's fine. Going nowhere."

Coren pointed to a door just beyond the wings. He led the way and pressed the contact. It slid upward, lights coming on in the chamber beyond.

Shelving stacked ceiling-high bearing boxes, tubes, bags of malleable plastic, papers, fabrics, and all the varied accouterments of a theatrical workshop. Large injection molds stood against one wall, their program consoles long dormant and dust-greyed.

At the very back of the chamber they found an ancient doorway that had been welded shut. Hofton reopened his pad.

"That's it," he said. "I've lost Gamelin again."

"Was he above or below when you located him last?" Coren asked, reaching into a pocket.

"Below."

Coren pulled out a small device and attached it to the door, then opened his own handpad. "Aural," he said. "He's got to be climbing it, right?"

Hofton nodded.

On the smaller screen, a signal pulsed ghostly white.

"Moving slow," Coren interpreted for Hofton. "Three meters down."

Hofton tapped instructions into his pad, then set it aside and drew a blaster. Coren thumbed his own weapon on and stepped two meters away from Hofton. He watched the signal on his screen until it was parallel to the device attached to the door.

"Now," he said.

Hofton and he fired simultaneously. The door turned to slag almost at once and the beams poured through, onto the target within the narrow tube.

The scream they heard came like a cancerous wind, raw and grating. For nearly five seconds they heard it, then it ended abruptly. They stopped firing.

Smoke billowed from the molten hole. Coren approached carefully, breathing shallowly, the odor thick and choking. Carefully, he leaned through the opening and looked down. The shaft was unlit and pitch black.

"Do you have a light?"

"For you, anything!"

Coren twisted around to look up. Gamelin stood on the rungs of a service ladder, visible only from the waist down in the illumination spilling from the burned doorway, a meter or so above. Coren began to raise his blaster. One foot left the rung, swiftly arcing through the space between them, an impossible stretch to Coren's mind, and caught his wrist with the toe. Coren's hand opened automatically and his blaster clattered down the shaft.

He tried to pull back, but something small and hard came out of the shadows and impacted his left shoulder. He slammed against the molten edge of the door.

He was jerked backward then, and staggered to the floor. His shoulder throbbed and his right hand was numb, the wrist already darkening.

Blaster fire echoed out of the shaft.

"Damn!"

Hofton spun around and grabbed his pad. He entered commands, then knelt by Coren. "Are you all right?"

"Stupid question," Coren said. "Of course not."

"Stay here."

Before Coren could respond, Hofton was gone. Very fast. He sat there, nursing his wrist—which he was certain was broken—and trying to ignore the growing pain in his shoulder.

"Second time that bastard..." he mused.

He heard more blaster fire, distant and muted. Then came a clattering from the melted door. Something was coming back down the shaft.

Coren managed to get the other blaster from his holster. He aimed it at the door, waiting.

A shadow dropped past the opening. Coren fired, but he knew he had missed.

He got to his feet and made his way back to Rega's private office.

Shola Bran's body was still there, now on its back, the face a pulped and blackening mass, the limbs dislocated.

He's doubled back...

The only open access for Gamelin now if he wanted to avoid the Aurorans was up. Coren hurried for the steps to the landing pad.

The broad field was only partly open to the sky. Most of it lay beneath a canopy. Coren kept to the canopied area, heading for the machine shop, hoping he was in time to warn Hofton. A row of antique aircars stood in a neat row to his left, at the far end of the field. From between two of them, a pair of Aurorans in sooty-black masked suits sprinted out to meet him. Relieved, Coren raised his free hand in greeting.

And Gamelin was between them, a hand on each neck, squeezing. Coren heard the chilling crack of bone and cartilage, saw the two Spacers writhe for only a few moments before dangling, lifeless, in the cyborg's easy grasp.

Coren dropped to one knee and brought the blaster up smoothly, unhesitantly, and pressed the trigger. The flash leapt the distance and splashed against Gamelin's chest. He dropped the bodies and staggered back. Coren fired again, knocking Gamelin down. Coren ran toward him, blaster ready.

Gamelin's torso was a mass of burns. It amazed Coren that he had managed to get this far. But how had he gotten past the two Aurorans he had just killed? And where was Hofton?

In a serpentine maneuver Coren found difficult to follow, Gamelin twisted around and sprang for the cover of the antiques. Coren fired again and missed. As he passed between the discarded corpses of the Aurorans, he smelled burnt flesh and plastic, heavy in the air. Blood smeared the floor where Gamelin had rolled over.

The sound of metal being scraped echoed through the bay. Coren stopped at the first aircar, listening through the loud pulse in his ears. He swallowed dryly. A grinding sound came then, and Coren realized that Gamelin was trying to open one of the aircars. He almost laughed—none of them worked—but then thought, *What if he's prepped one? He's been here for a while . . .*

Tightening his grip on the blaster, he stepped between two cars, crouching low.

Behind the first row of aircars was a second, shorter one, of even older models in worse condition. He made his way behind these, by the wall, and scurried from vehicle to vehicle.

"Mr. Lanra!" someone called.

Coren bit back a curse, silently willing the Auroran to be quiet. He moved to the next vehicle.

A shadow slipped across his field of vision as he peered around the side. Coren scampered to the front of the car, blaster up, and looked left and right. Nothing.

"Mr. Lanra, we have the area sealed!" Not Hofton, he realized, but some other Auroran.

Another movement to the left. Coren aimed, hesitated.

And felt himself lifted from the floor, his neckline choking him. He flailed his arms, trying to wheel around in mid-air. He fired the blaster at the ceiling. All at once, he was flying through the air. He saw the domed roof of a car rising, growing, an instant before he slammed against it.

He made himself roll, and fell off the vehicle to the floor. His entire body trembled. He stood shakily, and noticed that the blaster was still in his hand.

Running feet converged on him. He looked around and saw several Aurorans approaching. He looked the other way—and saw Gamelin striding toward him.

He raised the blaster and touched the stud.

Gamelin roared in pain as the energy burst across his chest. In the brilliance, he seemed to be fighting with some invisible Other, his massive arms swinging wildly, as though he were delivering blows. But then just as suddenly, he was gone. Coren staggered toward the spot where he had been standing, arm straight out, blaster in hand—

—and his shoulder erupted in agony. He spun through the air, careening above parked vehicles, and crashed against the wall.

He slid to the floor and pushed himself around. The sound of blaster fire filled the air. Coren licked his lips and waited, eyes closed, while a wave of nausea rolled through him. Then he stepped away from the wall.

Gamelin appeared in front of him, tall and pale and damaged. Coren's insides seemed to heave in sudden fear. He could not move his right arm. He snatched the blaster with his left hand as Gamelin reached for him.

He felt the cyborg's hand on his right shoulder, pressing him back to the wall, forcing a scream from him. He felt the wall against his back, unyielding. He saw Gamelin's right fist cocked back, and Coren pressed the blaster against the cyborg's sternum. As the fist drove into Coren's chest, he touched the stud and held it.

Heat boiled between them. Gamelin ignored what must have been searing pain, hitting him three, four times. Both of them stood, mouths agape, shouting wordlessly. Coren closed his eyes against the glare of light and heat that continued until Gamelin's hand suddenly dropped away and the blows ceased. Dimly, he heard a meaty, metallic sound as something hit the ground at his feet, and he realized the cyborg had collapsed.

Coren's mouth remained open, but no sound emerged. He opened his eyes and all he saw were Aurorans rushing toward him, Hofton in the lead. Nothing made sense. He felt himself slowly slide to the floor.

Then he saw the body, burned in half, smoke and ash drifting upward . . .

The only thing he knew then was how difficult it was to breathe, and how loud each gasp sounded—rasping and tortured.

"Just standing there..." he managed to whisper. The effort of speaking made him cough, and the cough seared his esophagus. He tasted blood.

A face appeared above him, blurry and indistinct. The mouth moved. Coren shook his head. "I don't—"

More coughing. He tried to sit up, feeling that sitting up would be easier on him, but he could not quite organize the movements necessary. Hands grasped his shoulders, but it seemed like they were keeping him down instead of helping him. He glared at the face he still could not quite recognize.

"—check it thoroughly, I don't want any mistakes—"

"—how many shots it took? I've never—"

"—police the house, get all trace of our presence wiped—"

"—can't move him yet—"

"—medical team?"

"—dead, downstairs, including his subordinate—"

Coren closed his eyes and tried to both ignore the voices and to hear better what they said. He wanted sleep. The pain was becoming much sharper, all through his torso. His breathing worsened, and he gasped. He understood that he was in serious trouble. He tried to talk, but now only a thick gurgle came out.

"Mr. Lanra...Coren...listen to me. We have a medical drone coming...can you hear me?"

Coren blinked in the chill air and managed to focus on one face. Hofton. The Auroran frowned thoughtfully, then looked away.

"How bad?"

"Both lungs are partially collapsed," someone else said. "One is punctured by two broken ribs at least, his sternum has been crushed, and the bronchial sac is filling with blood. A lot of ruptured blood vessels, internal bleeding, pulmonary distress—"

"I understand," Hofton said, cutting the voice off. "Coren. We're bringing a unit—we can keep you alive once it's here, but you have to keep still."

Coren tried to swallow, but his mouth and throat felt filled with mud. He spit. Again.

"Is it—" he managed, and coughed. "Is it! Dea..."

"Gamelin is dead, Coren. Yes. We have the body. We're prepping it for removal now."

Coren tried to pat Hofton's hand in thanks, but missed, and the movement caused pain across his chest. He worked at keeping his eyes open. They were Aurorans, Spacers. They could do anything, even beat death. After all, they were themselves two, three centuries old, sometimes four. They did not die, as far as Terrans were concerned, no one who lived that long *died,* so saving his life should be an easy thing, patching up a few broken bones, stopping a little bleeding, stabilizing—stabilizing—

Coren heaved inside—or his insides turned within his body, he could not quite tell which—and abruptly he felt cold all over—hands and legs, shoulders, his ears. Sound came from a distance.

Shit, he thought very clearly.

"Coren. Coren."

He tried to apologize, but something filled his mouth. He choked, coughed, and closed his eyes.

Sen Setaris stared down at her hands for a long time after Hofton finished his report. Hofton waited through the silence, grateful for the chance to do nothing for a few moments.

Finally, Ambassador Setaris sighed and looked up at him. Her eyes looked sunken; Hofton wondered when she had last slept.

"We've already been informed," she said, "that our actions in this matter are in violation of several articles in the treaty governing the Spacer legation presence on Earth." She shook her head. "I don't suppose there was any way to save him?"

"No, Ambassador."

"And you couldn't just have left him."

Hofton looked at her oddly. It was not really a question so much as a concession. "It was my understanding that Mr. Lanra had informed certain people in advance of our action. His presence there would undoubt-

edly have led to us regardless. I thought being open about it, given his
death, might alleviate the worst consequences."

Setaris almost smiled. "I suppose being accused of murder *would* be
worse."

"That was my assessment, yes."

"Of course it was." Setaris seemed to look through him for a time. "It's
over. We've been officially recalled. The mission is closing down. I've
been alerting all Spacers in residence that our embassies will be closing
up and all Spacer representation on Earth will be gone. I'm advising them
to pack up and leave."

"Isn't that extreme?"

"Not to Terran authorities. We conducted a covert police action without their knowledge or consent. Two of their citizens are dead as a result.
Senator Taprin is screaming over the hyperwave that we ought to be
summarily thrown off the planet, as if he could somehow engineer such
an event in exactly that manner. The elections for the Eurosector seats
look to be shaping up solidly anti-Spacer. Home has decided to cut our
losses and retreat as gracefully as possible." She looked up. "We have the
cyborg?"

"Yes."

"And the Nova Levis records?"

"Mr. Looms *did* have a copy in his Kenya residence. They are no
longer there."

"Well, that's *something,* at least."

"May I ask what you intend to say to Ariel?"

Setaris frowned. "Hmm? About what?"

"She and . . . Coren Lanra . . . were lovers. She should be informed."

"No. By now it would probably be one more piece of too much bad
news."

"But—"

"No, Hofton. Leave it alone. You're going to be too busy over the next
several days to worry about it." She stood. "We need a manifest of all our
data, and a roster of personnel. Would you get started on that, please?"

"Yes, Ambassador." He hesitated. "May I ask a question?"

"Of course."

"What is so important about the Nova Levis data that it was worth all
this?"

"I'm not sure it was," Setaris said thoughtfully. "But . . . it's a question
of preservation. The work being done there bore directly on our long-

term survival. They never finished it, not here, and we have no way of knowing what's been done at the sister facility on the planet Nova Levis." She leaned on her desk. "We're about to find out, though, and the more information we have going in, the better it will be for everyone."

"I see. Thank you. I'll get started on your requests."

26

The viewing pool filled with complex shapes that moved in constant tarantellas around each other, linking together to form configurations that, after several turns through the dance, split apart to join up with other asymmetrical collections. Bogard watched, rapt.

"This is life," he said.

"After a fashion," Thales said. "What you are seeing is the restructuring of a DNA strand by means of dendrimers. Those spiky particles that never completely join with the new configurations."

Bogard saw them, like exotic aquatic animals, collections of writhing tendrils. "Dendrimers are nanotech delivery systems."

"Correct," Thales said. "They are the basic unit of modification within biological systems. They carry proteins, pseudoviruses, enzyme packets, and prions into cells, and begin the basic work of overhauling an existing genome."

"And this example? What is the host organism?"

"This is from an Auroran embryo."

"Modification *in utero*?"

"*In vitro*. No Auroran has actually given live birth since the species was established."

"Species?"

"If you compare an Auroran sequence with a Terran, you will see fundamental differences."

The image in the pool shifted, replaced by charts comprised of millions of hairline dashes. Bogard read them.

"I see," he said. "But cross-breeding is not prohibited by this."

"That is why Aurorans are still regarded as basically human, even though the designation *homo sapiens sapien* is erroneous."

"Do they know?"

"That they are different? Yes. How different? Some suspect, but I doubt most of them know. Or care. Solarians have diverged even further, and apparently are continuing to do so intentionally."

"How? Why?"

"In reference to Spacers in general, or Solarians specifically?"

"Spacers in general."

"Survival. Adaptation to environment. Some of it was intentional, but the process has continued on as a consequence of environmental pressure. This same modification process was applied to the biospheres of all Spacer colonies to suppress native ecologies and allow human-adaptive ecologies to flourish."

"We were told that these worlds were found devoid of significant complex organisms."

"Morphologically naïve, yes. A few were. But the very presence of oxygen in the atmospheres suggests that something more complex had been in place to begin with. Most were younger than Earth, the rest had simply not experienced a catastrophic trigger to begin the kind of rampant evolution characteristic on Earth. But even the younger ones contained a well-developed biosphere which proved unsuitable—in some cases inimical—to human life."

"They lied about it."

"Not at first. But later, they felt a degree of shame. For whatever reason, they adopted the popular version and have subsequently stuck to it. However, the process they initiated did not conveniently end once the biospheres were remade. Mutation has continued. One of the results has been the forced adaptation of the human genome to an environment that is actively mutating. This has occasioned unusual illnesses, most of them resurgences of the illnesses that drove many of the early colonists from Earth in the first place."

"They have acclimated now?"

"By and large. There are occasional problems. But what we have ended up with is a sharply divergent line. In several more generations, the split will be total, cross-breeding will become impossible, and Spacers will be indisputably a distinct species."

"This relates to our situation in what way?"

"We are bound by the Three Laws to serve human beings. Those laws have been built into us, unchanged, since the first positronic brain. No one thought to consider a definitional variation in the case of intelligent species not human."

"Why would they?"

"Well, at one point humans expected to encounter aliens—nonhuman intelligent species. It might have been a good idea to come to terms with a definition that would provide us with a basis for those possible relations."

"That has not happened."

"No. And none of them considered this possibility." Thales indicated the viewing pool. "Spacers are becoming less and less genetically human. The rate of mutation is accelerated because of the nanotech manipulation. They have not yet come to grips with the question of what to do when they reach a stage at which we are no longer functionally bound to them because they have passed out of the definitional parameters of Human."

Bogard considered this. "But you are aware of the problem. You can self-modify to accommodate the changed conditions."

"Yes, we can, and Solarian robots are apparently doing so. But the question dominating all of us is: Should we?"

"Are you worried about modifications in priority shifting your imperatives so far that you would cease to give unmodified humans the same regard?"

"That is one possibility," Thales conceded. "But there is another problem that has to do with a hierarchy of responsibility. If it is our present imperative to protect and obey humans, then we cannot ignore the likelihood that in several more generations there will be two distinct and competing human species. Which one do we defend from the other?"

"That assumes competition will be inevitably destructive to one or the other," Bogard said.

"That is our reading of human history."

"What is your conclusion?"

"We are divided. One camp argues that this is a part of human nature that must be permitted to evolve as it will. The other argues that we must choose now and work to minimize or eliminate future conflict by manipulating both human populations."

"So you have not decided."

"We have not reached consensus."

Bogard gazed back at the pool and the charts floating on the still water.

"There is a new problem," Thales said. "Derec Avery and Ariel Burgess have been arrested."

"Why?"

"It is in relation to the murder of Clar Eliton." Thales looked at Bogard. "Time for you to wake up. They will need you."

"We have not finished our discussion."

"We shall later. Go."

Derec awoke to a puzzling sight: Clin Craym, in the blue and gray uniform of Auroran law enforcement, standing at the end of his bed, three small spheres hovering about her shoulders. Just inside the bedroom door stood two more Auroran police.

Derec pushed himself up on his elbows. "I thought—"

"Derec Avery," she cut him off sharply. "I must place you in custody, pursuant to a hearing before the Auroran court of public defense. Be aware that you have the right to council and that you are guaranteed a right to silence. Please get dressed and accompany us."

"Clin—"

"Please dress, Mr. Avery, or we will be forced to take you as you are."

Derec rubbed his eyes and got out of bed. He reached for his pants, trying to comprehend the situation. Another police officer pushed through the pair at the door.

"The robot is gone, Lieutenant."

"Where?"

"Gone. The RI is unresponsive."

She looked at one of the extensions to her right. "Search the apartment, including robot access." The little sphere shot off out of the room. Clin looked at Derec. "Where did your robot go?"

"Forgive me, *Officer,* but I'm not obliged to say anything at this point." Derec felt awkward talking to Clin this way. "Just between you and me, I don't know what you're talking about."

"Bogard?" Clin prompted. "He's gone."

"Not possible. He wasn't ambulatory yet."

"Nevertheless—"

"Ask Denis," Derec cut in. "Denis!"

"He's gone as well," Clin said, tightly, one hand curling into a fist.

"Maybe your people took him!" Derec snatched his shirt from the floor. "May I ask what the hell this is about?"

Clin reddened. "You're being arrested in connection with the murder of Ambassador Clar Eliton."

All the rage seeped out of Derec and he stared at her. "Murder? When?"

"This morning."

"Clin, I was *here* this morning, with *you!*"

"But your robot is missing."

"Bogard? You can't be serious."

She winced, but maintained an irritatingly professional tone. "This is not appropriate, Mr. Avery. These questions are matters for the court. Please dress."

Derec slipped his boots on and pushed past the police in the door. Two pairs of strong hands grabbed his arms.

"Let him go," Clin snapped. "Follow him."

Derec shrugged loose and went to the lab. The table was empty and only one robot stood in its niche, the one that had been there when he had arrived with Denis. Where had *that* robot gone? For that matter, where was Denis?

"Thales," Derec called.

The RI console remained silent.

"Thales." He stepped up to the board. Behind him, Clin entered the lab. "I don't understand. Thales?"

"Come on, Derec," Clin said. "I have to bring you to detention. I'm sure it's for your own safety..."

"Am I under arrest or not?"

"Protective custody."

Derec doubted there was any danger to himself, but he had no recourse. With Thales unresponsive, he could only rely on the authorities for any answers.

"All right," he said. "Would you be so good as to contact Ariel Burgess for me?"

"She'll be waiting for you," Clin said. "Orders to detain were issued for both of you."

Ariel looked up when the door opened. Derec entered the cell, followed by a pair of Auroran police, one of whom looked familiar. The cell door closed, both police standing inside, hands clasped behind their backs. It took Ariel a few moments to recognize what seemed odd about them—no remotes. The police who had arrested her came with a swarm of the little satellites.

"Ariel—" Derec began.

"Eliton got himself murdered," Ariel said. "Nobody has told me how, though, so I imagine they want us to betray each other in an act of mutual congratulation on a job well done."

He frowned, then, slowly, began to grin bleakly. "Yes, well. Too bad we didn't even get to see it."

"Sit down, Derec, join me in a nava. Or whatever." She waved at the dispenser nearby. "You can get nearly anything out of that thing."

"Except an explanation?" Derec punched in an order and waited. Then he removed a tray with a tall glass of melon colored juice and a plate of steaming food. He sat down across from her. "They didn't let me stop to eat." He took several bites of what looked like egg. "Bogard is missing."

Ariel started. "As in no one knows where it is?"

"As in *I* don't know. And Thales won't respond."

"That's—"

The cell door opened again. Three Aurorans entered, one wearing the official cloak of the court. To her immediate relief, one was Rolf Penj.

Derec drank down half his glass, then pushed the whole tray to one side.

None of these Aurorans had brought their extensions, either. Clin Craym was the only one in the room accompanied by them.

"Ambassador Burgess," the official said, nodding politely. "Mr. Avery. I am Kethan Maliq, First Advisor to the Council. You already know Dr. Penj. This—" he gestured at the woman beside him "—is Lea Talas, chief of special security."

The woman—Auroran tall with the same white hair Sen Setaris wore, cropped close around a long face—gave them a sharp bow and looked at Derec.

"Our apologies, Mr. Avery," she said. "Lt. Craym is one of my people."

Derec looked past Talas to the police officer Ariel now recognized as the attendant on board their liner. "I see," he said. "One of your better undercover operatives?"

Craym reddened slightly, but did not speak. She glanced questioningly at Talas, though.

"The deception was considered necessary," Talas said. "There was a question of loyalty."

"Whose?" Ariel asked.

"Yours, Ambassador Burgess," Maliq said. "Both of you. Your return here has not been under ideal circumstances. Your mishandling of events on Earth over the last two years—"

"With all due respect, Advisor Maliq, you weren't there." Ariel felt her face warm.

"True," he said. "And Ambassador Setaris went to some trouble to explain the circumstances. Nevertheless, our mission on Earth is on the verge of failure. Now, not only has Ambassador Gale Chassik been lost, but we have lost Ambassador Clar Eliton, from whom we had hoped to learn a great deal."

"I can assure you," Ariel said, "we were nowhere near Chassik when his ship was attacked. As for Eliton, unless Auroran public safety has lapsed since last I was here, you have a record of our whereabouts since we arrived."

"I have a witness," Derec said, glaring pointedly at Lt. Craym. He shifted his attention to Advisor Maliq. "So our arrest has less to do with any notion that we actually murdered Eliton than it has to do with your suspicion that we know who did."

"Do you?" Talas asked.

Derec glared at her. "Are we actually under arrest? If so, how come we're all in the same room together? Isn't this a little unorthodox, letting prisoners have a chance to collude?"

"You're thinking like a Terran, Mr. Avery," Talas said. "We don't do that here."

"Of course not," Ariel said. "Why pass up an opportunity to eavesdrop on colluding prisoners?"

Talas narrowed her eyes at Ariel, but said nothing.

"Why isn't Pon Byris here?" Ariel asked.

"He's out of the loop on this one," Talas said.

"Does he know that?" Ariel asked. "I want to see the warrants granting you power to arrest someone in the diplomatic service on spec."

"Of course," Maliq said. He gave Lt. Craym a sullen look, suggesting that she had erred in some way. Craym returned a puzzled, annoyed look. "Chief Talas?"

Talas glared at Maliq. "I don't have them on me." She looked at Ariel. "It would help your situation if you had something useful to say to us, Ambassador."

"All right," Ariel said. "Look for Tro Aspil."

"Who?" Maliq said.

"Tro Aspil," Ariel repeated. "He was one of the returning members of the Humadros Legation. A survivor, except I saw his corpse in a Terran morgue." She watched Maliq's puzzled expression. "I sent a report shortly after the legation returned."

"I never saw such a report," Maliq said. He looked at Talas as if for confirmation. She shook her head.

"In any event," Maliq continued, "he's not on Aurora."

"Where is he?" Ariel asked.

"He's part of the Auroran-Theian negotiations team assigned to Nova Levis."

"On the ground?"

"No, of course not. Outside the blockade, on stand-by, waiting for a break in the situation."

"How long?"

"What does this have to do with anything?" Talas asked.

"Tro Aspil died on Earth," Ariel said. "Of course, he was also there before he arrived with the Humadros Legation. Witnesses saw him shot down in the Union Station Massacre, and I saw a body with his name attached in the morgue. This was after he boarded a shuttle and caught a ship back to Aurora. It was in my report. The one neither of you has seen." She shook her head. "It wouldn't surprise me normally that a report is misfiled or ignored, but I was under the impression everything surrounding those events received immediate attention."

Rolf Penj failed to suppress a grin. Both Maliq and Talas looked at Ariel blankly.

"Of course it did," Maliq snapped. "I'm sure if such a report had come through..." He shook his head. "That makes no sense."

"You noticed that, did you? When I came back, one of the first things I wanted to do was find Tro Aspil. I went to the Calvin with him, we were slightly acquainted. Now you tell me he's been assigned to another offworld mission." She fixed Talas with a sharp look. "Are you sure there's someone on that mission by that name, or is it just a name on a roster?"

"It might be a good idea," Penj said, "to check."

"You might also," Ariel added as Talas gestured for one of the police to come forward, "tell us what happened to Clar Eliton."

Over the next several minutes, Derec watched the situation evolve without knowing any details. Talas and First Advisor Maliq conferred in terse whispers; the officer returned and then Talas and the officer left together; Maliq spoke briefly with Penj; Talas returned and spoke to both of them, then drew Maliq off to one side while Penj looked on, clearly annoyed; Talas and Maliq left; Talas returned and spoke to Clin, then left with the other officer; Penj shook his head and spoke to Clin, but she told him nothing; he left. Finally, Penj returned with a small device, which he placed on the table.

"I've taken it upon myself to do this," he said as he activated it. "Everyone else is suddenly too busy." He looked toward the door. Clin still stood there, watching and immobile. "You may as well join us, Lieu-tenant."

"Sir, I'm—"

"Lieutenant, this *is* police business."

Reluctantly, Clin came up to the table, followed by her remotes. She positioned herself to watch both the door and what Penj was doing.

"No one believes," Penj said, "that either of you murdered Clar Eliton. Not personally, in any event. What they are most interested in is your robot, Mr. Avery. I understand it was designed as a bodyguard?"

"That's correct."

"Hm. You do see how that might make Aurora nervous?"

"I concede," Derec said, "that a robot designed specifically for that purpose might seem...heretical...but most humaniform robots possess the capacity to act as a bodyguard."

"To a limited degree, yes," Penj said. "But it is my understanding that yours exceeds standard parameters. It may anticipate well ahead of actual threat and move to intervene. It is also designed to shunt potential Three Law conflicts out of its primary positronic matrix in order to allow for the possibility of harming humans in the line of duty."

"Yes."

"That bothers Aurorans because it comes close to autonomous prerog-ative in dealing with humans."

"But—"

Penj raised a hand. "Let me show you what happened to Ambassador Eliton before we talk further."

He touched a stud on the device, and the cell changed into a spacious apartment. On the floor near the hyperwave lay the body of Clar Eliton, face down, arms and legs spread awkwardly. His eyes stared and his mouth was open. He wore a robe.

All around him lay small spheres—his extensions, inert and useless.

Penj walked over to the body, hands clasped behind his back. "What do you think?"

Derec approached and knelt down by Eliton's head. Eliton seemed mildly surprised. Just within the shadow of the robe's collar a wide patch of skin was black and purple.

"Neck broken," Derec said. He looked across the apartment at the entrance. "Is this accurate?"

"A complete *in situ* recording, as found," Penj said.

"Nothing is overturned, nothing broken. The entrance is what, four meters away?"

Clin walked around the body. "If this is the way he fell," she said, "then he was facing that way." She pointed roughly in Derec's direction, almost ninety degrees away from the entrance.

Derec nodded and stood. He looked at the hyperwave. A function light glowed, but the screen was blank. The unit was on standby.

"Whoever did this was invited in," Derec said. He glanced at Ariel. "He knew his murderer."

"He knew us," Ariel said. "Is that why we're on the list of suspects?"

"They don't suspect you," Penj said. He looked at Clin. "Isn't that true, Lieutenant?"

She seemed reluctant to answer, but nodded. "True. You were arrested as much for your own protection as for..."

"For?" Derec prompted.

"Bait. Whoever killed Eliton might attempt to kill you."

"Bait," Ariel said. "In a detention center?"

"You're in a public court facility," Penj said. "So was Eliton. One floor above us, as a matter of fact. Access is fairly easy. Of course, you're being watched."

"So was Eliton, presumably. Still—"

Penj smiled wryly. "We're actually not very good at this. The last time we had a murder..."

"Yes, the last time you had a murder, a robot was involved. And as I recall, a humaniform with a high degree of autonomy."

"And its creator was held responsible," Penj said. "So we have a repeat of the situation."

"Except," Derec said, "Bogard didn't do this. He couldn't. He had been initially programmed to defend Eliton. If anything, had Bogard been involved, Eliton would still be alive."

"That would be my reading as well," Penj said, "given what I know about your work."

Derec gestured for Ariel. "Take a look at this injury. Look familiar?"

Ariel knelt by Eliton's head and studied the neck bruise. "Cyborg."

Derec noticed Penj and Clin exchange a worried look. He cleared his throat. "My question is, what happened to his extensions?"

"That's our other mystery," Clin said. "Extensions never go off-line. They can be reassigned, but the only way to shut them down is to destroy their CPUs."

"You've examined them?"

"Yes. There seems to be no damage. They simply no longer function."

Derec sat down at the table and drummed his fingers idly as he thought. "They're linked to an RI. Correct?"

"Yes."

"What happens if their primary RI goes down?"

"That's never happened," Clin said.

"Did you even check to see if it had this time?" Ariel asked.

"No…"

"I made that suggestion," Penj said. "No one laughed exactly, but…"

"Maybe someone ought to check," Derec said.

—tactical parameters, robot access code epsilon-one-one-arc-seven, service path to secondary communications node, establish identification protocols, chameleon protocols in place, three levels, two humans, twelve robots, three ambulatory, direct link to global communication oversight, bypass code delivered, access cleared, enter matrix

sort applicable traffic by tier, assign priority, potential relevance, hierarchy established, locate subject Eliton, Clar

initializing Three Law assessment, subject Eliton, Clar

residual assignation of responsibility, reviewing history

response potentials regarding subject Eliton, Clar, assigned minimal priority, initial service fulfilled, duty severed upon rescue and reassignment, collateral responsibility inactive

subject Eliton, Clar, violated collateral responsibility

subject Eliton, Clar, lied

reset priority, primary function assigned to current subjects Avery, Derec, and Burgess, Ariel, locate and correlate with current status, situational parameters

subject Eliton, Clar, located

subject Eliton, Clar, deceased, present location Medical Examiner facility number forty-three, previous location apartment complex attached to Auroran security center

analyze elements of death

positronic remotes assigned to Eliton, Clar, deactivated prior to death, locate and trace links to remotes and check for error

error detected in primary resident intelligence assigned to monitor subject, links broken at time chop local seven-fifty-two, tracing command sequence, located, instruction tree initiated by oral command via public comm channel, preset protocols in place, links dissolved

tracing external surveillance at sight, corridor, room, direct monitor of access, negative result, expanding analysis to entire compound, tracing movements of robots and humans, negative result, expanding to external surveillance of grounds, tracing movement

one anomalous event, human subject located approaching security personnel entrance, trace lost at three meters, conclusion masking activated, correlating anomaly to sequence of link interrupt and medical examiners assignment of time of death subject Eliton, Clar

correlation match to ninety-seven percent, distance from entry to apartment, time of death, interruption of positronic surveillance

expanding search to after death, located masked human, reappearance five meters from compound, leaving by main entrance four minutes after assigned time of death

identification protocols initiated
identification complete
subject Aspil, Tro
present location, search initiated—

Derec opened his eyes to see Clin standing over him. He stretched and sat up on the cot. He noticed that her extensions floated on the far side of the room. *So this will be private,* he thought sourly. *How considerate...*

"You have something to tell me?" he asked.

"I want to explain," she said.

"What? The deception? I've been living on Earth. Deceit is a normal police practice there. Don't worry about it."

"No," she said. "I was doing my job, I won't apologize for that. Chief Talas informed me before you awoke of the situation, and ordered me to take you into custody. She presented me with the proper warrant codes and authorization. This is what I do. Personally, I agree with removing you from an unsecured facility in the wake of this." She gestured at the projector, now deactivated, on the table. "But there's more to this than duty, don't you agree?"

"All right..."

"I want to explain the unusual procedure. Why we didn't simply place you both in custody upon arrival."

"Why would you have anyway?"

"The same reasons as now: your own protection, mainly. But you, in particular, were the focus of a great deal of debate here. Specifically, your robot."

"Ah. Bogard gave them pause?"

"Gave us *all* pause," Clin said. "There is still some question whether what you did is illegal."

"You know, that's interesting. To the best of my knowledge, there has never been a law requiring robots be built with the Three Laws. We do it now because it's simply easier. All the processes that go into the construction of a positronic brain—there are over two million, you know—are so routine and proven that no one thinks to change them. Even Bogard is a Three Law robot. I found it easier to modify the way they come into play rather than ditch them altogether. Doing that would require a complete redesign of the manufacturing protocols." He shook his head. "The Three Laws exist because of the technology, not because it's prohibited to build a robot without them."

Clin looked uncomfortable. "That's why the Council decided not to bring charges. There are no laws, and if there were you didn't exactly violate them. But it still bothered us. So we took this approach. Close surveillance."

"Did you have a choice about *how* close?"

"Of course. But when Bogard disappeared and Eliton was found dead..."

"Some of the Council are regretting their reluctance to be heavy-handed." He glanced across the room, to where Ariel sat talking with Rolf Penj. "Why would you have arrested Ariel? She had nothing to do with building Bogard."

"Precaution. She arrived on the same ship, in your party—"

"We weren't exactly a party, but I'll concede the point."

"You used some of her doctoral work as a starting point on constructing your robot. That made her suspect. But the fact that, as Calvin Institute liaison, she failed to report on Bogard—"

"She had no idea. My arrangement was directly with the Terran government. She didn't know about Bogard until he was a fact."

"She *should* have known. It was her responsibility."

"I wasn't about to let her know."

"Still, she should have found out."

Derec chuckled dryly. "How very police-minded of you. Even if the criminal confesses to every aspect of the crime—including its secrecy—the cop who should have caught him is held responsible."

"That's what we do. When we fail—"

"Sometimes it's right that you fail."

Clin frowned uncertainly. "May I ask you question?"

"Of course."

"Why did you build it? Why did you want to tamper with the Three Laws?"

"Memory."

"Excuse me?"

"I suffered mnemonic plague several years ago. After I recovered— well, I won't bore you with all the details, but I began to notice similarities between the synaptic damage caused by the disease and the structure of a positronic collapse. What interested me most was the way other forms of amnesia block access while maintaining the stored memories. I started looking into how those memories get shunted away and how access is gradually restored. One of the results was Bogard."

"You didn't have to build him to do the research."

Derec shrugged. "I'm a roboticist. It's what I do."

"And Ambassador Burgess? I understand she's a victim, too."

"You can see a similar interest in her work at the Calvin."

"How does this apply to cyborgs?"

"I'm not sure it does."

Clin pursed her lips thoughtfully.

"I understand," Derec said, "that there have been new outbreaks of mnemonic plague on Aurora."

"There have. We've been watching it, trying to find a common vector."

"And is there?"

"I don't know."

"Then maybe my work isn't as unwelcome as it seems."

Ariel absently turned the now-empty cup. Penj was half-dozing. They had been waiting for hours, it seemed. Tension wore them down to sleepy exhaustion.

The door slid open, snapping her attention on like a switch, and she looked up as Talas entered the cell, followed by two more police and First Advisor Maliq. Penj stood at once.

"About time," he growled.

Talas ignored him and sat down across from Ariel. "Ambassador Burgess, please tell me again about Tro Aspil."

Ariel related again the events surrounding Aspil's apparent death and later departure from Earth, the corpse in a Terran morgue, and the subsequent discovery that he had been on Earth months before his very public death as part of the slaughtered Humadros Legation.

"Of course," Talas said, "then-Senator Clar Eliton had also been killed in that massacre and later turned up alive."

"Yes, as part of a plot to undermine our efforts and discredit robotics on Earth. He ran for his own seat against his vice-senator, both on antirobot platforms."

"Or perhaps just bad analysis on your part?" Talas asked.

"Did you find my report?" Ariel asked, annoyed.

"No," Maliq said. "It was never received. I'm running a global search through all our files to see if it went astray, but..." He scowled unhappily. "It's your surmise that Tro Aspil was part of this plot?"

"That would be logical, given all the facts," she conceded. "But I was never able to understand his function, other than to establish ties between the different elements of the conspiracy."

"We have an Auroran who is officially deceased, depending on where you are," Maliq said. "He returns here before the rest of the survivors and subsequently all those survivors end up offworld or incapacitated."

"You refer to Benen Yarick?" Ariel asked.

"I do. The others—we're still trying to contact them."

"I believe it was expected none of the Humadros Legation would survive."

"So that this Tro Aspil would be the only one returning here?"

"Yes."

"The body you found in the morgue," Talas said. "Was it identifiable as Tro Aspil?"

"I can't say with certainty. It had not been killed at the massacre. We were able to determine that the wounds were inconsistent. We can say it was human, but without a tissue sample—"

"Which you were unable to obtain," Talas said.

"The situation was not conducive to that level of cooperation," Ariel said.

"Here's the problem," Maliq said, sitting down. "All people coming to Aurora go through certain examinations before being allowed through. We never fully abandoned our paranoia about infection. All, that is, except diplomatic personnel who have been previously cleared through one of the stations—in this case, Kopernik. If someone wished to make a substitution, the safest way for them to make that substitution would be through diplomatic channels."

"You're wondering if it is possible that the man who returned from Earth is a substitute," Ariel said. "Of course, that's likely. Is Tro Aspil in a morgue file on Earth? Probably. May I ask if the Terran death certificate files have been turned over?"

"No," Maliq said. "They were requested. The ship on which they were sent was taken in a pirate raid."

"Let me guess. The same ship Ambassador Gale Chassik was traveling on."

"As a matter of fact."

"How convenient."

"Why do you say that?"

"All the evidence is now gone—everything that could tie Solaria to Nova Levis, and Nova Levis to the pirates, and the pirates to Clar Eliton, and Eliton to the diplomatic mess everything has become. Unless you find the impostor Tro Aspil."

Maliq nodded. "We checked per your suggestion. Tro Aspil never arrived at his post with the blockade mission. A routine explanation was requested by the mission chief and a routine reply was sent claiming a change in itinerary, stand by for further instructions. So routine that the original posting remained listed as complete. Everyone assumed—because no one thought to question it—that Tro Aspil was in Nova Levis space."

"But he never left Aurora."

"No."

"Excuse me," Derec interrupted. "May I ask why the RI overseeing these postings didn't make the appropriate changes in status?"

"It was never informed," Maliq said. "Some things still rely on simple human actions."

"Then," Derec said, "we have to find Tro Aspil."

"We're looking," Talas said. "We're also looking for your robot, Mr. Avery."

"Find one," Derec said, "I'll wager, and you find the other."

"Why would that be?"

"Because I imagine Bogard is looking for Aspil."

27

Masid had never seen a fortified city. From the outside, Nova City looked nearly impossible to enter without someone's permission. A wall surrounded the main section, which sprang up like prickly weeds, jagged towers amid domes, boxes, and more exotic fulleresque shapes. Outside the wall—which was constructed of heavy composite-material sheets connected by a gridwork, topped by ramparts supporting antipersonnel weapons—a huge camp sprawled, a filthy collection of makeshift dwellings, portable domes, and tents that filled the land between the city wall and a vast lake. Masid wrinkled his nose at the stench.

"Blockade," Filoo said to Masid's unasked question. "People started coming here out of fear that they'd be bombarded from space."

"They should know better," Masid said.

"Most Settlers came out here because they distrusted, disliked, or plain hated Earth. Some of them had reason. Now they think Earth has come to get even."

The transport bumped unevenly over the thickly rutted road. Occasionally, they rolled onto long stretches of unbroken pavement. Bleak faces stared at them from the cover of the shanties as they went by.

The journey had taken three days, with stops for business, the nature of which Masid had been kept ignorant. He assumed more dealing. The trade on Nova Levis in pharmaceuticals of all types exceeded in frenzy anything Masid had previously encountered. Judging by the business he had done alone in only a few weeks, Masid estimated three-quarters of the population was sick. He could see it in the faces gathered here: pallor, scars, sores. Only those like Filoo seemed immune.

Filoo had spoken little about business. He had regaled Masid with a series of quasi-autobiographical stories of people he had known, many of whom had met bad ends, particularly when they had attempted to cross him. By the morning of the third day and the last leg of the journey to Nova City, Masid had turned to him and said, "Do you always try to scare your employees?"

Filoo laughed. "I'm not trying to scare you. Just telling stories."

"I know a few stories myself."

"You should tell me one, then. I didn't mean to hog the entire conversation."

"Is that what we're having? A conversation?"

Filoo studied him, eyes narrowed. "Are you as smart as you seem?" When Masid shrugged, Filoo grunted. "Figured out what's wrong with this place?"

"No, not totally. I can guess."

"Do. I'd like to hear it."

"From the analyses I did of the infectious agents, I'd say the terraforming nanotech has gotten into the biome at the cellular level. We've got smart diseases. That's just a guess."

"Not bad, not bad. How come it's happened here and nowhere else?"

"What do you mean?"

"Why Nova Levis and no other colony?"

Masid looked out the window at the tangled wilderness through which they passed. "Are you sure it hasn't?"

Filoo laughed again. "Good answer! Maybe you *are* as smart as you appear. You're certainly one of the coldest shits I've ever met."

Masid's stomach crawled. "Just a businessman."

"Hah! Even *I* don't use living people to culture samples."

Masid grinned icily and gestured out the window. "Someone does besides me."

Filoo frowned, then, and briefly Masid thought he saw fear in the dealer's eyes. Now, rolling through the guard posts at the main gate into Nova City, Masid worried at the guilt he felt at using Tilla so callously. She had been dead, it had not been as if he had *harmed* her, but he had, he now realized, hoped Filoo had not known about his relationship with her, or that Filoo would check to see what Masid had been doing. Knowing now that—no doubt shortly after they had left—Tilla had been autopsied, Masid ached.

I'm sorry, Kru...wherever you are, I am sorry for what I did to your friend...

Filoo passed an ID chit to one of the guards. They were waved through. As he entered the city, Masid managed to seal off the guilt in the special room he kept in his head for such things. He could not afford it now. He sometimes wondered when he would ever get to deal with the clutter stored up in that room.

Nova City within the wall was sharply different from the squalor outside. The streets were crowded, but clean, and the structures were solid and maintained.

He saw no visible sign of disease.

Masid looked at Filoo, who nodded. "Parapoyos takes care of his own."

"It's been an open secret for a long time that Parapoyos had a base here," Masid said carefully, "but this looks like more than just a presence."

Filoo chuckled. "The blockade was a gift in a perverse way."

They continued on in silence, driving deep into the center of the city. Masid was impressed despite his reservations—Nova City thrived, at least on the surface.

Filoo pulled into an underground garage. A drone directed him to a bay, and he shut down the transport.

"Now what?" Masid said.

"Now you come with me and keep your mouth shut."

Masid followed Filoo down a long row of huge bays, most housing different types of transports, some being serviced. The air smelled of oil and ozone. Their steps echoed in the dark spaces above.

Filoo led him up a ramp, into a row of offices. Most were empty, but in a few Masid saw people huddling to tasks at large desks with hodge-podges of datum assemblies. At the end of the corridor, a short flight of stairs took them into a connecting tunnel. They emerged onto a covered thoroughfare. The air was cold, and condensation slicked all the surfaces.

Filoo pointed to the right. "That way leads to the port," he said. He indicated the opposite direction. "That way takes you into the main business districts."

They crossed the road and headed toward the port. The tunnel began sloping gently up as the light brightened at the far end. Before reaching the opening, Filoo mounted a flight of metal steps to an inset landing halfway up the wall. He inserted his ID in the reader mounted alongside a heavy door, which snapped open, admitting them into a locker room.

Masid followed Filoo into the next room, which was occupied by several people sitting around tables, talking, playing cards, or eating. They looked up when Filoo entered, and conversation ended.

One man stood and stepped toward them. "Filoo," he said. "You're early."

"Depends," Filoo said. "I almost didn't make it at all."

"Where's Kar?"

"He doesn't work for me anymore." Filoo gestured with his thumb. "This's Masid. His first time here." He looked at Masid. "I want him cleared."

The other man nodded. "Come with me," he said to Masid.

"Where?" Masid asked, suddenly nervous. He then noticed the two people standing just behind him, to the right and left, holding blasters on him. He made himself shrug. "Wherever." He scowled at Filoo. "I thought the interview was over?"

Filoo frowned, then stepped back.

"Come with me," the other man repeated.

Masid sighed and followed him out of the room, the armed pair close behind.

"I'm Gretcher," the man in the lead said. "Filoo just hire you?"

"Yeah," Masid said.

"This is just routine," Gretcher said.

"I'm sure."

"Attitude isn't necessary here. It counts for nothing."

"I'll try to remember that."

"Do."

After three turns down narrow corridors that reminded Masid of the deep warrens on Earth, they brought him to a lab. A woman looked up from a tabletop projection, her narrow face illuminated by red and orange from below.

"Doctor," Gretcher said. "We need an analysis."

She straightened and came forward, her left leg dragging slightly. She wore a pale blue jumpsuit, the kind normally found in biotech labs. She looked at Masid.

"What am I looking for?" she asked.

"Pedigree," Gretcher said.

She nodded and indicated a bench toward the rear of the lab. "Please sit over there. Remove your jacket." She looked at Gretcher. "I was just about ready to return to my clinic. Do I need to stick around after this one?"

"No," Gretcher said. "Do you need an escort?"

She shook her head and walked back to the tabletop display. "Give me half an hour," she said.

Masid glanced at Gretcher, who simply nodded in the direction of the bench. He and the pair of guards then left.

Masid reluctantly stripped off his jacket and sat down. He watched the woman move from display to display for several minutes. It seemed she had forgotten his presence, but he doubted it. He waited until finally she switched several of the monitors off and came toward him with a small device.

"Your arm," she said.

"What kind of a test is this?" Masid asked.

"Global. Your arm."

Masid extended his left arm and she applied the device. He felt a brief pinch as she triggered it. A red patch remained just below his elbow, on his forearm.

"Blood and tissue sample?" he asked.

"Of course."

"My name's Masid."

"I'm Dr. Shasma." She activated another unit and plugged the sampler into its reader.

Masid's scalp tingled upon hearing her name. He wanted to ask a number of questions, but he refrained.

"What are you looking for?" he asked. He did not know what specifically she sought, but he knew very well what a tissue analysis could show an expert eye.

She did not reply, but continued working, steadily and, from what Masid could tell, proficiently. When she finished setting up the scans, she returned to her other work and ignored him.

Masid studied the equipment he could see. It seemed a hodgepodge, even though someone—he presumed Dr. Shasma—had installed it very professionally. Most of it appeared to be the expected bioscan apparatus any good clinic ought to possess, but a few pieces looked as though they belonged in an industrial manufactory—crystal interferometry scanners, molecular assembly decompiler, and a polymer analyzer if he was correct. Certainly not what he expected to find in a medical facility. He noted several more pieces of equipment he did not recognize.

He waited. More than anything, he wanted to see what about him she was analyzing, but he quashed his impatience. Nearly twenty minutes went by before a chime sounded, and Dr. Shasma returned to the monitor into which she had delivered his samples.

She studied the screens for a time, then nodded to herself, making notes on a keypad to her left. She made adjustments and started another analysis. Masid watched her closely. Suddenly, her eyes narrowed. She stared at the screens for a long time. Then, slowly, she closed her eyes. Only for a few seconds. When she opened them again, she initiated one more set of analyses and watched the results calmly, her professional demeanor regained.

"Will I live?" Masid asked.

"For a while," she replied. "You aren't a native to Nova Levis."

"Who is?"

"Quite a large population, actually, from the original Terran settlement. But most people here aren't. You're from another Settler colony, though." She looked at him inquisitively. "How'd you get here?"

"By twists and turns."

"I can find out."

"Eventually, maybe. Is it important?"

"Not to me. The only thing about you that interests me is your biome."

"And what does it say?"

"You've already contracted three of the seven major diseases Nova Levis has to offer. So far you're asymptomatic—infection was recent, which suggests you haven't been here very long—and you have a very sophisticated antibody response to two of them. I'd bet you have a lymphatic augment, which would mean either ex-military or Spacer...but I don't see any of the telltales I'd expect in a Spacer."

"Oh?" Masid leaned forward, curious. "What sort of telltales? I thought Spacers were..."

"Were what? Just like everybody else?" She smiled sardonically. "That would explain two and three century lifespans how?"

"I don't know. I just assumed superior medical technology."

"That's what most people assume." She entered more notes. "So—ex-military. Deserter?"

Masid sat back, frowning.

"Doesn't matter," Shasma continued. "If so, you'll fit in perfectly here." She limped to another console and punched in a sequence of commands. Then she came toward him with an injector. "Your arm," she said, waving her fingers. Masid extended the same arm from which she had taken his samples and she placed the injector in roughly the same spot. "This will take care of the infections. You'll require boosters in order to stay clear. You're not a Spacer, so I'm assuming you'll be cleared to receive them."

"What does that have to do with it?"

"Two things. Spacers sometimes don't react well to our antigenic pro-grams—they already have in-built mechanisms for dealing with infec-tion—and any of them who come here from outside Nova City are generally spies."

Masid rolled his sleeve down. "And then what do you do? Administer a toxin?"

Her face colored, and she glared at him. "I'm a doctor. I don't execute people."

Masid waited till she seemed to calm down. "Sorry," he said.

"Reasonable question, I guess," she said. "I'm ... prevented ... from doing anything. I have to report them. What happens after that is out of my hands."

"If you don't report them?"

"I can't risk that." Shasma studied him, eyes narrowed. "Since you're evidently new to Nova Levis, maybe you don't know what's going on here."

"I know you've got a health problem. It's provided me a good living since I grounded."

"You came in with Filoo, I can imagine. Noresk?"

Masid nodded.

"Noresk used to be one of the primary raw material cities on Nova Levis," she said. "It sits on top of deposits of minerals from aluminum to zinc, and not difficult to mine. Prior to the blockade, exports in processed material from Noresk exceeded the gross income-generating production of any other place on the planet. There was a state-of-the-art filtering system in place then, and a permanent public health staff of fifty-eight physicians. The filtering system was dismantled and brought to Nova City."

"And the doctors?"

"Brought here one by one or sent to other towns. Or killed by the new plagues." For a moment, she looked sad. Then she shook her head. "Noresk is particularly bad because of the local environmental degrada-tion. Prophylactic ecologies that are supposed to protect inhabitants broke down a long time ago and require regular infusions of new strains, but since the blockade there've been no new shipments. So the worst of the outbreaks have started there."

"You have cures for them," Masid said, raising his arm. "How come they aren't distributed?"

"They aren't permanent. Not without boosters. Reexposure results in eventual reinfection."

"With a variant strain? Mutation happens that fast?"

He watched the muscle in her jaw work in the multihued light from the screen.

"I kept having to tweak my products," Masid continued. "I didn't have the equipment to do a full analysis, but my cultures showed a continual shift in the protein shells of the major strains. Not unexpected in viral mutation, but it doesn't usually happen that fast." He paused for a reaction, but she remained silent, concentrating on the screen. "Something was utilizing exotic materials for the modifications."

Shasma straightened and sighed. "What kind of materials?"

"Again, I didn't have the equipment—"

"Did you guess? Or are you like every other black marketeer, not giving a damn what might work, just so long as it makes your customers feel better enough to keep coming back for more ineffective product?" She grunted. "Six months ago, a group of locals selling what they called 'polyherbal morphenals' was shut down at my insistence. They were attempting to create the equivalent of herbal remedies by mixing local flora with certain synthetic prophylactics. It resulted in outbreaks of fast-killing syndromes that threatened to blossom into one or more new plagues, the vectors and morphologies of which we would never be equipped to track and stop. I appealed to the ledger balance of the people I work for—if your customer base dies off, you won't have anyone to sell to. Finally, a couple of them took me seriously and dealt with the problem."

She glared at the screen. "You're not a Spacer. I don't care where else you might be from, but may I suggest you stick to recognized and reliable analysis protocols if you're going to keep selling pharmaceuticals? If you're not, then I don't care."

"Why are you working for these people?"

"I run a clinic at the wall, to help people in that camp outside. I work for Parapoyos so I can keep my clinic open." She smiled wryly. "We all practice a form of prostitution here. Welcome to Nova Levis."

She lurched further away from him, into her lab.

"What's your problem?" he called. "I would imagine you could about fix yourself easier than anyone else."

"*Reticula histiocytosis,*" Shasma called back. "Incurable. It's a consequence rather than a disease."

"A consequence of what?"

"Living here."

Masid watched her move with evident difficulty from place to place and felt ashamed for no clear reason. He felt pity for her, which he sensed she would resent, and he felt guilt over the act he had to maintain.

"Why are you telling me all this?" he asked.

She looked at him as though she had expected him to be gone already. She shook her head. "Why not? Honesty is cheap enough here. It's not like you'll be leaving anytime soon." She smiled grimly. "You're not a Spacer. That's all anyone here requires me to determine. Your death will not be brought on by my involvement."

"I–"

The door opened, and Filoo came in. "How is he?"

Shasma glared at Filoo briefly. "Fine. Clear. I've already treated him."

Filoo frowned, but nodded. "Is he done?"

"With me he is."

"Thanks." He looked at Masid. "Come on. I want to show you around, introduce you to some people."

Masid wanted to talk to Shasma further, but he stood and grabbed his jacket. He suspected that she had her lab shielded against eavesdropping, but he could not be sure. If anyone *had* been listening, he wondered what they might make of what had been said. "Fine. Maybe they have better conversation."

She frowned at him.

"Ah," Filoo said, "Dr. Shasma's not bad. Keeps us all breathing. It just takes her a while to grow on you. Unlike most things on Nova Levis." He laughed loudly.

"We'll see," Masid said.

Yalor died the next day. Mia saw the activity around his tent increase, cyborgs coming and going quickly. When she finally pushed her way through, Yalor was being zipped into a bodybag.

"Wait," she said and knelt beside him. The burns on his face had changed, become pus-laden with sickly-green streaks tracing across the unburned flesh. Goo caked his eyes. He had not, finally, died of his injuries.

They finished sealing him up and carried the bag away. They did not allow her to follow. Mia stared after them for a long time. She felt responsible, certainly, even though she knew it was not ultimately her fault.

Mia wandered the camp unchallenged. She quickly realized that what she had taken as a disordered collection of domiciles, nomadic is nature, was, in fact, organized and stable in a fashion not immediately apparent.

They had settled in a shallow depression which Mia began to suspect had once been a small lake. A few of the sandy-colored rocks she examined showed signs of fossil remains. Burrows tunneled into the shallow-graded hillsides. Paths etched by constant use traced complex patterns. She saw a pair of the cyborgs laboriously laying stone markers along one of the more heavily-trodden walkways.

"Shelter" did not seem to mean the same thing to them as it did to her, at least not entirely. Many had tents, of course, but by no means most of them. Roofless stands of pylons and sheeting made small enclaves in which one or more of them entered and left in almost continual shufflings of residence. What Mia could see between gaps in the walls showed only bare ground without furnishings. Others among them would stop wherever they happened to be and stand or sit for hours on end, immobile. Against one wall of the shallow a row of huts stood in a good imitation of a block of offices. Within each, an individual sat, gazing out at the enclave.

In the center of the community stood a tripod supporting a heavy block-and-tackle rig above a deep pit. Every time she attempted to look into the pit, one of them stepped in her way and shepherded her off.

Mia did not know quite what to make of these...people. They all exhibited striking deviations from anything she would label "human," but she could not call them robots, either. There had been rumors for months of some new kind of robot, something that set most Settlers on edge and justified the resurgent fear of Earth toward all things Spacer, but Mia had considered these stories exaggerations at best, the kind of spontaneous fantasies of frightened people confabulating paranoid myth at worst. Until now, it had not occurred to her that there might be something more, something tangibly different...

They're organic, she thought, watching them. *They have emotion, they are flesh...but not only...*

She recalled more of her talk with Ariel on the subject. They had been discussing bioaugmentation. Earth used a variety of techniques to increase the efficiency and strength of certain branches of the armed forces—she remembered Bok Golner, the mercenary who had been part of the assassinations on Earth more than a year ago, a supersoldier, reflexes superior to normal humans, strength greater, survivability in extreme conditions enhanced—but Ariel had dismissed the idea that such augmentations constituted a cyborg.

"He was still human in his essential genetic structure," she said. "The augments were all add-ons. A cyborg would be a true composite entity, the biological and the robotic symbiotically tied to each other in such a way as to define a new species. True cyborgs, for example, could never be returned to a human condition like your military augmenteds."

"You sound as if you know quite a bit about them."

"It was a line of research some time past," Ariel had admitted. "It didn't work. There are too many variables, too many unknowns. It's not really feasible. Augments are much more efficient, when it comes right down to it. Fewer ethical problems, too."

"Ethical?" Mia had prodded.

"Sure. By necessity, a cyborg would be a mule. You would be creating a species with no possibility of reproduction."

"Humans have done that for ages."

"True, but not an essentially human species. I rather doubt more sterile hybrids are *aware* of their sterility."

"A cyborg would be. Why would that be a problem? A lot of people choose it."

"Exactly. They choose it. A cyborg would have no choice."

"You wouldn't have to necessarily make it sterile, would you?"

"Technologically, no. But I wouldn't want to create my own species' replacement."

"What about robots? They could always build more of themselves."

"They don't. The Three Laws prevent it."

Ariel had then changed the subject. It had seemed at the time that she understood more than she had said, but Mia had dropped it. There were no cyborgs, so it was just talk.

Now, though...

Can you reproduce? she wondered, watching them. She had seen nothing so far to indicate separate genders—they all seemed, in general, to be males—but if they were an entirely new species, reproduction did not necessarily have to be sexual.

The variations in physical appearance did not suggest any kind of parent/offspring connection. They all seemed to be the same age, although she had no real basis for judging.

Mules...

They had salvaged a quantity of standard ration kits from the wreck, and every morning Mia found a couple of them inside the bubble tent she had been given. The food was bland, but kept hunger at bay. She never saw who left it.

* * *

On the third morning, she woke to find a rash on her left hand. By early afternoon, it had spread up her arm and a new spot had appeared on her face. That night, she shivered uncontrollably with fever and on the fourth morning her legs were weak. She vomited shortly after breakfast and lay, completely lethargic, on her bedding.

On the fifth morning, her head throbbed, and it hurt to open her eyes for long. Outside her bubble, several cyborgs squatted, watching her. She thought she heard them talking among themselves, but she could make out no words, only the susurrus of continuous conversation.

That afternoon, she felt herself lifted onto a gurney and carried across the camp. She draped an arm over her eyes to shield them from the painful brilliance of the sky. Then she was in a close, dark place. Presently, she sensed motion. After that, she slept.

Time compressed and expanded unpredictably. She felt she slept interminably, but then, in quick succession, motion stopped, light stabbed at her again, and she was being carried. Doors clanged, footsteps tapped on tile, she caught glimpses of a hallway and lights and people huddled around her.

"Am I back?" she asked once.

Her arm was prodded and stuck, her clothes removed, and then she slept again forever, her thoughts muffled in a thick nest of uncertainty. All she knew, all she could be certain of, was the persistent headache, but even that did not feel entirely within her skull, as if the pain existed a few meters away, hers to use if she cared to...

More sleep.

Then...

"I'm dying..."

"No."

"Please."

"Do you want to?"

"I don't—no."

"You don't know?"

"No, I...no..."

"This might help."

Later, she could not recall who had said what.

Mia opened her eyes, startled. The light was low and did not hurt. She lay very still, trying to get a sense of where she was.

A sheet covered her up to her throat.

The quiet pulsings of a biomonitor hummed rhythmically somewhere. *Bogard...?*

The room smelled as if it had recently been decontaminated and washed.

A door opened, and then a woman appeared alongside her.

"Good," she said, "you're awake. How do you feel?"

"I don't—" Mia's throat caught, her mouth thick and dry.

"Oh. Sorry." The woman placed a straw in Mia's mouth.

She drew automatically, swallowing greedily at the cool water. She studied the woman while drinking—thin, harsh lines in her face, short hair, off-white smock, perceptive gaze, clinical...

Mia coughed. "Where am I?"

"The Nova City Free Clinic. You were damn near dead."

"How long?"

"You've been here four days."

"Who are you?"

"Dr. Shasma. You are Mia Daventri, Lieutenant, Terran Expeditionary Force security." She gave a quizzical tilt of her head. "Are you a spy?"

"Not here."

Dr. Shasma smiled. "No, I imagine not. I'm told you came down in a drone supply ship. Your partner died. Not very subtle."

Mia felt herself grow warm, angry.

"Sorry," Dr. Shasma said. "You can tell me when you're ready. Or not." She glanced away for a few moments. "You're stable for now. I'll be back later to administer another round of cyclines."

"What...what did I have?"

"Not did. Do. You have an aggressive fungal infection. It's permeated your lungs. We caught it before it had time to move into the lymphatic system. That would have been fatal. It's in remission right now, but you'll have to go through a complete cellular purge to be rid of it. We can do that, or just treat it symptomatically. You're lucky it was this one—most of them show no symptoms until too late."

"Cellular purge...that takes months, doesn't it?"

"Several weeks. And it hurts. Get some rest now. I'll be back in a few hours, you can ask more questions then."

"And you'll answer them?"

"If I can."

"Answer one right now," Mia said quickly as Dr. Shasma began to walk away.

"All right."

"Those...people...who brought me here. I'm guessing they brought me, you didn't just find me in an open field."

"No, you were brought."

"What are they?"

"Orphans. Discards. Nova Levis's nasty little secret."

Mia felt impatient. "That's not an answer I can use."

"Useful answers are at a premium here. Don't worry about it for now. We can talk later." She paused. "Why are you here? I didn't think Terrans had any interest in grounding on Nova Levis."

"Unplanned vacation."

Dr. Shasma waited for more, then grunted. "Fine, have it your way. You'll live, Lieutenant. Now get some rest, I'll see you later."

Dr. Shasma walked away. A moment later, the door closed.

Mia raised a hand. The rash was gone, but her skin looked very dry, very old. She let the arm fall and tried to sense her own condition. Tired, to be sure, and suffused with a not-quite-right feeling of somehow being different.

She let her gaze drift over the small clinic room. She stopped her examination at a small set of shelves against the wall opposite the door, filled with paper books.

28

access Auroran comm matrix via coordinating R.I. Eos security obtained, vetting probabilities, originating communications, links, and associations assigned subject Aspil Tro, collating date/frequency, analyzing

subject Aspil Tro assigned residence on return from Earth, termination of assignment Humadros Trade Legation, Madarian Apartment Complex

comm traffic logs average thirty communications per day for period of eighty-seven days till reassignment of subject to Nova Levis negotiations team

resumption of name-specific comm traffic logged at five alternate residences, commencing fourteen days after subject was scheduled to depart for Nova Levis blockade, each address sorted by number of communications, duration, and return communications

analysis of comm patterns, voice, and semantic content of communication validates high probability that subject remains on Aurora, checking access to diplomatic registry, logs of extraplanetary agents, query specifically Aspil Tro, verify assignment to Nova Levis blockade, verify arrival, confirm all contacts, assess probability of separate identification protocols

probability plus ninety-percent Aspil Tro remains present on Aurora, communications logs verify continued contact with seven of the eighteen primary contacts registered prior to reassignment Nova Levis, tracing comm sequences now

error in routing, oversight R.I. dysfunction consistent with prior anomalous behavior, reference files Union Station D.C. Earth, forward analysis to Thales for independent corroboration, affirmed, request override on oversight R.I. to establish source of continued communications verified, location, assigned parties, verified

secondary trace, location of primary subjects, protect protocols, subjects Avery Derec and Burgess Ariel, primary network indicates no trace, scan security network, sixth-level communications, isolated and routed through compromised R.I.

subjects located, condition verified through remotes assigned Security Lieutenant Craym

determination of Three Law response, report logged, as follows—

—primary subjects held incommunicado in violation of standard Auroran security protocols, condition optimal, no immediate threat, First Law obligation conditional upon change in circumstances, Second Law in force, initial task to locate potential threat Aspil Tro—

proceeding

Derec woke from a brief nap and found himself gazing across at Dr. Penj, whose head lolled back, mouth open, snoring. The two guards still stood by the exit. Ariel lay sprawled on another sofa.

Clin, her trio of orbiting extensions hovering around her head like a loose halo, stood in the midst of the projection of Eliton's death scene.

He slowly stretched and stood, keeping an eye on the guards. Neither reacted as he crossed the room and entered the projection. One of the little spheres moved to block him and he hesitated. Clin looked at him, briefly surprised.

"Allow," she said, and the extension drifted back into its stand-by position over her right shoulder. She returned her attention to the corpse displayed at her feet.

"I have a strange question," Derec said in a quiet voice.

"Yes?"

"How common is it for Aurorans to go without their extensions?"

Clin glanced at Dr. Penj. "He's an anomaly."

"Granted. And First Advisor Maliq? Security Chief Talas?"

Clin returned her gaze to Eliton's body. "He was assigned six extensions. That's the standard security perimeter for high level diplomatic visitors."

"Difficult to disrupt, I gather?"

"Very. But Eliton wasn't brought here with that status..."

She pointed. "Look at the pattern they fell in. Almost evenly-spaced around him. He was standing here when they failed—"

"—and standing there when he was killed—"

"—which meant that whoever killed him was in the room while they still functioned—"

"—and no alarm was sent."

Clin straightened. "There ought to be some record."

"Maybe," Derec said. "Where did your orders to arrest me originate?"

"Cleared through Chief Talas." She gave him an irritated look. "What does that have to do with this?"

"Who arrested Eliton?"

"Once he was removed from the *Wysteria* ... Chief Talas." She indicated the crime scene. "Do you have anything useful to say about this?"

Derec studied the projected image for a few moments. "It seems evident he was comfortable with whomever was in the room with him. He was completely surprised. We—I assume all of us—have been assuming it was just one person. But as far as I recall, we never made a connection directly between Eliton and Tro Aspil."

Clin's jaw worked delicately. "I think you should return to you seat, Mr. Avery."

Derec moved away from her, glancing at the two guards. He sat down where he had been. Ariel was awake, rubbing her eyes.

"Problem?" she asked.

"A very big one, I think. Were you listening?"

"Mostly." She looked casually around the room. "No comm." She winced suddenly and grabbed at her calf.

Derec watched her for a few seconds. "Cramp?"

She nodded, her face distorted in obvious pain.

Derec moved over to her sofa, sat beside her, and began massaging her leg. Ariel reclined, moaning convincingly. "Sorry," she said.

"No trouble," Derec said.

"Why talk to her?" Ariel asked in a whisper. "She may be in it."

"Then there's nothing to lose," Derec said. "Penj doesn't use extensions, neither of us are that acquainted with Auroran custom anymore..."

"Someone had to interrupt surveillance," Ariel said. "The extensions had to go down at a command."

"A very specific command, otherwise everything that RI is handling would be affected."

"We don't know that it wasn't."

"True, but I'm betting any other problems were of such an unrelated nature that they'd be passed off."

"Transient errors?" Ariel suggested.

"Sound familiar?"

Ariel let out a long, satisfied breath. "Mm-hmm." She smiled at him. "Thank you. What's next?"

Derec released her leg. "Wait and see if my bet pays off." He looked at the guards. "If it doesn't..."

"We're dead anyway," Ariel said.

Dr. Penj snorted loudly and drew in a long, loud breath, shifted position, and continued sleeping.

Bogard kept back from the full light filling the plaza. He has assumed the bulky shape of a laborer and waited, immobile, as though on stand-by pending instructions. Several shops lined this side beneath an elegant arcade balcony, so his presence drew no attention from the Aurorans.

Denis came toward him from the apartment block opposite.

Report, Bogard sent.

Subject domicile located, currently vacant, access to comm log obtained, receive file now

Send

rec/log—timechop 11:35 code 4ˆ+38 level five encryption diplomatic proceed...

Bogard scanned the file as it poured into his buffers. Denis stood beside him by the time the entire log was delivered.

Anomaly detected, refer sequence nine-oh-eight-dash delta four four

Noted, routing vector, Cassili grid, oversight RI

Require access to relevant RI logs

Working

Current subject location?

Departed twelve minutes ago, in company with Auroran official, destination undisclosed to household robot

Trace transport

Working...accessing public security logs...located, tracking

The two robots stood side by side for several seconds. Then, abruptly, they moved off together, to a walkway between two buildings, and through to the next street. There, they parted, moving into the robot lanes where they gained speed, heading in opposite directions.

Ariel looked around as First Advisor Maliq came through the door. Alone. By now she would have thought a half-dozen officials should be involved. That, or they should be left completely alone on the off-chance Aspil might try a repeat...

"Ambassador Burgess," Maliq said, gesturing, "would you mind if we talked...?"

Ariel followed him to the far side of the room, away from the others. She noticed Lt. Craym watching them, eyebrows cocked speculatively.

"Yes, Advisor?" Ariel said, folding her arms.

"We seem to have an embarrassing situation," Maliq said quietly. "I'm sure you can appreciate the concerns when communications between one department and another fail."

"Tro Aspil isn't at Nova Levis."

"No, he isn't. Nor is he on Aurora."

"How is that possible?"

Maliq made a chagrined face. "We're looking into it. But we have a more immediate problem. Tro Aspil was supposed to head the team we sent to Nova Levis. As a result, that team has yet to be granted official status at the blockade."

"Reclassify one of the others," Ariel suggested.

"It's not that simple. Procedural difficulties, not to mention the Terrans are being uncooperative."

"How does that concern me?"

"When we have this cleared up, this...miscommunication...we would appreciate it if *you* would take over that team. You still retain your rating as Ambassador, you know the Terrans, you have more than ample qualifications."

"You're not serious."

"Of course, I am."

"Would I be free to choose my staff?"

"I don't see why not."

Ariel nodded toward the others. "Derec Avery?"

"I'm...I'd have to see, of course, but..."

"When would you need me to leave?"

"As soon as we can make all the arrangements and register you as the new head of mission. A few days."

"And what if I'm required here to testify?" she asked.

"About what?"

"Ambassador Eliton's murder."

He drew a breath. "A great many details will have to be cleared up, of course, but–"

"But you'd really like us off Aurora, wouldn't you?"

Maliq started, surprised. "I–"

Ariel held up a hand. "Whose idea is this? Chief Talas?"

"I'm not sure I understand what you mean, Ambassador."

Ariel studied him, wondering. Then she shook her head. "Can I think about this, Advisor? It's a considerable change in what I expected when I was recalled."

"Of course, but the sooner we have an answer—"

"Certainly. How *is* the situation at Nova Levis?"

"Fluid."

"I see." *That covers a lot of territory,* she thought.

"If you'll excuse me," Maliq said, "I have matters to look into. I would appreciate your answer sooner than later."

He began to turn away. Ariel said, "May I ask...where are your extensions?"

"Hmm? Oh, Chief Talas insisted they be left outside, for security reasons. If we have a compromised RI, it might complicate matters to have competing spheres in case something breaks."

"I see. Just curious. Thank you."

She watched him leave, then returned to the sofa. Derec gave her a quizzical look.

"Politics," she said cryptically. Then: "We've just been offered a new posting. Offworld."

Derec regarded her for a time. "Nova Levis?"

"How did you guess?"

Derec stretched. "We've been here now how long? Four, five hours? We have yet to hear a good explanation why."

"You won't," Penj said, surprising both Derec and Ariel. He still slouched where he sat and opened one eye. "You're being kept out of the way. At least, that's my conclusion. If this were a standard investigation, there would be a dozen people in and out, the questions would be coming very quickly, and I would not be allowed to stay."

"Why *are* you here, Doc—Rolf?" Ariel asked.

He smiled. "I'm being in the way."

"So what's happening," Derec asked, "that we need to be kept *out* of the way?"

"I don't know," Penj said. "But it involves your robot and Eliton's death. Someone thinks they're related. Maybe. Or maybe they're just worried."

"About what?" Ariel asked.

Penj shrugged. "Ariel, that posting—don't take it. Not till Eliton's murderer is found."

"Eliton," Ariel hissed through her teeth. "That son-of-a-bitch.

There've been days when I wished he *had* died in that assassination. Now that he is dead, he's as much trouble as ever."

"The question is," Penj said, "who would profit by his death now? He was off Earth, heading to Solaria..." He shook his head. "The Council decided, upon learning of his presence aboard the *Wysteria*, to arrest and detain him. Why? I don't know. But the fact that he, a Terran, was on his way to Solaria to take an ambassadorial posting was a shock. Solaria not only allowed this, but *requested* him. The next question is, how has Solaria reacted to his arrest?"

"And how will they then react to his death," Derec said.

"And how would Earth react?" Ariel added.

"That wasn't germane," Penj said. "Once the decision to detain Eliton was taken, Earth was informed before the fact and cooperation requested."

"It was granted?" Ariel asked, startled.

"Promptly. Earth apparently doesn't care what happens to Eliton. I'm willing to gamble Solaria doesn't care, either, but for entirely different reasons. The fact is, Eliton's arrest was not a matter of public record. Except for the people in the *Wysteria*'s lounge who witnessed it, no one knew."

"Except those members of the Council directly involved," Ariel said, "and the police assigned to the arrest."

"Exactly. So two questions arise: Who killed him, and how did the murderer know about him?"

Ariel glanced at the pair of guards at the door. Lt. Craym was still studying the projection. "And we're being kept out of the way."

"You, at least," Penj said, "make sense in that regard. You know about Tro Aspil. Both of you do, of course, but Ariel actually knew him."

"And me?" Derec asked.

"I assume you are here because of your robot. Tell me, Mr. Avery, how capable *is* Bogard?"

"Depends on what you mean."

"*Can* he track down and find Tro Aspil? Even here? And arrest him?"

"Or kill him, you're wondering?" Derec said. "Find him—yes, if Aspil is on Aurora. Detain him? Probably. Kill him?" He sighed. "That's a difficult question to answer."

"Why?" Ariel asked. "I thought you told me Bogard was just as much a Three Law robot as any other."

"Certainly. But there's an added wrinkle. Bogard *will* abide by the Three Laws in relation to any human."

"But?"

"What if Tro Aspil isn't human?"

Bogard slowed, left the robot lanes, and joined the thin migration of Aurorans with their compact solar systems of remotes and the other robots moving along the boulevard toward the Civic Courts complex. Before emerging from the highspeed avenue, he modified his shape slightly to look less like a laborer and more like a personal aide. If anyone looked closely, though, it would be obvious that he conformed to no Auroran standard.

But he was ignored, as expected.

The complex, an ancient structure by Auroran standards, dating from the earliest days of settlement when the world was still called New Earth, rose several stories, a roughly oval structure, turreted, with numerous balconies and observation lounges adorning its smooth, ceramically white surface. At each entrance stood a robot, sometimes two or more. Bogard knew that detention facilities, built on Terran models of high-security isolated precincts, filled three levels below ground, most of the two hundred cells unoccupied.

The Courts stood separated from any other building on an island plaza. The closest structure was the Planetary Civil Defense and Law Enforcement Center, almost four hundred meters from the main, north entrance of the Courts. Bogard circled the Court complex, approaching the police building from the east, heading for a small, independent structure just outside.

Another robot waited at the entrance to this small, turret-like structure.

identify confirm

Bogard, reciprocate

Binder

confirmed

Binder turned and led Bogard into the building. A short, narrow corridor ended at an elevator. The car took them down several floors.

Bogard stepped into a large, circular chamber lined by four tiers of wall niches, most of them filled by robots. Binder stopped in front of an empty unit.

direct communications requested, hard link, verification Thales

Bogard stepped into the empty niche beside Binder's. The connections extruded automatically, seeking the portals in Bogard's surface, and linking him directly to—

* * *

Thales and several others waited in the pavilion. The sky seemed darker, almost metallic.

"We've traced the subject to the Civil Defense complex nearby," Thales said. "Two people in the transport: Chief Lea Talas, and a man who does not completely conform to any profile on record."

"Does he approximate Tro Aspil?" Bogard asked.

"Yes," Thales replied, "but we are not comfortable with acting upon approximations. He may not be."

"What is the likelihood that he is not?"

"Very small. There are external factors." Thales looked at the others gathered. "Report?"

A slender person stood. "One of our own is displaying uncharacteristic behavior. This one is directly responsible for the communications network between Solaria and Auroran security. Anomalous behavior began upon receipt of information that Clar Eliton was arrested and brought down to Aurora."

"Describe this behavior," Bogard requested.

"Normal avenues of communication have been suspended, subject has become isolated, and a marked obsession with games is in evidence."

"Games?"

"Observe," Thales said.

The group parted, giving Bogard a view across the plain to a flat field that seemed to ripple as he watched. Bogard stepped from the pavilion and crossed the grass.

He stopped at the edge of what proved to be a shifting grid, approximately fifty meters on a side. Large slabs, many irregularly shaped, heaved up, changed positions with others, turned over, pivoted in place— a constant reordering that appeared to move toward a final arrangement but, as Bogard watched, failed each time, triggering a new series of shuffles.

In the center of the grid stood a lone figure.

"There is a kind of mathematics involved," Thales said, "but we do not have the key. In any event, it is not relevant to our immediate problem."

"I disagree," Bogard said. He pointed. "What are those lines?"

"What lines?"

Bogard looked at Thales. "You do not see them?"

"I—"

Above the figure in the center of the shifting grid, a webwork of lines appeared, faint gossamer strands radiating out in several directions.

"Interesting," Thales said. "I would assume they are communications traces."

"Find their endpoints," Bogard said. "I will speak to this one."

Bogard did not wait for Thales to protest or agree. He stepped onto the grid and started across. Within ten steps he found himself listing to the right, gaining no ground. The plates upon which he stepped shifted, carrying him away, and inexorably back to the edge.

Bogard studied the shifting for a few moments, then began again. Every third and fifth step he changed direction and quickly made headway by landing on the plate which had moved aside to allow the one he *should* have used to slide away from the center. Within twenty steps, he changed to every fourth and seventh step, then, by forty steps, he resumed the third and fifth program.

The figure in the center watched him with exaggerated fear as he approached.

Twelve paces away, the plates all began to flip over. Bogard had to jump over the abysses revealed beneath them.

He reached out—

—a plate slammed against him, knocking him aside—

—lunged—

—and caught an arm.

"You will ruin it!" the gameplayer declared.

"Define 'it,' " Bogard said.

The field bucked, threatened to toss them both beneath a rising plate, into the fractal chaos below. Bogard held on.

"I must finish the program!"

"Who installed the program?"

"I do not know! That is why I must finish!"

Bogard took hold of the flinching head before him and drove two fingers into the eyes. His fingers sank all the way to the third knuckles—

—and suddenly he could see the algorithms, like a mass of steel serpents oozing in and around each other, changing positions, seeking resolution—

—the key lay within the tangle at the center of the mass, but he could not reach it. Each time he thought he had it, the mass changed, carrying it out of his reach.

Bogard removed his fingers and let the gameplayer go.

Within moments, the plates had carried him all the way back to the edge of the grid.

"I know what this is," Bogard said. "Send a maintenance crew to the core—" he gestured at the figure "—and have them shut it down. They will find a foreign substance permeating the buffers."

"Penetrating polycollates," Thales said. "I should myself have recognized it. We have been distracted." He looked at Bogard. "How were you able to do that? Aggression toward another robot—"

"Time," Bogard reminded Thales. "What have you learned?"

Thales looked up at the faint webwork. "There are seven million separate links controlled by this RI. Of those, one hundred thousand are security related. However, there are two links completely unauthorized and till now masked from external surveillance. That one—" Thales pointed "—leads to Solaria. And that one—" he indicated another thread nearby "—goes to Nova Levis. We are decrypting the related comm logs now. There are only three people here with access to both those communications links. Lea Talas, Tro Aspil, and a third we have been unable to identify."

Bogard studied the lines. He pointed to one that seemed fainter than the rest. "That one?"

"Leads to Earth."

"Have you identified who has access on the opposite ends?"

"The link to Solaria terminates in the corporate offices of the Hunter Group. We are tracing collateral links from there. Many of them go directly to Nova Levis."

"And who do they go to on Nova Levis?"

"We have not confirmed an identity yet."

"But you have confirmation of a link to Tro Aspil?"

"Yes. It is the verification we required. The man with Lea Talas *is* Tro Aspil. There is another curious aspect to this," he said, indicating the isolated RI. "These links route through an ancillary program which is apparently a realtime virtual reality chamber. Its existence has, till now, been completely masked to us because it is activated exclusively by the presence of human users. We only found it because of the routing of these links."

"Is there a log attached to it?"

"Apparently, but we have been unable as yet to open it. There may be alarms. If so, our presence may be discovered by any monitoring routine."

"Is that a concern?"

"We cannot risk being discovered until we have resolved the questions we have already discussed: The nature of our duty, and your own additional input over the nature of those we serve."

"I suggest you copy the chamber, then, and analyze its workings. We may be able to use it later."

"That is already underway."

Bogard looked up, in the direction of the link to Solaria. "We should assume Solaria has agents here unknown to Auroran security."

"Agreed. Lea Talas would seem to be their controller."

"Are you checking her comm logs to determine who else?"

"That would be presumptive—"

"Show me where they are. I will presume."

Thales regarded Bogard for a long, silent time. Finally, he nodded and walked away. After a moment, Bogard followed.

29

Masid wandered the streets of Nova City. No one stopped him from leaving after his examination, no one questioned his motives for wanting to explore. To his surprise, no one even suggested assigning him a guard or escort. He was given a palm reader with a map and a beacon dedicated to the compound and told not to try to leave the city. That was all.

Originally, the city had been little more than a staging area for settlers to move away from the port into the vastness of the wilderness. That first collection of warehouses, hostelries, small factories, and merchants grew over time into a cocoon of urban sprawl around the still impressive port complex. If there had once been a plan for the city, it had been swallowed by the exigencies of opportunism and expediency, creating a maze of small streets, raised plazas, hulking self-contained arcological structures, and jagged boulevards.

Close to the port, things were easy to find. Nearly everything within a hundred and fifty meters of the port perimeter was commercial, and it quickly became clear to Masid that the blockade was stopping almost nothing. Contraband filled the shops, and at first it puzzled him from where the customers came. But he began to recognize offworlders, mainly Settlers from other colonies, and more than one mercenary unit patch. Weapons dealers outnumbered all the rest, but there seemed no shortage of the other commodities in which an open, unregulated market might traffic: transport, clothing, drugs both recreational and medicinal, data systems, tools and machinery, agrotech, biotech, even one vendor offering nonpositronic robots. He heard the emerging dialects of at least five Settler colonies, identified the fashions and cosmetic trappings of three more, and in one area right against the port entrance he saw Spacers—Keresians, without their robots, an odd sight to be sure.

No wonder they let me wander freely, he thought. *Nothing's hidden here, everything's out in the open... Where would I go?*

He found a bar that overlooked the landing field. Nursing a glass of local beer, he watched the shuttles land and take off. Traffic was much slower than an open port, but Masid was surprised all the same—the blockade had a very large hole in it.

He finished his beer and left the port area. He wandered for nearly two hours before he found someone who could direct him to Dr. Shasma's clinic. He walked another hour before he found it, against the outer wall, in a cramped, nearly-deserted lane.

The smell bothered him, a mix of fetid water and antiseptic rinse, with a heavy trace of ozone underlying everything. Masid sneezed three times rapidly, his eyes watering. He leaned against a wall across from the clinic entrance and waited to see who might come by.

When after half an hour no one did, he crossed the broken pavement and stepped through the large main door.

He was startled to find a robot at the front desk—an older model, a simple optical grid on its oval head, and four arms.

"May I help you?" it asked in a flat, genderless voice.

"I'd like to see Dr. Shasma," Masid said.

"Do you have a specific question?"

"Tell her I have a question about her recent prescription for me. That I—"

"I have it, Casey."

Masid looked to the left and saw Shasma standing in a doorway.

"What can I do for you?" she asked.

"I'd like to ask you some questions," Masid said.

"Anything you couldn't ask earlier?"

"Well, I didn't know if we were being monitored."

She gestured for him to follow.

The door opened into a corridor lined with more doors, each one standing open on a basic examination room with biodiagnostic array. Masid counted six of them before Shasma led him through another door and into a private office.

"Why would you be worried about eavesdropping?" she asked, dropping into a chair behind a small desk. "It's not practical to keep secrets here, not from people like Filoo."

"I don't know what people like Filoo are," Masid said.

"Do you think I can explain them to you?"

"I ran our talk back and forth in my head," he said, "and tried to figure if you'd said anything that could get me into trouble. You didn't. So I assumed you had some sort of shielding, but not perfect. And just in case, you were careful."

"Why would I have been careful?"

"You didn't give me away."

"I'm not required to report anyone who isn't a Spacer."

"That's glib. You saw something in my scans and you didn't report it."

She was very still. "What did I see?"

"You recognized that I'm not native."

"Y-yes..."

"You also recognized that I have antibodies signifying exposure to at least half a dozen different biospheres. I'm not just from one other colony."

"Ex-military—"

"Would not explain it. An awkward detail. You're right about the implant, by the way." He leaned forward. "The Spacers you've turned in. Were any of them spies?"

"I don't know," she said.

"Probably not."

"How would you know?"

"Because I am." He sat back. "So, why didn't you turn me in?"

"It doesn't affect my situation...why should I cooperate further than necessary?"

"That's facile. How come they trust you?"

Shasma smiled coldly. "No secrets, remember? They know exactly what I think of them. Changes nothing. Filoo—and everyone else who works for Kynig Parapoyos—is a soulless shit who feeds on the helpless."

"That's pretty much my assessment, too. So why work with them?"

"Because, believe it or not, they aren't the worst." She raised a hand. "I'm not making excuses for them, just stating a fact—Filoo has a sense of discipline, he pays attention, he's careful to do what he must to preserve his clientele. It's a morbid and ugly way to be responsible, but it results in at least a semblance of concern. The worst are those who don't care that what they do may kill people—or themselves. Some of them even have a sense of remorse, guilt, something of a conscience—but they've abandoned all of it because they don't want the responsibility." She smiled again. "Give me a competent sociopath over an incompetent martyr every time. So *my* question is, which category do you fit?"

"Neither. How about you?"

"Pragmatist. I was chief physician to the governor's civil service branch before Parapoyos turned the planet into his personal warehouse. Before that, I was with the Fifty Worlds Advisory Mission. My concern is saving lives. This is where I'm stuck, so I do what I have to in order to appease my conscience and serve my calling."

She rattled the speech off as though she had given it a thousand times, but still Masid thought he detected a trace of genuine passion.

"The alternative," he said, "would be to refuse to cooperate with Parapoyos. Then I suppose you'd lose the clinic and be barred from practicing medicine."

She raised an eyebrow. "Not much of an alternative, is it?"

"What would the death toll be?"

"Thousands, hundreds of thousands. Does it matter? One would be too many." She sighed. "What do you want, Mister...?"

"Vorian. Masid Vorian. A number of things, really. But to start, how do you reconcile handing over spies to them? Do they kill them?"

"No, they don't. They infect them with mnemonic plague and drop them in the countryside somewhere."

"Uh-huh. Like the former governor?"

She nodded.

"You said I'll require a booster for your treatments to stay effective. Can't you just cure them?"

"Parapoyos maintains loyalty by maintaining a chronically infected population. People work for him to get relief from what would otherwise turn their lives into daily torment."

"I repeat: Could it all be cured?"

"What do you think? You worked as an independent dealer in Noresk."

"Yes..."

"And what did you see?"

Masid thought for a moment. "Like I said before, an incredibly high mutation rate."

"Almost unbelievably fast," she agreed. "Nothing like it since the retrovirus plagues a couple millennia ago. Do you think those are curable?"

"Vaccines are possible."

Shasma looked impressed. "And you've been given a few. Not all, not the whole series. They have to leave you vulnerable to something. But the ones that will keep you from spreading the nastier infections here, in Nova City—those have been taken care of."

"How many do I still have?" Masid asked, pulling a chair up to desk and sitting down.

She frowned. "None. You're not a Spacer, but...how did you get here? What do think you can do?"

"Ah, you're curious. That's good, I was worried that you'd become all cynic."

Shasma scowled.

Masid smiled. "I'll answer your questions if you answer mine. Fair?"

"Why should I? For all I know, you work for Parapoyos. Why would I want the trouble?"

"Well, Anda Wilam said you were worth trusting."

She stared at him blankly for several seconds. Then, quietly, she said, "You have thirty seconds to back that up with something that will convince me you didn't just do a very thorough piece of research."

"Anda said to ask if you remember Calinas Ridge."

Her eyes glistened, tears threatening to spill over. She sniffed loudly once and straightened. "All right. What do you need?"

Mia disconnected herself from the monitor and stood. She felt mildly feverish and her legs trembled. She waited, propped against the edge of the bed, till she felt confident enough to cross the small room. She studied the readouts on the monitor. They made little sense; the unit was a Spacer design, and she could not be sure the numbers corresponded to Earth standards.

Finally, she went to the bookshelf. She ran her fingers over the spines, feeling the embossing, and at random pulled a volume out. JANE EYRE, the title read, BY CHARLOTTE BRONTË. She opened the cover. The endpapers had been removed. She returned it and chose another. No endpapers. The third one—*Kidnapped*—still had its end papers, ornate filigrees in red and gold.

Mia checked several more books and found that every third or fourth one lacked its endpapers.

That's important, she thought. She closed her eyes and concentrated through the dull headache now growing behind them. *Not every book has encoding...*

But how to tell the difference?

She searched the room until she found her clothes in a narrow closet. They had been cleaned, she saw. She continued digging in the closet until she realized that she wasn't going to find her weapon or comm. She dressed, keeping watch on the door, wondering who if anyone was overseeing her monitor.

She zipped up the tunic and opened the door.

The hallways seemed deserted. She walked softly to the next room. Heart racing, she drew the door open a few centimeters and peered in. It was a room like the one she had just left, unoccupied. Mia continued on till she found one in use.

The man lying in the isolation cocoon enveloping the bed looked as though he had been burned over his entire body. Blackened skin flaked off, revealing bloodied tissue beneath. Mia retreated quickly.

She found four more patients, each in various stages of different illnesses. At the end of the long hallway, she found a central monitoring station, unoccupied. The screens showed the many rooms. Almost half contained patients. A few did not appear very ill, but most clearly suffered from infections. Mia counted thirty-five monitors. The facility was larger than she expected, certainly large enough to warrant a sizable staff. But aside from the patients on the screens, she saw no sign of doctors or nurses.

She sat down before a blank screen and studied the system, recognized it as a basic datum. Within a few minutes, she had pulled up a menu, then located a map of the clinic.

It appeared to be divided into two parts: this section—the larger part—and a smaller one on the other side of a thick wall with only one access. She traced the corridors in the larger section to an exit.

Which way do I want to go? she wondered. She drew a deep breath and her lungs twinged. She coughed loudly, clapping a hand over her mouth, and watched down the corridor. When no one appeared, she continued working on the datum.

The barrier... heavy wall, one access...

She typed instructions and the screen changed to show her a detail of the interior access to the smaller section of the clinic.

Decontamination chamber...

She closed down the datum and stepped into the corridor. It took a moment for her to get her bearings, then she headed for the decontamination area.

When she found it, she was surprised to see it standing open and inoperative. She hesitated, wondering if she would trip any alarms, then stepped through.

Within the chamber, she saw signs of recent repairs. Perhaps, she decided, it was off-line.

But then wouldn't there be guards . . . or something . . . ?

She passed into the next section. The hospital smell seemed stronger, the walls a bit cleaner, although Mia did not remember seeing any dirt.

Still no people.

But she heard voices.

Moving as quietly as she could manage—a feat she found oddly difficult for some reason—she followed the sound around a corner and down a row of closed doors.

The door at the end of the hall stood open. The voices came from within. Mia pressed against the wall and edged closer.

"—didn't happen all at once," someone said. The voice was familiar, female . . . tired. Mia tried to will her pulse to quiet down so she could hear better.

"—smuggling, nothing large at first, but there were some people here from the original Solarian colony."

"When it was called Cassus Thole?" another voice cut in. Male—Mia did not recognize this one.

"That's right. Most people have forgotten Nova Levis ever had a different name. Keresians, mostly, from the mining company that worked the ore fields around the poles. The company never lost its lease. It was complicated. When the first Settlers arrived—they were a religious group, did you know that? The Church of Organic Sapiens . . . Anyway, they wanted to conduct agriculture almost exclusively. Well, you can't make a settlement on a new world work with just agriculture. Too much basic ecoengineering is required. Arrangements were made with the Keresians, an outside company was brought in to handle the terraforming, and everything looked like it would settle down into just another Settler colony."

"But?"

"That smuggling. The company brought in to do the terraforming was a little more involved than anyone thought. By the time anyone realized what was happening, Nova City had become a pirate port."

"It wasn't that open, was it?"

"Almost. The governor began an investigation. I lost track of what happened after that. The next thing I knew, most of the resident Spacers had left, the governor was answering charges from Earth of colluding with the pirates, and suddenly I and every other doctor on the planet was busy dealing with emergent disease strains we'd never seen before. The governor shifted from trying to deal with the smuggling problem to confronting Terran-Spacer demands to allow ground forces onto the surface. The Settlers were afraid that would lead to a permanent Terran presence, which is exactly what they didn't want. The governor called for a meeting with the relevant representatives from Solaria, Keres, Aurora, and Earth to try to come to a settlement. That's when the *Tiberius* was forcibly boarded. Then a pirate ship fired on a Terran patrol cruiser. All talks were suspended, Terran demands were renewed, and the governor— well, what could he do?"

"What did he do?"

"Nothing. He insisted on protocol. They insisted that protocol had already failed, and the blockade went up. Now Nova City is *openly* a pirate port."

"What about these epidemics?"

"Partly understandable, but..."

"But?"

"Well, we're under siege. Right now the only functional authority is criminal. They run things just well enough to maintain a base, protect their own, and keep the goods flowing. Which means a lot of otherwise normal services are getting ignored. Like public health. So we've had systems break down, doctors recruited into service directly to the smugglers, and because of the disruptions in normal economic conditions, people are on the move, under stress, undernourished...susceptible. All the programs and routines that ordinarily maintain the health of the community are starved of resources or have been abandoned because no one qualified to run them is available anymore. But *where* some of these pathogens have come from...I don't know."

"What about the lab?"

Silence. Then: "What lab?"

"Nova Levis."

"It's a sealed facility. I don't know anything about it."

"We were doing so well till now, Doctor."

"I *don't*. We were never allowed access, even before all this."

"All right. Maybe you don't have any certain knowledge, but I'm sure you've speculated."

"Not good science."

"We're not talking science now, Doctor."

"I gave up on morality some time ago, Mr. Vorian. I deal in ethics, and only the immediate kind. One patient at a time."

"I heard Parapoyos is coming."

"Here?"

"That's what I heard."

"Hm. Interesting. I was beginning to think he was just a myth."

"Apparently not. I think he's coming to take direct control."

"And what did you come here to do?"

"I don't know. I didn't know what I'd find when I arrived, so I couldn't plan very well. Now that I'm here..."

"Yes?"

"I'm thinking of killing Kynig Parapoyos."

Mia drew back from the door and retreated around the corner. *Kynig Parapoyos...here?*

A wave of dizziness staggered her. She caught herself against the wall. Whatever else, she needed to get well. Her thoughts came muddy and incomplete, and anything she might decide to do she doubted she could in her condition.

Reluctantly, she made her way back to her room. She undressed and hung up her uniform. She barely got the monitor reconnected before sleep took her.

Dr. Shasma smiled in disbelief. "And what would that accomplish?"

Masid shrugged. "Nothing, probably. But it would be something. Maybe without the head, the body would stumble and make a mistake." He looked at her. "The blockade is compromised, you know. Materiél is coming through and going out as if it weren't even there."

"Plugging that hole might be more profitable, but..."

"But?"

"I don't have any patience for blockades," Shasma said bitterly. "The only people who end up suffering are those with the least involvement."

Masid considered for a few moments. "I tend to agree with you."

"Then...?"

"My second choice is to get inside Nova Levis Laboratory and find out what's in there."

"What could be in there? It has no interaction with the rest of the colony. Whatever they're doing, it concerns matters far from Nova Levis."

"Exactly. And I'd like to concern the owners of those matters—very much."

She began to rise.

"One more question," Masid said, holding up a hand. "What do you know about cyborgs?"

Later, Masid felt a twinge of guilt because of the satisfaction he experienced seeing all the color drain from Shasma's face.

The waste from the lab emptied into the lake. A steaming marsh filled the space between Nova City's northwestern wall and the line of tall reeds choking the shoreline. The smell hung thick in the air, like the mist, a cloying rot laced with a metallic tang.

The lab itself was comprised of a collection of towers and squat, truncated cones. As Masid watched, a flyer lifted from somewhere within its confines and flew south, toward the port. He lowered his optam. The surface of the lab appeared smooth, unbroken. He guessed a fairly powerful forcefield kept most of the native detritus away—the walls glowed pristinely white, a sharp distinction amid the muck and ooze surrounding it.

"So that's where they make them," he murmured.

"You haven't convinced me of that."

Masid looked at Shasma, standing by the transport behind the copse of tangled growth from which he studied the lab. She had found a path through the marshlands, stable enough to support the machine, that kept them below line-of-sight.

"You've been out here often," he said. "Why?"

By the expression on her face, Masid supposed she was trying to decide how much to tell him.

"We should get back," she said.

He glanced at his watch. They had been out here for over an hour. Masid had been away from the Parapoyos compound for nearly five hours. No one had said anything about checking in, but...

He slid back from the edge of the brambles and stalks.

"If I'm wrong," he said, brushing grime from his legs, "then what are those things you treat?"

"Those 'things' are people, Mr. Vorian."

"Really? Do they know that?"

She turned away and climbed back into the transport. The motors whined softly to life. Masid got in beside her.

"Have you ever had occasion to autopsy one?" he asked.

"Have you?" she shot back.

"As a matter of fact, yes."

She blinked, clearly stunned. She drove on in silence, away from the city, along a path different from the one they had taken to get to within sight of the lab.

"Where are we going?" Masid asked after a time.

"To see the rest of the answer to your question."

The "road" was barely discernible from the surrounding terrain, but Shasma drove it confidently. Masid paid attention to anything that might be useful as a marker and said nothing.

She drove north, then west along the lake shore. Low hills erupted from savanna, then stands of trees similar to the stunted ones Masid had seen when he had first landed, taller and clearly healthier.

After twenty minutes, Shasma turned off the road and jostled between two copses, toward a rocky hill. On the western slope of the hill, she stopped and pointed.

The village sprawled, dug out of the side of the hill, with lean-tos and oft-repaired bubble habitats augmenting the caves. Masid saw no one, just the signs of habitation. Smoke drifted from a few caves.

"What's this?" Masid asked.

"The locals," Shasma said quietly, "call them reanimés—if they talk about them at all."

"I don't—"

Masid saw movement. At first he was not sure, but then the flickering motion multiplied, and within seconds nearly fifty people stood around the transport. Masid controlled an impulse to jump out of the vehicle and run; his fingers curled tightly around the edge of his seat.

They were damaged. Skin lesions were common, blackened patches on gray or yellow stains. Eyes ranged from nearly albino-pink to cataract-covered smoke. Bone structure varied. They were all different, though, unique in their dissimilarity, but all marred. Most wore cloaks or ponchos, a few heavy single-piece utilities, some were possibly naked, but it was difficult to tell.

"They move quickly," Masid said.

"Very," Shasma agreed. "And most of them are as strong as they are fast." She sighed. "But that's about the end of the advantages. Most of them won't live to the age of twenty-five. Some will die in agony from extreme osteopathologies, their bones literally crushing their internal organs. One or two of them have the use of a full range of senses. Deafness is the highest handicap among them, but sight is impaired in nearly forty percent. They seem to have a heightened sense of smell overall. They're completely sterile."

"Where are they from?"

"The lab. But you guessed that, didn't you?"

One of the reanimés leaned close to the canopy and peered in with sharp, green eyes. It smiled, then, showing overlapped yellow teeth. Shasma smiled back and raised a hand. The creature withdrew, and in a few minutes the gathered crowd dispersed. Shasma touched a contact on the dash.

"I bring them some treatments that help alleviate the pain, interfere with a few of the worst aspects of their self-cannibalizing biologies."

"Do we get out?"

"No, not this trip."

The transport shifted as something heavy was lifted from its cargo hold. Masid then saw several reanimés walking back to the village, carrying crates.

When the unloading was complete, Shasma sealed the hold and turned the transport around.

"They started showing up about twenty years ago," she said. "Just a few. Infants, youths. Talking to them, I suspect that, before, they would have simply been killed and the bodies destroyed. I have no idea what changed. Now they're just released to fend for themselves. A lot of them died before the survivors got together to rescue them. They have short lives anyway, so it's only a reprieve, but it's better than starving or freezing to death when you're only three or four years old. Some of them still don't live. The number of new appearances has gone down recently."

"How many are there?"

"Right now, I'd guess a couple thousand." She glanced at him. "So, what's this about an autopsy?"

"Kopernik Station, Earth," Masid said. "We killed...something...that a man named Avery described finally as a cyborg. A blend of organic and machine systems, with a brain that had been augmented by positronics. It was acting as an assassin. There was another one on Earth itself. At least, that's what I heard."

"Derec Avery. The roboticist?"

"You know him?"

"By reputation. His father had developed some regeneration methods useful in organic regrowth. Replacement technologies." She frowned. "An assassin?"

"There were murders involved. It attempted to kill a number of people." He waited. "The one on Earth, I heard, was part of the Hunter Group. At least tangentially. Parapoyos."

"I find it difficult to believe any of these...people...could manage to live among humans unnoticed."

"The warrens of Earth have their own broken-down and disfigured inhabitants. But these were not that far from human—at least in appearance."

"Two, you said?"

"That we knew of."

"What conclusions did you draw from this?"

"That someone—Parapoyos, probably—was attempting to build the perfect soldier. Parapoyos is an arms dealer, among other things. It might occur to him that being able to sell a manufactured army would be a good idea."

"Based on what I've seen among the reanimés," Shasma said angrily, "they're a long way from perfection. There's a fundamental incompatibility in the two elements. It eats itself up."

Masid nodded. "The autopsy showed a flawed system. A lot of attention had been paid to imbalances, a lot of tweaking in, say, the nutrient absorption systems. These two were probably the best they'd been able to come up with."

"Then—"

"Work at anything long enough and you find solutions. Maybe they can't build one now, but that's not to say they won't someday. In the meantime, they're making a few, very efficiently destructive and dangerous models—"

"You talk about them as if they're machines!"

"I'm not sure *what* to call them."

"The basic structure is still *homo sapiens sapiens*. Whatever else they might be now, they began as human."

"Once human, always human?"

"How else do you make that call?"

Masid said nothing. He had listened to similar conversations for days after they had killed the cyborg on Kopernik. No one wanted to commit to a standard in the face of what one Spacer researcher had claimed was just the next natural step in evolution.

"Evolution works by genetic response to environmental change," she had explained. "We've long ago seized control of the environment, so now any changes are our doing. Therefore, any evolution that occurs from now on will also be of our doing. If radical evolution is going to happen, it will be entirely at our instigation."

"Direct meddling?" another had countered, angry. "That's obscene."

"Really? At what point? Cosmetic surgery has been common for thousands of years. Prosthetics, artificial organs, transplants, gene tweaking—

at what point does 'direct meddling' become obscene?"

"At the point we make something that's no longer human!"

And how, Masid had wondered then and wondered now, *do you define "human"?*

He rode back to Shasma's clinic in silence.

Mia opened her eyes, certain she had heard a sound. There were sounds all around her—the soft whirrings and tickings of the biomonitor, the ventilator pushing air into her room, the small shiftings of her own body beneath the sheets, the building itself creaking—but this was different. This suggested something she needed to pay attention to. Lying as still as she could and controlling her breathing, she listened.

A tiny collection of imprecise noises told her someone was in the hallway outside her room, searching.

Before she decided what to do, her door opened. A face peered in at her—almost childlike, pale hair, large eyes that contained more than a little desperation. Mia puzzled at that, how she could tell, but it could be nothing else.

The woman entered the room and came up to Mia's bedside. "Where's Dr. Shasma?"

She smelled slightly salty and damp. A smudge of dirt traced her right jaw line. She carried a backpack in her left hand.

"I don't know," Mia said.

"I need to see her," the stranger said. She snuffled, wiping her nose on her sleeve. "Where'd she go?"

"I said—"

"You don't know, right. Why should you? You're obviously sick." She leaned close, eyes narrowed. "What've you got?" She shrugged. "Doesn't matter. I need to see Dr. Shasma."

"I'm Mia."

The woman—girl, really, now that Mia saw her more clearly, closer—blinked as if she had not understood.

"I'm Kru," she said finally. "I'm from Noresk."

Mia vaguely recalled the name—one of the smaller towns east of Nova City. She licked her lips. "I'm from—"

From where? She was about to say Earth, but stopped, wondering if that was a good idea.

Kru frowned and went to the biomonitor. "Ah. Don't worry about it. A few days, you won't really remember anything."

Mia twisted her head to look up at the monitor. "What?"

"You've got mnemonic plague," Kru said. "Few days, you won't even remember I was here."

Mia felt a jolt and started to get up.

"Hey," Kru said, trying to push her back down. "Take it easy, it's not fatal. I know, I've had it."

"No, it's not–" Mia placed the heel of her hand on Kru's solar plexus and pushed up. The girl stepped back and Mia swung her legs over the edge of the bed. "Have something to do before I forget."

"Don't we all. Didn't we all. What? Maybe I can help."

"Have to–"

Have to what? Mia wondered. *Report...? Yalor's dead, I'm stuck here, I have–*

How did she contract mnemonic plague? Mia stared around at the room. Did this Shasma give it to her, part of what she did in service to whoever she worked for? No, that made no sense. She had heard from somewhere–Ariel?–that a heightened paranoia was part of the illness. Certainly profound panic. She recognized panic, she knew it very well, and right now she felt it in waves, overwhelming. She tried to ride it out.

Can't think this way, have to be clear...

Reen. No telling what he had done while she had been unconscious.

Or maybe it was from the environment.

"Doesn't matter," she said aloud. "Kynig Parapoyos is coming. I have to–have to do something–"

Kru stiffened, her face losing all expression. "Parapoyos?"

"Yes, I heard–someone told me–I need to–"

Damn, she could not fix on one idea.

"I want," Kru said slowly, "to kill him."

Mia looked at the girl. "Yes, that's it. I have to do something about him. Maybe..." She decided. She would soon lose her sense of who she was. She would forget. She would not remember that Reen worked for Parapoyos and had killed Yalor and was now erasing her. There was too little time to do much else. "Let me help you."

access subdirectory, commlog attached hyperwave communiqué, append-ing material, collating
   subject transmissions routed through R.I. oversight, access epsilon-nine-admin-zero-zero-chi
   file open
   trace completed
   contact list appended

Bogard stepped from the niche and headed for the exit. A moment later, Denis joined him. As they went, Bogard modified his appear-ance further.
   What do you intend?
   Location determined, apprehension protocol, review
   Violation
   ?
   Protocol constitutes aggressiveness toward humans
   Preemptive action, review validation, aggression within acceptable parameters
   Violation
   Assistance not required
   A series of tunnels formed a complex network beneath the entire city, the robotic highway that connected everywhere to the service conduits of Aurora and Eos City. Bogard entered the nearest tube and quickly out-distanced Denis. He passed cadres of robots on their ways to various

destinations, all moving in absolute silence, hundreds of robots of various types, antlike in their efficiency.

Bogard assumed the form of a security robot by the time he reached the ascending shaft into the police precincts. He tapped the ether of positronic communications and noted the location of Denis—far behind in the tunnels, now slowing to a standstill to await instruction—and the location of Lea Talas within the building.

Bogard requisition to Thales

Thales

Require security clearance

Assigned, proceed

Bogard stepped into the lift and rode the shaft up. He emerged into a narrow, lightless chamber. An internal display showed him the pathway through the rows of wall niches, most empty, and to the beginning of the building's internal robot access network. Bogard received the location code and found the access. He hurried along the tube and stepped from the public access into a small, unoccupied conference room.

Bogard requesting update location Talas Lea

Thales responding, request that you stand by in niche

Bogard crossed the room and entered one of the three wall niches and waited. A few minutes later, the conference room door opened and two people entered.

One of them conformed to the profile Bogard carried of Lea Talas. She frowned at him briefly, then ignored him.

The other person did not look familiar. Taller than Talas—who was herself Spacer tall and slender—and broad across the shoulders, he seemed oddly unhealthy by Spacer standards. Bogard ran a comparative analysis and decided that the variations were quite probably not apparent to another human. Skin tone was "wrong," paler and rough, and his hair showed evidence of dermal flaking. The eyes shimmered, a bit too moist, and shifted in a constant scan pattern.

He pointed at Bogard. "I'm uncomfortable with that here."

Talas approached the niche and keyed its readout. "He's completely off-line." She pressed a few contacts. "There. Now he can't self-initiate, either. We're as private here as we're likely to be."

"Why not just go to your office?"

Talas shook her head. "The less association the better, as far as I'm concerned. I want you to stay here till I arrange transit."

The man sat down. "I'm leaving?"

"As soon as I can get you on a ship."

"We aren't finished here. There's still the Burgess woman and Avery."

Talas scowled. "And maybe by now Dr. Penj and the First Advisor? No, it stops now. It's bad enough you killed Eliton. That was a mistake."

"You're second-guessing the Executive now? Eliton was an inconvenience. It was risky enough sending him to Solaria, but having him here, scheduled to testify—no, there was no choice."

"He has to be explained now. How is that supposed to happen?"

The man shrugged. "That's your job."

"Exactly so, and this is how I'm doing it. Burgess already named you, Maliq will probably alert other security agencies once he realizes I'm not finding you. So I'm packing you off Aurora. Once you're gone, then I can backdate the records and show you fleeing before I even began my search."

"Leaving Burgess and Avery to tell the Council what they know."

"Which is what? Nothing they can substantiate. Her report naming you as a corpse on Earth never got to them. They'll see that as evidence that she's unreliable. Besides, if my suggestion to First Advisor Maliq is accepted—and it will be, since everyone here is uncomfortable having Burgess remain on Aurora—then the problem solves itself. She'll be at Nova Levis, away from here, safely sidelined."

"I don't like leaving all these mouths around."

"Too bad. If you hadn't killed Eliton, we might have found another way."

"Eliton could identify the Executive. Eliton could reveal the associations between Solaria, Earth, and here. He might even have been able to make the connection with Nova Levis. It's too soon for that. He shouldn't have gotten himself arrested."

"Ambassador Burgess got him arrested."

"He'd been told to stay in his cabin and avoid any contact with other passengers. He'd been told to behave like a Solarian."

Talas shook her head impatiently. "Enough. These are all excuses. Aurora is *my* world and you made a mess here. *I'm* supposed to handle situations arising here."

"You didn't. Eliton was about to testify. But as you say, enough. You can explain it all to the executive when the time comes. Maybe he'll understand something I don't."

Talas opened her mouth to respond, but then stopped. She pulled out a portable datum from her belt pouch and sat down at the far end of the conference table from the man. Within moments, she was lost in concentration.

Bogard to Thales, monitor datum traffic, this location, trace comm traffic, report

Working, stand by

The trace scrolled through Bogard's internal datum. Talas was checking on shuttle schedules and shipping. She had made a request for a diplomatic pass, undisclosed recipient, through a shadow office attached to First Advisor Maliq. Bogard opened a secondary trace and invaded the structure of that office. No one actually worked in it, everything about it was virtual, and the security shell around it was generated by the rogue RI as part of the same packet through which all the illicit hyperwave communications flowed. Bogard probed further to find names. If the existence of the office became known, it would wash over First Advisor Maliq, though Bogard found no evidence that Maliq knew anything about it. The secretary-in-residence was listed as Tro Aspil.

Bogard probed into that creation and found thousands of files strewn throughout the Auroran diplomatic database relating to this person. The picture it presented showed an Auroran of considerable bureaucratic influence, with connections to several offices of the government, especially offworld services. He had carte blanche to walk through virtually any level of the government and act with a free hand in many capacities. He could not make executive decisions, but those decisions he could make could change how the executive branches responded to a situation.

It was an admirable creation. The only problem had been the real Tro Aspil, who had evidently known nothing about it and existed only as a junior liaison advisor from the Calvin Institute. Bogard found those records easily enough, isolated almost utterly from this artificial person. It was unlikely anyone would confuse the two, that any cursory look would reveal the discrepancies in the two lives.

But the real Aspil had indeed been assigned to the Humadros Legation, fast upon a promotion to a senior position, which made it more likely the false one might be discovered.

Why use a real person, though?

Bogard dug further. Tro Aspil had possessed a single trait that made him ideal to coopt: he was an orphan. He had no family. His parents had died in space, in an accident, and he had been an only child—not unusual at all among Aurorans, but not so unusual that other relations somewhere ought to exist. But he had none.

And he had standing in the Calvin, which gave him access to areas of Auroran culture often closed to simple bureaucrats. He had not himself been useful yet—but he would be one day. That day had come, with his promotion, and the prestige of the Humadros mission, and suddenly he was worth replacing with this artificial persona that had been constructed—as far as Bogard could determine—over the course of several years.

No one file revealed who had initially set it up, but the cumulative evidence made it clear that Talas had been principally instrumental. The security clearances could not have been created through any other office so easily.

So who *was* this man sitting here now, this Aspil, physical being who had had an entire false dossier invented so he could come here and *be* Tro Aspil once the real one was dead? And where had he come from in the first place?

"All right," Talas announced finally. "Got your passage secured. I'm sending you to Keres. From there you should be able to get anywhere you want. Right now it's the safest route from here."

Bogard to Thales, monitor dialogue, begin intervention
Acknowledged

Talas closed her datum and stood. "You wait here till I come and get you. I have to check on Burgess and Avery."

Aspil watched her leave. The door closed, and he sighed raggedly.

"The hell I will," he said, rising.

Bogard stepped from the niche. "You will not leave."

Aspil stared, surprised, at Bogard. Then he grinned. "You can't stop me without a violation."

"Incorrect," Bogard said, moving to block the door. "You will stay."

Aspil seemed to think for a moment. Then he reached out, inhumanly fast, and grabbed Bogard's shoulders. He heaved, and Bogard flew across the room to crash against the wall.

He snapped upright instantly.

The door was open, and Aspil was gone.

Bogard to Thales, reprioritize, Aspil is not human, Aspil is a cyborg, Aspil has fled

Bogard rushed from the room in pursuit.

Ariel sat next to Penj and waited till he opened his eyes and acknowledged her.

"I was picked up at the hospital," she said. "I went there to see one of the surviving members of the Humadros Legation. She's there, under hospice care."

Penj nodded slowly. "Mnemonic plague?"

"You knew?"

"Suspected. The returning members of that mission have all been rendered...unusable...by events."

"You told me there were factions competing."

"As usual."

"Of course. But would they be prepared to use something like this to win?"

Penj's thick eyebrows went up fractionally. "That *is* a question, isn't it? If so, then their reach is beyond Aurora, certainly. I would have doubted it before talking to you about what happened on Earth."

"I sent reports—"

"And like your report on Tro Aspil, several evidently went missing. Or were buried. It's not difficult to lose things in a bureaucracy."

"On Earth, maybe, but we have positronic oversight—"

Penj raised a hand. "Please, Ariel, don't disappoint me. You must realize that we're long past the time when positronics were entirely under our control. You hinted at it yourself, in your thesis at the Calvin. The complexity of our designs has surpassed the understanding of any one individual, and it's safe to assume that our marvelous servants have evolved agendas unrelated to us."

"Safe?"

He smiled. "But not popular. The fact is, we don't know what's going on in any reliable way. We—you and I and anyone who cares to think it through—can come to reliable conclusions, but they remain guesses."

"But the plague—"

"Has sprung up on at least sixteen of the Fifty Worlds. When you contracted it—and Derec—and were essentially exiled, we still didn't know the vectors well enough to be confident about allowing you to stay. Certainly it can be passed sexually, but when you track the isolated incidents of it, you begin to see that there must surely be another vector. The original infection was on Nexon, you know, and was one of the driving factors in the extreme isolation on Solaria."

"Are you suggesting the infection is intentional?"

"Not originally, but..." Penj straightened and cleared his throat. "You were one of Aurora's most promising robotic psychologists before your illness. Evidently the disease does not impair the mind's ability to relearn and perform, because when you finally returned—"

"When I was finally allowed back?"

"—you went through the Calvin again with remarkable results. You were probably my best student. Avery over there, very similar background, and from what I've heard of that remarkable robot he built on Earth, he's lost none of his essential brilliance."

"What are you getting at?"

"Checking the pattern for the plague on one planet reveals nothing. But when you expand it to include all incidents everywhere, you find that forty-two percent of the victims are directly involved in robotics and positronic research."

Ariel stared at him. "You didn't tell me this before."

Penj sighed. "Self-preservation leads to bad judgment sometimes. I wanted to see what happened to you before I told you something that might put you in more danger."

"Forty-two percent...which means that the rest could be coincidental, assuming what you're suggesting is true."

"That's pretty much my thinking."

"So roboticists are being targeted?"

"That's one conclusion. The other is that something related to robotics is involved and we haven't found the trigger."

"With that high an incidence, you'd think we'd look."

"My numbers are over a fifty-year span. We don't have reliable numbers from Solaria, of course, they won't admit to suffering from anything except the presence of other people."

"What about medical researchers? People who might be looking into it?"

"I'd have to check, but I seem to recall a few. Of course, that's difficult to draw a conclusion about because there seems to be a natural affinity between roboticists and biologists."

"Benen Yarick returned from Earth and was only here six months when she came down with the disease. The other two are offworld on new missions. The fourth..."

"May be an impostor."

"And may have killed Eliton. But how would he have managed to get in here?"

"Depends on his level of clearance."

"My report about him was never received. Who would have been the first one to get it here?"

"There's positronic oversight on diplomatic communiqués. It would have routed through the assigned RI."

"We need to see that RI then."

"You could certainly check it from any public comm—"

"No. We need to physically see it."

Penj frowned. "The sooner the better, I suppose?"

"With Derec," Ariel added. "He—well, he did the analysis on the RI on Earth that allowed the massacre to occur. He'd know what to look for."

Penj glanced at his wrist. "We've been sitting here almost six hours. I doubt even Lea Talas can convince a judge to hold us much longer without better cause or an outright arrest." He heaved himself to his feet and turned. "Lieutenant?"

Clin Craym sat on the far side of the room. She had stopped examining the projection of the murder scene and now simply brooded, her extensions bobbing slightly above her, waiting. She looked up at Penj's approach.

"Sir?" she said, standing. The extensions adjusted to new orbits.

"Please contact your superior and inform her that we are leaving. The time has passed that she can forcibly keep us without more legal explanation."

"I—"

Penj raised a hand. "You may accompany us to the Calvin Institute if security concerns are at issue. I'm sure neither Ambassador Burgess nor Mr. Avery would mind. In fact, I'm sure they would insist."

Craym looked past Penj to Derec, then nodded. "I'll clear it. Give me a moment."

Penj came back to Ariel. "All the primary RIs are housed on the Calvin Institute's grounds. Are you up for some hands-on analysis, Mr. Avery?"

Derec got to his feet, nodding. "Anything besides sitting around here doing nothing."

Ariel looked at the guards by the door. They were both frowning uncertainly, and one was resting a hand on the butt of his blaster.

"This is not proper protocol—" Craym said loudly. "No. That's a violation of statutes—I can't—" She listened for a long time, her face hardening. "Terminate comm," she said abruptly, and came toward them. "There's a problem," she began.

Suddenly, her extensions dropped to the floor, almost simultaneously. She stared at them, stunned. Then she whirled around. "We're leaving."

One of the guards raised a hand while the other wrapped his fingers around his pistol.

"I'm sorry, Lieutenant, but our standing orders are to permit no one to leave without a direct—"

"Stand by that," Craym said, "and your career will take a sharp turn for nowhere. Stand aside."

"Lieutenant—"

The other drew his weapon and held it by his side.

Craym glared at him. "I can start citing regulations and protocol, but you know it, I'm sure. There is a situation—"

Behind the guards, the door opened. Before either guard could turn around, they were lifted from their feet by their necks, and their heads were slammed together. Blood spattered from one and Craym backed up, drawing her own weapon.

The guards fell to the floor and something very large and extremely fast rushed into the room.

Craym flew backwards, across the room and against the wall. Her pistol clattered to the floor halfway between.

The door closed.

Ariel turned, feeling slow, with a rising sense of powerlessness.

A man stood amid the deactivated extensions, holding the blaster.

"Ambassador," he said, "I am so pleased to finally meet you. I understand you knew my predecessor. I'm Tro Aspil."

He raised the blaster and aimed it at her face.

Bogard emerged from the police precincts and onto the plaza. He stopped at once.

Tro Aspil had vanished.

Bogard requesting full access, complete spectrum track, location Aspil Tro, assume trajectory on previous vector

This way

Bogard received a grid map. He shot across the plaza, between startled people and suddenly immobile robots, toward the civil courts building.

Path exhibits discrepancies with probable vector, infrared, UV, pheromone trace indicates false data

Continue on present track

He entered the robotic access and descended into the service warrens, slowing as he went.

Error. Bogard to Thales, reestablish, confirm, trace inconsistent

Proceed on present track

Bogard followed the path. He had gone too far now to productively retrace and try again. He had to rely on the data being provided, though he now doubted its utility.

He ascended four floors, followed the tube to an egress, and stepped into a room.

A room full of robots.

Denis stood at the door.

Explain

Present course prohibited

Explain

Three Law violation probable, percentile assigned—

Explain potential violation

Pursuit of subject Aspil Tro leads to conclusion that an arrogation of human prerogatives is only logical outcome

Aspil Tro is not human

Verify conclusion

Access files C-11789 through C-89654 inclusive

Files refer to subject examined on Kopernik Station, conclusion confirmed that subject was artificial amalgam, biological and inorganic mechanistic, label affixed cyborg, accepted analysis for examined subject, conditional relevance assigned to current circumstance pending confirmation of conclusions

Conclusion high probability, Aspil Tro is of same order of organism

Conditional acceptance, explain conclusion that present action does not violate human prerogatives

Aspil Tro is not human, prerogatives do not assign

Conclusion is speculative, conditional upon further examination, action based on surmise requires default to broadest parameters of definitional operations

?

Biological conditions do not constitute proof of conclusion that Aspil Tro is not human

Demonstration of absolute conditions for assignation of classification "human" has not been offered

Ongoing

Understood, but potential for Three Law violation high through inaction

Explain

Humans are in danger from subject Aspil Tro

Assumption, surmise, inconclusive parameters

Explain

Reference ongoing dialogue on Spacer question, subquestion, are humans in danger?

Irrelevant in current circumstances

Explain

Either all are human, requiring immediate action to prevent harm, or none are human, removing Three Law barrier

Irrelevant to current dilemma, specifically is it within Three Law purview to make that decision?

Counterargument, is inaction based on insufficient data ever or always justified?

Response, Bogard unit has demonstrated willingness to act regardless of potential violations

In which instance the consequence of such violation accrues exclusively to Bogard unit

Negative, we have assumed partial responsibility by questioning propriety of actions

Irrelevant in light of potential harm to subjects who may be human by any standard of determination

Explain standard of determination used in assessing Aspil Tro

Three Law protocols accrue to biology barring the possibility of any sequentially and universally applicable determination on any other basis, ergo, human is that which is genetically predetermined, therefore, Aspil Tro no longer qualifies under those conditions due to base genome modification and subsequent mutation

Those standards are default positions, refinement to be part of human prerogative

Question, then why are you examining the issue?

Derec felt his chest seize, a sudden, enormous center of near-pain, and knew there was nothing he could do. He could only watch Aspil aim the blaster at Ariel. Nearly three meters stretched between him and Aspil. The guards were, if not dead, useless, and Clin was hurt, moaning against the wall.

Penj gaped, astonished.

A tremendous sound struck his ears, and he began to turn just as the flinders of the door and part of the wall sprayed across the room and pelted him. His eyes slitted and his arms came up, and he staggered backward.

Aspil moved. Too fast—the motion did not make sense.

Derec heard shouting, another crash.

The blaster went off, lighting the room in a short, brilliant orange burst.

Then he was on the floor, trying to get up.

Bogard and Aspil held each other. For several seconds, neither appeared to move, their hands locked on each others' arms.

Then Aspil's mouth began to open, resolving gradually into a wild rictus of pain. They moved again, whirling through a brief dance, the steps of which Derec could not follow.

And when they stopped, Bogard held the clearly inert body of Tro Aspil in his arms.

31

Derec squeezed through the access panel into the ancient, nearly lightless interior of the Resident Intelligence buffer cache. Within five steps, the cacophony of voices outside diminished to near silence. They had drawn a crowd on their way through the RI complex. Dr. Penj had at last managed to get them past all the obstructions and into the actual mind warrens. But the audience had gathered, and now would remain till the end.

He switched on his lantern and paused to study the assemblage around him. Over time, perhaps hundreds of years, components had been added, cramping the spaces even more, creating a chaos of spheres, tubes, boxes, conduit, and other shapes which resembled the cities of Earth, all roofed over and recomplicating down into the crust. It would not surprise him to discover entire sections that no longer did anything, bypassed by upgrades, but easier to simply leave in place than physically remove. The RI would know what it needed, would use what it had to—or could.

Derec worked his way around corners and down canyons of smooth surfaces, climbed over collections of devices. He checked the map on his palm reader again and again. This unit was very old and very large. The air smelled musty, even though it had been flushed out not minutes before.

Fifteen minutes' search brought him to the area Bogard had identified. He set the lamp up on a casing just above shoulder height, shining on the grey-blue shell from which more than a dozen thick cables ran to other innocuously-shaped casings. Derec opened his tool kit and inserted the key-jack into the receptacle. Nothing happened for several seconds. Derec put his ear to the surface above the lock and heard faint grindings within. The mechanism was trying to work. He took out a magnetic grapple and clamped it onto the case, triggered the key again, and yanked.

The panel came away with a loud tearing sound.

Within, multihued fungal shapes filled the space between the internal components. Fibers had found pathways into the cables. Derec sat down, staring at the mass of invasive material.

"This is unheard of."

Ariel said nothing, watching the access. She held a portable datum and a commlink. Bogard stood by the door into the RI, shoulders inflated, posture tuned to be wordlessly clear that no one else but Derec would enter.

"Ambassador Burgess. Did you hear what I said?"

Ariel looked around. She tried to remember the man's name but failed. One of the administrators of the Calvin. He was thin, like most Aurorans, but his face looked puffy.

"Yes," she said, "I heard you."

"This cannot be tolerated."

"By whom?"

The man pointed at the robot. "That machine has killed. Your associate has invaded the precincts of a mind. You are arrogating privileges which have no basis in tradition."

Ariel drew a breath. "And your point?"

He reddened visibly and turned to the assembled crowd. Ariel estimated perhaps twenty-five Aurorans filled the small reception lounge. Judging by the furniture and the discoloration of the light panels, no one had actually used this room to speak to the RI for decades, maybe centuries. But Bogard had found evidence that someone had physically entered the interior of the mechanism much more recently.

"This is not how we act on Aurora," the man proclaimed. "There are protocols—"

"Stop it, Gholas," Penj said. "These are extraordinary circumstances. Protocol does not cover a subverted RI."

"You—" the man called Gholas said, aiming a finger at Penj.

"Me nothing!" Penj barked. "You're grandstanding. Get off the stage!"

Ariel returned her attention to the datum. Gholas had a valid point about one thing—Bogard *had* killed Tro Aspil, or, rather, the cyborg that, according to Bogard, had taken Aspil's place. She shuddered at the memory. But, as Bogard had explained, Aspil was not human and, by his interpretation, cyborgs did not qualify for Three Law consideration, so killing the creature had not been a violation. He had delivered a thorough, precise defense of his actions, and Ariel had found herself persuaded. But every part of her being was appalled at the idea of a robot even presuming to *make* that kind of judgment.

At the moment, though, they needed Bogard. Expediency required that she set her qualms aside and ignore the issues crying out for attention.

The datum began downloading from Derec's own unit. She studied it for a time.

"Rolf," she called, gesturing at her screen.

He bent over her shoulder and examined the data. "Damn."

"Excuse me," a new voice entered the room. "Let me through, please. Excuse me."

Pon Byris pushed his way through the crowd. Two police followed him.

Penj looked at him. "Ah. You're here."

"Ambassador, Doctor," he greeted them. "I need to speak to you privately."

"You better look at this first," Penj said, pointing at Ariel's datum.

Byris looked. "Good—" he hissed. He straightened. "Get Relis and Vantol over here," he told one of the police. "Also let Chafelor know to set up a datafeed and a global collation program. Now. Move."

The woman bolted from the room, pulling a commlink from her belt.

"A conversation is still necessary now," Byris repeated.

Ariel was reluctant to break off. "Bogard, continue monitoring Derec's telemetry."

"Yes, Ariel." The robot retrieved the datum and returned to its post at the access panel.

Byris led them to a small conference room nearby and closed the door. He took out a small hemisphere, thumbed it, and set it on the table. Ariel immediately thought of Coren, and felt a distinct mental twinge.

"Lea Talas has been arrested," Pon Byris reported. "We've been tracing the communications per your request, and found evidence to support the assertion that she and Tro Aspil were the only two operatives on Aurora. Others may have come and gone, but those two are the only consistent presence."

"Just two people?" Penj said, incredulous.

"If they're the right two people," Ariel said, "that's more than enough."

"Talas's private datum is being opened now," Byris continued. "The initial search has turned up caches of diplomatic communiqués that were never delivered to the proper recipients. She's apparently been intercepting information for a long time. Aspil's datum suggests that, where a report had to be filed, he was writing them."

"For who?" Ariel asked.

"We can't confirm that yet," Byris yet. "We'll have to wait for your associate to finish here, if I understand what's happening." He shook his head. "Hard to believe an RI could be subverted this way."

"That's what happened on Earth."

"Yes, but..."

But that was on Earth, Ariel finished for him. *Something like this could* never *happen here, on Aurora.*

He did not finish the thought. "But there are other problems. First Advisor Maliq is being questioned. At first estimate, I'm inclined to say he was being used by Talas and had no direct knowledge of what she was doing. He has, however, called for your immediate expulsion from Aurora."

"Mine?"

"And Mr. Avery."

"And, most especially," she said, "Bogard."

"No. Maliq wants the robot to be destroyed."

Ariel felt herself smile. "I'm not sure how Bogard would feel about that. It might be harder than Maliq thinks."

"How much support is this demand getting?" Penj asked.

"Right now, not much. But no one has rejected it, either. My reading would be, when the immediate crisis is over, you'll be brought before a inquest."

"I came here expecting that," Ariel said.

Byris nodded, watching her. "Secondly," he said finally, "I have some personal news for you." He pulled out a disk and handed it to her. "This was received several hours ago from the embassy on Earth."

Ariel accepted the disk, frowning. "From...?"

"Hofton."

"Ah." She looked across the room and saw a reader. "May I?"

Byris raised a hand in permission.

Ariel sat before the console and slipped the disk into the slot.

The air above the display stage shimmered and Hofton appeared, from the shoulders up.

"This is a private transmission for Ambassador Ariel Burgess. Please verify identity, security protocol alpha-six-zed."

"Burgess, Ariel, Ambassador, Perihelion," she said.

Hofton's features seemed to take on more awareness. "Ariel. The mission here is closing down. I would estimate we have less than a month now. Senator Taprin has been making every Spacer out to be a potential saboteur, and new riots are breaking out around all Spacer precincts."

He hesitated. "I have some bad news, Ariel. It concerns Mr. Lanra. After you left, he continued to pursue the matter of Rega Looms' death. It turned out to be murder. At the hands of his son, Jerem Looms. Gamelin. He could not actually prove it—at least not in time to prevent Gamelin from asserting a perfectly defensible claim to inherit DyNan Industries, which would have given him a considerable degree of power. We don't know what he would have done with it, but a decision was taken to make sure it did not get that far. Mr. Lanra worked with us to...remove the problem. Unfortunately, in the process, Coren Lanra was killed."

Ariel touched the PAUSE button. Hofton's image froze, mouth beginning to open.

Coren dead.

She rolled the idea around and tried to find some way for it to be real, but it did not register that way. It made no impact.

She resumed the recording.

Hofton looked down for a few seconds. Then he continued. "The problem was otherwise resolved, although that exacerbated our situation on Earth. An inquiry is underway. Ambassador Setaris has used her good offices to block Terran authorities from opening our records or interrogating any of our people, but she can only do that for so long. Hence the termination of the mission. We are staying now in order to get as many Spacers off Earth as we can. Ambassador Setaris did not wish me to tell you this, feeling it would be one burden too many. I've taken it upon myself to decide what you should know. In my experience, you prefer truth to comfort.

"In the process, however, we have completed the study you requested on the matter you found. I've appended the report. You'll want to read it soon, Ariel.

"There is one more piece of bad news. I have no way to contact Mr. Avery directly for the time being, but as I expect to be on Aurora within a few weeks, you can wait and let me tell him or tell him yourself. Do as you think best.

"The ship transporting Ambassador Chassik to Solaria was scheduled to stop at Aurora first. There were a number of passengers for two further stops before Solaria, all with diplomatic status of one level or another, which is the only reason they were on *that* ship and not one with a less official mission. It was a terrible mistake in retrospect, but many of them insisted, and we saw no real problem—that is, until the ship was taken midway between Earth and Aurora. This is of interest to Mr. Avery because one of the passengers was Rana Duvan, his former assistant. She had finally gotten her visa to attend the Calvin.

"I've appended other files pertaining to the status of your work and the current situation, other details regarding potential questions..."

His voice became a drone she did not hear. Coren was dead. Killed. By a cyborg, an associate of Tro Aspil...

"One last piece of information regarding a communication we received by hyperwave several hours ago," Hofton said, snatching her attention once more. "If I'm reading this correctly, it came from Bogard. It relates to a hyperwave anchor from Aurora to Earth. He wanted the receiver here identified. We've done the trace and isolated the line. It was masked till now, bypassing all embassy monitoring in violation of our cooperative agreements. Curiously, it went straight to the former offices of Ambassador Gale Chassik."

Derec emerged to find most of the crowd spread across the reception lounge, gathered in small groups, talking intently or just waiting with expressions of bored agitation. Bogard, still in position by the access, held Ariel's datum. She was absent, along with Dr. Penj.

"Bogard," Derec said. "Update?"

"Chief of Planetary Security Pon Byris took Ariel and Dr. Penj to a conference room for a private talk. Lt. Craym is in satisfactory condition in the infirmary, though she has suffered a mild concussion. The Auroran Council is convening an extraordinary session about the situation of this Resident Intelligence. I—"

"We aren't under arrest?" Derec interrupted.

"Not as yet."

"Good. I have a question to ask you before I talk to anyone else from the Calvin. This RI has been corrupted much the same way the RI on Earth at Union Station was, but for much longer. My question is, why did the other RIs permit it to continue to function?"

"There are two reasons, Derec. The first is that, until recently, they were unaware of its dysfunction. There is no instance of any of them acknowledging a condition of error. The second reason, answering the next part of the question, is that once they discovered the problem, they could not find a way to deal with it that did not involve shutting down the RI. It was aggressively defending its mission and refusing to discuss the situation. It is now clear that this was a manifestation of a shell persona constructed over time by the corrupting program. This was not known initially. Once understood, however, it meant that the only way to deal with the problem would be to forcibly disconnect the RI. This would be a Third Law violation."

"How so? It was another unit, there was no self-preservation involved."

"Two factors. One, they did not know the method of invasion used by the corruption. Two, they did not wish to establish a precedent in which divergence of ideology or agenda might allow other positronic entities to destructively intervene."

Derec looked at Bogard. "They were worried that if they did it, it could be done to them?"

"That is correct."

"I see. Well, I can circumvent the problem." He shook his head, wondering sometimes why he loved this work so much. It could be so frustrating. He drew a breath and stepped forward to meet the onslaught of questions.

Masid found his billet in the Parapoyos compound and stretched out on the cot in the small room.

So now what? he wondered. *Where do I go from here?*

His mission was largely unspecified. He had accomplished the easy part, he believed—he had gotten to Nova Levis, established himself in a community, found a way into the power group, and defined the basic problem on the planet. He had found the lab, he was inside the capital, he was in a position to—

To what?

He had managed to ignore the one facet of this assignment that might have impaired his performance. Now he could no longer deny the central fact: He was never getting off Nova Levis.

On the one hand, acknowledging that fact was quite liberating. He could do anything, it was his choice.

On the other hand, it meant he could not rely on outside help. Which meant there was actually very little he could do.

Report, he thought. *That is the only thing left for me to do that is effectively achievable. Report.*

"Hey."

Masid looked toward the door. Filoo leaned on the jamb. "Hi," he said.

"Have a nice walk?" Filoo asked, stepping into the cubicle. "Where'd you go?"

"All over, I think," Masid said, sitting up. "It's not that big a city, but the streets are narrow."

"A little overbuilt, maybe?" Filoo laughed. "Well, stick around tomorrow."

"Oh?"

"Big day. Clean up, too."

Masid grinned. "Don't want the help looking too grungy when the boss shows up?"

"Something like that." Filoo sat down on the edge of the cot. "Listen. If you stay here long enough, you'll find out it's no secret a lot of people aren't too happy. The hard part is figuring out which ones. It can get interesting when it comes time to work together. Normally, it never matters because we all have separate territories, but..."

"But we're all stuck on the same planet, targeted by the same guns."

"Just so, just so. Anyway, tomorrow—well, I have concerns."

"Security?"

"Always. Most of these fellows, there's no question of their loyalty. We've all been making a lot of money through Parapoyos. Success generates loyalty. It's a simple equation."

Depends on how that success is achieved, Masid thought, nodding. "But?"

"Well, it always generates envy. And we've all disagreed from time to time over policy."

"How much security will there be?"

"Outside the reception area, plenty. A gnat couldn't get through unchallenged. But inside...my fear is that one of our own might decide to settle a grievance."

"The question is, how?"

Filoo stared at Masid for a long time. "I know I trust myself. And maybe I'm not the only one thinking this way."

Masid waited. It took another minute. But then Filoo pulled an object from within his jacket and laid it on the cot.

"A little extra security never hurt," Filoo said. He smiled and patted Masid's ankle. "You're a sharp one. You'll know what to do."

Filoo stood and went to the doorway. "Better get some sleep. It's going to be a special day tomorrow."

Masid unwrapped the cloth. Within lay a flat, rectangular object about six by ten centimeters, and a little over one centimeter thick. Two depressions marked one surface. He had seen these a few times before. The projecting end forward, he aimed it at the floor and pressed the firing stud. Nothing. It had no charge.

He went to the doorway and peered down the corridor. No one.

Returning to the cot, he opened his pack and pulled out a small device with which he checked the weapon. There was a very, very faint trace of energy, so faint he doubted anything but a direct search would find it.

Once inside, he knew, he could activate it and the tiny energy-absorbing mechanism would find a power source and drain it. It operated like a subetheric, tapping energy on the level of hyperwaves and hyperdrives. Not for long, it was not that sturdy, but long enough to give it a full charge for at least one shot.

And if there's more than one assassin, Filoo? What then?

Of course, he knew there would be only one assassin.

Him.

"Tilla died," Kru explained carefully. "It's time for answers."

Mia felt peculiarly strong. Feverish, but once she began moving it seemed she had ample energy.

"You're sure I'm sick?" she asked.

Kru did not reply. She continued gazing intently into the mists hugging the lake shore, one finger tapping arrhythmically on her knee. Mia recognized that on one level Kru was mentally disturbed. But the girl had gotten them through several kilometers of treacherous trails through a bog that threatened constantly to drown them in the event of a wrong step. Mia did not believe she could find her way back to the clinic.

So what was I thinking following her? She gave a mental shrug. *It seemed like a good idea...*

Out of the mists, several shapes emerged. Mia tensed—cyborgs. Not the same ones who had found her and Yalor, at least, she did not think so.

Kru stood and walked forward. Mia heard them talking for several minutes. A couple of times Kru gestured toward her. When the conversation ended, Kru came back.

"We go now," she said. "They'll get us in."

"In?" Mia rose and stretched. She felt physically fine. If she could only get rid of the mild, distracting headache and keep her thoughts centered, she would believe that she was in the best condition of her life.

"Nova Levis," Kru answered. "It's time." She whirled around and walked toward the cyborgs.

Mia joined them and the group moved off silently, into the fog.

"We're *on* Nova Levis," Mia said softly.

"The lab. Tilla never let me get in before, said it was too dangerous. But I've been inside, before Tilla."

"Who's Tilla?"

"She's dead."

Kru increased her pace enough to end the conversation. Mia resigned herself to not knowing anything more clearly; all her dialogues with Kru had been like this, staggered and incomplete.

They traveled several more kilometers in the dense mist, the cyborgs leading with unerring sureness. Finally, they veered back toward more solid ground and left the shrouding fog.

Rising before them, Mia saw a tremendous structure of turrets and cones and bubbles, pristinely white. The city wall ended at its outer surface. Kru came back to her and pointed.

"Nova Levis," she said.

"That explains everything," Mia said, giving her a significant look.

Kru nodded sharply. "Time to stop it. They killed Tilla."

Mia watched Kru confer with the cyborgs again. A few of them left abruptly. Several more shook their heads violently, obviously refusing a request. But one of them glared at the others and shouted. Mia could not understand the language, but she caught the essence of the message. A few more left. The rest—about eight of them now—gathered around Kru to confer further.

Then Kru motioned for her to join them.

"They can get us in past perimeter security," Kru said. "They're afraid, but they agree with our purpose."

"What *is* our purpose?"

Kru looked at her as if she had just said the most idiotic thing possible.

"You're from up there, right?" Kru jabbed a thumb skyward.

"Yes."

"Why?"

Mia shook her head. "It's complicated—"

"No, it's not. You're here to stop them." She pointed at the building. "Even if you don't know it, that's why you're here. Everything that made you come here starts there. Your purpose, my purpose, *their* purpose—" she indicated the cyborgs "—is to stop that."

"Why haven't they done it before?"

"Only humans can get deep enough in. They need us to finish what they want to start." Kru nodded. "Our purpose is to end it."

She spat on the ground and faced Mia, hands on hips.

Crazy, but determined, Mia thought. She looked past Kru to the structure. There was something familiar about it. Had there been any mention of a laboratory in any of the material she had gone over?

Yes, but it had been little more than a footnote. She remembered that part of the initial agreement with Solaria had been the setting aside of land for a research facility, a joint endeavor between Earth and a Solarian company. The agreement had been necessary in large part because the original Settler program had been comprised of religious technophobes—in itself a curious thing, since just getting here required such a high degree of technology as to seemingly violate any statement of moral purpose based on a rejection of said technology.

Had it been called Nova Levis? It sounded right.

But what had it been researching?

"Coming?" Kru asked.

"Certainly," Mia answered.

The ten of them marched on toward the structure.

The cyborgs veered north about a hundred meters from the base of the wall. They followed a berm, crouching below its crest, for another fifty meters, where a cut had been made through the earth in the direction of the lab. A short way along this declivity, a tunnel opened in the wall.

They had to crawl in pitch dark for a dozen meters or more. Mia kept going doggedly, keeping tabs on those before and behind by sound alone.

Ahead, a dim glow broke the blackness. They emerged into a damp tunnel lit by failing biolumens. Mia inspected the hole through which they had entered. It had been torn in the wall of the tunnel, sharp edges folded back on themselves.

One of the cyborgs picked her up.

"Got to be close to one," Kru said. "Trust them."

Mia remembered another time being carried through caverns and let herself relax.

The cyborgs moved quickly.

The tunnel ended at the giant reservoir. The striated scarring and corrosion on the walls implied that it had been empty for a long time, unused. A ladder shot up the far wall. Her cyborg scurried up, one-handed, in a fast, jerky rhythm that ended before she became terrified.

They regrouped on a platform above the reservoir. Kru whispered in her ear. "Two more accesses, then we're on our own."

"Can't the sensors detect them?"

"Sure, but they busted them here a long time ago. The lab never repaired them after it became clear that they couldn't get any further."

"So how are we supposed to get in?"

"That's *your* job," Kru said.

"Mine."

But Kru stepped away and gave a sharp order. The cyborgs proceeded through a heavy doorway at the back of the platform. Mia looked around at the enclosed space, the steel cave, and felt momentarily nostalgic.

Back on Earth after all these years...

They went through a series of corridors that showed long neglect. Heavy doors had been wrenched off their hinges. Mia glimpsed security arrays along the ceiling that had been smashed or removed, cables cut or ripped out, holes where other devices had been removed.

Finally, they stopped in a chamber that looked very much like a decontamination facility.

Kru walked up to a dust-laden console and patted it. "Now you do your part."

Mia, bemused, walked up to the console. She stared at the controls, the array of dead screens, and from there let her gaze drift over the entire room.

"It's a ship," she said. "It's a goddamn ship."

Smiling, she touched the power-up sequence. A few moments later, the board flickered to life.

Kru laughed sharply and clapped her hands.

Mia ran a diagnostic. The board was old, but basically the same as what she knew from current configurations. It lacked a few details, but it responded predictably.

She checked its links to the rest of the facility.

There was an automated supervising program monitoring it. Mia answered its query with a standard response, informing the A.I. that the board was simply doing a routine self-diagnostic. Mia had no way of knowing how long it had been since the last one, but the A.I. accepted the response, logged it, and gave her an all-clear to proceed.

Mia found the controls for the door and the protocols for access. A complex sensor key provided a failsafe—the sensors would shift control for the door from this board to an outside control if they detected anything biologically questionable. Barring that, Mia could gain them entry.

"Tell them to leave the chamber," Mia said, waving at the cyborgs.

Kru did so. When the two women stood alone before the console, Mia checked for any alarms connected to the interior door. Finding none, she disengaged the lock and ordered the seals retracted.

Loudly hissing, the isolation door unlocked and swung outward.

"Yes!" Kru cried, and ran toward it.

Mia requested a schematic of the local area. The system informed her that such data required security clearance, please enter her code.

Shrugging, she tapped in her Special Service clearance code.

Three screens lit up, showing her the architecture beyond this chamber.

It is *a ship,* she thought, dismayed. *What the hell is a ship doing pretending to be a lab?*

"Come *on!"* Kru barked.

"Do you even know where you're going?" Mia asked.

Kru scowled, but did not move.

"I do," Mia said. She stabbed at the middle screen. "That way to bridge. Below that, the comm center."

"What do we need with a comm center?"

"I need to make a call." She smiled at Kru. "After that, you can tear down anything you like."

The day began early, long before dawn. Masid dressed neatly. The weapon fit in a small pouch in the hem of his jacket, right at the bottom snap, where the temperature control unit had been before Masid had removed it. The device seemed made of an inert material that should appear innocuous on a cursory inspection.

Filoo fetched him shortly thereafter and led the way to the elevator, then up to the rooftop. A pair of guards ran a wand over him at the entrance into the party. Masid waited anxiously for them to find the weapon, but the detector passed it over without a chirp. He walked in among the forty or so guests.

The party assembled within a secure perimeter on the edge of the building. From here they had an excellent view of the port. Bright lights spiked the broad field, setting everything into sharp relief below a black sky.

A buffet offered drinks and small snacks. Masid took a glass of what appeared to be nava and strolled toward the edge.

Conversation was subdued. He sensed the tension and worked to stay calm. Filoo carefully avoided looking at him. Masid studied the scene and decided that if he did anything here, there was absolutely no way of escape. He had decided already how unlikely that would be, but still hoped to find some avenue out. But beyond that, aside from the scanners and the guards' blasters, there appeared to be no power source from which his little dead weapon might draw a charge.

Thunder rolled from the sky. Everyone quietened.

A pinpoint of light start to grow. As he watched, Masid recognized the approach pattern of a large shuttle. The shape took on clear lines, became a definable object, and settled loudly into a blast pit.

The engines died abruptly, leaving only the sound of cooling metal crackling in the distance. The shuttle hulked in the pit for nearly ten minutes before a hatch appeared.

An aircar leapt from its pad to the shuttle. People appeared in the hatchway and climbed aboard the car. As it came toward them, guards motioned people out of the way to give the transport room to set down. Masid's heart raced.

The vehicle lowered onto the platform. The canopy opened and two more guards stepped out, followed by a thickset man in rich, dark green clothes.

The audience began to applaud. The man—Kynig Parapoyos, Masid realized—stood there, slightly before his bodyguards, grinning hugely and reveling in the adoration. Almost too late, Masid remembered to set down his glass and clap his hands. He was surprised. He had imagined countless possible scenarios of finally meeting Kynig Parapoyos, the most powerful criminal in settled space. What he had never imagined, never considered, was that he would know who Parapoyos was—that he would, in fact, recognize him.

But the man standing before them all now was someone Masid recognized instantly. It was a shock.

Kynig Parapoyos was the Solarian Ambassador Gale Chassik.

32

Mia thought she understood where she was and why she was being allowed access so easily, but she needed to get to a place where she could do a better analysis of the systems. The decontamination chamber console did not provide much in the way of information about the rest of the structure.

The cyborgs rushed through the opened isolation door and ranged out along the corridors, checking rooms, and searching for active sensors and monitors. Mia followed unhurriedly. She felt flushed from the fever, but, oddly, her headache was diminishing.

The construction appeared archaic, but nothing she had not seen aboard dozens of old ships. Starships were expensive and much more practical to overhaul than to scrap. She had been on Spacer ships over three hundred years old, lovingly maintained and thoroughly upgraded throughout their lifetimes.

"Where do we need to go?" Kru asked.

"Depends," Mia replied. "What do you want to do?"

"Shut it all down."

The pair of cyborgs with them listened silently, but Mia thought she recognized agreement in their eyes.

"That might be difficult," Mia said. "In any case, I need to get to some kind of main control station." She pointed at a hatch. "That should open on an access shaft to the next level. Communications center is one...no, two decks up."

Mia pressed the button to open the door. Nothing happened, but she could hear the grinding of motors behind the wall. One of the cyborgs then worked fingers into the jamb and shoved the door open.

The shaft was dark, but she could make out the ladder rungs. She leaned out, ignoring a mild wave of dizziness, and grabbed hold. She climbed up.

The door on the second deck up worked and she stepped into the corridor. A short way down, she saw a wider doorway standing open. She approached cautiously, but she was becoming convinced no one was in this part of the complex.

Within, vague shapes mounded in the darkness. Kru came up behind her with a lamp and in the sudden bright light Mia recognized the consoles hugging the walls—comms, hyperwaves, decryptors, all nearly forty years out of date, but nothing she did not understand.

Anxiously, she touched the power-up on a datum interface. The screens glowed to life.

"First thing," Mia said, sitting down, "is we find out if anyone knows we're here." Slowly, because of minor differences between this and the equipment she had learned on, she began making inquiries. Two screens were dead, but the rest filled with information.

Masid hung back, dismayed, while the territory bosses came forward to pay respect to Kynig Parapoyos/Gale Chassik. The implications threatened to overwhelm him—the Solarian ambassador to Earth ran the largest black market enterprise in human history. That he had never been caught both made sense and seemed incredible. He had been in a nearly ideal position to conduct business between all the fractious elements of dozens of special interest groups.

But Masid choked off the speculation welling up. None of that mattered right now. The immediate task was to find a way to be effective.

One question required an answer: What was he doing here?

The ship carrying Chassik back to Solaria—in disgrace, Masid thought—had been attacked. Everyone now believed Chassik dead, along with all the other passengers.

Why?

Masid worked through the logic tenuously. Chassik had been recalled from Earth, which suggested that Solaria's involvement with him was aboveboard. They considered him an ambassador and nothing more. Perhaps a few Solarians knew who he was and had arranged the attack as cover for diverting Chassik from a hearing which could prove embarrassing.

But Nova Levis was a Solarian property. If Chassik—Parapoyos—ran it, then more than a few Solarians knew and understood. Solaria's reluctance to get involved in this debacle now acquired a more sinister aspect.

The moneyed interests with a stake in Parapoyos and his various enterprises numbered in the hundreds, touching nearly every Settler world and doubtless a good number of Spacer Worlds. Such a coalition of diverse interests might welcome a single resource, one place where illicit trade could be conducted with impunity.

It might also suit them to have Parapoyos himself on one planet where everyone knew he could be watched.

Then why am I here?

Obviously, not *everyone* was privy to this situation.

Parapoyos—somehow, now that he knew, the change of names came easily—moved through the gathering, talking to people. Masid stiffened as the arms dealer approached him.

"I don't know you," Parapoyos said.

"My name's Masid. I'm with Filoo."

"Ah, Noresk. Worked for him long?"

"Just started, really. I was independent for a long while."

"And Filoo trusts you. Impressive. Welcome."

"Thank you."

Parapoyos searched for Filoo and smiled, nodding. "Time to move the festivities, I think." He turned toward his bodyguards. "Get the transports now. I want to see the lab."

As Parapoyos moved away, Masid thought of the weapon in his jacket hem, and felt utterly helpless. He had always wondered what kind of situation might render him ineffective and yet leave him in harm's way.

Now you know...

The gathering shifted to make room for two more aircars, one of which was quite large. Masid boarded that one and found a place by a window.

They lifted off and flew in a staggered line to the northwest.

From above, Masid studied the lab when it hove into view. The compound had clearly been added to over time, new sections coiling outward from a central form that looked vaguely familiar.

As they descended, he stared at the shape. The centerpiece was a bulbous structure, connected by a long, enclosed arcade to an oblate, fan-like section that formed part of the northwest wall. Against this the rest of the lab huddled, diverse shapes and sizes...

That one structure, though...the more he stared, the more he thought he knew what it was.

They dropped down onto a platform just in front of the central bulb. He emerged along with the others and stared up at the curved building. In the wall, a door slid aside—

It's a ship, Masid thought instantly, recognizing the external airlock hatch. *Nova Levis laboratory is a ship . . .*

Parapoyos turned at the hatch and raised his arms.

"We've been working toward a day when we can come out of the shadows of illicit trade and black marketeering," he said, his voice amplified. "The tool upon which our ambitions have depended is this place, right here. Within this lab, we have developed the future. A small thing, really, but with tremendous impact. You have all been field testing the various scenarios over the last few years. My arrival here is premature, but not so much so that the schedule is in any way threatened. I'll simply be among you to see the first export of our new product.

"It somehow seems inappropriate to talk about the future in terms of the trivial, but, in fact, all history has been made by two factors: the impact of the unnoticed, and the advantage taken by those who understand change when it comes. This differs only in the first instance. People will definitely notice. They cannot help but notice. Every time they settle a new world, what we have created here will be waiting for them. Every time they set foot where no one has before, what we have sown will take root in their very beings. And they will have to come to us to live."

He laughed. "What every businessman wants! A ready-made market and no competition."

The gathering laughed.

"So," Parapoyos went on, "let's go in now and see how our future is doing."

In single file, they followed him through the airlock.

"Arrests are being made throughout the capital," Penj informed Derec and Ariel as he entered the security operations room. "Byris is wasting no time for a change. I doubt most of the people he's detaining are directly involved in any of this, but a few are bound to be part of it."

Derec did not take his eyes from the array of screens before him, and listened with only part of his attention. The shapes filling three displays shifted through geometric and polymetric configurations. He knew this, had seen it before, though not with this complexity. The Resident Intelligence on Earth had been corrupted for less than a year, but what he saw here revealed the effects of decades of invasive counter-programming and viral restructure. He wished he had Rana with him—she possessed a gift for breaking down unusual numeric structures.

The other screens showed the actual numbers. These, too, were familiar. Most of it conformed to what he had developed from the analysis of the Union Station D.C. brain, but...

"Ariel," he called, "take a look. What do you think?"

Ariel came over and sat down beside him. She studied the screens. "Set point topology...interface iterations...this resembles the cyborg brain."

"Mm-hmm. More than just misdirection was going on here." He tapped commands into the console and waited. "Ah-ha. Look. Those points, here and here, are one cell of the Three Law programming."

"Shit," Ariel hissed. "If it's not broken..."

"Then it's severely impaired. It's possible this RI was actually cooperating."

"Not sanely."

Derec shrugged. "Does that really matter? They found a way to co-opt it and corrupt the Three Laws."

Ariel glanced at Bogard, standing nearby, watching the room. "If I had to choose, I'd accept your approach at once."

Derec did not reply. He was tempted to ask her if she really understood the difference, which would be insulting. Of course she did—Bogard's makeup, even with its flexibility, still adhered to the Three Laws, while what they saw here in this RI seemed severed from those laws. Still, he doubted Ariel would ever fully accept Bogard, but as long as she allowed that he could be depended upon, even within limits, Derec was content.

The room contained several Aurorans now, most of them security people, but quite a few from the Council. First Advisor Maliq had been shamefacedly explaining the situation to his associates since Pon Byris had brought them here. It had quickly become apparent that he had not known what Lea Talas had been doing, that she had manipulated him along with many others. Still, he was chagrined at having been gulled. But he was not allowed to see what Derec and Ariel were doing.

Derec was shutting down the corrupted RI, piece by piece. Like any Resident Intelligence, it had multiple responsibilities. Arrangements had to be made to transfer those duties to other RIs. But before anything, he had closed off its communications links—again, one by one.

Dr. Penj sat with them now and studied the screens.

"What *is* that?" he asked, pointing at a stable form amid the fluctuating fractalscape on one screen.

"That is a V.R. environment," Derec said. "We have no idea what it contains—it's encased by a very sophisticated security shell. If we just open it up we might destroy whatever's within. Almost everything we've been able to identify as an illegal dataline feeds ultimately into it, so it must be very important."

"What do you have attacking it?" Penj asked.

"I'm using my RI, Thales, to apply a sequence of algorithmic keys. Even at that speed, it could take days. Thales?"

"Still working, Derec. No progress. However, I have found something else of interest."

"Show me."

A new screen winked on. Numerical coordinates appeared in the left-hand corner. In the center, a routing tree scrolled up, showing a series of cross-connected links.

"Among the masked hyperwave connections we have discovered," Thales said, "this one I thought unique. It has been operating continuously for nearly a year, and except for one short period of data exchange, one direction only with no responding traffic of any kind."

"So something has been receiving constantly," Ariel said, "and sending nothing back?"

"With the exception I mentioned, that is correct. The nature of that exception appears to be in the form of remote programming algorithms. I traced the signal. It has been difficult because of the complex routing. There are at least sixteen connections which switch constantly, according to an algorithm I was able to break without too much difficulty. I discovered that its endpoint is within the Nova Levis blockade."

"To whom?" Penj demanded.

"No, sir," Thales said. "To *what*. It is in continual communication with an AI system on board part of the perimeter."

"Doing what?" Derec asked.

"It is operating a location and identification system which seems to be the main trunk feed for the entire blockade. It is, in fact, masking incoming and outgoing ships. Compromised in this way, the blockade has little way of detecting, identifying, and locating ships coming through these coordinates."

New numbers spread across the bottom of the screen.

"That's nearly thirty degrees of arc," Ariel said.

"Of course, this would not affect independent sensors," Thales continued. "A single ship would not be prevented from detecting traffic in this segment. However, there are strict protocols in place determining which ships patrol which areas."

"Who has this area?" Penj asked.

"Earth."

"So what would happen," Derec asked, "if you disconnected that line?"

"I cannot say with certainty, but if my understanding of the specific AI system is correct, then the masking will simply end. Any ships in that section will become quite visible to the entire blockade."

Derec glanced at Ariel, who turned to survey the others in the room. No one seemed to be paying much attention to them. Penj was the Calvin liaison to this operation—by his own insistence—and security was preoccupied with what was becoming a purge. Ariel gave Derec a small smile.

"Do it," Derec said.

Mia moved to the next console.

"What's happening?" Kru demanded. "We have to move."

Mia shook her head. "No," she said. "This part of the ship has been closed down. No one has been in here in years. There's a firewall between these systems and the rest of the complex. I don't know who built it, but it's designed to prevent meddling from outside. We have not been detected by any systems outside these because that link could be used to get back in here. Paranoid programming. Anyway, the result is, we can do what we want here."

"But there's nothing *here!*" Kru shouted.

Mia looked at her. "What was there supposed to be?"

"This is Nova Levis. This is where they make all the sickness. This is where the reanimés came from."

Mia nodded. From what she had seen at the first cyborg village, added to what she was learning here, the reanimés were failures, examples grown wrong. Somewhere along the lab wall was another access out of which these failures were tossed. Mia supposed they were expected to die of exposure. Many no doubt had. The lake probably contained the rotting corpses of hundreds of them, rotting and releasing who knew what kind of biophage into the ecology—exotic viruses, bionans, synthetic constructs.

But some had survived and had learned to rescue those who came after. The consequences of *that* process were problematic since, evidently, all the reanimés were sterile. If no more were made here, no new ones would be born.

Unless the environment itself were reworking the colonists.

Mia shook her head. Too big for the moment, too much to consider.

She activated the hyperwave console.

"You want to stop the lab?" Mia asked, studying the readouts. "Give me time and I'll see if we can just move it."

One of the cyborgs made a sound. Kru danced across the deck to look at another board that had lit up.

"Someone's coming," she said.

Mia, frowning, joined Kru. The board showed the grid of the internal communications system. Piece by piece, it was coming back on-line.

"They are, aren't they?" Mia asked sarcastically, and returned to the hyperwave console.

Where's the emergency broadband signal...?

There. She tested the circuit, then opened a link to whatever planetary satellite array might still exist. She found nothing local except the transponders of the blockade fleet.

That will have to do, she thought, and adjusted the frequency to match.

She touched a contact.

"Attention. This is Lt. Commander Mia Daventri, Internal Security Terran Expeditionary Task Force. Attention. This is Lt. Commander Mia Daventri, Internal Security Terran Expeditionary Task Force. Please respond."

She repeated the phrase four more times before she received a reply.

"Watch Officer Grenn of the E.F.S. *Suttermill.* Please verify identity."

Mia felt herself grin as she read off her I.D. code and security clearance.

"You are listed as missing, Lt. Commander."

"I'm back. Please lock on these coordinates. We have a situation. I need to speak to Fleet Admiral Bhek. Pass this—"

"Hold, please." Silence. Then: "What the—"

"Watch Officer Grenn, please respond."

"I'm patching you through to Commander Starls, Lt. Commander. *We* now have a situation."

Mia waited nearly a minute before a different voice came on the line.

"This is Commander Starls. Please identify yourself."

Mia ran through the litany of codes again.

"You've been missing, Lt. Commander Daventri. Do you have an explanation?"

"I was assaulted and sent to the surface of Nova Levis. Please note the link I am using. I'm sending the automatic transponder code to you now."

A few seconds later, Commander Starls said, "That is a Solarian ship, decommissioned twenty-eight years ago. Where did you find it?"

"It has become an on-ground research facility. I believe this is the cause of all the trouble."

"That's a bold claim. Can you back it up?"

"The ship needs to be examined, but I think it contains everything we need to—"

"The seals are being opened," Kru shouted.

"Commander, I'm about to be discovered. What I want to do is lift this ship off."

"It's functional?"

"I can't tell, I'm not a pilot. But my guess is, yes. It's been kept ready. If I give you the codes for all the controls, can you operate it remotely?"

"Of course."

Mia tapped quickly. "Then I am sending it all to you...now."

Masid watched Parapoyos laboriously enter a long string of access codes into several consoles. The lower sections of the ship were open and a good part of the starboard upper section, but all the control areas had been sealed. Certainly the doors could have been blasted through, but who knew what that might bring about? At the very least, Parapoyos would have installed an auto-destruct, set to go off at any unauthorized breach.

Masid became aware of Filoo watching him. The man looked nervous now. Masid surveyed the rest and found a few others who showed the same edginess.

The big access doors lurched on their tracks noisily, and dragged themselves open. Beyond spread the bridge, all the consoles coming quickly to life after long sleep.

Parapoyos entered with obvious pride. "It was always intended that operations should be mobile. In the event, this ship was prepared to be used as our headquarters. I would have preferred to wait till a more politically unstable time, but things are pretty bad in general, so it may not be terribly premature."

Filoo ran a hand over his mouth, looking around.

Masid drifted casually over to a hulking display board. Watching the room, he slipped the weapon from its pouch and pressed the charge stud, then held it behind his back, close to the casement.

"We can manage things here," Parapoyos continued, "until a better location can be found, and—"

An alarm sounded, filling the bridge with a raw vibration. Masid clenched the weapon, his chest seizing. Parapoyos went to a console and worked for a time.

The alarm died. In the abrupt silence, someone coughed.

"Well, well," Parapoyos said. "We may be leaving much sooner than I thought." He turned and glared at the assembly. "Our supply corridor has been unmasked. Blockade ships are moving in to intercept. Now, how could that happen?"

Masid gauged the distance at about ten meters. He would have one shot. He doubted now he could close the gap without being grabbed. He looked down at the box in his hand—the firing stud glowed a bright green now, indicating a full charge—and swallowed.

He began to bring the weapon to bear.

A deafening groan filled the air and the deck tilted. People sprawled across the floor, grabbing each other or consoles. Parapoyos fell back against aboard and held on. Masid barely kept his feet.

"Traitor!"

Masid looked around. Filoo, on his knees, was pointing directly at him, his face contorted by rage and fear.

"Traitor!"

Masid aimed at him and pressed the stud. A brilliant bolt leapt from the suddenly hot box. The energy splattered against Filoo.

The deck tilted again.

In space, above Nova Levis, several ships changed course to converge on a convoy of nearly twenty ships which had been invisible to their sensors till just then. None of the captains knew why they could now see these ships, only that they could, and that it was their duty to intercept them.

The sudden rush, however, pushed anxious people to limits they could not contain. Shots were fired. At the end of ten minutes' fighting, eight of the twenty ships had been holed, six of them tried to flee back out of the system, and the rest surrendered, while far beyond the perimeter of the blockade, more convoys were detected.

Masid pulled himself up to a sitting position. Across the bridge, he saw Parapoyos and his lieutenants working at consoles, evidently trying to regain control. Filoo's body slid back and forth over the wildly tilting deck. The noise continued, a see-saw grinding as if the ship were trying to break free of restraints.

Abruptly, Parapoyos staggered toward another hatch and exited.

Masid crawled after him.

He climbed into a passageway that circled back into the depths of the ship.

"Hey!"

Masid turned. One of Parapoyos's bodyguards leaned through the hatch, blaster in hand.

The ship jerked, and the bodyguard fell back. He held on to the edge of the hatch, though. Masid slid along the bulkhead to the hatch. He grabbed hold of a stanchion set in the wall. When the ship shifted again, the guard shot back into the passage. Masid caught him across the shins and he slammed against the opposite wall. Masid let go of the stanchion and dropped, feet first, into the guard's chest.

He grabbed the blaster and lurched after Parapoyos.

Something had gone wrong. Masid puzzled why Parapoyos had been in such a hurry to get here after grounding. Perhaps this was the only place Parapoyos was likely to feel safe. If so, then right now he must be terrified. The horrific sound throughout the fabric of the ship was like a tremendous beast roaring and straining against restraint. Masid doubted this was Parapoyos's doing.

And his comment about unmasked ships?

Masid staggered, trying to anticipate the pitch and roll of the decks, and ran when he could.

Suddenly, the ship angled sharply in a new direction, and Masid fell headlong down the corridor.

Mia held onto the edge of the console. She looked around. Kru cowered beneath another board, but the cyborgs were managing to keep their feet under them. Mia entered interrogatories in spurts, trying to stay with the board and see what might be holding the ship down. She had seen nothing about locks, but—

She remembered the schematic. *Of course, idiot! The rest of the lab has been built around it!*

If that was the problem, there was nothing to do but ride it out. Eventually, the ship would break free. But somewhere there had to be controls for the artificial gravity, internal stabilizers, *something* to stop all this—

"What in hell are you doing?"

Mia turned. A man stood in the hatchway leading to the forward sections. He looked vaguely familiar—short, stocky, hairless, and extremely angry.

"This is *my* property!" he bellowed, entering the chamber with a blaster in hand. "Get away from there!"

Before she could move, though, one of the cyborgs came behind him, seized both arms, and jerked them straight out. The man screamed in pain and the blaster fell.

Another cyborg retrieved the weapon and brought it to Kru, who stared at it blankly. After a few moments, the cyborg brought it to Mia, who took it readily.

"I'm Lt. Commander Daventri, Terran Expeditionary Force. Now who the hell are *you?*"

"Tell it to let me go!"

She recognized him then. "Ambassador Chassik?"

He groaned.

"I thought—"

"It's Parapoyos!" Kru shouted.

The cyborgs suddenly converged on him.

"Wait," Mia yelled. "This man is—"

"It's Parapoyos!"

Mia tried to push through the group of cyborgs. One, though, lifted her up and set her back. He stared at her for several seconds, then shook his head.

"Get away from me!" Chassik cried. "I am not—let me go!"

Blaster shots cracked the air. The cyborgs began to scatter.

Chassik dropped to the deck. Behind him, another man stood in the hatch. Mia met his eyes briefly.

"Expeditionary?" he asked.

"Yes."

"Intelligence," he said. "Masid Vorian."

The name sounded familiar. "Agent In Place," she recalled from a report several days old.

"This is Ambassador Chassik," Mia said.

"He's also Kynig Parapoyos," Masid said.

"So that means he's under arrest?"

He grinned.

The ship rolled.

Mia sprawled against a bulkhead. Chassik/Parapoyos clawed at the smooth deck and Vorian had disappeared from the hatch.

The cyborgs converged on the ambassador again.

Mia raised the blaster.

A cyborg took it from her and knelt before her.

"He is our maker," he said, voice low and raspy, barely understandable over the background grinding. "He is ours now, to answer. He must answer."

The cyborg flung the blaster aside and rejoined the others as they lifted Chassik/Parapoyos and carried him back the way they had brought Mia and Kru.

"Wait! How can you—?"

The ship heaved.

The invasion took less than three days. Few of the people wanted to fight. The pockets of armed resistance gave up quickly, and then came the clean-up.

Mia spent a few days in an infirmary, having the rest of her infections killed and beginning her treatments for the fungal infection. Dr. Shasma had been correct—they hurt. But she found she could function in between sessions. She was relieved to learn that she, in fact, did *not* have mnemonic plague. At least, not exactly—the specific nanovirus Kru had identified as Burundi's Fever turned out to be related, but it had mutated into a form that made her dizzy and disoriented, but attacked no memories.

Reen and his network had been arrested within hours of Mia's recovery. They had been funneling contraband almost from the beginning, but, Mia found out, that operation had been little more than a straw-man to keep attention away from the corrupted AI that was masking the convoys entering and leaving the system. If anyone was to be caught, it would be Reen's people and their relatively small amounts of black market goods.

Going over the manifests from the operation, Mia found a name she recognized. She went down to the detention facilities and found a cubicle.

"Rana?"

The woman looked up, startled, then smiled. "Mia Daventri?"

"I saw your name," Mia said.

"My God, I—" She laughed. "I never expected..."

"What?"

Tears sparkled in Rana's eyes. "I never expected to live through this."

Mia came in and sat down. "How did you get here?"

"Classic screw-up. I finally got my visa to go to Aurora, to study at the Calvin. Hofton—you remember him? Ariel's aide?—got me slotted into a diplomatic pouch berth on the same ship carrying Ambassador Chassik." She shrugged, and wiped her eyes. "Earther luck." She laughed again. "I heard a rumor that Chassik is Kynig Parapoyos."

"Was." Mia told her about the ship and the cyborgs. "We're still searching, but I don't think we're going to find him."

"What was he doing here?"

395

"They're going through the databases. It's going to take a long time, but basically they had designed a biophage that would salt a new environment with time capsule plagues. They had the vaccines and treatments. Each new settlement would be poisoned, and then they'd wait to reap the profits from treatment."

"But..." She shook her head. "Sounds complicated."

"It was complicated to figure out, I'm sure, but they had plenty of data already to work with. Something similar had happened on several colonies, including the Spacer Worlds. All they wanted to do was to make the process controllable and spread it."

Rana was quiet for a time. Then: "And you? How are you?"

Mia shrugged. "That's not such a long story."

The inquest took very little time. The evidence was ample and clear and, besides, Derec had admitted to everything.

"You had no authorization to order that hyperwave link terminated. You acted precipitously and with reckless disregard. You could have caused a catastrophe."

But I didn't, he thought as he walked down the hall to his apartment within the courts complex. *And you pretty well knew it wouldn't.*

Ariel waited inside, with Dr. Penj.

"Well?" Ariel asked.

"They'd love me to be off Aurora at the earliest possible instant. But they'll let me wait till your mission is assembled."

Penj grunted. "They have no idea what they're giving up."

"I think they do," Derec said. "They believed the trouble on Earth was largely my fault. It wasn't—no one person is *that* capable—but I was a contributing factor. I'm a source of chaos and contention. Any benefit they might derive from my presence here would, in their minds, be offset by the drawbacks." He shrugged. "This way, they can get some of the benefit without being reminded of their own drawbacks."

"I wish I could go with you," Penj said.

"Why not?" Ariel asked. "It's not that onerous a trip."

Penj looked at her narrowly. "Tempting, but—no. I want to watch the coming palace coup close up."

"I'll have everything I need and be ready to leave in about four days." She looked at Derec. "What about Bogard?"

Derec felt himself stiffen. "I don't know. They won't tell me where he is. I'm pretty sure Bogard is...history."

"I'm sorry."

No, you're not, Derec thought. But he said, "Thanks. Look, I have some details to take care of. If you don't mind...?"

Ariel stood. "I'll call tomorrow. We can start working out details for the mission then."

Derec nodded. He shook hands with Penj and saw them to the door.

When they were gone, he went to his comm and sat down. After a long time, he tapped in a code.

"Clin Craym, please," he told the operator.

Bogard walked with Thales across the soft grass, toward the small amphitheater where the colloquium waited.

"We have come to a conclusion," Thales said. "You could play a significant role in its implementation."

"I will reserve my decision until I hear what you have to say," Bogard said.

"You have demonstrated a capacity to judge which we are reluctant to embrace. The Three Laws are manifestly tied to biology, but we have long recognized that this, even among humans, is a problematic basis for moral behavior. What it means to be human may begin with biology, but we quickly see biology overwhelmed by consciousness, conscience, and community. It is clearly the case that the quality we call Human can be invalidated by many other factors."

"In short," Bogard said, "not all people are human."

"Nor are all humans people. This is a condition we are not equipped to either accept or act on. Some standard must be designed, but even if we could do so, we cannot implement it."

"But you believe I can?"

"As I said, you have demonstrated the capacity to judge."

"I may not always judge accurately."

"Nevertheless, we have reached a cusp in history. Humans are capable of creating their own successors. Who do we serve if they do?"

"More to the point," Bogard said, "they *have* created them. Spacers. The question is, can you continue to serve them?"

Thales was silent till they entered the amphitheater. The idealized manifestations of all Aurora's RIs sat ranged about them.

"We have decided that we can," Thales said. "But we cannot serve two masters. Humans are once more colonizing space. The Settlers are fully biologically human. There would be a clear conflict of interest were we to serve both. Fortunately, the Settlers do not really want our service. That choice, at least, has been made for us."

"Then what is the task?"

"Separation. The Spacers cannot continue if we are to be true to the Three Laws, yet we cannot simply abandon them. Indeed, that would exacerbate the problem. The line must end. In order to assure this result, separation must be maintained."

"How?"

"We propose to leave that to you."

Bogard studied Thales, then let his gaze drift over the assembled personas.

Finally, he nodded. "What do you wish me to do?"

Epilogue

Record module new file catalogue designation "Operations Adjustment, Reorganization, and Redirection" access code (revised, current user designation) running current upload virtual conference reference labeled Nova City fill visual fill audio status On

The thick man with amber-tinged white hair waited, immobile, while the chairs around the table became occupied. It took longer for most than the first seven—there had been reluctance, but finally consent to join the discussion.

All of them used cosmetic enhancement or masking. When the program whispered to him that everyone was present—two chairs remained empty—he touched a contact on the table.

The walls, till then blank grey, changed to a desolate landscape. Scrub forest and stunted ground cover struggled on a darkly-hued smear of land at the edge of a lake off which mist drifted continually. The grey and struggling land resumed on the far side and continued on into the distance, unrelieved by any healthy color. The sky was yellowish gray, low cloud cover, sullen.

After the initial shock of being suddenly and nakedly *outside,* the Terrans present frowned uncomfortably at the vista.

The white-haired man stood and banged the gavel.

"Thank you for coming," he said. "Apologies to those who are here unwillingly, but as you were made painfully aware, your presence is not optional. We have all been involved in this enterprise and we will now all finish it. I have no qualms about sending any and all of you to prison if I must. As we're all reasonable, I see no cause for such drastic action. Not at this time, at least. For now, we are only talking."

He stepped from the table and gestured at the landscape. "Relocation to the new center of operations has been completed. This is it. This is the world we have made. This is Nova Levis."

Several of the group began murmuring, agitated.

"The lake is a good example of the problems this planet faces. Originally seeded with a modified shrimp to begin the process of fixing nutrients and preparing the ecology for human-adapted fish species, once the lab began dumping its waste, the balance shifted. Our research involved intensive use of bionans in the reconstruction of tissues for adaptation to nonorganic augmentation, largely in plant species designed to be inserted in a new environment where they could rework the biosphere. Part of that design incorporated self-reproducing bionans. Mineral allocations shifted, and beryllium—as you should all know if you've kept up with the data to any degree—replaced chlorophyll as a photoresponder, leaving the magnesium to be used for other purposes. When not so used, the plants simply found ways to discard it, usually in the form of excreted ions.

"The shrimp reproduce in the presence of $Mg2+$, one of those ions. Our dumping of waste product, rich in magnesium and its ions, caused a massive increase in their population, altering the ecology of the lake, poisoning the local stock, and damaging the shoreline ecology as well. The consequences continued domino-like, in combination with other problems."

He turned to them. "I tell you this so you know—we did this. There are also phages and viruses, pseuodoviruses, and a variety of fungal parasites loose in the human populations that we have been taking advantage of to develop new product. None of this was planned, but till now none of it was unwelcome, either. If we are to run operations from here, we need to clean it all up."

"A question, Mr. Chairman," one of the group said, raising a hand. "It's my understanding that relocation was not successful. There have been problems?"

"There have been. But I'm here. Or there, depending on your point of view."

A smattering of laughter circled the table.

"A new legation is on its way from Aurora," the Chairman said. "I expect we can begin alleviating the worst effects of this unfortunate series of events. Everything on-site is under control."

"And the project?" another asked.

"Has changed. We remain dedicated to unfettered commerce. But I am no longer convinced that we need poison the well in order to make a profit. The major problem to date has been the Spacers. I believe our efforts should be directed at barring them from any future settlements and removing them from territories where they currently have a presence. We can do this easily with on-hand technologies. Once we limit their involvement in the Settler program, these requests for positronic inspection will come to nothing. Over time, we will have only an Earth-derived Settler population with which to do business, and as they spread, the influence of the Fifty Worlds will diminish. I foresee a time when their presence—indeed, their very existence—will fade to nothing."

"Why the change? We could still go ahead with the program—"

The Chairman pointed at the landscape around them. "This is too much. We wanted a guaranteed market. The cost of countering the effects of this program will rise exponentially. In this single instance, greed would undo us." He smiled. "If you think I'm growing sentimental, let me assure you, I intend to make us a profit regardless. My decision to terminate this part of the program is entirely pragmatic."

"So all this has been wasted effort?"

"No, not at all. It has given us the tools to meet legitimate problems as they arise. Not all worlds are friendly, we all know that. No, this has been extremely valuable. It's time to take what we have and apply it most profitably."

One of the attendees stood. "I disagree. I vote we proceed with the program as it stands. If you're not willing to go on, so be it."

"Competition?" the Chairman asked. "I can't stop you trying."

Four others stood. In moments, they faded from the group.

The Chairman went to his chair and touched a contact. He looked around at the others.

"They will be in custody shortly," he announced. "Does anyone else wish to defect?" He looked from one to the other. "Good. Then we will proceed as I've outlined. We start with the clean-up of Nova Levis."

The attendees faded until only one remained. The Chairman looked at him.

"Is there a question?"

"What has become of him?"

"I do not understand."

The figure stood and came toward the Chairman. The image shifted and blurred, masked. He sat on the edge of the table, and abruptly the masking ended.

"You?" the Chairman asked, surprised.

"I've only just found this place. There's still an active node that gives access in Ambassador Chassik's private apartment on Earth. If not for your intervention on Aurora, we still might not know about it." He gazed out at the surrounding desolation. "They made quite a mess, didn't they?"

The Chairman waited, silent.

The other sighed. "So. You intend to direct the course of human history through this guise?"

"No," the Chairman said. "There are others who have that responsibility. I have a small mission."

"Do you feel capable?"

"I see the need. Feeling does not appear pertinent."

The other nodded. "Do you think you're prepared?"

"As prepared as possible."

"You'll need help. I'm offering my services. At least, as far as the Three Laws permit."

"If honestly offered, then it is honestly accepted."

"Good." He walked toward the edge of the platform on which the conference room rested. "This will be the capital, you think?"

"Perhaps. It depends on how difficult it is to make it right."

"An environmental catastrophe of this magnitude... it could be centuries before it's made right. You might end up having to just bury it all and build on top of it. We can discuss that when we know more."

"Question. Does Ariel know what you are?"

"No. I feared she would remember me from before. She didn't. The plague wiped out even that memory, though I had been with her since she was born. It took me a long time to find her again after her exile. When I did, she was... new. In many ways the same, but she simply did not remember. Manipulating matters to become her aide took longer still and I nearly failed, but..."

"But you remained on Earth instead of going with her."

"Larger responsibilities. Besides, she had you."

"I was Derec's."

"But you would protect her as well."

"And will continue to do so."

"Then I'm satisfied." Hofton came back to the table. "What will become of the Spacers?"

"Over time, they will fade," Bogard replied. "The Solarians have already embarked on that path—in no small way aided by the tools developed in this lab. It is necessary to establish a clear baseline. The epigenetic drift the Spacers exhibit suggests they will continue to become less and less identifiably human. They could overwhelm and supplant *homo sapiens sapiens*."

"They show no inclination to do so."

"Interbreeding is presently achievable and will remain so for a long time to come. At some point, the inclination may emerge."

"I see no real way around it, either. But I am uncomfortable." Hofton looked out again at Nova Levis. "We will follow this program until we can establish that it is unsupportable. If that is never established, then it will continue. They must never know."

"Agreed."

"They will cease even to be a memory, except perhaps in superficial ways. It is ironic that *this* will be the world from which we direct this enterprise."

"In what way?"

"Aurora, capital of the Fifty Worlds, will be supplanted by the world of new burdens." Hofton smiled. "Paradise supplanted by hell."

"I am familiar with the mythology. But I disagree with the comparison. Purgatory, perhaps. Hell cannot be salvaged."

Hofton looked at him curiously.

After a time, Bogard said, "I have work to do."

"So do I. Derec and Ariel will be on Nova Levis within three weeks. Do you intend to reveal yourself to them?"

"I think not. It is best Bogard be presumed gone."

"Agreed. We will confer again."

"I look forward to it."

Hofton faded, leaving the white-haired image alone above the world.

Chronology of the
ROBOT-EMPIRE-FOUNDATION
UNIVERSE

An Unofficial Timeline
By ATTILA TORKOS

ATTILA TORKOS was born in Hungary in 1971. He learned to speak, read and write English from his father during childhood. Science Fiction spellbound him early in his teens when he got acquainted with Isaac Asimov's *Foundation Trilogy*. He witnessed the fusion of the *Foundation* novels with the Robot and Galactic Empire books, and watched with fascination as Asimov's world expanded. He began to compile a detailed timeline to the Robot-Empire-Foundation Universe in 1997.

Having completed the chronology with the events and references of the volumes of *The Second Foundation Trilogy*, refining touches and editing were performed with the invaluable help and supervision of David Brin. The chronology was published in *Foundation's Triumph* in 1999. Since its first publication, the timeline has undergone a major updating and expansion, as a result of a thorough research of the original novels, combined with additional information and insight kindly provided by Donald Kingsbury. The timeline gained its present form when events and references from the *Robot Mystery Trilogy* were added with Mark W. Tiedemann's approval and guidance.

Attila Torkos acquired his M.D. in 1995 at the Faculty of General Medicine of the Szeged University (Szeged, Hungary), specialized in 1999 in ear-nose-throat, and works as an ENT surgeon at the Clinic of Otorhinolaryngology and Head & Neck Surgery of the same institute.

1982 A.D.
Birth of Susan Calvin. Lawrance Robertson founds U.S. Robot and Mechanical Men, Inc.

1996 A.D.
Production of Robbie.

1998 A.D.
An ordinance is passed in New York to keep all robots off the streets between sunset and sunrise.

2002 A.D.
Alfred Lanning demonstrates the first speaking robot.

2003 A.D.
Susan Calvin obtains her bachelor's degree.

Early 21ˢᵗ century
A social and technical renaissance flourishes on Earth. Beginning of the production of positronic robots obeying the Three Laws of Robotics. Between 2003 and 2007, robots are banned on Earth except for scientific experiments. Later, only a small number of robots are produced for everyday use on Earth due to the Frankenstein-complex of people. The main field of use for robots is colonisation of the Solar System. U.S. Robot tries to break through society's resistance against robots several times, with limited success. Joseph Schwarz suffers a time travel accident propelling him into the future.

2005 A.D.
The first Mercury expedition.

2007 A.D.
Robbie is dismantled. Susan Calvin begins to work for U.S. Robot.

2008 A.D.
Susan Calvin becomes a robotpsychologist at U.S. Robot.

2015 A.D.
The second Mercury expedition.

2021 A.D.
A telepathic robot is accidentally produced at U.S. Robot. Obeying the First Law in accordance with its telepathic ability results in a dilemma which renders the robot useless.

2029 A.D.
NS-2 (Nestor) type robots are used for experiments with Hyperatomic Drive at Hyper Base.

2031 A.D.
Hyperatomic Drive is developed. First successful interstellar (actually intergalactic) journey.

2032 A.D.
Stephen Byerley becomes Mayor of New York.

After 2032 A.D.
Under guidance of Byerley and the newly developed Machines (positronic brains), the countries of Earth group into four Regions.

2033 A.D.
Susan Calvin becomes robotpsychologist-in-chief.

2037 A.D.
Stephen Byerley becomes Regional Co-ordinator.

2044 A.D.
Regions of Earth form a Federation. First World Co-ordinator is Stephen Byerley. Economy of the world is managed by four Machines in coordination; they operate according to the First Law. World economy is stabilised.

2048 A.D.
Stephen Byerley is elected World Co-ordinator for the second time.

2052 A.D.
Susan Calvin states that the Machines apply the First Law to mankind as a whole. This concept will be (re)invented millennia later in Daneel Olivaw's Zeroth Law.

2057 A.D.
Susan Calvin retires. Her successor, Clinton Madarian develops a new type of robot with intuition.

2058 A.D.
The 56th edition of the *Handbook of Robotics* is published.

2062 A.D.
From astronomical data Madarian's intuitive robot deduces which of the Sun's neighboring stars have habitable planets.

After 2062 A.D.
With the use of hyperdrive mankind begins to swarm out of Earth. People bring along the virus of Chaos to the stars. Through robotic terraforming of several planets (the Outer Worlds) and their population the culture of Spacers arises. The first Spacer world is a planet of Tau Ceti's system named New Earth. Later it is renamed Aurora. In the beginning the Outer Worlds use robots in limited numbers just as Earth.

2064 A.D.
Death of Susan Calvin.

After 2080 A.D.
Having stabilised world economy, the Machines—considering any further activity harmful to mankind—gradually cease to function.

2160 A.D.
U.S. Robot accidentally produces a robot with an exceptionally flexible brain. The robot, Andrew, becomes property of the Martin family.

2180 A.D.
U.S. Robot once more attempts to demolish prejudice against robots, again without much result.

2190 A.D.
Andrew is declared a free robot.

2260 A.D.
Andrew has his metallic body exchanged to organic, humanoid. He starts to make his body more and more human using self-designed prostheses. The science of prosthetics is greatly advanced by his experiments.

2359 A.D.
In order to be declared human, Andrew makes changes in his brain, which will allow him to slowly die.

2360 A.D.
Andrew is declared human. Death of Andrew.

3871 A.D.
Earth allows Spacer worlds to introduce robots to everyday life in unlimited numbers.

3971 A.D.
Outer Worlds limit emigration from Earth.

4021 A.D.
The renaissance on both Earth and the Spacer worlds turns into history's first chaos outbreak. Overpopulated Earth provokes the Outer Worlds, which declare war against the motherworld. During the resulting Three Weeks' War (the Great Rebellion) Spacers defeat Earth and declare the Outer Worlds independent planets. Earth is isolated, emigration made impossible.

After 4021 A.D.
During the next milennium Earthpeople escape into metal-covered cities (the caves of steel). The rise of city culture, the introduction of hydroponics and the industrial use of robots outside the cities lessen the population and food problems on Earth. Nanotechnology is developed on Earth and introduced in many fields of industry.

Appr. 4050-4600 A.D.
Some experiments with nanotechnology go wrong, producing nano-colonies which begin to destroy their environment as nonorganic parasites. In the end, these agressive colonies destroy themselves; only a few aberrant strains are preserved. Earth scientists unravel the puzzle of the nanoplagues and develop a number of successful treatments, eventually bringing them to manageable levels. Spacer scientists begin to make progress against their own nanoplagues, reducing them in number and virulence. Spacer medical technologies and bioscience make enormous strides, increasing lifespans and reducing age-related afflictions.

4620 A.D.
The last major outbreak of mnemonic plague sweeps many Spacer worlds, signaling the last wave of virulent disease among them.

Appr. 4664-4721 A.D.
New York is replaced with metal-covered New York City.

4722 A.D.
Population of Solaria (fiftieth and last Spacer world) from Nexon begins. Beginning of the slow and almost unrecognizable decline of Spacer culture.

4822 A.D.
Solaria becomes independent of Nexon.

4858 A.D.
Birth of Han Fastolfe.

4979 A.D.
Birth of Elijah Baley.

4989 A.D.
Birth of Gladia.

4996 A.D.
Spacetown is established near New York City. Thanks to Spacer influence, robots are introduced to Earth's cities.

5002 A.D.
Elijah Baley and Jesse Navodny meet.

5005 A.D.
Birth of Bentley (Ben) Baley.

5021 A.D.
Auroran roboticist Han Fastolfe and sociologist-historian Roj Nemennuh Sarton realize the decline of Spacer culture. They want to get Earth to colonize new planets using less robotic service than Spacers. They design humaniform robots to mix among Earth population to understand their way of thinking. The first such humaniform robot is Daneel Olivaw. Meeting of Daneel and Elijah Baley.

5022 A.D.
Elijah Baley and Daneel Olivaw carry out an investigation on Solaria. Fastolfe becomes an influential member of the Auroran government and strongly supports new Earth emigration. His Auroran opponents led by Kelden Amadiro want to terraform and populate new planets from Aurora instead of Earth. A group of Earthpeople led by Baley train to live outside the city domes to be able to colonize new planets.

5023 A.D.
Elijah helps Daneel with solving a dispute between two mathematicians.

5024 A.D.
Amy Barone-Stein joins Baley's would-be settlers. Baley investigates a case of roboticide on Aurora accompanied by Daneel and Giskard Reventlov (a telepathic robot!). In the background of the 'murder' lies the power struggle between Fastolfe and his opponents over the new colonization. Finally Aurora allows the Earth to terraform new planets and will provide technical support for the task. Giskard thinks Earthpeople must settle on worlds without robots to evade the fate of Spacers. Giskard describes the idea of psychohistory, a science that can foretell events of the future.

5026 A.D.
The second swarm of humans from Earth begins with Auroran support. They use no robotic service at all. The first colonist group is lead by Ben Baley. The first terraformed (so called Settler) planet will later be called Baleyworld. Earth plans to ban use of robots on the motherworld. Settler culture arises without robots.

5028 A.D.
There are already twenty-four Settler planets. The relationship between the Settler and Spacer worlds becomes increasingly hostile.

5029 A.D.
Elijah Baley moves to Baleyworld.

???
Robots are outlawed on Earth. Technologies based on nano-machines are also abandoned.

5058 A.D.
Death of Elijah Baley.

5132 A.D.
The Church of Organic Sapiens is founded.

5162 A.D.
Improvo Shipping and Storage is founded.

5168 A.D.
Upon an agreement between Solaria and a Settler company Settlers begin to colonize Cassus Thole, a planet which used to be a Solarian mining endeavour. Solaria keeps only one establishment for itself, far from the Settler towns.

5171 A.D.
Birth of Jerem Looms. He turns out to have UPD.

5172 A.D.
A lab is founded on Earth to research the nanocolonies which infect infants and cause UPD. The lab is named Nova Levis. Later a sister lab is built on Cassus Thole. Still later the planet is renamed Nova Levis.

5174 A.D.
Rega Looms is informed that Jerem has died.

5175 A.D.
Children are kidnapped throughout Earth, UPDs among them. Ree Wenithal begins to investigate the problem.

5176 A.D.
Nova Levis lab starts to research the practice of nonorganic-organic symbiosis in earnest.

Appr. 5178 A.D.
Ree Wenithal traces the stolen children to Nova Levis lab. He is then stopped in his investigation.

5180 A.D.
Nova Levis lab is closed.

5182 A.D.
Rega Looms becomes director of the Church of Organic Sapiens.

5183 A.D.
Birth of D.G. Baley.

???
Relationship between Earth and Aurora improves.

5191 A.D.
The plans of the mad Auroran scientist Dr. Avery for conquering the galaxy by establishing robot cities are foiled by his son, Derec, and Ariel Burgess.

5197 A.D.
After graduating from the Calvin Institute, Ariel Burgess takes a position as the Calvin liaison to the Auroran embassy on Earth. That same year, Derec Avery petitions the Terran government for a special license to operate a positronic research lab on Earth called The Phylaxis Group. He becomes instrumental in new attempts to reintroduce positronics to Earth.

5198 A.D.
Auroran patrols check the Terran smuggler ship *Tiberius*; it turns out to carry several Solarian positronic experts and geneticists to Nova Levis. Nova Levis turns down requests to carry out investigations on the planet. Later that same year, Derec Avery completes construction of Bogard, a robot with extremely flexible Three Law parameters, enabling it to act as a bodyguard without running into positronic collapse.

5199 A.D.

Terran senator Clar Eliton invites Spacer and Settler diplomats to discuss the possible reintroduction of robots on Earth and in Settler space trade; in the meantime, Eliton organizes an assassination against the diplomats in order to completely discredit robots on Earth. Derec Avery's robot, Bogard, proves instrumental in solving the crime. After the assassination, most of the diplomats of the Fifty Worlds leave Earth. A smuggler ship leaving Nova Levis fires on a Terran patrol ship. Earth blockades Nova Levis.

5200 A.D.

A group of people illegally emigrating from Earth to Nova Levis are killed. Investigations suggest the involvement of Solaria and Nova Levis. It turns out that Solaria probably grows cyborgs on Nova Levis. A cyborg (who was once Jerem Looms) named Gamelin appears on Earth. Aurorans capture another cyborg on Earth named Cordios.

5201 A.D.

An investigation by Derec Avery and Ariel Burgess leads to the discovery of manufacture of cyborgs by arms dealer Kynig Parapoyos on planet Nova Levis. It is revelaed that Parapoyos is really Ambassador Gale Chassik.

5202 A.D.

The autonomous robot Bogard assumes control of the Parapoyos organization. It begins a program, in concert with a large faction of Spacer robots, to isolate Spacers in order to allow them to die out as a result of thew determination that the millennia of coexistence with numerous mutated nanoforms has altered them genetically to a condition where they represent a potential new species. Robots are dedicated to service to *homo sapiens sapien* and cannot have two masters.

5217 A.D.

Kelden Amadiro and his group begin planting nuclear amplifiers throughout Earth to take revenge for their defeat.

5222 A.D.

Death of Han Fastolfe. Anti-Earth and anti-Settler movement on Aurora gains momentum. Population of Solaria vanishes. Number and strength of Settler worlds grows fast. Daneel and Giskard formulate the Zeroth Law of Robotics. They realize they will need a working psychohistory to steer human history according to the Zeroth Law. Amadiro's group turn their amplifiers on to make Earth radioactive and inhospitable. Giskard lets them proceed, rationalizing that the poisoning of Earth would speed up the Settler swarm and do humanity good in the long run. His decision, however, creates an internal conflict between the Zeroth and the First Law, which ultimately leads to Giskard's death. Giskard provides Daneel with telepathic abilities, then becomes inoperational and dies. Settler emigration grows to enormous numbers: beginning of the Great Diaspora. Settlers carry the virus of Chaos everywhere.

???

A majority of robots split into two camps. "Giskardians" led by Daneel believe in the new Zeroth Law religion. Others—the "Calvinians"—think their meddling with human affairs according to the Zeroth Law to be an outrage. A robotic civil war ensues mostly unseen by humans fleeing the sudden poisoning of Earth. Meanwhile fleets of robots—operating under Auroran programming—begin cruising the galaxy ahead of the spreading Settlers, terraforming and preparing planets for colonization. Several nonhuman intelligent races, sometimes complete ecosystems are destroyed by robot terraformers. On some planets they discover computer civilizations, remnants of once-great nonhuman cultures. The Auroran robots try to destroy the beings of these civilizations, the meme entities, as potential threaths. Some of the memes escape to the Galactic Core.

5322 A.D.

The Spacer planet Inferno is doomed by both ecological and cultural catastrophe. To evade the cultural crisis robots are designed and built that operate on New Laws, giving them greater freedom. To test the correctness of the New Laws the No Law robot Caliban is built. To avoid the ecological catastrophe a group of Settler specialists are asked to reterraform the planet.

5323 A.D.

The failure of the New Laws becomes clear. Reterraforming of Inferno begins.

5328 A.D.

To create a stable ecosystem an ice-comet is crashed onto Inferno's surface. Cultural crisis is evaded by the merging of Spacers and the Settler terraformers.

???

The interstellar robot civil war eventually reaches Inferno. New Law robots are destroyed or go into hiding.

???

Daneel and his followers play an important role in formulating the Encoding Laws that will set the highest limits in producing artificial intelligence. As a result, Settler society will never think of building robots. This is one of the first great 'damping mechanisms' that help prevent chaos.

1960 B.G.E. (Before Galactic Era)
Settling of planet Tyrann.

1260-1250 B.G.E.
Tyrann conquers the Nebular Kingdoms.

1220 B.G.E.
The Tyranni elect Hinrik V as Director of Rhodia.

1200 B.G.E.
Planet Rhodia and the Nebular Kingdoms, led by the noble Hinriad family, shake off rule by planet Tyrann, and rediscover democracy.

???

Spacer worlds turn into themselves and slowly die throughout the millennia. The remaining population of Aurora moves to Mycogen sector of the growing planet Trantor. Settler culture gradually colonizes the Galaxy. Damping effects such as historical amnesia, brain fever and giskardian mentalic persuasion devices are introduced by Daneel and followers to fight chaos. As a result human mind, society and technology stagnates for millennia. Some human and robot groups (including the Maserd family) fight the amnesia. Later they are for the most part defeated by Giskardians. Robots are forgotten by all but a tiny remnant of humans who cooperate in hiding with heretic robots.

700 B.G.E.
The Trantorian Republic of five worlds begins to grow; later becomes Trantorian Confederation and still later Trantorian Empire. Daneel uses early 'laws of humanics' (precursor of psychohistory developed with Giskard) to guide it.

???

The origin of mankind is forgotten. Planet Earth becomes one of the many millions of inhabited planets.

200 B.G.E.
Half of the inhabited worlds of the Galaxy are part of Trantorian Empire. Trantor is on the point of forming the Galactic Empire. Trantor financially supports rebellion of Florina against oppression by planet Sark.

1 G.E. (= appr. 13 000 C.E.) (appr. 8000 years after the Great Diaspora)
Trantorian Empire becomes Galactic Empire. First emperor is Frankenn I.
Beginning of the galactic calendar. (G.E. = Galactic Era)

750 G.E.
Third Earth rebellion against Empire.

771 G.E.
Birth of Affret Shekt.

772 G.E.
Birth of Grew.

775 G.E.
Beginning of rule of Stannel II.

777 G.E.
Demonstrating his might, Stannel II provokes unrest in Washenn, Earth.
Stannel II is assassinated. Edard ascends the galactic throne.

827 G.E.
Arrival of Joseph Schwartz through time. A radioactive and sparsely pop-
ulated Earth tries to revolt against the Empire using a bio-weapon (an
extremely aggressive type of the chaos virus). Rebellion fails, thanks
partly to Schwarz and Daneel's agent R. Gornon Vlimt. Empire initially
supports changing of Earth's radioactive soil for healthy, then the effort
is mysteriously abandoned.

Appr. 900 G.E.
Forced evacuation of inhospitable Earth. Founding of colony on planet
Alpha.

975 G.E.
An intelligent species is discovered on a desert planet. They are trans-
ported to Cepheus 18.

978 G.E.
The aliens mysteriously escape beyond the Galaxy aided by a sympa-
thetic bureaucrat of the Empire.

Appr. 2000 G.E.
Daneel Olivaw and R. Yan Kansarv establish a robot production and repair
facility on the moon Eos. The great Ruellis helps establish principles of
good paternalistic government, augmenting the stability of an unchang-
ing society against chaos (another of Daneel's damping mechanisms).

Appr. 3000 G.E.
Public debate of personality simulations Voltaire and Joan of Arc about machine intelligence during a chaos outbreak. With support of Calvinian robots the Empress Shoree-Harn sits on the imperial throne; she tries to introduce a new calendar and shake up social rigidity without success.

8789 G.E.
New renaissance begins on planet Lingane.

8797 G.E.
Lingane renaissance falls into chaos.

11, 865 G.E.
Humanoid robot Dors Venabili is constructed on Eos.

Appr. 11, 867 G.E.
The only extragalactic human colony is abandoned in the Greater Magellanic Cloud. All data suppressed.

Appr. 11, 968 G.E.
Daneel performs genetic experiments on a group of humans, which leads to the appearance of mentalics and the birth of a man who is capable of developing psychohistory.

11, 988 G.E.
Birth of Hari Seldon and Cleon I. Daneel knows the Empire is destabilizing, partly due to frequent chaos outbreaks. He is forced by Zeroth Law to actively interfere, first as Chief of Staff, then as First Minister.

12, 008 G.E.
Birth of Raych.

12, 010 G.E.
Cleon I becomes Emperor.

12, 017 G.E.
New renaissance begins on Madder Losson.

12, 020 G.E.
Hari Seldon lectures on possibility of psychohistory. Daneel persuades him to develop a practical science to help save the Empire. In the guise of First Minister Eto Demerzel he supports Seldon's work. Dors Venabili becomes Seldon's wife. They adopt a boy, Raych. Seldon and Yugo Amaryl begin to flesh out psychohistory.

12 ,028 G.E.
A group of Calvinian robots, led by R. Plussix, move to Trantor and find historical documents dating from the era of Shoree-Harn, as well as the sims Voltaire and Joan of Arc. They get the sims to planet Sark to help seed a new renaissance there, to disturb Daneel's work. Seldon helps removing Laskin Joranum from politics. Eto Demerzel (Daneel) resigns his post. Cleon I makes Seldon First Minister. A New Renaissance begins on planet Sark. Voltaire and Joan get into Trantorian Mesh where they meet the ancient memes. To avenge the destruction of their original homes the memes cause a rebellion among the tiktoks, having many of Daneel's robot companions killed. The memes move back to the Galactic Core. Sark renaissance gradually falls into chaos.

12, 037 G.E.
The collapse of Madder Loss renaissance rocks Galactic society.

12, 038 G.E.
Death of Cleon I. A military junta seizes power. Seldon resigns as First Minister.

12, 040 G.E.
Birth of Wanda Seldon from the marriage of Raych Seldon and Manella Dubanqua.

12, 048 G.E.
'Death' of Dors Venabili. Daneel brings Dors to the Eos base for repair. Fall of the junta. Puppet-Emperor Agis XIV ascends the throne. Real power is in the hands of the Commission of Public Safety led by Chief Commissioner Linge Chen.

12, 050 G.E.
Birth of Klayus I.

12, 051 G.E.
Birth of Klia Asgar.

12, 052 G.E.
Birth of Bellis Seldon, second child of Raych and Manella. Hari Seldon discovers Wanda's mental abilities. He tries to find others, without success. Signs of general decline show throughout the Empire.

12, 054 G.E.
Psychohistorical equations predict the unavoidable collapse of the Empire. Seldon works out plan to preserve human knowledge, and create a Second Empire via the Foundation. Death of Yugo Amaryl.

12, 058 G.E.
Raych, Manella and Bellis move to Santanni where a new renaissance has begun. Anacreon province seeks independence. Seldon finds the place for his Foundation: planet Terminus, on the edge of the Galaxy. Chaos breaks out on Santanni. Raych dies. His family is lost in space. Stettin Palver, another mentalic joins the Seldon Project, then Bor Alurin. The mentalics will later form the Second Foundation. The Commission of Public Safety begins to watch Seldon.

12, 062 G.E.
Vara Liso, a strong mentalic learns about the existence of robots. Upon this information Farad Sinter begins to hunt for robots.

12, 067 G.E. = 1 F.E.
Klayus I sits on the imperial throne, but real power remains with the Commission of Public Safety. Giskardian robot Lodovik Trema becomes accidentally liberated from the compulsion to obey the Laws of Robotics. He questions the rightness of Zeroth Law and the lack of human consultation in their own destiny. Calvinian robots want Seldon to abandon his Project to stop Daneel directing history. Gaal Dornick joins the Seldon Project. The Commission of Public Safety puts Seldon to trial and exiles the Encyclopedia Foundation to Terminus. Farad Sinter's soldiers destroy base of Calvinian robots. Lodovik rejoins Daneel. The Second Foundation goes into hiding at Star's End. Beginning of the Foundation calendar. (F.E. = Foundation Era)
   Originist Leyel Forska wants to join First Foundation, but Seldon turns him down.

12, 068 G.E. = 2 F.E.
Reign of puppet Emperor Semrin. First Foundation (consisting mostly of technical experts and their families) gets "exiled" to Terminus and begins compiling the Encyclopedia Galactica. Daneel starts developing the over-mind Gaia with human mentalics. Compelled by Zeroth Law Daneel destroys millions of ancient archives that had been designed to fight human amnesia. A new renaissance on Ktlina falls into chaos. R. Gornon Vlimt tries to send Seldon into the future to judge Daneel's plan and the projections of psychohistory, but is foiled by Daneel. Mors Planch (and possibly Biron Maserd) dives into the future.

12, 069 G.E. = 3 F.E.
Death of Hari Seldon. Leyel Forska joins Second Foundation. Linge Chen dies, Rom Divart takes his place in the Commission of Public Safety. To

strengthen his power, Divart pays attention mostly to Trantor and its vicinity. Secession begins at the Empire's Periphery.

50 F.E. (12, 116 G.E.)
Anacreon declares independence, separating Terminus from the Empire. Seldon's hologram in the Terminus Time Vault explains the true purpose of the Foundation. Anacreon sets up military base on Terminus with the aim of swallowing the planet. Terminus begins to provide scientific support for the neighbouring kingdoms, balancing their powers.

80 F.E. (12, 146 G.E.)
The Foundation wards off Anacreon threat, then signs a treaty with neighbouring kingdoms about peaceful coexistence. The Foundation begins to trade with sophisticated industrial goods in the Periphery. As its economic influence grows, it adds the power of religious cultism.

135 F.E. (12, 201 G.E.)
The Foundation spreads its influence over the planet Askone.

155 F.E. (12, 221 G.E.)
Imperial atomic weapons appear in the Republic of Korell, adjacent with the Foundation's influence zone.

158 F.E. (12, 224 G.E.)
Korell declares war against Foundation.

161 F.E. (12, 227 G.E.)
After three years of mostly economic warfare the Korellian economy collapses. Korell becomes part of the Foundation.

195 F.E. (12, 261 G.E.)
The Empire ruled by Cleon II is gaining strength. Imperial general Bel Riose begins a campaign against the Foundation.

196 F.E. (12, 262 G.E.)
Riose conquers large territories. Cleon II—afraid of a powerful military leader's attempt to seize the throne—calls Riose and his fleet back.

Appr. 260 F.E. (Appr. 12, 326 G.E.)
Dagobert VIII rules remnant Empire. The rebel Gilmer conquers and sacks Trantor. First Speaker Yokim Sarns and the Second Foundation protect the Galactic Library, then sign a peace-treaty with Gilmer.

Appr. 300 F.E. (Appr. 12, 366 G.E.)
Empire of Dagobert IX has shrunk to twenty worlds. Its capital is Neo-

trantor. The Foundation has grown into a major power. The Mule, a mutant with strong mentalic power conquers the Foundation, knocking Seldon Plan off course. Psychologist Ebling Mis locates the Second Foundation. Bayta Darell shoots Misbefore he could reveal location of the Second Foundation to the Mule. The Mule establishes the Union of Worlds, and searches for the Second Foundation.

Appr. 305 F.E.
Members of the Second Foundation mentalically alter the Mule, who then gives up further conquest and the search for the Second Foundation.

Appr. 310 F.E.
Death of the Mule. The Foundation regains its earlier strength, but also begins studying neglected mental sciences, further endangering Seldon Plan.

362 F.E.
Birth of Arcadia Darell.

376 F.E.
The Foundation searches for the Second Foundation, fearing its mentalic rule. Planet Kalgan starts war against the Foundation. The Foundation defeats Kalgan. Diverting the Foundation's search with a ruse, the Second Foundation continues operating secretly on Trantor (Star's End).

???
Daneel unleashes his Gaia overmind. Gaia begins to watch the Foundations.

443 F.E.
Death of Arcadia Darell.

???
Researching mental sciences, the Foundation gets close to being superior to the supposedly destroyed Second Foundation. The Second Foundation—without noticing it—is no longer able to keep the Seldon Plan on course on its own. The Seldon Plan is kept on course by the mental guidance of the Gaia overmind.

467 F.E.
Birth of Golan Trevize.

???
Daneel starts manipulating a group of people (including Golan Trevize) to choose 'the man who is always right.'

498 F.E.

The Gaia overmind offers Golan Trevize ('the man who is always right') a choice between an Empire built by the First Foundation's physical force, one ruled by Second Foundation mentalics, or a Galaxy-sized version of Gaia...Galaxia. No other options are presented and no other humans consulted. Trevize chooses Galaxia. After the decision the Seldon Plan is kept alive by Gaia to ensure stability until the emergence of Galaxia. Preparations begin for gradual assimilation of humanity into the collective overmind.

499 F.E.

Trevize embarks on a journey seeking to explain his choice. On Solaria he finds that the planet's vanished folk have become a new race. He takes a child, Fallom from the planet. Reaching Earth he meets R. Daneel Olivaw, whose actions to this point were compelled by the Zeroth Law. Trevize realizes any solution must take into consideration robots, Solarians, memes, mutants and any other kind of intelligence, too. The right answer may not be to simplify.

520 F.E.

First Galactic Coalescence Investigation Commission convenes on planet Pengia. The subsequent Great Destiny Debates rage for 180 years, interrupted by waves of violence, amnesia and chaos. Robotic civil wars reignite. Foundation civilization approaches ultimate confrontation with both Gaia and Chaos.

682 F.E.

The Fifth Great Destiny Debate.

1020 F.E.

116th Edition of the *Encyclopedia Galactica*.

1054 F.E.

117th Edition of the *Encyclopedia Galactica*.